I0585426

STOLEN
TIME
JENN LEES

COMMUNITY CHRONICLES BOOK 2

Copyright © 2018 by Jenn Lees

All rights reserved.

This book is a work of fiction. The names, characters, places, and incidents are products of the writer's imagination or have been used fictitiously and are not to be construed as real. Any resemblance to persons, living or dead, actual events, locale or organizations is entirely coincidental.

No portion of this book may be reproduced in any form without written permission from the publisher.

This novel is written in British English.

Cover by Fiona Jayde Media

www.fionajaydemedia.com

To my husband Frank,
The man who would travel through time for me

Contents

Chapter One

Scottish Highlands 2056 AD

S cott Campbell rested his finger on the trigger of the L115A3.

Watching. No, he'd give them a chance.

He lifted the telescopic sight of the long range rifle and viewed his quarry from his vantage point above. His Militia silently settled into place behind him. The tips of the Scottish Highland mountains glowed orange as the setting sun dimmed his view of the bandit group—about a dozen of them—setting up camp below him amid the heather and gorse, sheltered by large grey boulders. This was an unfamiliar group of simply dressed, woollen-cloaked campers. Scott repressed a shiver as the mist settled amongst the mountains and the cold from the ground beneath him seeped through his clothes, chilling his skin.

Still watching.

A scraggy-haired youth slipped saddlebags off the back of a mule and placed them next to the growing pile. An older man in torn jeans directed proceedings. A middle-aged woman lit a fire as a scrawny lass brought cooking pots and utensils from a packhorse. So far, the only stolen goods on this group of reprobates were not of the human kind. Not slavers then. Still he watched; he had to be certain. The people in his Community must be safe.

The soft murmurs of Scott's crew settling-in surrounded him. This reconnaissance should be for nothing. At least it would give the youngsters with him some more experience. Experience never went astray.

Guilt nagged at him, but he pushed it aside. He needed a break from the compound and this exercise was an excuse—the emotions at home were growing too intense.

He glanced up at the darkening peaks ahead. The world's trauma had barely touched the Highlands. The cities hadn't been so lucky. It had been a long time since he'd been in Glasgow. Man, that'd been a mess. He'd walked away, past looted buildings and crumbling infrastructure, never to return.

Scott had chosen to take the first watch. His eldest boy, Rory, joined him as others hunkered down for the night behind the rocky outcrop where they had perched. Rory was a quiet lad, and smart.

"So, tell me, if ye loved someone, and one day ye will." Scott shifted his gaze from the rifle's sight and now looked at his son.

A smile tweaked at the corner of Rory's mouth.

"If ye had a chance to be with them again, once ye'd lost them, would ye?" Scott asked, then returned to watching through the sight.

Silence was Rory's first response. Scott didn't mind, he would get a considered answer eventually. One worth waiting for. He slid his glance back to the eldest of his twin sons.

"Now that depends on the means of acquiring the chance." Rory's deep red hair seemed brown in the fading light. "Would I do *anything*? Maybe. Would I risk danger to do so?" He pursed his lips and scratched his wispy beard. "I'd weigh up the risk against benefit. If I was sure I would see them again, and I couldn't imagine life without them..."

Good lad, wise enough to not give advice. A warmth settled in Scott's chest as he turned his attention again to the camp below. The youths in the group were removing saddles and tack from the horses and mules and tying the animals to a line for the night. The young lads were rowdy and undisciplined. Scott gritted his teeth. He had to be sure these people were just one of the usual groups of desperates trying to survive in this world. Slavery was rife and nowhere was safe. Well, his Community was. And he was determined it would stay that way.

The quiet whisper of static followed by low-voiced conversation floated along to him. The lass in his Militia group on communication-duty, padded up the slope from her position with the portable radio, to their secluded shelf in the hillside, her brown buckskins and dusky-green homespun camouflaging her in the night.

"Sir, you're wanted at the compound." There was an urgency in her voice and a frown creased her brow as she dragged a rifle from her shoulder.

"Verra well. I'll go back." Scott knew what the problem would be. "You stay here with the others, Rory. If ye and your brothers need to come, I'll send a message for ye."

Scott strode down to where they'd tethered the horses and leaped onto his Highland Mountain horse. Scott galloped his stallion to a lather along the trail. He seemed to fly through the Western Highland night, by lochs glistening in bright moonlight, with the silent mountains gleaming as they observed his journey by their feet. The electricity-generating windmills on the hill behind the compound glowed a dull white in the moonlight, spinning like crazy long-limbed ghosts. The sentry called as Scott approached the high walls of the compound and the sturdy iron gate slid open, revealing light spilling onto the main building's courtyard. It had once been a farmyard but now the farmhouse, animal sheds, and other buildings formed part of the complex that was the Invercharing Community—and home.

Flinging his right leg over, Scott landed beside his stallion and patted the deep-brown neck, warm and smooth under his hand. He loved this animal and would miss him.

A long shadow approached from the doorway. The doctor was quiet; her mouth a straight-line matching those on her forehead. His heart missed a beat.

"Has she gone?" he asked.

"Not yet, but soon." Her voice was soft and full of sympathy, as she would use for those who mourn.

He ran inside.

***

Present Day

The shard of metal protruded from the man's eye. It had pierced cornea and lens, and now the clear fluid of aqueous humor trickled down his cheek.

"Please lie down on the trolley, Mr McNabb, and we'll have a closer look at you." Caitlin Murray directed the sheet metal worker to Bay Four in the emergency department of Edinburgh Royal Infirmary.

The sheet metal worker who had *not* worn his protective eye-gear. It was her last shift before her annual leave, and it had been a killer. Only one more hour to go.

Sound assaulted Caitlin on every side. The hum of professional conversation, the beeping of monitors, IV pumps and blood-pressure machines, and the emotion-packed voices of patients and their companions filled the air. With all the bays taken, patient-occupied trolleys now lined against the walls. As Caitlin went to fetch an ophthalmoscope and alert the intern to call an ophthalmologist, a bony hand grabbed her arm, digging in above her elbow, while the scent of stale urine wafted into her face.

"Nurse! Nurse!" The elderly woman had been there for hours; her daughter had left two hours previously.

There was no available bed on the wards, so the elderly woman waited on a trolley. Caitlin had seen it before—a granny dump—an over-taxed carer in need of a break hoping for a hospital admission for her elderly relative. The old woman's sunken eyes and flaccid skin, the signs of dehydration, told Caitlin the woman's family was not coping.

"It's okay, the ward will have a bed for you soon." She patted the woman's arm and then continued her journey to the equipment trolley.

She passed the end of Bay Two where her team partner Jan had been working. She glanced in to see how she was going.

"But we've been here two hours already! And before that, we were in the waiting room for three." The man in his late thirties spoke through gritted teeth, frustration boiled in his voice.

Throughout the busy day, one demand after another had prevented Jan from attending immediately to the man's wife in Bay Two. Caitlin had tried to help her team partner and get to Bay Two herself but without success. Over the buzz of the ED, the man's frustration was giving birth to aggression. Jan glanced at her, pleading in her expression as the man's verbal output took on harsher tones.

'Want help?' Caitlin mouthed.

Jan took a step away from the man and moved toward Caitlin, with an imperceptible nod. The man's hands clenched into fists.

Oh, how I hate calling a Code Grey and having to bring security in.

"Sir, I'm Caitlin. What's your name?" She would try anything to deflect his simmering anger.

"Miles." His voice was tight.

"Miles, I'm truly sorry you and your wife have had to wait for so long." She kept her voice gentle and even. "It's been a busy day, and we also find it concerning when we can't get to everyone in the time frames we would like to."

His fists, which had pressed into his sides, loosened their curl.

"I understand your frustration; we feel it too. Your nurse, Jan, is ready now." Caitlin turned to Jan. "I've got something to deal with and then I'll give you a hand, Jan." Caitlin paused and looked directly at Miles' wife. "We'll be with you soon, okay?"

The woman was pale and dark lines curved under her eyes as she leaned back against the trolley's pillow. She nodded, a slight flush beginning on her cheeks from her embarrassment at her husband's behaviour. Caitlin felt for him; he was looking after his wife in a difficult situation.

***

At the end of the shift Caitlin shut her locker door, now dressed in civvies, and with her nurse scrubs in the Change Room laundry basket.

"You handled that well, *Duchess*." Jan's warm hand rested on Caitlin's shoulder.

Caitlin groaned inwardly. Jan meant no harm with the nickname which had stuck since they graduated over a year ago, but the twinge of guilt rose in her stomach as always.

"So where are we going for drinks? Got to celebrate you gettin' a place in the Master of Nursing program. We'll make you a super ED nurse yet." Jan turned to Milla. "You comin' for a drink to double celebrate her success and freedom from here for a couple of weeks?"

"No, I'm sorry I can't." The older woman grimaced. "We are meeting with our Financial Planner. Pension funds and all that. I'm thinking of retiring soon."

"Jan, have you organised something without asking me?" Slight panic swirled in the back of Caitlin's mind.

She was about to let her friends down because of tonight's family commitment. She took a breath, bracing herself for the inevitable scorn from Jan who constantly reminded her of all she benefitted from since she started living with her aunt and uncle.

"If you have, I can't do it," she said. "It's my uncle's birthday and the family doo is tonight. After all they've done for me, I can't miss it."

Jan's shoulders drooped. "Not even a quick drink?"

"No, you know what the traffic's like. I need to leave now."

Milla and Jan were quiet for a few moments, Jan's shoulders sinking deeper.

"So where will you be holidaying?" Milla broke the uncomfortable silence.

"I'm just staying at my uncle's estate this year," Caitlin replied. "Be nice to relax and ride."

"Just going to *The Estate*. *Only* riding my horse this year. Not gallivanting around Europe. That's *so* tiresome." Jan put on a toffy accent and gave a false yawn.

Caitlin shook her head. If only Jan knew of the loss leading to her so-called life of privilege since her aunt and uncle had taken her in.

***

The drive to her uncle's Scottish Lowland estate took the usual ninety minutes due to the traffic out of Edinburgh. Caitlin stopped at the shops in the small village right before the gatehouse to the estate. She walked past the supermarket, hardware and hunting goods store to the Post Office, where she bought a birthday card to go with the present for her Uncle Kieran. She smiled to herself as she thought of her gift for him. Once back in her car she drove the short distance before turning into the driveway next to the gatehouse and approached the main house. Her chest warmed at the sight of the large trees that dotted the neat green lawn edging the drive, which stretched its way toward the stately home. On either side of the two-storey grey-stone Georgian building, barley fields rippled like the wind on still water.

Caitlin called it a house; Jan would call it a mansion. A smile tugged her mouth. Whatever it was, it had become her home. She rented a flat in Edinburgh close to work, but this was where family lived, and that was her *home*. Her *only* family since her mother died. Uncle Kieran and Aunt May had kept a room for her, it was a comfortable place. They spoiled her, and she loved them for it.

It was late in the day when she parked her two-door run-about at the front of the house. It looked a little shabby next to her cousins' luxury class sedans. The setting sun angled beams of gold through the front doorway and large windows, illuminating the paintings hanging on the walls of the main entrance of this stately home. Scenes of Scottish lochs hung beside portraits of past lairds. A fan of Lochaber axes glinted next to a display of claymores mounted on the bare-stone wall. Caitlin walked around the back to the kitchen door. All her cousins would be there tonight, even though none now lived at home. Family gatherings were always a large event in this house.

Caitlin entered the kitchen. The radio was on, as usual, and platters of food sat on the large kitchen table: cold meats, smoked salmon, antipasti, dips, and oat cakes. The smell of gourmet party-pies and vol-au-vents wafted from the oven. No-one was in sight. They would all be in the drawing-room already. As she left the kitchen, the news item on the radio caught her attention.

US stock markets tumble to an all-time low.

It was never a music station, always someone *talking*. Caitlin stepped down the corridor. The bronze statuette of a twelve-pointer stag sat on the marble hall table.

So Scottish.

Laughter floated through the open door down the hallway.

"Here she is!" Uncle Kieran's deep voice greeted Caitlin as she entered the drawing room.

"Happy birthday Uncle Kieran." Smiling she placed the wrapped present in his lap and returned his hug, his strong aftershave lingered in her nostrils.

"Ooh. Wonder what this is?" He unwrapped the present and laughed as he folded the paper and set it aside next to the rest of the folded, used wrapping paper.

They all laughed.

"Really cuz? A deerstalker?" Theresa's deep blue eyes looked directly into hers.

Theresa would be ready to give Caitlin the 'appropriate gift' speech once more. Caitlin had already decided she'd ignore her.

What do you give someone who has everything, *really* has everything? Caitlin thought.

"Now, now, Theresa. Caitlin's presents are always fun, aren't they, darling?" Uncle Kieran gave Caitlin a kiss on the cheek. "Thank you. I love it. I shall wear it on next week's shoot." He placed it on the coffee table in front of him, beside the designer label watch and cologne, and the Fabergé egg.

"So, are you coming to Majorca with us, Caitlin?" The other deep voice belonged to her favourite cousin Martin. He pushed his long fringe out of his eyes as his intense, intelligent stare fixed on her.

"No, I'm staying here." Caitlin craned her neck to look him in the eye. "Want to keep my riding skills up."

"Well, come say hello to your great-aunt and give me a hug." The crisp voice came from a high-backed chair in the corner where Great Aunt Meredith sat.

Caitlin stepped across the room and obediently hugged the elderly woman. Her bony frame seemed thinner, but the resemblance to her own mother remained. It brought a tightness to her chest as it did every time.

"So where is your boyfriend?" Aunt Meredith asked.

"She doesn't have one." Theresa supplied the information, as usual.

"And why not?" Aunt Meredith asked Caitlin. "A beautiful and intelligent young woman such as yourself should be well and truly married by now."

To Great-Aunt Meredith it was *all* so clear.

"Aunty, when I find the right man," Caitlin said. "I promise you'll be the first to know."

"You are being too fussy, girl." Aunty Meredith crossed her arms over her bosom.

"No. The guys my age are just *boys*," Caitlin said.

"She wants a *real man*." It was Theresa once more and her derision was at full pitch.

With her back to her cousin, Caitlin rolled her eyes. Aunty looked up as Caitlin stood over her.

"Well, they are, Aunty, and I'll not settle for just anyone." She hoped they all got it. This topic was becoming tedious—again.

"You're not coming to Majorca," Monica piped in, "but you'll be getting your room redecorated, won't you?"

"Oh no," Caitlin said. "It doesn't need it."

"Yes, it does! It's been the same *pink* for three years."

"But I like pink." Caitlin's stomach tightened.

Arguing with her cousins was sometimes futile. They were so used to having the latest and the best. And by the *best*, it meant the most expensive designer label. Caitlin's stomach knotted. She couldn't justify what her cousins always thought was theirs by right. She'd stand her ground for as long as she could.

"I don't want a change to my room. But thank you anyway," She said.

Caitlin walked over and gave Aunt May a peck on the cheek. She had watched her closely throughout this exchange. Aunt May understood. She was wealthy, but she had come from working-class roots. Caitlin loved her family, but sometimes, like now, the cringe-o-meter was off the scale.

Chapter Two

C aitlin swung her leg over her mare and landed lightly on the stable floor. The ride had been invigorating and the scent of horse comforting. Aunt May and Uncle Kieran had been tense over breakfast. She hadn't heard the full story, but through the farewells to her great aunt and her cousins, she had sensed something about today's stock market activity was making them nervous.

They always watched the stock market closely since floating their electronics business ten years ago. The company was now in Europe as well as the UK. Uncle Kieran had made his fortune since then. They were regarded as 'new money', but they didn't seem to mind—this Scottish Lowland country estate and a flat in London, plus a personal wealth which they had never disclosed to Caitlin—but was substantial—was nothing to sneer at.

"Yoor uncle's lookin' for ye, miss." Andy leaned over the stall door. "And we've taken on a summer hire to help me with the grounds for a wee bit. Giant of a man, ye will nae miss him." Andy's balding head shone in the morning light filtering through the stable's high windows.

"Very well," she responded over her shoulder as she left the stable.

It was good news as Andy was an excellent groundsman but getting older and needing the help to maintain the large estate.

As she strode to the kitchen door, her mobile buzzed in her jacket pocket. It was Jan.

Milla has lost her Pension Fund. Jan texted.

What? How?

The Stock Market crashed. Haven't you heard? Jan replied.

No.

People are losing money. Jan text. *Ask your uncle.*

Okay.

Caitlin ran upstairs to her uncle's study. The noise of the television came through the closed door—it was turned up loud. Aunt May glanced at her as she entered.

"Something terrible is happening." Aunt May returned her attention to the news.

'Stock Markets fall world wide. DOW, FTSE 100, S&P 500, Nasdaq, Hang Seng all down 55 percent since opening today.' The BBC Television News ticker made its way across the bottom of the huge television screen on the wall of the study.

Uncle Kieran stared at the television, one arm across his chest as he stood, the index finger of his other hand tapped his upper lip and his brow furrowed. Something he always did when deep in thought. The main news item reported in-depth the current stock market crash and the resulting fall-out.

The tension in the room hung like a fog between its occupants. Aunt May, who usually never stood still, sat down heavily on the Georgian sofa and made a call on her mobile phone. Uncle Kieran rushed to his mahogany desk and opened his computer. Caitlin stood behind him and peered over his shoulder.

"I can move stock electronically," Uncle Kieran muttered to himself.

Caitlin guessed he was trying to prevent further losses. Her bottom lip pinched as she chewed it. She had grown used to the lifestyle she had with them, and quite enjoyed it, so different from her financially tight existence with Mum. But Uncle Kieran's wealth had not come easily. They had both worked hard and she admired their work ethic.

"Are you okay, Uncle?"

"Oh, we'll ride it out." Uncle Kieran sounded optimistic.

"If we do, we'll be the only ones!" Aunt May said.

She always seemed to have a greater understanding of the vagaries of the stock market and Caitlin found herself inclined to pay more attention to her aunt's comments.

"You'll be alright even if you lose a chunk, won't you?" Caitlin asked.

Aunt May glared at her. "The market has lost over half its value. Our net worth has dropped by at least thirty percent."

"We'll be alright, darling." Uncle Kieran's fingers clicked over his computer keyboard.

"My friend has lost her pension." Caitlin stepped from Uncle Kieran at his desk and sat beside Aunt May.

"She's not the only one. And there's a run on the banks." Aunt May pointed to the television.

The live feed showed queues outside banks, people wanting to withdraw their money before the closure of banks lost it all.

"We still have the cash in the safe, don't we?" Aunt May asked.

Uncle Kieran nodded and pursed his lips, but his eyes stayed on his computer screen.

"How much exactly?" Aunt May asked.

She rarely discussed their finances in front of Caitlin. Caitlin's stomach twisted.

"Maybe twenty," Uncle Kieran answered.

Caitlin assumed he meant thousands.

"Is it as bad as last time, Uncle?" she asked.

"Hmm. Just a wee bit worse. It depends on how quickly it bounces back." Distracted by his share reshuffle, Uncle Kieran didn't elaborate further.

"People lost their jobs and homes last time," Caitlin said. She couldn't keep the question or the concern out of her tone.

"Aye, it may well happen again, Caitlin," Uncle said. "People seem to be exceptionally nervous about this one. Too many got hurt in 2008."

"What about your business?"

"It's alright at the moment, but if the companies that buy from us fold, or can't afford my electronics then..." Uncle's lips screwed to one side.

At least hospitals were secure. You always needed nurses, right? She'd be okay job-wise but what about Uni? Her phone buzzed in her jacket again. Caitlin slipped out of the room, they didn't notice her go; Aunt May's focus was on the television reports and Uncle Kieran stared at his computer screen.

Caitlin walked down the hall, the atmosphere of stress and mild panic she had sensed on entering the room remained with her.

This is really serious.

She passed works of art—some by famous artists—ceramics, bronze sculptures, and other collectibles, as she always did. But she wasn't admiring them today. Her mobile buzzed again.

My father's work has laid him off already. It was Jan once more. *He's checking he still has a pension.*

Poor Jan, she still lived at home with her parents.

So soon? Caitlin text back.

Yep. It sounds like he's not the only one. Jan replied.

Sorry. Caitlin text.

After a pause, Jan text. *Will have to get more shifts at work.*

Yep. Caitlin text back.

What else could she say? Jan would think that she, *The Duchess,* would be okay because of her Uncle Kieran's wealth. But *this* crash would diminish even that.

Caitlin stayed in her room for most of the day. She ventured downstairs a couple of times, but everyone was glued to the television, so she went back to her room, snuggled into her cushions on the four-poster bed, and continued reading for her university post graduate studies, trying to distract herself. She had little savings in her own bank account, having paid her own way through university and had only worked a little over a year as a nurse. She had gone to university to study nursing straight from school and her Mum, being a single parent, had little to spare and her inheritance had been small.

More text messages from Jan interrupted her reading. Other friends had lost shares and the rush on banks had caused some to close their doors only to announce by the end of the day that they had closed permanently. Two of 'the big four' banks had folded, including Caitlin's. Wow, all her meagre savings gone in an instant! Other banks called mortgages in. Caitlin went downstairs to tell her aunt and uncle.

They were eating their dinner in front of the television news in the study. They *never* ate dinner out of the dining room.

"There's rioting in London." Aunt May abandoned her meal and placed the plate precariously on the edge of the Chippendale coffee table. It threatened to tumble onto the Chinese silk rug.

The television showed footage of a mob smashing the glass doors of a bank, shoving past security guards, and dragging staff out onto the street. Other clips showed people exiting broken shop windows with as many goods as they could carry. Crowds ran and the riot police were manoeuvring into position. Uncle Kieran picked up the remote and turned over to the Scottish news.

"Glasgow too!" Uncle Kieran's voice held a shocked tone Caitlin had only heard once before when she told him of his sister's death. The day her mother died.

Chapter Three

C aitlin spent the evening watching the unfolding of events on the television with her aunt and uncle. It felt so far away, even Glasgow's troubles.

Unbelievable.

When she finally went to bed, disturbed sleep was all she had. She woke several times to stare at the dark canopy lining of her four-poster bed. Morning came, and she went down to breakfast. *What would be next?* Her eyes were gritty after spending the night contemplating a future without any money apart from her income from her job, which meant no backup savings and life would be harder. How would she pay university fees? She wouldn't presume on her aunt and uncle.

The backdoor closed with a bang and Andy staggered into the breakfast room.

"Andy? You look as white as a sheet, man. What's wrong?" Uncle Kieran's teacup was mid-way between the saucer and his mouth.

"Och, I've just been getting some groceries at the wee village." His Highland accent lilted through his amazement. "There's a mob o' strangers smashin' things. Must be from the city for I dinnae ken anybody." Andy's eyes were wide as he shook his head.

Uncle Kieran's teacup remained motionless for only a moment longer. "I'm going to check a few things. Won't be long, darling." He gave Aunt May a brief kiss on the forehead and left with Andy.

Aunt May's butter knife clattered on her plate. Caitlin jumped as she turned to her aunt who had already risen from the table.

"Go check every window along the front of the house is locked. The housekeeper and I will do the back and sides." Aunt May said over her shoulder as she strode through the kitchen. "And close the wooden shutters!"

Caitlin strode through the rooms on the lower floor checking and locking each Georgian sash window and closing those with shutters. From her position in her bedroom on the second floor, Caitlin could see right down to the gatehouse. If she stood at an angle to the left of her window, the far end of the main street of the village came into view. As she stared at the smoke and movement in the distance, her neck prickled and the hair on her scalp rose.

A hand covered her mouth, stifling her gasp, and a muscled arm came around her, pinning her arms to her sides.

"Please dinnae scream... I mean ye nae harm... I am here to take ye to safety." A deep gravelly voice whispered into her ear with a broad Highland accent.

Caitlin stiffened and grunted behind the man's hand. Her heart pounded as she took in her predicament.

"Now please just hear me oot! I seriously mean ye nae harm." The man's voice became more intense as she struggled. His masculine scent surrounded her as strongly as did his arms. "Ye are, or will be, in danger soon if I dinnae get you oot o' here, Caitlin."

How did he know her name? And he spoke like he knew her, his tone one of familiarity.

Stay calm Caitlin, think!

Her room was so far away from anyone else's in this big house, screaming was not an option. She needed time to plan an escape—she'd talk him around. She had dealt with aggressive people at work and staying calm to dispel any violent behaviour was her usual plan of action. Her training kicked in. She slowed her breathing and let her shoulders relax. He released his hold on her.

She turned and stood with her back to the window. He was tall, with dark-blond hair and a neat beard, and blue eyes typical of Highland families. His broad shoulders and muscled arms filled a shirt that stretched over his well-formed torso. His size and army-type attire were incongruous against the backdrop of her pink lace-curtained four-poster bed covered in frilly scatter cushions. Was he the summer hire Andy had mentioned? Why had he snuck up on her? Her muscles tensed, and a shiver of fear began at the base of her skull. She was no match for him in physical strength.

Time to talk!

"How do you know my name?" Despite trying to stay calm, her voice quavered.

"Caitlin Murray, ye would be surprised how much I actually ken about yoo, lass." He smiled. "My name's Scott. Your Uncle Kieran hired me to work here for the summer. Andy told ye aboot me, aye?"

He moved to stand in front of her bedroom door, effectively barring her exit. No staff had ever behaved toward her like this—cornering her. Her eyes flicked to the bedside table. With the internal phone by her bed, she'd call the phone in the kitchen. Aunt May might be there. His eyes narrowed slightly as he followed her glance.

"Your family is losing millions and the average person their wealth." His gaze returned to her. "Although most of them are losing everything—investments, superannuation, their life savings, their homes, which will be seized by the banks. The economy is in decline. People will lose their jobs. Your family, on the other hand, and all the similarly wealthy, will ride out this storm and survive it. This will nae please the average 'Jock in the street' and life for the wealthy is about to become dangerous."

It seemed a weird time to be giving a running commentary on current events. She stood straighter and clenched her sweaty palms into fists. How does this crazy know Uncle Kieran is worth millions? So, he was going to abduct her, was that it? For ransom? A plan formed. Distract him with questions, take him off guard, make her move.

"You mean 'the peasants are revolting'?" she asked.

"Aye, I ken ye know your history. Dinnae joke about revolutions. Some of the rich will recover and the poor will become poorer. The United Kingdom, Europe and eventually the globe will sink into disarray and chaos after this economic crisis." His deep voice rumbled in steady, measured tones and his stare was intense.

"The world economy has crashed before. It recovered. It will do the same this time." Caitlin swallowed and inhaled deeply as she flicked her long blond hair behind her shoulder. She continued her direct gaze, trying to ignore her thudding pulse.

"No. It does nae." He crossed his arms over his chest, making him look even larger. "The rich people of the world have been ignoring the past for far too long. It will now catch up with them." His shoulders rose as he drew in a breath. "People *will* die. Cities will be torn apart. The world will never be the same. There's going to be food shortages, disease, wars!" He flung his hands around him expansively as if trying to explain the unexplainable. "That's why I am here for you Cait, to keep you safe while the world goes crazy. I have my vehicle packed but we need to go the noo', before they come to ransack the place." He moved toward her.

He called her Cait. Only her mother ever called her Cait. Her thumping heart came into her throat for a moment. She took another breath to steady herself.

"We are off the road here," she said. "And we can lock the gate and doors."

This halted his advance.

"Ye really think that will keep that mob out? Caitlin, they're all fired up and comin' here. I need to get ye out of here. Now!"

The room faded out briefly and as the floor began to shift, Caitlin reached for a post of her bed. She quickly refocussed, and the room ceased its slow tilt. He spoke like it was inevitable. In any other situation, he would come across as intelligent and articulate—normal— apart from his theories of the present crisis. She'd continue with her plan—talk and distract.

"I can't go with you." She shook her head.

"Well, ye have no choice." He crossed his arms as the fingers of his right hand tapped his left bicep. Tilting his head, in a way only a Scotsman can, his tone was persuasive. "Please come with me willingly. It's for to keep you safe lass. Och! You're so *young* here! Ye dinnae ken anything. Just have a wee look oot the window. The mob's on its way here!"

Caitlin blinked, not wanting to take her eyes off the man but the conviction in his voice compelled her. She turned side-on, viewing out of the window and keeping an eye on him. At the far end of the long driveway there was movement. A group of men had come through the open gate and were trekking up the driveway to the house. As she turned fully to the window to gain a better view, her pulse seemed to miss a beat. The mob carrying cricket bats and iron poles parted from behind as it made an avenue of honour for a car, its occupants waving guns and knives.

A warm rough hand grabbed hers. She flinched away from the man as she turned.

"Caitlin, ye must come with me now. We'll go out the back way, aye?" He raised his brows and intense blue eyes engaged with hers.

She didn't want to go with this stranger, a stranger who acted so familiar with her. Yet danger marched up the driveway. He claimed to be the summer hire. That meant Uncle Kieran and Andy trusted him. *Aunty...Uncle Kieran!* They were out there! Her leg muscles tensed as her hand came to her mouth.

"What about Aunty—" Caitlin began.

"*Now,* Caitlin!" His voice was firm as his grip encircled her upper arm.

He dragged her out of her bedroom and down the passageway. Passing the hall table on the right, she grabbed the bronze statuette of a Highland Mountain horse. So intent on their flight, he didn't turn as she feigned a stumble. Swiftly she raised the small, heavy object and let the weight of it crack onto the back of his skull.

He halted mid-stride, his grip loosened as his hand flew to the back of his head and his whole body flinched in pain. She glanced at his face for a nanosecond as she ran down the corridor and headed for the kitchen. His expression was one of shock and surprise as he crashed to his knees.

Chaotic voices became louder as she approached the entrance hallway on the way to the kitchen. Clanking metal and the thudding of sturdy wooden furniture on the oak floor greeted her as she turned the corner, her flight bringing her right into the centre of the mob. The men with cricket bats stood around the lobby table, which they had dragged over to the wall displaying the armaments. Two men dressed in jeans and T-shirts were ripping claymores from the wall. A younger guy with a shaved head jumped down to the floor and brandished the sword, waving it around as if he knew what he was doing.

"Well, hello!" Hands grabbed her upper arms.

A man either side of her jerked her backward, forcing her toward the dining room. Her heels dragged along the carpet.

"Let's see what's under all this posh clothing, eh?" The one on the left sneered into her face.

Caitlin's heart pounded. She let out the scream she'd been holding in. Her breath now came in short, sharp pants. They flung her on the dining room floor. She rolled over, regaining her footing and took in a deep breath, preparing for another scream. The Turkish rug loomed bright red before her eyes as she pushed up with her hands to stand. Rough hands grabbed at her jeans, pulling her T-shirt up from behind.

A grunt sounded from the doorway. The hands ripping at her clothes fumbled. Then the man fell beside her. Blood dripping from his mouth. Eyes staring.

Caitlin spun around. Scott stood behind her holding high a bloodied claymore. He lowered it onto the man in the doorway who was rising from a fall. The man's shoulder buckled with the force of Scott's blow. He fell to the ground and didn't rise.

"Caitlin." Scott's expression was severe. "Will ye come with me *now*?" His chest rose and fell rapidly with his exertion. "We are running' out o' time, lass."

Caitlin opened her mouth to answer as Scott reached out and grabbed her arm in a firm warm grip.

"Stay behind me," he ordered as he led her through the dining room and to the back of the house, to the old servant's stairs unused for years.

"Are you sure you know where you're going?" With a shaking hand, she pulled her T-shirt down to cover herself.

"Certainly do." His voice was gruff as he faced ahead, intent on their escape. He strode with purpose, like he knew where he was going.

Once down the stairs they reached a door Caitlin had never seen before. A hot ring of pain burned around her upper arm where Scott held it in a vice-like grip. If he let go, she would make a run for it. But he held her firm as though he read her thoughts.

"What about Uncle and Aunty?" Her voice sounded ragged, even to her own ears.

"My only concern is you, Caitlin," he said.

"Let me go. Now! You're hurting me."

"Dinnae run away on me, lass!" he spoke firmly.

He shouldered the door, and it flew open. Dust particles rose in the air and mould hit her nostrils. She squinted at the bright day outside. Sounds of the mob filtered through from the front of the house.

Loud. Angry. A cold sensation in her chest fought with her heart trying to escape it. Now this tall stranger was dragging her to his vehicle. Those thugs were plundering the house, just as they had almost plundered her. For the moment Scott seemed the safest option. Reluctantly she let him tug her to his four-wheel drive vehicle as he threw the sword aside. Caitlin landed heavily in the front passenger seat as he pushed her inside.

"But Aunty and Uncle!" She yelled up at him.

"Put your seat belt on." He slammed the door, ignoring her pleas for her family's safety.

The lock clicked shut. He ran around the front of the vehicle to the driver's side. The door clicked unlocked for the few moments it took for him to jump in. Then it clicked locked again.

So, he doesn't trust me.

"Keep your head down." He started the engine and skidded past the back of the house, making his way to the far driveway to avoid a head-on confrontation with the mob.

Chapter Four

The back driveway came out onto the main road which led into town one way and to the north the other. Scott turned north.

"So where are you taking me?" Caitlin asked.

"Somewhere safe, Cait. Don't worry."

The vehicle jerked to a halt as the seat belt dug into her neck and burned. Across the road leading north two cars were alight. In front of these a group of men with metal poles—broken signposts most likely—stood as a further barricade. Scott cursed under his breath as he skidded the car around and headed into the village.

Ahead, rubbish littered the street, and the breeze picked up a long sheet of plastic wrapping blowing around the feet of distressed shop owners, their hands hanging by their sides as they stood in front of their businesses. Glass covered the footpaths and road. Apart from the stunned locals, the street was empty, with no sign of the mob. Scott drove cautiously through the rubble, the tyres crunching over the broken glass.

Following the road through the village, they approached the gatehouse to the estate. Caitlin's breath caught in her throat as she looked along the driveway. The mob still massed at the front of the house and some men moved along smashing the lower floor windows. Others were dragging out the furniture and paintings.

"There's Andy!" she yelled. "We've got to help him."

Scott ignored her.

She tried the car door. Still locked.

"We have to help him. Uncle Kieran's probably with him!" she screeched, frantically shaking at the door catch.

Caitlin's heart pounded. Her head swam.

Uncle! Aunty!

Scott accelerated past the end of the driveway. She yelled with all her might as a large man swung his fist toward Andy's head, using full force to land the blow. She let out a strangled cry as Andy crumpled to the ground.

"No! Go back! We've got to help them!" Her empty lungs burned with their struggle for air.

She punched out at his arm trying to hit his face, but he was out of reach. Scott drove on, raising his arm to block her futile blows. It was like punching a concrete wall. Her knuckles crunched as pain shot up her arm.

"Scott!" Her voice was hoarse now as she pleaded with him. "Let me out. We have to help them."

"Quiet!" His shout was deafening.

Caitlin flinched. He scowled at her and continued to drive, glancing constantly at the rear-view and side mirrors. His breathing came loudly through his nostrils, matching her own ragged breaths. A silence settled in the vehicle's cabin, its engine the only sound as Scott read the road signs. This man was hard-hearted or a *psycho*. What had she got herself into?

"You've let them *die*," she said.

"No, I have nae."

"How can you be sure?"

"I ken, that's all."

Caitlin glanced back trying to get a glimpse of the house. Now in the distance smoke rose from the stables.

"Bonny! My mare!"

What if she's caught in the fire? What if they stole her? Or killed her! Caitlin's throat tightened. But it was more from seeing Andy slump to the ground.

She would never forget it.

Never. And the fact that *this* man would *not* go back!

"Caitlin lass, we cannae go back." Scott's voice took on gentler tones. "It's too dangerous. Your uncle and aunt survive. I dinnae ken for certain about that nice old man Andy."

He drove on in silence.

How could he know that? The crazy-man-theory was looking more and more plausible. She glanced at the equipment in the back of the 4WD. It was boxes containing who knows what—camping gear and guns? She recognised gun covers from the shoots her uncle held at the estate in summer. Why did he need guns? Emotions swirled within her; chilling fear tempered by the subtle warmth of curiosity.

"How do you know?" Caitlin asked. "You can't *know* —"

Scott's raised index finger silenced her. "I'll stop up ahead and we'll talk. Give me your phone." He held out his hand. "You're welcome, by the way."

"For what?" She took her mobile out of her jacket pocket and slammed it into his open palm. "Oh, yes. Thank you for saving me from the bad men."

She repressed a shiver and tried to keep up the bravado. If she made him think she was compliant, she might be able to lull him into a false sense of security and then make a run for it. Another run for it. He drove until they came to a secluded wooded area off the road and then parked.

"I must explain it to you. But not all at once, for ye will have trouble accepting it. The reason I am here. You see... och how do I say this?" He ran the thumb of his left hand over his brow as he sucked air between his teeth. "I've been trying to think of a way to make it easy but there is nae one." He lifted his head and looked her directly in the eye. "So Cait, I'll just go right with the truth. I'm from the future and I'm here to protect you."

Caitlin blinked, and nothing came out of her mouth, no matter how much she wanted something to.

"In the future," he continued, "I know you. And you, young lady, are a great leader. You see, I need to keep you safe during this time, so you can do your job in the future and help the world get back on its feet." He paused and blinked a few times as she held his gaze and took deep breaths.

"You mean like *Terminator*? You're not an android, are you? I knew the crackpot-theory was going to win in the end!" She grabbed for the door handle.

"Now Caitlin, give me a chance!" He restrained her with a firm grip, his massive hand encircling her right arm. "I'm no' a robot."

She looked at him with squinted eyes. "If you're from the future where it's a mess, how do you know what a terminator is?"

"You made sure people rescued books and made anyone who remembered a movie to write the story down," he replied.

"Really?"

"Aye. Really." He slowly nodded his head and his mouth became a thin line.

"How do you know me?" She kept her eyes narrowed.

"I know you well."

"No. That's not what I asked. But you claim you know me well. Tell me something about myself. Prove it!" Caitlin glared at him.

"Ye have a dark mole," he said, "on your upper inner thigh very close to—"

"Wait a minute!" Caitlin gulped. How the hell did he know *that*!

"I said I know you." His voice rose to a defensive squeak.

"What else?"

"The cause of death recorded on your mother's death certificate is not correct," he said.

"How *not correct*?"

"The young doctor who completed the form wrote Sarcoidosis instead of Lymphoma," he replied. "Sarcoidosis was the initial, but incorrect, diagnosis. Sarcoidosis mimics many diseases. The doctor had nae looked far enough into your mother's history when she came to write the death certificate."

"Now, you could have somehow got those records yourself and found that out!" A coldness began in the pit of Caitlin's stomach.

"And you refused an autopsy," he continued his revelations. "They wanted to perform one because your mother had undergone surgery in the previous two weeks. But you said that ye knew what she died from, and ye wanted her buried untouched." His Scottish accent lilted throughout his explanation.

No one else was in the room with her, the doctor, and her mother's corpse when that conversation occurred four years ago. Only someone whom she herself had told would know this.

And she had told no one.

Caitlin sat straighter, breathing deeply. His grip remained on her arm as she still held the door handle. He raised an eyebrow.

"Are we good then?" he asked. "Can I proceed?"

"I'm not totally convinced you're not a crack-pot. And I really want to know how you know *all* this stuff about me." She chewed her bottom lip. "What do you propose to do with me now?"

He sat back in the driver's seat a little, having released his grip. Mirroring her, he now chewed his bottom lip and stared intensely.

"Okay." He leaned forward on the steering wheel. "The plan is to take you somewhere safe to ride out the chaos which is erupting."

"What then? A couple of weeks hiding away and then you take me back to my family?"

He shook his head. "Remember I said I'm from the future?" He hesitated. "Well, this anarchy and world-wide chaos will last for years." He paused only slightly to acknowledge her exclamation of disbelief. "And my plan is," he continued, "to take you to a secluded place in the Highlands and ride it out."

"The Highlands! What's in the Highlands?"

"Not much in the place I'm going to take ye, and that's the point. Now, we should get movin'." He looked her directly in the eye, ensuring he had her attention. "Please, Caitlin, will ye promise you will nae attempt to leave me? This is all for *your* safety. We will keep listening to the radio, and ye will see that today was just the beginning."

Caitlin returned his direct gaze but made no reply. In the present situation locked in a vehicle, escape was impossible. She settled down for the drive to the Highlands, determined she would find the means of escape once her circumstances changed.

They journeyed for an hour or so without speaking. Caitlin tried to absorb everything he had told her.

"You say my aunt and uncle survived. Can you at least let them know where I am?" she asked. "Or just that I'm safe?"

"No, Caitlin. No one can know your location. It's for your own safety."

"Why the *Highlands* for heaven's sake?"

"I grew up there," he smiled. "I know parts of it full well, ye ken. Have you ever been there? And I dinnae mean Inverness or Loch Ness and all the tourist places. Have ye been to the *real* Highlands?" Caitlin shook her head. "The Highlands of Scotland are wild and beautiful. Some parts are so remote ye can spend days there and never see another soul. Ye may as well be on another planet. It's ideal for what we need."

Caitlin repressed a shiver.

"Aye, it's cold, and it's windy," Scott continued. "*And* it almost always rains, but I have equipment and warm clothing and stores to see us through till I can stock up a larder with game."

"So, you've really thought this through?" Caitlin glanced again at the stores, camping gear and guns in the back of the 4WD. Like a Doomsday prepper would collect. "You sound like the conspiracy theorists in the USA. The ones who prepare for the end of the world by going out to the wilds and living 'off-grid'."

"Exactly." He nodded. "That's what we're doing."

"And you are trying to convince me you're not mad. I'm having difficulty here!"

He smiled and tilted his head slightly as though she was behaving exactly as he had expected.

Chapter Five

C aitlin was deep in thought as they drove to the Highlands, contemplating everything Scott had said, plus the fact the vehicle held weapons. They drove past Stirling with the castle sitting on its rocky base to their right. At Perth, they took the road to Crieff, then Crianlarich through the Trossachs National Park. The countryside of vivid green flashed past, lush and verdant. Higher hills were turning purple with the heather coming into flower. Grey, pebbled burns and rivers flowed fast with brown brackish water through spectacular valleys with cloud-capped mountains on either side.

At Bridge of Orchy, Scott ordered her to stay in the car. He opened the door and got out, glancing at her as he locked it again. Her gaze followed him as he walked to the Inn and entered the reception area. After a moment he reappeared with a man following him. Scott pointed to the large aerial attached to the vehicle and spoke to the man. Caitlin wound the window down slightly. Both Scott and the hotelier spoke the Gaelic. Scott was fluent. Caitlin didn't like to stare, so she watched him while he wasn't looking, as he spoke to the hotelier.

Scott was older than he first appeared, maybe in his mid-thirties. He had the tell-tale smile lines at the sides of his eyes. He appeared fit and healthy looking, well-muscled with broad shoulders and strong hands. *And handsome.* Not 'pretty-boy' manicured-handsome, but rough 'lived-life' manly-handsome. He was articulate and bilingual. He had an animated conversation with the hotelier and smiled often, such a contrast to the gruff, serious man who had dragged her from her home.

Once back in the car, Scott handed her a bottle of water and a bag of crisps. He drove in silent concentration, drinking his own bottled water. Caitlin watched the scenery flitting past, her vision in sensory overload. They drove through Rannoch Moor with lochs nestled beside the road and purple heather-covered moors stretching for miles either side. She wound the window down further; the air held the faint scent of heather in bloom, the freshness of clean mountain water and the warmth of a summer's day.

The warmth entered her being and momentarily settled some of the chill harbouring there. Green mountains rose behind the moor, but there was little traffic.

"Where are all the tourists?" she asked. "These roads are usually thick with them."

"Aye, the tours have cancelled due to the troubles, and we're a step ahead of those who eventually flee north." Again, he spoke like it was fact—past-history.

Then the scenery changed. It was as if they had turned a corner and the world at once became larger. The mountains were steeper and higher with darker summits, and *so* close to the road. Caitlin craned her neck as she looked through the passenger side window. A white-grey cloud-filled sky obscured the craggy peaks of the mountains. Waterfalls cascaded over grey rock, pounding their way to earth; burns tore along the glen between the twin rows of imposing mountain peaks. A still loch, mirroring the cloud filled sky, sat to Caitlin's left. She let out her breath.

"Amazing, isn't it? We are now in Glencoe." His voice held respect.

Caitlin nodded but stayed silent. Scott turned off the main road to a track that led them closer into the mountain range to the north. They passed through the forest at the base of these mountains and turned into the hillside to a much narrower track.

"Now we walk." Scott stopped the vehicle.

"What about all of this?" Caitlin pointed her thumb over her shoulder to the equipment in the back of the vehicle.

"That we carry."

Scott placed a weighty backpack on Caitlin's shoulders. He gave her two duffle bags to carry, one in each hand. They dragged her shoulders downward. What? He expected her to carry this heavy stuff? Caitlin thought.

The track began by entering a small wood of Scots pine trees, with pale-orangey-brown trunks, almost skin coloured, and green pine needles iconic of the forests in Scotland. She looked at them with fresh eyes. Usually pretty, but now she memorised them as the eventual way to the road. She followed Scott through the copse, their feet crunched the pine needles, which carpeted the ground. Relief swelled within her and wearing good running shoes added to her resolve. The wind blew slightly, hissing through the pine branches, and wafting the distinctive scent into her face.

While passing a bend on the path, Caitlin dumped the gear and made a run for it. Her heart pounded. It wasn't only from exertion, but her adrenalin-fuelled desire to escape this possible mad-man. She glanced back before turning the bend. Scott was shaking off an over-stuffed rucksack.

She ran hard. So hard her thigh muscles burned, and her knees trembled from the unaccustomed exertion. She ran for five solid minutes. She then turned and continued a brisk sideways walk, searching behind her. He's fit and athletic. He'd be coming around the corner any moment, surely?

No, not yet.

Caitlin continued her flight. She pushed herself hard, endeavouring to put more space between herself and *him*. Her breath seared her throat. Her T-shirt stuck to her sweating back.

Further along the grassy track, Caitlin's heart pounded as she gasped for air. The damp sweat running down her back travelled parallel to the chill developing in her spine. Was she rid of him? She flicked her head around. Still no Scott.

A movement flashed in her peripheral vision. Caitlin turned with a gasp as Scott lunged from the gorse at the side of the track. He tackled her to the ground. They landed on a patch of grass, surprisingly soft against her back. He was on top of her.

Straddling her. Pinning her down. He grabbed both of her wrists in one hand and held them above her head on the ground amongst her hair. Her hair tugged at the roots. Burning. She fought against his strength. It was useless. His weight bore down on her, his strong thighs held her immobile.

"Caitlin!" Scott pointed the index finger of his free hand in her face. "It can be like this if you want it to! Dinnae be foolish girl. Och, you have a lot to learn! Do not forget I ken this place like the back of ma hand." His face reddened, and fear drained her strength.

She pushed against him with her legs, puffing from the exertion. Scott was too familiar with her, and he'd overpowered her—again.

"I chose it because, as you are now, ye would not survive in it without me. So, trust me Caitlin Murray, it's in everybody's interests, and especially your own. Aye?" Scott grabbed her chin and forced her to look at him, his voice rising "Are ye understanding me, lass?"

Caitlin widened her eyes and stared back, determined to show her defiance and none of her fear. His blue eyes stood out in his stern face.

She gave a slight nod. Scott let her go and lifted himself off her. She wanted to scream at him but bit her tongue. She must now keep to her plan of making him think she would comply. That way, she'd be able to take him by surprise with her next attempt at running away. She pushed herself off the ground, staggering. Warily she followed him to the place on the track where she had begun her flight.

This guy was clever, she thought. Caitlin picked up the backpack and duffle bags as Scott reloaded himself with equipment, and the trek continued. Her mind spun, options for escape fast eluding her. They approached a small, abandoned crofter's cottage, a grey-stone with peeling white paint and a slate roof, a neglected vegetable garden and an attempt at an orchard. Inside, was renovated to a liveable interior; cool inside despite the summer's day. They took off their overstuffed backpacks and unloaded the equipment and supplies.

"Now, I have one more load to bring from the vehicle and then I must hide the 4WD," Scott told her. "Due to your escapades on our journey here, I am much later than I originally thought. But I must do it. It may be dark before I return. Glencoe is a scary, cold place at night on your own. Remember, there was once a massacre here. They say ghosts roam. Och! I'm nae bothered, for you see, I'm a Campbell." Caitlin looked blandly at him. She wouldn't respond to his humour. "Caitlin? I'm serious. Please stay here and don't try to leave. I'll be back as soon as I can. Okay?" His Scottish burr accentuated in his earnestness.

"Yes." She had no choice. She would lose herself in this valley of steep sided mountains and night almost here. "Are you really a Campbell?" she asked.

"Aye, lass. But I dinnae treat people the way my ancestors did."

Caitlin peered out the front window and watched him walk away through the small, grassed area at the front of the cottage. He had locked her in. Her mind went to the story of the Campbells massacring the MacDonalds of Glencoe, breaching the sacred trust of guest and host, the Campbells were the guests turning on their hosts and murdering most, even pursuing them through the winter snow.

The cottage comprised of one very large room with three doors to rooms at the kitchen end. An Aga was in this kitchen section. The housekeeper of her uncle's estate said solid fuel stoves were the best thing to cook on, but this one was stone cold. In the wall at the other end of this main room was an open fireplace, also chilly and empty.

Caitlin ran her hand along the length of the wooden kitchen table, the timber's grain somehow comforting. She sat on the green fabric covered sofa at the living room end of the cottage. It had two armchairs to match. It was old. Well, everything was old. And not antique old, just *old*. Caitlin coughed as she patted the cushions, raising a slight cloud of dust. She left the two bedrooms at the kitchen end of the cottage unexplored as boxes of supplies caught her attention. Wandering over she briefly rummaged through the contents of a box on the floor near the open fireplace. A musty scent emanated from the old books inside.

The last of the daylight waned as Caitlin stood by the front window. Mist covered mountains were on every side, giants peering down at her through a green and white monochrome.

She jumped as the gate creaked. Scott closed the gate to the small front garden, the wind lifted his hair. His expression was one of contentment as if he had enjoyed his invigorating afternoon in the great outdoors of Scotland. Maybe he *was* okay if not a little weird regarding the whole end-of-the-world thing. But not a kidnapper holding someone to ransom, or a rapist, or a murderer, despite his roughness with her earlier. He had just seemed determined, even though it *was* scary. He said he was from the future though.

"That's right! How did he travel through time if he's from the future?" Caitlin vocalised her thoughts. Huh, she sounded as crazy as him.

"A Time Machine. The prototype actually." Scott's voice came from behind her.

Caitlin turned with a start. He was standing close, looking down at her, his usually hard features softened.

"So, you brought all this stuff with you? In the time machine?" She took a small step backward.

"No." He shook his head and chuckled. "I brought money and bought everything once I got here."

"Even the 4WD? How much money did you bring?"

"A lot. I still have plenty," he said. "You see it lost its value, paper money that is. There was plenty of it around, but it was nae worth the paper it was written on, so tae speak." He smiled at his own witticism. "People still hoarded it in case the value ever returned. So, there was plenty to share."

"People *shared* it with you?" she asked.

"Aye, the people we live with. There were pockets of people who survived the chaos and eventually we gathered together into small communities of survivors dotted throughout the world. We communicate with other Communities worldwide by Citizen Band Radio."

Caitlin sensed her eyes and mouth were open wide. She shut her mouth.

"I told you worldwide chaos would ensue from the recent stock market crash," he said. "If ye still dinnae believe me, just keep listening to the news on the radio. I've got one here and I'll get it set up after dinner."

"Okay let's see if all your predictions come true. One question though. Where do I sleep?" Wherever it was, she was determined she would bar the door.

Scott gave another chuckle.

"You'll be relieved to know there are two bedrooms in this crofter's cottage. Most untraditional, I might add." He spoke over his shoulder as he locked the front and back doors.

Chapter Six

McSweeny

S hit happens. Wasn't that a T-shirt? McSweeny's daughter was a lead weight in his arms as his muscles trembled. The lorry had come from nowhere. He had been cautious approaching the intersection as all the traffic lights city-wide were now out. The lorry had clipped the back end of their car and spun it around. It was the lamp post that did it.

Michelle and Daniel. In one split second, his wife and son, gone.

He looked down at Kiera. She was pale and tiny beads of sweat balled on her forehead. Since the stock market crashed, life had been a nightmare. *Hadn't he done the right thing?* The bank had called in the mortgage on the business. He'd laid their employees off first, then the inevitable bankruptcy and closure. He'd convinced Michelle to pack up the house, load everything up and head for their shack in the woods before the bank called in *that* mortgage. They'd be safe in their hut until the madness ended.

What a fool he'd been. So naïve to think anything would be safer.

Shit happens.

Well, it had. He'd carried Kiera's small body the half mile or so to the new Edinburgh Royal Infirmary. She was quieter now and had not made a sound since he'd entered this frantic place they called the Emergency Department.

"Miss! Nurse! I need someone to look at my daughter!" His own voice was desperate pleading in his ears.

"Jan, can you get that?" The older nurse briefly lifted her head and viewed him in between running from one patient to another.

"Okay, Milla." The younger nurse made her way toward him, her eyes intent on Kiera in his arms. "What's your name, sir?"

"McSweeny," he replied. "A lorry hit our car. We ended up wrapped around a pole."

"Please come with me." The nurse led him to a trolley, one of many lined against a wall, the only empty one.

He placed Kiera gently on it. She made no sound, or maybe she had, but he couldn't hear her over the beeping machines and loud voices surrounding him. The nurse placed her stethoscope on Kiera's chest, then flicked her eyes up to his, she blinked a couple of times.

"One moment Mr McSweeny. I'll be right back." She walked away.

McSweeny followed her progress to a guy with a stethoscope draped around his neck, standing by the trolley two places down. She tapped him on the shoulder and spoke quietly to him. The noise in the frantic ED drowned anything she said, but the nurse glanced back over to him a few times.

He approached McSweeny and stood close enough for him to read his name badge. *Doctor Kumran*. The doctor put his stethoscope on Kiera's chest and listened. He pulled her eyelids open. Kiera only stared—blank. McSweeny didn't need them to tell him. Another hole formed in his chest, fashioned after the other two.

"But there's not a mark on her!" McSweeny cried.

"Abdominal injuries most likely have caused her to bleed internally, Mr McSweeny." Dr Kumran's dark-brown eyes peered directly into his. They were tired eyes, but they held compassion.

The holes in McSweeny's chest grew larger.

All of them gone.

Shit happens.

The surrounding noise continued, swamped him. He released Kiera's body from his grip, unaware he'd been holding her.

He needed to get out of this crowded place. He walked outside, leaned against the concrete wall, and breathed.

Why? He'd tried to do the best for his family in this ridiculous situation the world was now in. Tried to be a good father and husband. Tried to take them to safety, protect them. Wasn't that his job? Didn't seem to matter now. Everything had changed.

After he buried them, he'd find what he could, and do what he did best—buying and selling. Keep business going. Ride it out and possibly survive. That was all that mattered now—and being on top when the world got right again.

Chapter Seven

C aitlin awoke in the back bedroom, its double bed squeaked and sunk in the middle and she had spent the night in its dip. Something else that was *old*. She focussed on the task at hand. The remoteness and wildness of this place thwarted her plans for escape. She got up and dressed hastily in the cold bedroom. She opened the door after removing the chair she had put against it the previous evening. Scott sat at the kitchen table, eating. A wave of warmth from the Aga hit her face.

"I can offer ye tea and toast," he smiled. "The Aga will soon have heated enough water for a wash. Ye can take a bath if ye wish."

"No, thanks."

A small radio sat on the kitchen bench broadcasting the news, as it had done the previous evening.

"Well then," he said. "Today we need to stow these supplies."

"Okay." Resigned, she helped Scott to set up the crofter's cottage with the equipment and stores he had brought. She unpacked tinned vegetables, tinned soup and hot dogs, and condensed milk and dry foodstuffs which she placed on the shelves in the pantry.

The radio continued in the background, constant news and commentary; any usual programmes abandoned in light of current events.

The stock market continues to fall, with no sign of recovery... the radio news announced.

"You enjoyed yourself shopping?" Caitlin unpacked the fourth box of tinned tuna.

"Aye. I've never been in a supermarket which has nae been looted," Scott said. "In fact, I've never been in a real supermarket before."

Riots continue in London, Manchester, Birmingham, Southampton, Glasgow, and Edinburgh... the radio continued in the background.

Edinburgh? Her peaceful Edinburgh? Were her friends okay? And her cousin Martin? Her flat? The Hospital would be swamped. What did they think of her? Under these circumstances, she would have gone to work, annual leave or not.

Scott had also brought potatoes, pumpkins, apples, and pears which he placed in the cold cellar. He must have spent some time at this cottage in preparation prior to bringing her here. There were enough fresh food supplies to last quite a while.

After a full morning of unpacking, her stomach grumbled. She picked up a loaf of sliced bread.

"Shall I make sandwiches for lunch? Tuna? I think you have enough." She hadn't kept the sarcasm out of her voice.

One side of Scott's mouth curled. "Aye, tuna will do just fine, lass. And ye ken how to make bread?"

"No. Should I?"

"Aye, for once the loaf is finished all the bread we'll have is what ye make." The rest of his mouth curled into an amused smile.

Well, he won't be laughing when her bread failed, she thought. Apparently, it was a skill; one she didn't have.

Caitlin sat at the long kitchen table eating her tuna sandwich, facing the back window which gave a good view of the cottage garden with its vegetable patch and fruit trees growing against a drystone wall, facing north. She glanced at Scott sitting opposite, his eyes on her.

"Why don't we get the autumn and winter vegetables planted this afternoon?" he asked. "I have bought seeds. I'll dig the beds."

Caitlin stopped chewing her tuna sandwich. A vegetable garden was part of a long-term plan—long-term in a place where she was still reluctant to be. She looked away and swallowed.

Calm down, Caitlin. Feign compliance, remember?

After lunch, Caitlin followed Scott to a medium-sized shed not far from the backdoor. He got a spade from the supply of tools and began turning over the soil in one of the raised beds. Caitlin had gardened little in the past and had only vaguely watched her aunt in the flower beds, nothing to do with vegetables and food production. Scott turned the sods and broke up the soil with the back of the spade. He looked like he knew what he was doing. Chewing her lip, she opened the packets of seeds. The winter spinach seeds were quite large and star-like, they were gritty between her fingers. Parsnips seeds were not.

"Aren't these carrot seeds?" she asked.

"No." Scott broke some soil up in his hand and, holding her hand, poured the seeds from hers to his.

Caitlin flinched at his touch. He never hesitated when it came to touching her. His hand was warm and rough, and his eyes flicked up to hers when she flinched.

"Mix them with the light soil," he said. "This way, they don't clump together, and you get the seedlings growing spread out and the parsnips have room to grow."

Scott instructed her on how to hoe back and cover the seeds once sown. Caitlin smiled at the smell of the earth, the grit on her hands and all the promise a seed holds. Scott smiled back and nodded. Her smile froze as she reminded herself of the permanency of a garden.

No, she had to go along with it. She had to fool this guy.

Caitlin put the garden equipment away in the shed, vaguely toying with the idea of running back into the house with the spade and beating Scott over the head with it. She took a breath and silently shook her head. She'd never pull it off. He'd see her coming a mile away *and* it would spoil the illusion of her compliance.

In the shed there were torches, batteries, and tools, knives and a gun locker which held guns, she guessed. Quite an armoury.

Why does he need so many? There were more guns in the pantry. She recalled that was where Scott locked the ammunition away, the key always on him. And amongst the stores in the cottage, was a citizen band radio which went with the very large aerial previously attached to the vehicle. Scott had missed out little. He had bought clothing, cleaning products and toiletries, including feminine hygiene products. *That* was embarrassing—Scott seemed to be used to living with a woman.

Her back ached and dirt clung to her hands, its fine grit clung to her face. She walked inside to have a wash. Scott had taken logs from a small woodpile near the shed and was now feeding them into the Aga. She wandered over to the bathroom and looked in. A medium sized bath sat along the back wall and a sink with a mirror above it was to the side of the door. A separate loo was the next door. There was also a long drop outside, which she believed would stink eventually. She stepped out of the bathroom.

"Ye'll be wanting a bath now," Scott stated matter-of-factly.

Well, as a matter of fact, she did want a bath now but was not going to have one while *he* was around. She didn't answer him as she went back into the bathroom and checked the door. No lock. A hasty wash then.

"No, I'm fine. I'll just have a wash." She made her way to the pantry where the soap was and took a cake. "Where will I find a towel?"

"Behind the door on the shelves." He nodded in the direction of the bathroom.

Yeah, she should have guessed that, because it's where she would have put them. Once back in the bathroom she shut the door behind her.

He had better stay where he is.

Washing quickly, she listened for any noise coming from behind the door. When she opened the door, Scott was not at the table, and she hadn't heard him leave. He came out of the pantry and walked toward the Aga where a pot sat with steam rising.

She exhaled and the tightness disappeared from her shoulder muscles. So, he wasn't a pervert. Well, not today, anyway.

Dinner was a silent meal. Her back still ached and, to be honest, she felt like she had worked a full shift in the ED. After she'd eaten, she went to her room without saying goodnight and placed the chair against the handle of the door once more before laying down on the lumpy mattress. Rolling into its middle, she recalled bread took a long time to make.

Chapter Eight

"You always have a loaded gun ready." Caitlin's gut tightened.

She would ask him more, but that would be probing... she didn't want to get personal.

"Aye, that I do." Scott rested the rifle on his shoulder, handling the weapon with ease as if it was an extension of his arm. He reminded her of the gamekeeper on her uncle's estate. In fact, the gun itself looked familiar. Just like the rifle her uncle used on shoots.

"Is that a Remington?" she asked.

He jiggled the rifle while a slight blush came to his cheeks and remained silent.

"Have you stolen my uncle's gun?"

He took a long pull of air. "Och. We need arms and your uncle had a gun locker full o' them. The mob would have used them if I did nae bring them with us."

"You've got more? You mean you stole them *all*?"

"They're for your protection, lass." Exasperation tinged Scott's voice. He looked her up and down. "'Bout time you learned how to defend yourself."

Caitlin raised her eyebrows. "Me? Fighting?" Her indignation over his theft of her uncle's guns gave way to surprise, which was more at his offer—it showed his trust.

"Aye, well. Not just yet," he said. "You need to get fit first. Ye do ken what exercise is?"

"Of course I do! It's important to your health."

"Aye but, from the look of you"—he squinted an eye— "ye have nae done much of it yourself, like."

"Humph!"

"Okay, then," he said. "How many miles do ye run a day?"

"I don't run."

Scott tilted his head. "I can see that, lass. Time to start. Get your trainers on."

"They're already on," she snapped. "They're the only shoes I brought!"

He slung the rifle over his shoulder by its strap and started jogging out of the garden, flicking his head, indicating she was to follow.

He jogged with a smile and a relaxed gait. Caitlin kept up with him, her breath coming easily. Scott headed to the right of the familiar track which had led them from the hidden vehicle by the Scots pines. Leaving this track, Scott ran past a grey boulder sitting beside a gorse bush.

"Ow." She brushed against the gorse as she passed.

"Aye, it's prickly. Be careful."

Her arm stung, and her thigh muscles started to burn. Scott stopped a little way further to check a piece of green string across a gap between boulders.

"Good. It's still intact." He tightened the green string and scanned the area.

Birdsong floated out from a nearby copse of rowan trees, their clumps of red berries reminiscent of Christmas. She followed Scott's gaze but there was nothing.

"What's still intact?" Her voice was breathless.

Scott pointed to the green string. "My markers."

"String? Thought you'd have landmines." Her sarcasm slipped out.

"Good idea." He raised eyebrows.

"What!"

He recommenced his jogging without answering. They left the clump of rowan and made their way up an incline onto the nearby moor. Caitlin's cheeks cooled as the chill wind brushed past her, catching her jacket. As they jogged across a carpet of grass and heather, purple and white patches caught her peripheral vision while her heart beat loudly and the burn in her thigh muscles increased.

"There's peat over there. We'll cut some to burn another day." He turned around and jogged backward, inspecting her. "When you're a bit fitter."

"I'm fine." Her words came between puffs. Her face was hot and her forehead becoming damp.

"Keep up, lass." He grinned and turned ahead.

Was he slowing down for her? The burn in her thighs was greater and her calves were tight. A sharp knife-like sensation hit in her side.

"Ow!" She gasped and bent forward.

In her vision, Scott's booted feet arrived in the purple heather in front of her. "Okay. Enough running for today. We'll finish checking the boundaries though."

This took most of the morning of that day. It seemed he knew every inch of this place. He was right; it was as familiar to him as the back of his hand. Caitlin's legs dragged, and her heart sank. Even though she had now seen most of the boundary markers, there was still no familiar way out, except the copse of Scots pines. She was certain now he would never let her out of his sight when away from the cottage.

***

Her throat was warm where Scott's hands covered it, a ring of pain crossing over her windpipe. The rough pressure of his thumbs neatly pressed against her carotid arteries. If she let him continue, she would pass out.

"What did I tell you, Caitlin?" He raised his eyebrows, his mouth so close, his warm breath brushed her face as he spoke.

"Clench my fists." Her voice sounded strangled. "And force them up between your arms."

"Go on then." He nodded.

Thrusting her clenched fists upward with all her strength, she connected with his solid forearms, loosening his hold on her and wrangling her way out of his grasp. She fled.

"Well done," he said. "Now come back. I have more ways of killing you."

"Can we do something else?" She dawdled back to the middle of the patch of green grass near the vegetable garden beds. The seedlings had sprouted, and shafts of green were increasing in size daily. The sun shone dully, and the sky threatened a late summer shower. It had been another long day, and her arms were heavy with weariness.

"We could look at weapons," Scott suggested.

Caitlin picked up her pace and was soon back in front of Scott.

"Guns? I know shotguns and rifles. We do clay pigeon shoots as well as duck and pheasant shoots on uncle's estate. I was sometimes the ghillie, reloading for the guests." She smiled and nodded.

Scott crossed his arms as he stared down at her, his eyes narrowed slightly.

"Not today," he said.

You mean, not ever.

Her shoulders slumped. "What then?"

"Anything else." His mouth held a smirk to one side.

Caitlin curled her lip and shook her head slightly. "Anything else? You are going to have to elaborate. That means explain further." She crossed her arms.

"It means *anything* can be a weapon," he leaned toward her, his lip now curling in the ghost of a smile.

She slouched as she tilted her head to the side. What was he on about?

"Go inside and bring something out." He raised his arm, pointing to the backdoor. "Anything except the obvious, like the kitchen knives."

Okay. She strolled inside, walked past the knife block and wandered around the living area. Near the fireplace, the musty scent emanating from the box in the corner caught her attention. *Yes!*

Caitlin sauntered outside, shoulders straight, chin held high and hands behind her back. *This will stump Mr Martial Artist.*

Walking straight up to him she waited till she was almost toe-to-toe, then she thrust the book into his abdomen. She expected a grunt. None came. The hard-back landed on a solid wall of muscle, as hard as its own cover. Caitlin gulped.

"Oh aye. Giving me a difficult one, you think. I told you *anything* can be a weapon." He held the book lightly in his hand and flipped it. "Keep still while I demonstrate."

He stepped even closer, slowly pushing the book, edge first, into her face. It landed at her nose, and he pressed it there. "One hard thrust and the bones of your nose will be in your brain."

"Oh wow." Caitlin's eyes were wide and her imagination in overdrive as she envisioned septal fragments entering the frontal lobe and severing vital blood vessels.

As self-defence training finished for the day, an internal struggle began within Caitlin. Could she fight this man, once she knew a thing or two? No way, he'd overpower her in a second. She got the impression as he was training her, that he was awesome as a fighter. Her admiration for his skills surprised her. He was truly capable of defending himself and this place if he had to. And, if she could believe him, he'd defend her.

*****

Thwack. Thwack. Through the rain, the throwing knives hit the old wooden crate repeatedly. A sense of achievement pervaded Caitlin's mood. She had mastered it. Well almost. The knives just did what she wanted. She had the knack. Despite the cold wet trickling down her neck from the rain, warmth arose within her, at this skill successfully learned, but there also had been a niggle of discomfort developing.

"I feel a little guilty enjoying learning how to be violent." She turned to Scott, her smile awkward.

He stood beside her, hair wet and curls standing prominently. His expression was softer than usual.

"Well, lass ye are quite good at it. You may well need it one day, so don't feel guilty, aye?"

His voice was gruff, always with his gravelly Highland burr, but his manner kind. She imagined his expression if one of those knives went into his chest. Pain momentarily stabbed her own chest. She would never do that to him. If she ran, she would just go, and try not to hurt him in the process.

***

After several days of weapon training, Scott turned his attention to teaching Caitlin hunting skills. They left the cottage for the day to hunt for squirrel and rabbit. It rained on and off, but Caitlin wasn't cold as the sun still shone between showers, making the rain look like drops of milk through the sunshine. There must have been a rainbow nearby. Scott squatted down on a rabbit trail as he set a loose wire snare. His hair was wet and small drops of water collected on the ends of the strands of dark blond now overhanging his face.

"So, the poor wee rabbit hops along, all happy like, and then suddenly, his head's in a wire noose which is getting tighter and tighter the more he struggles?" Caitlin put her hands around her throat.

"Aye, lass. It *is* a trap for food, after all." He looked up at her, his stubbled chin glowed ginger as it caught the afternoon sunlight.

"How do you know all this survival stuff? Where did you learn it, Scott?"

"Learning how to survive is how I learned it." He replied through tight lips.

"What about stalking deer?" she asked, changing the subject.

"There's two of us, "he replied. "Do you think we'll be able to eat all the meat of a deer between us before it goes off? We won't hunt deer until I've got something sorted to preserve the meat."

They returned from hunting and Scott made Caitlin stay back while he went ahead to check their cottage had not been chanced upon. She was on her own now and escape was possible. But her legs stuck to the path, immobile. She wet her lips as she peered ahead toward the cottage. Smoke rose out of the chimney from the Agar, its warmth proving the bread dough she had left beside it. She flicked her hair behind her ear as she reflected on her achievement, she'd mastered bread making easily. The wind moved the tops of the trees which edged the cottage garden where the vegetable seeds she had sown were growing. Now the permanency of this vegetable patch was comforting. Her pulse rate increased as her legs remained immobile, her window of opportunity for escape closing rapidly.

Scott returned and reported the cottage was undisturbed, so they began their walk home. Behind Scott, Caitlin stared ahead at his broad shoulders. Did his solidity have anything to do with her feelings of security? But it was still unfair! She huffed behind him as she walked along, again pushing down the resentments which had sat at the edges of her thoughts while she had tried to make sense of it all, and how she now found herself with this perfect stranger who treated her like he *knew* her.

"I just wanted to establish my career!" She burst out, and now it had started, there was no way of stopping it. "I wanted to be normal, like anybody does!" She stomped on. "But instead, I'm stuck here..." She almost said, 'with you!' but bit it back. "The world's going mad out there and according to you...and the news...it will never be the same again."

Her splurge of rage released some of the frustration. Her heart rocked against her ribs. She'd expressed her feelings to him!

He turned, the broken open shotgun over one arm and two dead rabbits dangling from the other. His blue stare held an understanding she had not encountered before.

"Everyone's life got disrupted, Caitlin. You're not the only one whose future was not only put 'on hold' but changed forever. Many a child, who was lucky enough to grow up, never got the education nor the proper nourishment he would have if the world had nae changed as it did. Sorry, but on that score lass, ye are nae special."

"Just suck it up then?"

"Aye," he said simply.

He made it sound like *she* was the Code Grey, the aggressive distressed patient, needing placating. Why did she blurt all that out? Now he knew how frustrated and vulnerable she was.

She followed as he turned and kept walking. There had been no judgment from him, only understanding. That made it even more difficult.

Once back at the cottage he hung the rabbits. A news report was on the radio. They were now sporadic. This report revealed that the violence and looting which had begun in the cities was spreading. Not only had looting occurred in all the major shopping centres, but attacks on other homes of the wealthy had occurred as it had to her aunt and uncle's stately home. Some families within her aunt and uncle's social group had suffered injury and loss of life. None of the other news reports had mentioned the attack on her Uncle Kieran's estate specifically. Each news report on the radio had confirmed Scott's version of events. The world out there was now a very different and dangerous place.

"I hope Uncle Kieran and Aunt May are all right," she wondered out loud.

"They survive, Caitlin." His strained voice came from the pantry as he locked the shotgun away in the gun locker. "How many times do I have to tell you?"

What *did* he know? How much was he *not* telling her? A sudden pang of longing to see her aunt and uncle filled her, reminding her again that her sole human company was this man who had removed her from them, claiming he would protect her.

Chapter Nine

The only means of heating water, and most of the cottage itself was the Aga cooker which fed a boiler. The Aga, the open fire in the main room and the Copper, used to heat water for the laundry, required large quantities of wood from the nearby forest. Scott was in the habit of chopping a load of firewood daily. Scott had also shown Caitlin how to cut peat from the peat bog on a moor nearby.

Caitlin looked through the equipment stored in sturdy plastic boxes in the kitchen and pantry. The afternoon sun streamed through the window and warmed her back. The rhythmic thud of an axe on wood, a continual percussive sound in the background, had now ceased. Scott burst in through the backdoor. He pressed his left forearm against his chest and gripped it with his right hand, blood covered his shirt and he smelled of its metallic scent.

Time to be nurse. She sat him in the chair by the kitchen table.

"I am going to look at it. Tell me first, was it spurting when you cut it?" she spoke in calm tones.

"No."

"You cut it with the axe?"

"No." He huffed a little. "But I should have been usin' one. I was using a hatchet and a knot in the grain deflected it, and it slipped up the wood onto my arm."

"I'm surprised, Scott. I don't know you that well, but it doesn't sound like you."

"Aye well, I was gettin' distracted."

Caitlin blinked at him.

"My mind was wanderin' a wee bit," he tilted his head with his admission.

He released his hand and blood seeped out in earnest, but he stayed calm, with furrowed brows.

"You're not going to faint on me, are you? Do I need to lie you down?"

"No, I'm fine." Scott was emphatic. "In the red box in the pantry, you will find everything you need for a situation such as this. I hope ye can sew."

"I thought you knew everything about me?" She opened the box in the pantry. In it was a well-stocked medical kit, filled with minor procedure kits, a delivery, and neonatal pack.

"I ken you can suture, just did not ken if you have actually learned it yet," he said.

"Oh, I have, don't you worry."

Caitlin gathered what she needed: sterile cleaning solution, sutures for muscle and skin, local anaesthetic, dressing pack, dressings, and sterile gloves. As Scott's wound was still oozing, she rummaged in the kit and found a pair of small 'mosquito' sterile forceps to aid in tying off the 'bleeders'—the small blood vessels which were oozing in earnest.

"Why have I not seen that medical kit before? There are long expiry dates on everything and should stay sterile for years. Well done with that one Scott." She was attempting to take his mind off his injury. "Are you okay with Lignocaine? Got any allergies?'

"Aye nurse, I'm okay with Lignocaine, and no nurse, I don't have any allergies that I know of." Scott said 'nurse' with the typical rolling of the 'r' mid-word, which Caitlin found so appealing in a Highland accent.

Caitlin went about her suturing task, often checking Scott's face to gauge pain or faintness, but detected no expression showing this. The smell of cetrimide, freshly chopped wood, and Scott's slight body odour enveloped her. He flinched under her hand as she injected the local anaesthetic right into the edges of the wound. Once it was numb, she took the needle through his skin, tugging the wound edge as she pulled the suture material through. She got into her rhythm— the needle clicked as it locked into place in the suture-holder, then her wrist curved as she pierced one edge of the wound and brought the semi-circular needle round up through the other edge from underneath. She pulled the suture through, leaving enough to tie it off once she had wrapped it around the tip of the suture holder and pulled tight to form the knot.

"Are you feeling up to holding those sterile scissors and snipping where and when I tell you?" She asked him after the first suture was in place.

Scott looked up at her, checking she was serious, then nodded.

"Well get those scissors there without touching my sterile field, okay?" Caitlin pointed with the suture holder.

"Aye nurse." He obeyed with a lopsided grin.

Scott had insisted on removing his blood-soaked shirt prior to Caitlin cleaning his wound. Caitlin's eyes lingered on Scott's naked, lean and muscular chest. The heat rose up her neck and her cheeks burned. She turned and prepared the dressing to cover his wound.

"That's the Caitlin I know and love," he said to her back. "Cool, calm and collected in a crisis and able to perform her task without a hitch."

She turned around. His head was still at a tilt and his gaze intense.

"You've seen me do this before?" She wrapped his arm in a new crepe bandage.

He pointed to various places on his front, side, and back.

"Aye, lass. It's no' the first time you've sewn me up."

Caitlin inspected his scars. Some suturing was neater than others, and the scars revealed some wounds had healed better than others.

"Why so many scars?" she asked.

"Life's no' easy out there, lass," Scott said softly, "but I always had ye to care for me." Their heads were close. His warm breath stirred the wisps of hair at the side of her face, tickling her ear. She stood straight, and quickly removed her face from his.

"I'd better go and have a good look at these medical supplies you brought." Caitlin cocked her head in the direction of the pantry and left him staring after her, a faint smile on his face.

Chapter Ten

"Anyone ever asked you 'If stranded on a deserted Island what books would ye take?'" Scott had bought both battery-driven and kerosene lanterns for light when the late summer sun eventually set, and an abundance of reading material.

"Is that what you are asking me now?" She lay on the couch, resting her head on her arm, staring out of the window at the mountains behind the cottage. The evening sun slowly descending through the clouds made the sky the colour of heather in flower, indicating tomorrow would be a beautiful day. Hard to believe chaos had erupted in the world outside of this peaceful glen.

"It's what I asked mysel' when considering the reading matter to bring,' he said. "Ye see, I had to consider what you need to know in the future when ye lead."

Caitlin sat up. Again, he'd commented on her being some great future leader.

Is he serious?

"So, what did you bring?" She rummaged through the box directly in front of her. She held up a Dictionary and Thesaurus. "Why? What about spell-check and Google?"

"Computers break down and become rare," he said. "We have one or two. I never used one. Forget your Google. What ye called 'The Internet' crashed, permanently."

There were many history books, both modern and ancient and works of great literature.

"I often wonder where the world would be if people didn't ignore this wee book." Scott had a soft leather-bound tome in his hand.

"What's that?"

"The Holy Bible," he said.

"The Bible!"

"Dinnae knock it. Ye ken it predicted The Stock Market Crash?"

"Really?"

"Really. One day ye should read the Book of Revelation."

Caitlin screwed up her brow. "Put it on the list because I expect there are a few things here you want me to read."

"But you were well educated, Caitlin." He held another book and sat back looking directly at her. "All your education and opportunity have to pay off, aye? Ye have a responsibility to share your knowledge and the experiences ye have gained as a member of a privileged family. You must, and you will, use it for 'The Greater Good' as they say. *Noblesse oblige*."

It was a lot to take in. Caitlin blinked. Was she up to this? She hadn't gone to a Private school as her cousins had, but Scott was right, she'd had a good education and gained opportunities from her relative's wealth. She'd travelled, learned languages, sort of. Viewed historical sites and famous works of art. But leadership? Her only leadership experience was as a team leader at work. She could barely imagine leading a whole *community*, as Scott said she would.

"Where did you go to school?" Caitlin asked.

"Well, by the time I was school age, schools were not functioning properly because of the infrastructure collapse after The Stock Market Crash. My mother was a clever woman, and she taught me to read and write and do simple arithmetic. I read everything and anything I got my hands on, which was nae much. You taught me a lot, Caitlin. And the people of our Community. You insisted they educate the children. Many people who joined our Community as young adults, like mysel', had never been to school."

Caitlin sat back on the couch. "Wow. I never thought I'd have much impact on anyone."

"Caitlin, ye'll be surprised at how much influence you have on a great number of people."

They were both quiet for a while. Her gaze went from one box of books to another and then back to Scott. She broke the silence with another question.

"How did you choose which books to bring?"

"I tried to remember the books in our library at the Community. And I made sure there were ones with information about time travel," Scott said.

He inspected the books closely, particularly their publishing dates and edition numbers. There were books covering theoretical physics, biology, chemistry, politics, law, languages and other textbooks.

"Och... that's amazing," he said, an open book in his hand. "This is the same edition as the copy of *Homer: The Iliad* we had in our library. You ken I loved reading this, and it annoyed me it had a coffee cup ring on the inner sleeve. Ye see they were all old books we'd had for a long time...." he trailed off. His eyes opened wide, and he turned the book to show her the inner sleeve. There was a brown-coloured ring. "It's the same book!" he said.

"No." She shook her head. "Coffee stains all look the same."

"I *ken* this stain," he exclaimed. "How can you get coffee stains to be identical? This is *the* book. Wow, that means I brought it. Maybe I brought them all."

Caitlin was silent for a time, watching Scott while he continued to look at the rest of the books with his eyes wide, exclaiming often as he recognised familiar books from his future... *Allegedly.* Was he putting on a show for her, or was he serious? She pursed her lips. Her assessment of him as an honest man was in jeopardy.

"What else did you bring, Scott?" She stood, then dragged over another large box to where they sat and opened it.

Sitting at the top were a pack of cards, a game of Scrabble and a Chess and Checkers board. During the following evenings, card games became a habit. Caitlin always enjoyed playing cards with her cousins and these times with Scott were just as agreeable. She found herself smiling often.

"Chess now," Scott announced one evening.

"Oh no. I am no good at Chess."

"How so? The Caitlin I know is quite the strategist."

"Ask Uncle Kieran, he tried to teach me. I was hopeless!" She said Uncle Kieran's name without thinking. She rubbed her thighs and bit her lower lip.

Scott's eyes flicked from her hands to her face.

"So, you ken the rules then?"

"Aye. I 'ken' the rules," she imitated his Highland accent. Scott sat back and took a breath; a slow smile began at the corner of his mouth. Then he set up the Chessboard.

"In the future, ye have actually said to me that you love ma Hieland accent. Yet here ye are mocking me." He placed the queens on the board.

"Oh, that sounded weird. 'In the future,' 'You have said.'" She mimicked inverted commas in the air with her fingers with each of these statements. "Not grammatically correct, you know. My Higher English teacher would have a fit if she heard you."

"Well, we cannot all speak posh English, My Lady." His voice was mocking but light-hearted, and he added a slight bow of his head.

"Are you knocking my Edinburgh accent?"

"Posh Edinburgh accent," he corrected.

They both laughed. Caitlin's smile lingered. This was the first time they had genuinely laughed together.

"So, this time machine, how did it come about?" she ventured.

He hesitated for only a moment and looked her in the eyes. She returned his gaze without faltering. He swallowed as he sat back in his seat.

"Well, ye mind I said we lived in a Community?" he began. "We have all sorts living with us. Being mostly Scots, and Scots being mostly clever, we have a few brilliant minds amongst us. Thing is, with brilliant minds, the day-to-day tasks of keeping a Community going are quite boring to them. 'Mind numbingly so' to quote one. Of an evening, much like we are the noo', we would get together over a game o' cards or Chess and, naturally, we would discuss things. We covered many topics. One certain topic came up often—the concept of time travel." Scott paused. Caitlin continued her stare. "You see, it was the view that all we had to do was bide our time, protect ourselves and wait for the world to get its act together again. But unfortunately, it was nae happening quickly. Consequently, we had plenty o' time. So, the discussions got away from the theoretical and into the practical." Scott paused and chewed his lower lip, then he added. "Ye ken the physicist, lass. He's your cousin, Martin."

"Martin makes it to this Community?" Caitlin blinked. "Wow. So, he's okay?"

"Aye, lass. He's the brains behind the time machine. He and our engineers then came up with their plans for one."

Caitlin then sat forward with her elbows on her knees, trying to absorb every word Scott said. Martin was smart. They'd often discussed the concept of time travel while on holiday. It fascinated her—as a *concept*.

"Gradually, they collected what they needed. What people who joined the Community brought with them. Things from the black market. It's amazing what turns up on that." Scott continued, "So, with the assistance of a very clever mechanic, they built one. Theoretically, time travel in the backward direction used approximately half the energy in the universe." Scott smiled broadly. "Or so our physicist claimed. That's half of the sun, half of me, half of you. But our team found in reality, this was no' the case. It only took the energy contained in the object or living thing to be transported. We had to increase the amount of electricity our wind turbines generated for the Community, so we slipped in some extra for our wee secret project. They tested The Time Machine on small animals, then larger ones and tweaked it a bit and announced it should be ready for human trials. They had devised a mechanism for pinpointing times in history."

"So, that's how you managed to come here when you did? Right before the stock market crashed?"

"Well, I'd been here for about a month before I met you." His lips pressed together. She held his gaze in acknowledgment that their meeting was more of an abduction. "That's when I got this place sorted and bought all the equipment and stores. Also, kept an eye on the news, and you. Worked at the castle of your uncle's for a wee bit, as ye ken."

Caitlin moved the first chess piece, distracted by her thoughts. Scott had planned with care and regard for her. He cared about her in the future, or so he said, and he cared for her now, in this past. He had always been respectful and had not taken advantage of her. If he wanted to, she would be unable to stop him, the same as it was on this chessboard! She moved one more pawn; he had already taken three. She moved her bishop diagonally to the edge of the board.

Bishop's gone. Damn his knight.

She moved one of her knights, then another bishop. She tried moving a rook but lost it as well. Scott's queen edged ever nearer to her king, and she moved her own queen to save it.

How could it be checkmate already?

"Well, that was short and sweet." Scott cleared the chessboard and set it up for another game.

"Told you I was rubbish," Caitlin said.

"You just need tae practice." His tone was patient.

"You said you came via a time machine that was a prototype," Caitlin said. "Had any trials with humans been done?"

He shook his head.

"You mean you used a time machine that could have failed? You could have ended up anywhere! Or nowhere!"

"Aye." He raised his eyebrows and let out a slow breath.

"Why?" Caitlin blinked and shook her head slightly. He looked at her but stayed motionless. "Okay, I need to know. How do you know me in the future?" Her voice was firm, demanding.

"I am your husband."

"What?" she whispered.

Many thoughts raced through her head, at first few of them were coherent. Then her mind-spin settled. It was a fact to her now—he was a truthful man. All he'd predicted so far had happened. Why would he lie about this? If he wanted to use it as a ruse for sex, he would have tried something before now. He behaved like a man who loved her.

Her attraction *to him* was undeniable, even though she was uncomfortable at times, as, in some ways, she still regarded herself as his captive. She had come to realise it gradually and had tried to suppress it, but it was no use. It was there every time their eyes locked.

Her intense gaze had not lifted from him.

"If in the future, you are my husband, why have you left me to protect me in the past?" Her voice took on an accusatory tone.

Scott hung his head. Silent moments passed. He massaged the empty ring finger on his left hand.

"Well?"

He lifted his head. Tears were in his eyes. He opened his mouth and closed it again as if struggling with what he had to say.

"You died," he swallowed. "I went straight from your deathbed into The Time Machine and never looked back. We'd previously set The Time Machine for the date of one month prior to The Stock Market Crash hoping someday one of us would come back and try to change things. Vain hope that was. Caitlin, my love, I could not stand a world without you in it. So, I came to a world where you still are. I only want to be with you."

Chapter Eleven

C aitlin couldn't speak. Her arms began to numb, fingers first. *Dead!* She shook her head, her eyes never leaving his. She sunk deeper into the green couch. Dead? Well, everyone dies, why was she so shocked? Scott ran his tongue over his bottom teeth and wiped the moisture away from his eyes. Caitlin slid her gaze out the window. The bird's song settled outside as the peaks of the mountains turned from light to dark. Caitlin swallowed.

"So, are we married? Now? No," she shook her head. "But I haven't fallen in love with you. Oh, I don't know. I sort of *have* to now, don't I?" She directed her gaze back to him.

"Caitlin do not feel pressured in any way regarding any of this, please. I want you to love me because ye do, not because I've told you ye do. Let me tell you about us in the future. Aye?"

"Okay. How did I meet you?"

"I was a baby when the Stock Market Crash occurred—" Scott began.

"What!"

"Aye." Scott's eyes had dried, and he had composed himself. "My family struggled for years and then we returned to the Highlands, where my parents were from. But eventually they ransacked our home and we had to flee. I lost contact with my parents while we were travelling through Glasgow on our way back to our home in the Highlands. Glasgow was...well, you don't need to ken everything that's going tae happen. Let's just say Glasgow was in a *state* at that point in time. I ended up walking back here to Glencoe, and when I could nae find my family, I wandered for months. I went further and further north until one day I wandered into the compound of the Invercharing Community, which ye ran. Everyone was so kind and welcoming. Especially you, Caitlin."

Caitlin did the maths. "How old was I, and how old were you?"

"Aye, you have surmised correctly. There is an age difference between us."

"How much of a difference?" she asked. "I must have been an old woman when you met me."

"No, you were in your late thirties when I first met ye."

"That's old!" she said.

"No, it is nae. I'm in my late thirties now."

"You don't look it."

"Thank you," Scott said. "Neither did you. In fact, you never aged, ever. You looked fantastic all your life. Like ye do the noo, but with smile wrinkles."

Scott peered at her face. Caitlin stood, and leaving the abandoned chessboard, wandered around the room.

"So, how old were you?" she asked again. "You still haven't answered that."

"I was in my late teens when I met you. I'm thirty-eight now."

"I thought you were about that. Wow!" Caitlin spun to face him. "I was a cradle snatcher!"

"Aye, I was mature for my age," Scott chuckled. "What with everything I'd been through."

"So, you are roughly twenty years older than when we met? We were married how soon after that? We *did* get married? We don't live together unmarried?"

"Aye, there was a Minister an' all." Sitting straighter, Scott began a smile which lit his whole being. "We have seven children. Four boys and three girls."

"What?" Caitlin was silent for a while, knowing her face reflected her thoughts in rapid fire.

"Aye. Seven. We must repopulate the world, ye ken. All strong and healthy. You are so proud of them all."

"I get pregnant *seven* times and you say I still look great!" she said. "Love *is* blind."

"No, ye aren't pregnant that many times. Ye give birth to two sets o' twins."

Caitlin sat again, hard.

"For how long had we been married when I died?" she asked.

"As to when ye die, now Cait, I dinnae want to tell ye, as it's not good for anyone to know the exact time and circumstances of their death."

"What did I die from?"

"Cannae tell ye that, either," Scott answered through tight lips.

"Why not? I might be able to prevent it. What do I die of? Natural causes? Accident? Cancer?" she pushed.

"No' telling you. What's the use anyway? The future is the future and some parts o' it ye cannae prevent." He stood and crossed his arms over his chest.

"Maybe I can. It was lymphoma, like my mother, wasn't it?"

"I'm no' telling," he said.

"I *knew* it." Caitlin jumped from her seat. "Then there is probably something I can do to prevent it or forestall it."

"What's the point, Cait? Ye have nae been listening to me. There are nae hospitals—proper functioning ones anyway. Nae cancer screening to detect and treat early. No chemotherapy, effectively no treatments at all. The public hospital system does nae exist—infrastructure has collapsed. Private medical providers were too afraid people's need would overwhelm them, they'd be ransacked, so they shut down. Even those who would provide treatment on the black market did nae have enough to cure... you." He trailed off.

"So, you tried?"

"Aye," his shoulders slumped.

"I can do something to change it."

"No, ye cannot." He shook his head.

"But you've come back to keep me safe from whatever would harm me now," she said. "What's so different about that?"

"It's just different, Cait."

"Is it?" she demanded. "Is it!" she yelled when he did not respond. "So, it's okay for you to want to change things, but not me?"

She moved closer to him, her face almost against his. She blinked at the vehemence of her own anger welling up inside her. Then she recalled her feelings when she had worked in oncology and watched her mother die. Understanding soothed down her anger.

"Is it?" She repeated her question, this time her tone had less fume.

He still did not reply but continued to gaze at her. Tears welled in his eyes once more.

"What I will tell you is this—ye died well, my brave, beautiful Caitlin," his gravelly voice was huskier than ever. "Ye fought to the last, and then, as ye sometimes choose to do, you gave in gracefully. And I loved you till the end."

Chapter Twelve

"Put that down." Scott stood at the door. Caitlin was in the middle of cleaning a cupboard and sorting its contents into a more efficient order. "We are going fishing. Come on! We're going the now!"

Autumn had begun, and it was an unusually warm day.

"I'll take you to a spot I used to go to when I lived near here. If it's the right time of the year, ye can tickle salmon. Ever done that?"

"No. What do you mean *tickle*?"

It was difficult to keep up with him. Scott turned around, still walking ahead. Autumn leaves from the trees which made the back border of the property, swirled around him as they fell to the ground.

"Catch 'em, the fish, with your bare hands," he said with a grin.

They walked for the twenty minutes or so it took to get to the secluded place in the river where larger rocks surrounded the shallow water. The grey boulders were big enough for a person to lie on them and warm themselves. The sound of the gently swirling current was a constant comment on its own passage downstream. Caitlin stood on the grey pebbled shingle, her feet crunching into place, squinting her eyes against the glassy sheen of the sky reflected off the water. Scott placed his rifle on the bank of the river and spent time examining it, the current was slower near the edge. He pointed to the water and smiled.

"Ahh! There's one!" Scott said. "Quiet now, as any sound will scare it away."

He lay face down on a boulder and reached into the shallows with his right arm. Caitlin moved to stand near and observe the salmon tickling. He waved her away, so she stood back, recalling her shadow over the water would spook the fish. After some moments, his face beamed with joy. He pulled his hand out of the water and produced a wriggling fish, which he slammed on to the boulder to stun it. Scott got out his hunting knife and looked directly at her.

"So now you want *me* to stab it to death?" Caitlin placed her palm on her throat. "Uncle Kieran did it for me the one time we went fly-fishing."

Scott nodded and handed her his hunting knife. After a few tentative practice strokes, Caitlin plunged the knife into the fish's head near the gills. Scott grunted his approval. She grimaced. He spent the next two hours with his hand in the water and caught four more salmon. After he scaled and gutted them, he put them aside.

"Well, I don't know about you, but I'm going swimming." Scott had removed his shirt prior to cleaning the fish, and now the rest of his clothing followed.

Naked, he walked into the river where the current was not so intense but the water deep enough to swim. A slow smile crept across her mouth and her eyes would not leave him. The warm sun shone off his wet skin, giving definition to his musculature.

"Come on, Cait. Don't be shy," he said. "Swim in your knickers and bra if you must."

Caitlin hesitated, then removed her jeans and top and waded into the chilly water, goose bumps formed on her naked thighs. Her swim ended sooner than Scott's. He stayed in the water while Caitlin sunned herself on the warm rocks which dried her underwear and warmed her core.

She raised her head. The dark-topped mountains before her were fading purple to brown on the lower reaches. This view had greeted her every morning since her arrival. The solidity and stark beauty had become a certainty in her world. These ancient elevations would remain while the world outside tore itself apart. It comforted her. It was like opening the backdoor of the crofter's cottage to an old friend every morning when she would take in a deep breath of the crisp mountain air, almost in a ritual. The scent of wood and *clean* air invigorated her. This was why Scott believed the Highlands were a place of seclusion—why he loved it so.

Caitlin laid back on the warm rock and closed her eyes. She drifted off in a relaxed dose but was now alert to the distinct *scush-scush-scush* sound of a human walking through shallow water. As Scott made his way to her, she caught sight of him naked, wet, and built like an Adonis. Or Michel Angelo's David, which she had seen on a trip to Florence.

The edges of Scott's mouth began to curl. "Nae bad for a man nearly forty, aye?"

"Do you really want an answer?" she asked. "And can you cover yourself? You are walking up to me, wobbling all over the place."

His smiled developed fully. "Sorry Cait, but I find it difficult to be inhibited around ye. I have made love to you every day of my life since I was eighteen, ye ken."

Caitlin's face heated, and she averted her eyes. How should she process *that* information? She turned her head away as he lay on the boulder beside her.

"Every day?" she asked.

"Aye. Twice on Sundays." Scott spoke to the back of her head. "That's every day of my life since I was eighteen except for the past couple of months, of course."

Caitlin did not respond. She was at a loss as to how. Maybe it was difficult for him being with her but not *being* with her. She turned her head back to him. He closed his eyes as the sun's warmth dried his body, his ringlets dripping on the boulder beneath his head. It gave her a chance to have a good look at him from a physical assessment perspective. As the medical person, she was responsible for his health and wellbeing. Scott had good legs, quite muscled thighs and he ran fast when needed. He had well-defined abdominal muscles; no fat; very lean all over with a nest of chest hair between his shapely pectorals. His collar bones were prominent and neck muscles thick, his arms ropey-strong. She had been in his vice-like-grip a couple of times. Yes, a very healthy specimen.

Caitlin frowned and pursed her lips. The previous weeks had shown her a man who cared for her. Caitlin swallowed. She and Scott in any circumstance would be attracted to each other, would be together. It was undeniable.

Should she let herself fall in love with him? He's wonderful. He's attractive. He's from the future... Should she believe it...? she asked herself.

She paused.

Yes.

Scott relaxed and dozed, oblivious to her mental conversation with herself.

Should she allow herself to love him now as he says she does in the future? This was the crucial question. Caitlin found herself undecided.

Once dried and dressed, they picked up their catch of salmon and made their way back to the cottage. As usual, Scott made her stay back while he ensured the cottage was safe. The path from the river did not allow them a view of the cottage until they were almost upon it. Soon Scott ran back, his brows drawn and mouth tight.

"There are strangers, men, at the cottage!" he spoke quickly. "Stay down and dinnae move till I come back!" He paused then and added, "If I don't come back, make your way to the Inn at Bridge of Orchy. Tell 'em you're a friend o' mine. He's my uncle, but he does nae ken it yet. No, tell him you're my mother's cousin. Ye look a wee bit Highland. Wish ye spoke the

Gaelic though." His accent was thick with his stress. Then he ran back toward the cottage.

Caitlin sat behind the large rock positioned at the edge of the cottage's garden, at the start of the tall pines which formed the boundary. The sound of footsteps came from her right. With her attention on the cottage, she turned too late. A man grabbed her by the hair, his breath foul in her nostrils, the knife in his other hand went to her throat. Its cold metal against her neck, close to essential vessels. She submitted. No use getting killed. He might take her to Scott if she co-operated.

***

Scott squatted under the window out of sight of the intruders, overhearing their conversation.

"Looks like the occupants of this 'wee' crofter's cottage plan to be here for a while," one of the men inside the cottage said.

From their conversation and the noise of their activities inside, Scott estimated there were only two men. He crept to the shed where he hid a shotgun and cartridges. The semi-automatic would be better for close quarters than the rifle, which he left in the shed. He loaded the firearm with buckshot cartridges. His intention was to talk them into leaving and carrying a large weapon might help to persuade them. But if not, he'd be ready. He slipped beneath the view of the window. The sounds coming from inside the cottage suggested rummaging and opening boxes of supplies. Maybe they wouldn't have to surrender many. The intruders had Northern English accents and had travelled to Scotland to get away from the difficulties down south, most likely.

Securing the shotgun and loading it, he silently made his way to the side door and snuck up on the unwelcome guests, watching them unaware of him as he approached. One man had a packet of tampons in his hand.

"There must be a woman living here. Wonder where she is?" His eyebrow cocked lasciviously.

"Hello, friends. Can I help you?" Scott sauntered through the laundry area, the loaded shotgun casually slung over one arm, his hunting knife at his belt and his *sgian dubh* hidden in his boot as always.

His entrance startled the two men who were ransacking the larder. They had gone through the house—their possessions were everywhere.

"Well, hello there," the older of the two replied. "We needed some things and so we thought we'd take yours." Both men had gleeful looks on their faces, like children who had come across a hidden stash of supplies. Even as they spoke to Scott, they covetously eyed everything in the cottage.

"I can spare you some." Scott tried a generous approach, maybe these two were in a sharing mood.

As Scott spoke, the man holding Caitlin shoved her through the back-door pushing her in front of him, restraining her by his grip on a handful of her hair. It pulled at the roots; her scalp was burning. He still held a knife to her neck, its cold blade constantly reminding her of its edge. She looked to Scott, calmly awaiting his cue. Her heart knocked against her ribs and a cool sweat formed on her brow.

But Scott will handle the situation, she thought.

She kept her focus on him and swallowed. He returned her gaze—a barely perceptible twitch of his eye indicated she was to follow his lead.

"Well, well, well! What a beautiful woman you have here, young man," the older man, who was the spokesperson, directed his observations to Scott. "Want to share *her* with us?" He pointed at Caitlin.

Scott cocked the shotgun to his shoulder. "You will all go...now."

"No, we won't," the one holding Caitlin said emphatically. He looked her up and down, his eyes lingering on her cleavage.

Caitlin's stomach churned.

"Pity." Scott fired the shotgun at the older man.

The impact forced his body against the wall. It slumped to the floor.

Scott's hunting knife was in the air. It spun toward the head of the man holding Caitlin. She held her breath, immobile. The hunting knife flew past her face, the wind in its wake stirring her hair. It landed in the eye of the man restraining her.

She was free.

Scott fired the second shot, missing his nearing opponent, then leaned down to retrieve his *sgian dubh* from his boot. His attacker lurched toward Scott's bent-over form. *Pop-click*, his switchblade flicked from its handle, and poised. Caitlin gasped as the man stabbed Scott through his shirt. Ignoring the blood, Scott fully faced his opponent. The man was quick and obviously used to close-quarter fighting. Scott blocked a blow and caught the man's hand that held the knife. Scott overbalanced. They both went crashing onto the kitchen table. Scott landed beneath the man. The knife pointing to his face descended by the moment.

The two men in combat were closely face to face. Scott's opponent's expression a sneer of victory, unnerving Caitlin and melting her feet frozen to the floor. She grabbed the carving knife from the knife block as she passed the kitchen bench. She crept to stand behind the man bending over

Scott. The man held the advantage. Trembling, she gripped the knife in both hands and raised it higher.

Caitlin's first strike missed her target, the renal artery. She hit ribs and lung instead. Air hissed through his chest wall. Bone crunched. Caitlin shivered. She needed better aim. She thrust her arms down again with as much force as she could produce. Adrenalin increased her strength. The man stiffened in shock as the knife cut through flank muscle. Caitlin hit her target—over and over while Scott held him in place.

The frothy blood coming from the man's mouth sprayed onto Scott. Scott pushed the shocked man off himself and onto the floor. He placed his foot on the man's neck as he quietly bled out. The older man had succumbed to his chest wound. A trail of blood smeared down the wall as he fell, a deep red arrow pointing to where his body came to rest. Scott's shoulders rose and fell from his exertion; concern etched on his face.

"Your guy dead?" Scott wiped his face on his sleeve as he pointed to the man who had restrained her, now lying on the floor.

"I think so." Caitlin's whole-body trembled; her breath ragged from her efforts.

"Check and *know* so." His gravelly voice sounded harsh.

Pressing her lips together, Caitlin nodded and grabbed another kitchen knife, as the one she had used was still in the back of the man now on the floor under Scott's boot. She went to her assailant and checked for a pulse. There was one present. The man was still breathing but unresponsive. *Brain dead.*

"Um…" she began.

"What?" Scott's voice was sharp.

With a gurgle, the last of the life of the man under his boot ebbed away.

"With your hunting knife through his eye into his brain, this guy is brain dead. But not dead-dead."

"Well, make him *dead-dead* then."

"No, Scott." She shook her head. "I really can*not* do that."

With a comment under his breath, Scott left the now corpse he had been restraining with his foot and strode over to Caitlin's problem. Pulling his hunting knife out of the man's eye, he leaned over further and placed it against the man's throat.

"No, you can't do that!" she yelled.

"Caitlin, I ken ye are a nurse, but do you really want to nurse *this one* back to health?"

"No, of course not. But you can't kill him!"

"Aye Caitlin, I can. He was going tae rape then kill you. So, I can kill him. Gladly!"

"Take him outside away from here then. The cottage reeks of blood and shite already." Her stubborn determination returned as she faced him with her chin up.

After a pause, Scott went outside, dragging the man's inert body behind him.

Caitlin sat outside on the bench in the remains of the afternoon's sunshine. She breathed in the clean air. On her tongue was the taste of blood and faeces which lingered in the air inside their home. Her mouth was dry, and she shook, not only her arms but all over—the post-adrenaline rush. She had experienced this before at work, after a code. Saving someone's life, resuscitating a patient, has the same effect on your body as killing someone in self-defence.

Who would have thought? She steeled herself for the clean-up job that awaited her inside the cottage.

Twenty minutes later Scott returned. He was shaking and slightly pale. Blood stained his shirt.

"Is that your blood, or his?"

Scott looked at his side. "It's mine." He grimaced.

Caitlin moved close to him. Blood seeped through his shirt from a wound to his chest.

"You've been hurt! Let me look at it!" She lifted his shirt to reveal a knife wound five inches long. It was shallow and now only oozing slightly. "Looks like he has given you a long, but not deep nick, with his knife. It followed the line of your rib instead of going in between. Just as well, because if it had gone in and through to your lung, you would have a sucking chest wound. That involves Underwater Sealed Drainage, probably the one thing you didn't pack in the first aid kit of yours!"

Scott gave a snort, a half-laugh and raised an eyebrow.

"You've heard that sort of thing from me before, haven't you?" she asked.

He nodded silently, a half smile on his face.

Then relief surged within her. Relief that they were both okay. They had gone through a terrifying ordeal together and survived. They had each other's back. Scott was a man she could trust with all certainty. And now, for sure, she *would* trust.

Chapter Thirteen

Removing the other two bodies and burying them was Scott's task, which he completed after Caitlin sutured his wound. Then she took on cleaning the house. The blood, faeces and other bodily fluids that escaped from the corpses were difficult to clean, involving a lot of rags and cleaning fluids. Caitlin replaced items in storage boxes as Scott returned, sweat-soaked, covered in soil dust and weary from his task.

"The smell will linger for weeks! If we had the resources, I would rip this floor covering up and replace it." She had rolled up her sleeves and tied her hair back. Her skin was damp on the back of her hand as she moved a stray hair from her brow, a fine sheen of sweat from her exertions covered her face and neck. "It was untidy, but they hadn't actually got to taking much yet. I think we got off lightly on *that* score."

"They must have driven here in a vehicle of some sort." Scott rinsed his hands and face in the laundry sink. "I need to find and hide it. Just in case they have friends who recognise it and wonder where they are. There is still some time before dark. I will nae be long."

"Keep safe. Come back," she called after him as he left the cottage.

He returned forty minutes later carrying duffle bags.

"These guys have a car full o' stuff!" he said. "I hid the car not far frae here. Come with me and help me bring things back home."

They returned laden with guns and ammunition, knives, tents, food-stuffs, a portable telescope, newspapers, and magazines, more first aid supplies and a small dog. It was a sorely neglected terrier-cross which feared them initially but followed them back.

"Was it guarding their car?" The creature stayed close to Caitlin's heels.

"No, I don't think so. It just appeared. It wasn't bothered I was taking stuff from the car. We'll keep it—we need a guard dog."

"This scruffy, pathetic excuse for an animal is *not* a guard dog."

"Aye well. Ye take what you're given, ye ken. He'll bark when anyone approaches. That's all we need. An early warning system, aye?"

The dog, after a wash, was less messy and more acceptable to Caitlin.

"It's an outside dog, though. I still don't want it inside!"

"Aye, Missus."

Caitlin paused as she watched Scott lead the dog outside. *We sound like a married couple.*

That evening they looked at the books and magazines they had retrieved. They were old and predated the Stock Market Crash except for one or two. It seemed some news in print had continued for a short time. Scott and Caitlin read them meticulously. Scott looked through the papers with a lined brow. She assumed he was looking for evidence to present to her as further proof his version of current history was true. There were reports of wealthier homes broken into, and thefts and home invasions increasing as peoples' misfortunes such as unemployment, property repossessions, company collapse, and bankruptcy increased. There were also reports of the continued general chaos and violent protests happening in the larger cities in the United Kingdom and around the world. Food and other goods were becoming in short supply due to factory and food processing plant closures.

Caitlin searched for information specifically about her family members. Eventually, she found it in a scrunched piece of newspaper wrapped around a gun. She read the newspaper article.

'*Kieran Moffatt, Scottish Electronics magnate, and his wife May have fled from their country estate in Scotland. A mob ransacked their property and stole their possessions. No reports of injury to Mr and Mrs Moffatt or any family members but Caitlin Murray, the couple's niece, is unaccounted for. Their current whereabouts are unknown.*'

Caitlin was relieved to find her uncle and aunt were alive and safe. She guessed they were down in London somewhere. Scott was correct in his report of their survival.

Caitlin considered the situation they had encountered together today. After an incident of such intensity at her work, it was usual to have a debriefing session. They needed one now.

"Scott."

"Aye?" he looked up from the newspaper he was scouring.

"We need to talk about today."

"Hmm?" He put down the newspaper.

"But I want to start by telling you I believe you totally now. Your predictions continue to come true. The world *is* descending into the chaos you described. Today I experienced once more how bad the world can be now. We experienced it," Caitlin corrected herself.

Scott's shoulders relaxed. "I cannot tell you how pleased I am at hearing you say that ye believe me. As for today, it was difficult, and ye did well."

Caitlin shuffled in her seat, still uncomfortable about the deaths.

"You started the bloodshed Scott!"

"No, I did nae lass." His gaze remained steady.

"Yes, you did. You shot the old man first!"

"Caitlin if I had nae, they would have killed us after raping you." Scott leaned forward in his chair, his face firm with conviction. "*They* were the aggressors. *They* invaded our home. *They* refused tae leave." He poked the finger of his right hand into the palm of his left with each point. "*They* stated they were taking our supplies. And they had *you*! I'll no abide any o' that. I'll no stand by and see you hurt! *Ever*!"

Caitlin burst into tears, shaking. Scott came over to her, scooped her up in his arms and placed her in his lap as he sat in the chair, with his arms encircling her. He spoke into her ear quietly. It sounded like the Gaelic. It was soothing. Caitlin's trembling eased, and she relaxed into his warm chest.

"You killed a man today," he spoke into her hair. "This is your mind and body recovering from it. I hope ye never need to do that again. But Cait, thank you. You saved my life."

Caitlin lifted her face to his. "You have killed before. You killed the guy at uncle's house when I…"

"Unfortunately, life has made it impossible for me to avoid that. Aye, you know I've killed before."

"I saw another side to you, Scott. You were awesome. And scary. But I'm so glad I'm with you."

Caitlin's gaze flicked from his eyes to his lips and back again. Scott leaned his head closer. Caitlin moved to touch his lips with hers. They were soft and warm. His arms held her close; she sensed his strength under control, gentle. The scent of his warmth radiated from him. Scott pressed her to his body and continued their kiss, his response to her becoming more ardent. Her passion matched his. He ran his warm hands down her back and held the small of it and pressed her hips into him. She allowed him. He broke off their kiss.

"You're no' scared o' me though, Caitlin? You ken I only want to keep you safe? That's what I'm here for. I'd never hurt you, *gra mo chroi*."

"Yes, I know." Her heart pounded. He felt *so* good.

Scott kissed her again as he stood and held her close to himself. The length of his body, strong and solid against her own. They continued their kiss, both caught up in the sensations of mouth on mouth and body against body. He walked into his bedroom, easily carrying her dangling in front of him, still held in his embrace. His firmness pressed into her belly. *Whoa!* She pulled her lips away from his.

"No! Stop." She pressed both hands flat against his chest. "I'm not ready for this." She could no longer hold his gaze. He froze in the middle of both his hands caressing her buttocks.

"Ah. Okay then, Caitlin," the words came through heavy breaths. He put her feet on the ground and let go of her bottom. Resting his forehead on hers, he recovered his breathing. "Just tell me when ye are then, okay?"

She nodded mutely, a slow warmth rising to her cheeks, adding to his warmth which surrounded her.

"You ken I love you and am used to showing that I do in the way a man loves a woman, aye?" He still held her close.

She nodded again.

"Sorry." She disengaged herself from his embrace and walked to her room, surprised at how quickly a kiss had progressed to more. Scott *was* used to being married to her. But they weren't. Not now. Not yet. Oh, she had a *lot* to think about.

Chapter Fourteen

C aitlin rose early the next morning, her task was to wash the laundry. She collected wood from the woodpile and lit a fire under the Copper, a very large basin made of copper held in place over the solid fuel fire. When the water was hot enough, she used a pole to agitate the clothes to wash them. Then she emptied the Copper and repeated with fresh water to rinse. Today, to save time, she rinsed the clothes in cold water. She would *not* be doing *that* in winter. Way too chilly on the hands! Caitlin hung the clothes on the line as Scott emerged.

Caitlin had spent most of the night thinking. They needed to talk, but where would she start? Did she really want to? Scott stood shirtless in the back doorway, dishevelled and drinking his first cup of tea for the day. He walked toward her. Caitlin's eyes flicked from Scott to her washing and back again. She tried not to focus on his chest. Scott's sutured wound still looked fresh. She opened her mouth to speak, but Scott, staring at the ground as he approached, began the conversation before her.

"Caitlin," he said. "I've been thinking after reading those newspapers last evening. Soon crude oil refining will almost cease, and petrol and other fuels will become scarce. So, I will go and buy horses and a goat."

"Where?" Caitlin double blinked. *Not* the topic she imagined they'd be discussing. She wouldn't bring up the subject of the embarrassing moment of last evening, even if he didn't.

"Probably back to Crieff or near Perth even. It will take me a couple o' days. I'm going tae take the car we hid and sell it. Then I'll stock up on what I can carry on the horses."

What? Wait a minute, she thought. He was leaving her? After those guys yesterday? A tightness clenched the back of her throat.

"What if somebody comes?" she asked.

"There's nae avoiding it." Scott bit his lower lip. "We need transport when there is nae any fuel. Which will soon be the case. If both of us go, then I'll no' be able to carry as many supplies back on the horses." He stood close in front of her now, empty cup in hand. He smelled of man, and his body heat radiated from him; reluctance also, but the journey was a necessity. "Keep all the doors locked," he continued. "When you're out of the house, keep the nearest door to you open, carry a gun and a knife. Don't be out when it's dark. Keep the wee mutt nearby ye. He'll let you know when someone's coming." They both smiled.

Caitlin did a double take, as his previous order sunk in. "A gun? But you've never let me touch a gun."

She looked him directly in the eye. He still always had the key to the ammunition cupboard on his person.

"Well, I ken ye know guns," he said.

"You trust me now?" She stood taller, challenging him.

"Things are changed between us now, Caitlin. Ye trust me, and so I can trust you." Scott took the key from his trouser pocket and placed it firmly in her palm, closing his warm large hand around hers as he spoke.

Caitlin looked at his hand engulfing hers. She was uncomfortable again, memories of last night in her head and she didn't know how to even begin to talk about *that*.

"But what if somebody comes?" She hardened her voice.

Scott faced her full on, his eyes narrowed a little and the muscles in his cheeks tightened as he clenched his jaw.

"Shoot to kill." He nodded slightly with a firmness to his voice to which she was unfamiliar. Scott sounded like a man used to giving orders and having them obeyed.

She gulped. "But what if they're friendly?"

"Caitlin, you're nae fool. Ye ken how to read people. Trust your instincts... shoot to kill." That slight nod again. He turned away.

"Why a goat?"

"For milk and cheese. You love goat's cheese." He half turned back.

"I do?"

"Well, ye do in the future. You love feta." The knowing smile, always present when Scott announced something previously unknown to her about herself, showed up on his face once more.

Before Scott's journey, he barred both the windows. "Just in case someone tries to break one to get in to ye." He showed her the loading and use of a handgun as she was familiar with a shotgun.

***

Three days passed. Before Scott left, Caitlin had asked him to try to stock up on medicines such as antibiotics and lignocaine. "Because you keep cutting yourself," she'd teased. It was an attempt at light-heartedness. Her concern grew. First, for the fact he was leaving her, second that he was leaving her on her own and third, because he may not return. She turned over her anxieties in her mind. Scott would never do this out of choice, but there was a strong possibility something sinister or fatal could happen to him and she would never see him again.

The first two days Caitlin had browsed the books on medicinal herbs and inspected the wild plants in the garden. She found Feverfew, which she had read soothed headaches. Also, Chamomile, which she knew was an herbal tea used for a calming effect. There was even a plant which might be Echinacea, but she wasn't sure, as the climate would be too cold for it. She researched herbs, as she assumed medicine production may cease as well.

At night, she sat by the Aga and read—history books, mainly. Scotland's history fascinated her. As a people, the Scots had been either subjugated or not ruling independently, for most of the last seven hundred years of their history. This absolutely baffled her. Her Scottish ancestors were so fierce, even the might of the Roman Empire could not subdue them. How had the British managed?

Caitlin looked at the Gaelic language book. Scott had called her '*gra mo chroí*'. She found out it means 'my heart's love' or 'love of my heart'. She spoke little of the Gaelic herself, mostly road signs, as many in Scotland were bilingual. Having lived in Edinburgh most of her life, she had not heard the Gaelic spoken often. She loved its sound when Scott spoke it. She hoped to say something to him in the Gaelic when he came back. Something like 'I love you'. Scott would probably laugh at her. Figuring out how to speak the Gaelic, when she had read the road signs, was difficult. There were so many letters in the words that were *not* pronounced.

Caitlin's thoughts often wandered back to Scott—his strong presence, his knowledge, his protection. She was alone and vulnerable without him. She slept with the loaded handgun by her bed and throwing knives under her pillow, and practiced with the knives during the day, becoming accurate with them. Caitlin considered shooting practice, there were plenty of guns around, and now she had the key to the ammunition store, but the noise would attract unwanted attention. That's if there was anyone's unwanted attention to attract. The dog, which she had aptly named Scruffy, had indicated no one else's presence. She hoped he would bark and bite, and not just lick any intruders to death. By the third night, she allowed Scruffy in the cottage.

By the fourth night, Scruffy slept on the end of her bed. Caitlin tried to imagine how to continue without Scott. Not only how to manage without his wisdom, experience at surviving and his companionship, but how to live without *him*. She did love Scott, just for being him.

Before Caitlin's mother died, they'd had the 'finding the right man' conversation. Her mother concluded with her final words of advice on the matter. "When you find the right man for you, you just know. You know?" At the time, Caitlin believed it was a little simplistic. But now she knew Scott, she understood. Her breath caught in her throat. Her father had died so young and her mother had never married again. When Scott returned, she would let him know she was willing to marry him and live as husband and wife in the fullest sense.

The fifth day since Scott left came and went. That night Caitlin's heart ached, convinced he would never return or was captured, or killed, or lying in a ditch somewhere. She wiped her eyes and decided she would go to find him. Maybe she would. If not, it wouldn't be the first time she'd lost someone significant in her life. In many ways, the loss of her mother was still raw, especially when she felt alone, like now. But if Scott was dead, she'd grieve, get over it and move on. He'd said she would found a Community 'up north'. She should start packing for the journey. She wouldn't stay here—everything reminded her of him. She'd start that Community, as he said she would. Perhaps she would search for Aunt May, Uncle Kieran and Martin, as Scott had said they would survive this mess.

Late in the afternoon of the next day, Scruffy started barking. Caitlin ran inside the house and locked and barred the doors. She checked the loaded gun and turned off the safety. She sat by the front window, as Scruffy focussed his barking at that side of the cottage. Caitlin strained to hear what disturbed the dog as she tried to quieten him, but he barked even more. Then his barking changed. It was no longer a warning bark, but a welcoming one. He began scratching frantically at the door, trying to get out. Caitlin unbarred and opened it a crack to let him go.

"Well, then lad. Do I only get ye for a greeting? After all this time?" Scott's deep gravelly voice rang out informing Caitlin the intruder was himself. "Where's the woman of the house, then?" He sounded cheery but tired.

The front lawn muted the clip-clop of horses' hooves. She fully unbarred the front door and ran out to see Scott on a horse, carrying a goat over the saddle and leading a heavily laden horse behind him. On seeing Caitlin emerge, he swung his leg over and jumped off, then set the exhausted nanny goat on the ground.

When Caitlin reached him, she threw her arms around his neck. He returned her embrace with a firm kiss, which lingered on her mouth.

"I thought you weren't coming back." Caitlin's pulse raced as she spoke. Scott continued to hold her close to himself.

"Did you think I'd left you?"

"No." She shook her head. "I thought something bad had happened to you. You've been gone nearly a week!"

"Aye, lass. Sorry about that. It took me longer to find decent Highland Mountain horses than I anticipated. Ended up at the market outside of Perth. Got the goat there too. Just as well, as there was a woman selling black market medicines and such out of the back of a van. I've got you a great deal of supplies." His smile was tired. "The saddles I had to buy separately. Some people are guessing what we already ken about fuel, and horses were nae cheap. But people were nae going for stock strong animals, like these dun garrons." He patted the rump of the medium sized horse he had dismounted. It gave a quiet snort in response. "People are still looking at horses, like fancy ones, ye ken? Not solid workhorses, like these two which I got for a fair price. Also, they'll no require a farrier as this breed rarely need shoeing."

He showed Caitlin the money belt full of cash; it was not much depleted.

"Got a decent price for the car then?" Caitlin asked.

He nodded in reply. Dark circles lined under his eyes and he was un-washed and grubby.

"Apart from the horses, I bought everything quickly. Coming home took the time. The horses are heavy laden, and I've forgotten how far it is to walk. We're only three or so hours frae Perth by car but walking... sorry," he shrugged in apology.

The horses' heads drooped. Caitlin helped Scott unload and unsaddle them. He ambled stiffly as he carried the goods inside. After taking in the last of the supplies, he went straight to his room and laid on his bed. After a minute, he sat bolt upright. "Och! I need to secure the horses."

"No, don't worry about that," Caitlin said. "Part of the legacy of my privileged upbringing means I know horses and how to look after them. You rest. Leave it to me."

Scott laid back down on the bed still fully clothed. Caitlin went outside to the horses and led them around to the back of the cottage. She took out the two halters from the tack Scott had bought and put them on the horses after removing their bridles and saddles then attached long ropes to them. She secured them to star pickets which she'd belted into the lawn at the back. The goat followed. Satisfied the animals were secure, she returned to the cottage. The goat stood in her vegetable patch making a meal of some wilting self-sown marigolds.

"Oh, no you don't!" She removed the nanny from the vegetable garden and tied her up near the horses, much to the nanny's protestations.

"Animals!"

Caitlin entered Scott's bedroom. Scruffy had ensconced himself on the bed.

"Out!" Her whisper was harsh.

The dog got off the bed next to the sleeping Scott and trotted to the mat on the floor in front of the Aga, where he curled up and slept. Caitlin turned back to Scott. He was unkempt from roughing it for a week; his clothes were shabby, and he looked like a hobo. The smell of unwashed human and lived-in clothes wafted out from his bedroom. She pulled the door ajar and began unpacking the supplies he'd brought home. She silently prayed. She hadn't prayed for a while, but it seemed proper to express to someone her thanks and relief that Scott was home. Her mother brought her up to believe God would always listen.

Caitlin unpacked the medicines Scott had bought. There were paracetamol, oral morphine, antibiotics, lorazepam, antihistamines, and some anti-hypertensives. Injectable medicines including morphine, antibiotics, antifungals. Also, anti-emetics, anti-diarrhoeal, and aperients. Intra-venous fluids and heavy-duty vasopressors. *I'd better not ever need to resuscitate someone with those!* There were also adrenaline, hydrocortisone, and promethazine for allergic reactions.

"Syntocinon and vitamin K!" Caitlin's eyes widened as these were used in childbirth. "What else did this black market pharmacist sell him?"

Caitlin stoked up the Aga and ensured the boiler was full. They'd need plenty of hot water for Scott's bath and to wash his clothes. He was still sound asleep three hours later. The onion soup, which she'd made to tide him over until she cooked a proper meal, was well and truly ready. But he still didn't stir. She peered into the bedroom. Scott remained sprawled on his back in the exact position she had left him. And breathing. She took his shoes off and covered him. His beard was thick, and his hair, which had grown long in the past couple of months, curled around his face. Caitlin's vision blurred with tears. Scott's almost forty years were showing tonight. Must have been quite a journey. She pulled the door to and started eating without him. No sound came from his bedroom that night.

Chapter Fifteen

E arly next morning Caitlin awoke to the bang of the back door closing. It would be Scott returning from the outhouse. She dressed hurriedly and joined him in the kitchen. He scooped a ladle of soup into a bowl, his eyes puffy with sleep. Caitlin got the kettle boiling and made a pot of tea. She stoked the Aga to ensure there was still enough hot water. Scott ate and then Caitlin broached the subject of a bath.

"Why, do I smell that bad?" Scott said in between mouthfuls of soup.

Caitlin raised her eyebrows, nodded, and began to run him a bath.

The bath was hot and deep. After shedding the clothing he had worn for the week, Scott sunk deeply into it with obvious delight. Caitlin no longer averted her eyes. She would enjoy him, all of him. Caitlin picked up the clothes from the floor with the finger and thumb of one hand and exaggeratedly held her nose with the other, as she carried them out to the laundry. Scott chuckled and then stayed in the bath for a while.

"So, did you see all the medicines I brought back for you?" Scott called from the bathroom.

"Yes. Quite a collection there," she answered from the laundry.

Scott moved in the bath and caused what sounded like a tidal wave of water to spill over the edge and splash on to the wooden floor.

"Ye have nae put my shirt into the water, yet have you?"

"Yes. Why?" she answered.

"Noo!" Scott exclaimed. "There's something in my shirt pocket for ye."

"Stay calm. You're flooding the bathroom, Scott." Caitlin returned to the bathroom and stepped gingerly into the flood. "I emptied your pockets before I put your clothes in the Copper."

"Would you kindly bring the contents of my pockets in here, lass?"

The paper bag she retrieved from the laundry had long strips of plastic and were bumpy through the brown paper, like it held strips of tablets.

"That package is for you. I got it off the black market pharmacist." Scott sank back into what remained of the bathwater.

Caitlin opened the bag. In her hand were ten strips of tablets—the contraceptive pill. She gasped at the packet in her hand.

"Knowing you as I do, Caitlin Murray, you'll need these," he said. "My experience of you is that you are a very fertile woman." She didn't respond to his comments. "I thought it might be part of your hesitation... in well... ye ken... having sex with me."

Caitlin held the packets of the contraceptive pill, mouth tight.

"Sorry, I could only get ten month's supply," he added. "They should all still be 'in date'. It seems to concern you, about medicines being 'in date'. I bought all she had."

Caitlin lifted her gaze from the packet of pills. He was lying back, naked in the bath, waiting for her response.

"Actually, I haven't even considered the possibility of getting pregnant. I'm quite touched that you have." Caitlin took her gaze from him and returned to stare at the strips of contraceptive pill and swallowed. "In fact, I'm a little scared of my first time."

"Oh." He raised his eyebrows.

"What do you mean 'Oh'? You know I'm a virgin? Don't you?" she asked. If he knew her, he'd know that, wouldn't he?

"Well, all I ken is, on our weddin' night, well, ye were nae. And," Scott had a satisfied look on his face, "you kenned what to do all right!"

Caitlin's brow tightened as her eyebrows raised. *What*? Confusion buffeted her.

"So, you weren't the first?" she asked. "Who was?"

"I dinnae ken, as ye wouldn't tell me." He tilted his head.

"Oh." She blinked a few times.

There was a short, embarrassed silence between them. Caitlin didn't know how to respond to *that* piece of information.

"Ye ken there are things you can do to make your first time easier?" Scott broke the silence.

"How?" The word elongated as it left her mouth.

"Well, positions and such."

"Yes, go on." Her voice sounded strangled.

"Well, if you—"

"Oh, I see—" She interrupted. It would be slightly too graphic for her.

"Or..." his suggestions came easily now and he went on to describe other options.

Scott was on a roll, obviously used to speaking about such things to her. Caitlin kept quiet, her face heating the more Scott spoke. She focussed her eyes anywhere but on Scott, screwing up her nose, unable to prevent it, nor stop imagining what he continued to explain. Caitlin squeezed her eyes tightly shut and put both hands in front of her like two stop signs.

"Tsh tsh no... no... no... no more! Too much information for me at the moment. Okay?" She exited the bathroom.

Behind her, Scott got out of the bath, the swish of water echoed through the open bathroom door. Caitlin glanced back at him. A grin encompassed most of his face. He had wrapped a towel around his waist. He then put fresh hot water in the sink and began to shave off his beard.

Caitlin spun and strode to the kitchen to prepare food, trying to process *that* conversation. Scott entered the kitchen once he finished his shave and stood eating the last of the bread, still wrapped only in a towel. She washed the dishes in the sink while he cleaned his teeth.

"Haven't seen toothpaste in a tube for years. We make our own, ye ken." Scott walked right up behind her and wrapped his arms around her, resting them at her waist at the front. He breathed against the side of her face. "Nice, eh?"

"Yes." She jumped slightly when he first put his arms around her but then relaxed into his embrace.

Scott was warm, and his firm abdomen and chest contacted the length of her back. He kissed her neck. Caitlin shivered. They were nice shivers.

Scott held his right hand closed in front of her and then opened it to reveal two gold rings, one larger than the other. He gave her the larger ring and splayed the fingers of his left hand, inviting her to place it on his ring finger.

"Where did these come from?" she hesitated.

"From my finger, and yours." He spoke into her ear from behind, his breath warm on the nape of her neck.

She placed his wedding band onto his finger. There was a dent behind the knuckle and the ring fitted back into its home. He then held the smaller ring in his right hand and poised. Caitlin stood straighter, then offered her hand certain of the meaning of her action. He slipped the band onto her finger. It fit perfectly.

Caitlin clasped his hand with hers. "Are you saying we are married now?"

"Caitlin, we've always been married as far as I'm concerned." His warm lips brushed her neck.

"You said, in the future, there was a minister." She turned around in his embrace and faced him directly. "Well, if we are to be married now, there has to be a minister. It's got to be legal this time as well."

Scott opened his mouth, his expressions reflecting thoughts flitting through his mind all too quickly.

"I don't know where to find a minister to make it all official. The legal system is in the process of falling apart. I'm grasping at straws here, but would a Justice o' the Peace officiating do? He could give us a licence of some sort. That's all I have, Caitlin." He spoke softly, his shoulders lifted a little.

"How do you know a JP then?" she asked.

"You mind my uncle at Bridge O' Orchy?" he said. "The one who does nae ken I'm his wee nephew recently born to his sister Margaret?"

Caitlin smiled and nodded.

"Well, he's one," Scott said. "We can go back there and see what he says about it."

"But Scott you're tired and only just returned."

"Aye well, 'strike while the iron's hot' as they say." He tilted his head. "I'll finish getting dressed and we'll go as soon as we can, aye?"

Scott sped away leaving Caitlin standing at the kitchen sink.

**

They drove to Bridge of Orchy, where Scott found his uncle in the Inn. His Uncle Robert took them into his small office behind the reception desk. He was a man in his fifties and a similar colouring to Scott. Scott explained their wishes to him.

"Och, well noo'," Scott's uncle began, "It usually takes six to eight weeks to get a licence and have the ceremony done at the Registry Offices in Edinburgh or Glasgow. But as ye can imagine, with things the way they are the noo', the system is nae operating." He eyed them both carefully. "Tae do it that way will be nigh impossible, at present, ye ken. Ye look rather disappointed, lass," he asked Caitlin directly. "Care to tell me ye troubles?"

Caitlin stood taller. She trusted Scott's Uncle Robert was made of the same stuff as Scott himself, so she took a chance he would be an understanding man and open to the truth.

"Sir, I love this man and dearly wish to be married to him. I don't want to live with him as his wife, unwed. So, I ask you, at this present time, how are we to be legally married?"

Uncle Robert scratched his whiskered face for a while, the room silent apart from the rasping sound it made. He eyed them both.

"I can make you legal. If ye will sign a marriage contract, which we'll draw up. I'll officiate and put my mark to, with my wife and one other witnessing," he explained his offer. "That will suffice until they restore law and order and ye can replace this contract with a licence. Would ye be happy with that?"

Scott turned to Caitlin and raised an eyebrow in question. She nodded. They devised and wrote a marriage contract and attended to the process as Scott's Uncle Robert had described. As legally married as possible, they returned home as husband and wife.

After camouflaging the 4WD, they walked back through the copse of Scot's pines to the cottage. As the back garden of the cottage came in sight, Scott reached out to her, his warm hand enveloped hers and his wedding ring glinted in the pale afternoon sunlight. When they got to the backdoor, he turned and picked her up with little effort and carried her over the back step.

"Very traditional of you Scott," Caitlin said into Scott's face.

He was so close his blue eyes blurred in her vision. His ropey arms held her tightly to his chest, his body heat flowing through his shirt.

"Aye." His voice was soft in her face. "One of the older men in the Community, George, told me this is what you do when you bring your new wife home." Once inside the cottage, he set her feet gently on the floor. "Did it the first time we married too."

His hand lingered on her leg, then both hands moved to her waist.

"This *is* the first time we marry." She whispered back to his face. *Oh, so close.* She shivered at the warm caress of his fingers now on her inner elbow.

"Not for me, lass." Scott's fingers continued their journey to the nape of her neck where they ran through the strands of her long blond hair at the base of her skull. These hairs raised and joined the shivers arising from his touch. Gently holding her head in his hand, Scott recommenced his caresses. With his mouth on hers, Caitlin leaned her body close to his, aided by his other hand in the small of her back.

"Come to bed Caitlin," he whispered in his husky way.

His warm breath was on her neck. Then his warm lips. They moved up to her ear. And down again. His hands moved to cup each breast.

"What are you doing to me, Scott?" Caitlin had never felt like *this*. Her heart pounded as his touch became everything. She wanted him... more of him. *All* of him.

"Making love to you, my wife." His voice rose from her neck where his lips pressed her skin, their velvet touch causing feelings her body had never before revealed to her.

He took her by the hand and led her to his bedroom.

At the doorway she paused. "I've started taking the Pill, but it won't be effective."

"You've taken one already?" He smiled. "I have condoms, too."

His warm grip became tighter as he gently tugged her into the room.

***

"So, what if we do something now that changes the future?" They sat close together on the couch. "You came back to protect me," Caitlin said. "What if protecting me from something that will happen causes a change in the future?"

"Good question." Scott rubbed his chin. It was smooth and shiny, a contrast to the beard he had worn that very morning. "Give me a 'What if'."

"Okay," she glanced up at the ceiling. "You know how people say things happen for a reason? And we are like we are, because of the experiences we go through?"

"Aye," he said.

"Well, *what if*, because you are protecting me, I don't experience what I would've experienced and, therefore, I don't become the person I was when you didn't protect me?"

Scott blinked with each point she made, mentally following them, and finally nodded after a brief period of quiet thought.

"Cait, I've a confession to make." His tone was serious. She sat straighter. "You remember how I said the scientists had set The Time Machine for human trials," he bit his lower lip and then continued, "and the engineer had devised a gadget for pinpointing a date? And they set The Time Machine so someone could come and try to prevent things from happening so The Stock Market Crash didn't occur? Well..." He paused, staring at his clasped hands as they rested on his knees.

"Well?" She prompted him to continue, lowering her head and trying to look him in the eye.

"Well, it was nae meant to be me. I gate-crashed. Like I said, you'd just died, and I wanted to be with you. So," he shrugged, "I suppose I stole their Time Machine. Well, that particular journey, anyway." He finished with his lips together in a grimace.

"Oh." She lifted her head and fixed her vision on the ceiling again.

"Aye." His mouth made a sucking sound beside her as he resumed biting his lower lip.

"So, we may very well have changed things already?" She removed her gaze from the ceiling and fixed it on him.

"Don't know about that Cait, you see, I've been teaching you skills I ken you know in the future. You have the same strengths of character you display in the future. Ye are learning the same knowledge you had when I met you. So, to answer your question you raised before—in a nutshell, I don't know." He blew out and his breath stirred his fringe.

"I suppose, in a way, it doesn't really matter. Life is so full of possibilities." Caitlin voiced her ideas, thoughts which had run through her head ever since Scott announced he'd travelled through time. "They're all determined by every decision we make. Large or small. Important or trivial. Each life lived follows a course that is only one of many possible scenarios."

Chapter Sixteen

"I'm glad you thought to include facial cleanser and moisturiser in the toiletry supplies you brought." Caitlin stood in front of the 1960s style dressing table in her nightgown. The dressing table didn't match the bed. Nothing matched. "Wish you had thought of make-up though."

"You want makeup?" Scott came closer and stood behind her. His expression of disbelief reflected in the mirror.

"Yes, it's probably the only thing I miss. You could have let me pack before we left Uncle Kieran's."

"Caitlin! You were nae coming with me. Remember I had to drag you out of there! Seriously, you never wear makeup in the future. You had opportunities to buy it, but the choice was medicines for our people or makeup. Being the leader you are, makeup lost, every time. Besides," he put his arms around her waist, "you're a beautiful woman. You dinnae need makeup." Caitlin sank into his hug and smiled deeply. Scott was one of the few people who had seen her without makeup.

Scruffy growled at the backdoor. Then the sound reached human ears—a dogfight in the backyard.

"Oh, no!" Scott shouted as he grabbed his handgun and ran into the garden.

Caitlin hesitated and stayed in the doorway. A pack of dogs was attacking the goat in the small, grassed area in between the vegetable garden and where Scott kept the horses. The dogs were of large domestic breeds. They were rib-thin with mangy coats. And hungry. The nanny goat, tied to a star picket, couldn't escape. The makeshift corral Scott had previously erected, confined the horses which ran wildly and escaped the dogs by kicking out at them.

Scott aimed his gun for the dogs and tried to avoid the horses. Scruffy entered the fray. Scott's attempts to miss all their animals slowed his efforts to defend them and himself from the dogs.

The largest dog grabbed a thick part of the sleeve of Scott's jacket. Latching on, it skidded along the grass as Scott tried to shake it off. Its growls fluctuated with each thrust of Scott's arm. Scruffy worried the larger dog, nipping at its heels, risking becoming its next victim.

Caitlin collected her throwing knives as she stepped out of the house. The goat was dead. Two dogs ran off with the decapitated corpse. The other dogs surrounded Scott, drawing closer to join their leader. The pack mentality of these dogs was in play. Scott was their target. One of them chased Scruffy away. Fast and agile, he avoided their savagery. Then he returned to protect his master.

Scott fired the handgun. The dogs circled him while their alpha held on tight to his arm. The only light in the dark night came from the kitchen window. It illuminated a patch of the backyard. Scott was in the patch. Caitlin threw five knives in quick succession. She hit two dogs in the ribs. The one latched on to Scott's arm got a knife in the hindquarters. This didn't stop it. Caitlin's next throw landed in its chest. This weakened it. Scott disengaged himself from its jaws and shot it at close quarters. A muffled yelp, and it was dead. With their pack-leader lifeless on the ground, the other dogs scattered. Scott sat heavily on the grass.

Scruffy jumped to lick his face. "I'm okay, boy."

"Did the dog sink his teeth into you?" Fear cracked Caitlin's voice. "Come into the house and let me examine you in the light."

Due to the thickness of the jacket, the dog had sunk its teeth into the material, avoiding Scott's arm. There were not any tooth puncture marks in Scott's skin, but she made him rinse his arm thoroughly under running water for a few minutes, in case saliva was present. Then she wiped his arm with antiseptic. Caitlin put the jacket aside to wash.

"Frightened I'll become rabid, lass?"

"Not funny, Scott." She frowned. "So, domestic dogs go wild!"

"Aye, the smaller abandoned domestic dogs are usually killed by the bigger dogs. Then the pack mentality takes over. Not very long before 'Spot' becomes wolf like. I'll have to make a more substantial shelter for the horses. One I can lock them in tonight."

Scott returned to the backyard to settle the horses. The smell of the dead dogs spooked them. Caitlin had donned gloves, retrieved her knives and washed them in bleach. Blood was another vector for Rabies. She piled up the bodies to burn them.

"Oh! Poor baby." She found the head of the nanny goat. "The goat died because we tied her up." *Our fault.* "Poor baby might have survived otherwise."

"Cait, do you actually think the wee goat would have survived those dogs even if she were free? No," he let out a short laugh. "That nanny goat had nae chance, either way." He peered at her. "There's your maternal instinct surfacing."

"What! I'm not maternal."

"Aye, you are. You were braw with the bairns." He grinned. "Ye loved mothering your wee ones."

Again, another aspect of her character which he revealed to her, that was out of her current experience. It was slightly bizarre. She'd better get used to it. He was right—it surprised her how much he knew about her.

"I'm not convinced the dogs will return, but I want to err on the side of caution," Scott said.

Scott started constructing a three-sided lean-to onto the back of the outhouse. Caitlin helped. They hurriedly built a rough temporary lean-to under kerosene lantern-light, using the wood he had prepared for construction. It was fully enclosed and lockable. They led the horses inside where it was snug, but they were safe.

They both washed themselves in the laundry before entering the cottage proper. As they did, Scott turned to her while she stood next to the door.

"Once again, my woman has saved me from harm. Thank you." He put his arms around her waist and kissed her. Caitlin had her back to the wall, and he pressed her against it.

"Well, all those Chess games have paid off," she commented once his lips left hers.

"Hmmm?"

"You have taught me the moves of all the pieces. Right?" she put her arms around his neck.

"Aye." He looked down into her eyes, his focus intense.

"Chess mirrors life."

"How so?" His blue eyes never left hers.

"Well, in Chess, as in life, the queen always protects her king, right?" She covered his mouth with hers and ran her fingers into his hair, gripping a handful, and kissed him firmly on the mouth.

Scott returned her kiss. They made urgent love against the wall, just inside the cottage, her love for him brimming up inside until it peaked. He lent close against her while they recovered. He kissed her neck. She held his head and ran her fingers through his waves. He lifted his head back to look her in the eye and grinned. She returned it.

"I wanted ye so badly, he whispered. "I couldn't even wait till I got ye to bed. Look at us, I'm still fully clothed!"

He kissed her again and carried her to their bed where she held him tight and snuggled into his warm side.

I could get used to this.

Chapter Seventeen

Caitlin lay naked on top of Scott with her head on his front and his bare skin warm against hers. The rough hairs of his chest brushed against her cheek, his own unique male scent filled her head, as she moved with the rise and fall of his breathing. The sound of air in his lungs came through his chest wall. His breathing slowed, and he inhaled, about to speak.

"I've been thinking," he said.

"Yes, I thought so. Important, is it?"

"Verra."

She raised her head; his eyes were only inches from her own.

"Now mind, just because I've time travelled from the future," Scott said, "it does nae mean I'm an expert regarding anything to do with it, like.'

"Yes, okay." She raised her eyebrows in question.

"Well, you were always the smart one, answer me this—what happens when I meet me?"

Caitlin double blinked. If he was to be with her from now on, the possibility of him meeting himself in the future was indeed a great one.

"You could become my secret lover," she tilted her head. "I could have 'young you' as my new inexperienced husband and teach you a thing or two. At the same time, have secret trysts with 'old you', whilst you hide from yourself."

Scott's eyes went wide. "I cannae believe you said that young lady! What have I turned ye into?"

Caitlin giggled and buried her face in his chest.

"I'm serious!" he said to the top of her head.

"What did your theoretical physicist, my cousin Martin, say about that sort of thing?"

"The popular opinion regarding meeting yourself in another time," Scott said, "is it would cause a break in the space-time continuum, and the universe would implode."

"Really?" She lifted her head to look him in the eye again.

"Well, it is theoretical physics, just conjecture, as nothing like that has ever happened, yet."

"Oh, you mean the universe imploding?" She cocked a brow.

"Caitlin, you're not being serious about this." Scott frowned.

"Well, it hasn't, has it? Did it happen when you were there in the future?"

"No."

"Well?" she asked.

"But I had nae travelled back in time then."

"Hadn't you? Are you sure of that?"

He was silent with a furrowed brow.

"Did you see yourself?" she continued.

"No."

"Did I say anything about you being around or 'watch out to not go to the men's showers at a certain time or you'll see the 'old you'?" she asked.

"No," he answered reluctantly. "But that does nae mean—"

"I wouldn't worry about it, Scott. It obviously works out."

She'd finished with a platitude, but she had been pondering the same questions. How would it pan out? Would she have two Scotts? Will the world end, with the time-space continuum disrupted, as all the experts suggested? She nestled her face back onto his warm, bare skin and let out a long sigh. Way too mind blowing to even *know* where to begin contemplating *that* one.

***

Light spilled in through the back window across the rough wood table. Scott finished the last of the tin of hot dogs.

"Hot dogs again?" Caitlin half turned from the sink in front of the window.

"They dinnae make them anymore. Have nae for years, ken. Well, have nae processed food of any sort in factories for years. I mind ma mither giving me them when I was wee. Love 'em." He got up from his chair. "I need to get more stores."

"What do we need now?" Caitlin's brow tightened and so did her hand around the dirty dish in the sink.

"Chickens and another goat." He brought his dirty plate to the sink. "I heard of a sometimes market at Fort William every first Saturday of the month. Which it is tomorrow."

She turned to him and put her arms around his waist.

"Take me with you this time, please?" She looked up into his eyes.

"I can't leave the horses here on their own." He clattered the plate into the sink. "What if those wild domestic dogs come back?"

"Oh. And you think *I* will be able to save the horses from a pack of wild dogs without you?"

"What do you suggest then?" he asked. "Go on the horses not the 4WD?"

"Yes!"

"No!" he shook his head. "We will nae be able to carry as much on the return journey if we are on horseback."

"We'll ride the horses there and lead them as pack animals on the way back." Caitlin affected her best pleading expression. It had always worked on Uncle Kieran.

"Caitlin, it will take us at least five hours one way if we are walking them. Which means roughly a day's journey there."

"We can take a small tent, hobble the horses and camp overnight. It will be like a holiday. A minibreak!" The idea of an almost holiday was exciting.

"Caitlin, *mo chroi*, the world is a different place than when you were last in it. It won't be a picnic. It's bad out there. People like our last visitors are everywhere. Even a remote a place such as Fort William will have undesirable, no," he corrected himself, "*bad*, evil people there, who may do you harm."

"I'm not staying here!" she cried into his face. "Last time you left me, I thought I'd never see you again. I'll never give you the chance to repeat that. I'll take my chances with you beside me to protect me. I will not be without you again. I'm going, and that's it!"

She pulled a few steps away from him, arms across her chest in defiance. She expected, and waited for, more negativity from him. Was he going to *order* her to stay? If so, he will soon learn something *new* about her.

Emotions played across Scott's face. His jaw muscles clenched, and his eyes narrowed. She guessed he struggled with his desire to keep her safe and her need to be with him. With arms still crossed, she regarded his handsome face gently lit by the early afternoon's daylight coming in through the kitchen window. She wished more than anything to be always looking at his handsome face. Finally, his shoulders slumped only slightly, and his face relaxed with resignation. It was enough for Caitlin. She strode toward him.

"You know I never want to be apart from you again." She wrapped her arms around him. "I promise I'll be careful and do whatever you tell me to do, to keep safe."

"Caitlin Murray-Campbell, if I had nae been married to you for twenty years, that would have been our first argument." He returned her hug. "It is only that I have encountered stubborn determination in you before, and I ken when it is time to give in, because *you* won't. So, we should leave before daylight tomorrow. Pack lightly so we have room for what we will bring home, aye? I'll start securing the cottage and grounds. I hope my information is correct about a market tomorrow, or this will be a waste of time and effort."

Caitlin packed two days-worth of easily transportable and easy-to-cook food, the two-man tent, a bedroll and camping gear for making a hot drink over a campfire. Caitlin carried her throwing knives as usual, and Scott an easily concealed handgun.

They left at five am the next day. The weather was turning cold and wet. They wore their wet weather gear, long oil-skin coats over waterproof pants covering their jeans. The Highland horses' shaggy coats were thick and offered their own wet weather protection. Scruffy ran along at the horses' hooves for a while, but Scott soon scooped him up to snuggle next to him on the saddle.

They rode with the dark waters of Loch Leven on their right, until just before North Ballachulish where they crossed the steel bridge which traverses the loch as it narrows and flows into the larger loch, Loch Linnhie. They travelled with Loch Linnhie on their left, Ben Nevis on their right. Snow-capped and shrouded in mist, Ben Nevis stood as a grey and white benevolent giant, observing their slow passage by the loch.

The chill wind blew off the snow from the mountains to the west and the water to their left, smelling of moisture and cold as it blew through the trees. Caitlin's nose was numb. She pulled her coat tighter, stopping trickles of water from her face running down her neck as a fine misty rain persisted. In places, the waters of the loch lapped the shore next to the road. Now the high dark mountains were difficult to see through the rain's translucent milkiness, which persistently travelled with them. Her emotions welled within her at the sight of this cold beauty; it spoke to her soul. Maybe it was something to do with her ancestry. Scott turned in the saddle, saw her expression and grinned.

They rode on through Onich and past Corran, where the ferry still took vehicles to the other side of Loch Linnhie. They stayed on the east side of the loch where Fort William was situated further to the north. This, the longest stretch of their journey, took them three of the six-hours. Many hotels and Bed and Breakfast accommodations lined their route, now unoccupied by holiday makers. The locals who remained stared warily at them as they passed. Hotels now housed squatters or families on the move. Few vehicles passed by on a road Caitlin was sure would have been full of traffic and tourist coaches only months before.

At set intervals, Scott would hop off his horse and walk. He made Caitlin do the same. Scruffy had barked at the horses at first, until he nearly got a hoof firmly placed on his head by Scott's horse. They stopped once on their journey that day, for hot tea from a flask and biscuits for morning tea.

They arrived at Fort William a little before eleven am and made their way through the streets to the centre of the large town, past grey stone buildings with boarded or barred windows. Scott's information was correct, and the market was in full swing. It had commandeered the paved mall area by the old museum, now crowded and full of stalls. The clothes of the crowd that gathered were dull and shabby; most of them needed laundering. Body odour hung in the air. Most market goers needed a haircut or a shave or both and looked thinner compared to the average person prior to The Stock Market Crash. The stalls were rickety trestle tables, the opened boot of a car or the back of a van or cart. Litter lay sodden at the foot of the tables as the goods sat precariously on top.

One stall sold chickens and their first purchase was five hens and a rooster, and cages in which to transport them. Caitlin mused that the animal pens and cages were a different sight than the front of the museum was used to. Scott had devised a way of placing the cages holding their chickens on the horses for the return journey. They bought a pregnant nanny goat, which would assure them of a supply of milk.

The renewable energy, sustainability and self-sufficiency stall, which sold energy generating equipment, intrigued Scott. He raised his eyebrows and looked hopeful as he spied the small-scale wind powered electricity generating equipment.

"What?" Caitlin asked as a smile came to his face.

"Something I'm verra familiar with as we use wind power. Some Communities in the future have tapped into the many wind farms which exist around the UK." He stopped speaking, turned his back on the stall, and looked straight at Caitlin. Then he fiddled intently with the saddle of his horse and pretended to tighten the girth.

"Caitlin, do you see the man at the windmill stall? Dinnae look!" His whisper was harsh.

"How am I meant to see him if I don't look? Buyer or Seller?"

"Buyer," he said.

Caitlin surreptitiously viewed the man looking at the goods on the wind-power stall. He was in his mid-thirties and fit looking, plainly dressed and chatting amicably with the stall keeper.

"And?"

"We ken him in the future," Scott answered. "He is an electrical engineer who helped design The Time Machine. He and his wife live in our Community. They are Brendan and Rebecca Hamilton. Only, we... *I* ken them from about twenty years older than they are now."

"Why are you hiding from them? They don't know us yet."

"Oh," he relaxed a bit. "Just wanted to tell you about them, aye." His cheeks pinked.

"So, what's the plan?" she asked. "Do we meet now, or not?"

"Not sure. He would be right handy to have around for a wee bit," Scott said. "He's extremely practical. Could do with his know-how to install a wind-generated electricity supply. Our Militia kept me busy. I never did much *hands-on* with the windmills. They were slightly different models too. Might go peruse the wares."

"What if it's too early to meet them and we change things?"

Scott shrugged. "Look around. Brendan and Bec are the nicest people I know. Much nicer than some people we have seen so far. I'll see what happens. Leave it to chance, I suppose." He walked toward the stall, then turned back, a thoughtful expression on his face. "If we connect with them, we are Murrays, aye? Dinnae be callin' me Campbell. It'll confuse them and alert them to *this past* in the future, most likely."

Scott wandered over to the windmill stall while Caitlin held the reins of the horses which had the chickens in cages strapped on to them, and the leads of the goat and dog. Quite a menagerie. She looked around. Scott was right. Some behaviours of the other market attendees were questionable. Youths scuffled beside a food stall. Most wore tattoos; one caught her eye. If only he knew how badly his neck tattoos clashed with his paisley shirt!

The group had laughed and sneered all morning and had knocked over a worm farm at the Vermiculture stall. Dirt and worm castings lay scattered on the ground in front of the stall. Vermiculture! She'd considered a worm farm to be a promising idea when reading the self-sufficiency section of Scott's library.

The gang of youths wandered off past an overweight middle-aged man with unkempt hair and beard. He nodded to the youths while his eyes scanned the market. He looked directly at Caitlin and she quickly turned away. A chill at the back of her neck flashed when their gazes briefly connected. Caitlin moved herself and her menagerie closer to the Vermiculture stall and helped the stallholder clean up. She chatted with the stallholder and ended up with a box full of Tiger worms, which looked like a box of dirt. She glanced in the man's direction. The man-with-the-stare was gone. Scott returned as Caitlin secured the box of worms to a saddle.

"It's them all right, he said. "We had a wee chat and hit it off, as we do. He invited us to eat lunch with them. Brendan suggested a park nearby on the front road by the church. What's with the box full o' dirt?"

"Worms." Caitlin couldn't keep the excitement from her voice. "I'll start a worm farm to enrich our vegetable patch."

"Oh, aye?" He seemed distracted. "So, I've got a windmill, and some batteries lined up with the energy guy."

"How will we carry heavy batteries on the horses all the way home? They are the size of car batteries, aren't they?" Her voice rose a pitch.

"No, they're bigger. But I have a plan. I'm hoping Brendan and Bec will come to the rescue. Let's meet them for lunch. I've finished for now. We can get the other things after we've eaten."

The man from the windmill stall and a slightly plump and conservative looking woman, both in their thirties, ambled into the park in front of the church near the railway station.

"Brendan," Scott shook the man's hand, "this is my wife, Caitlin."

"And my wife Bec." Brendan responded.

"Oh, it's so nice to meet lovely, normal people for once." Bec grabbed Caitlin's hand in both of hers and held tight. "The world's a different place, you know."

"Unfortunately, yes." Caitlin smiled at her new acquaintance. "Lovely to meet you too. So, where are you and your husband from?" She gently removed her hand from Bec's.

"We are from Glasgow. Brendan is an electrical engineer, and I have been a GP these past ten years. What about yourselves?"

Caitlin turned her gaze to Scott for his cue. He nodded a fraction.

"I am a nurse. I was about to start post-grad study at university when it all happened."

What would Scott say about himself, having had no formal education or training in anything?

"Well for myself," Scott smiled, "ye could say I'm a 'Jack of All Trades' and definitely master of none. I spent some time in an army, but I mainly work as a gamekeeper, you could say. Ken how to hunt and so on."

Caitlin was glad he omitted 'time traveller from the future'. But was the army the Militia he had mentioned earlier?

"How have ye and your wife come to be up this way?" Scott asked Brendan.

"I don't know how much you have heard about what's been going on, but the cities are not safe anymore," Brendan answered.

"Sauchiehall Street wasn't the safest of places before The Crash, so you can just imagine," Bec added.

Caitlin offered Bec some sandwiches she had brought for herself and Scott.

"Oh, no thank-you we couldn't possibly," Bec said. "Not unless you have some of the doughnuts we bought at the food market."

"Doughnuts!" Caitlin exclaimed.

"Oh, please have some then," Bec offered, her face lighting up at Caitlin's response.

"I do feed my wife, ye ken," Scott commented. "Just no' had anything as exotic as doughnuts lately. Are you on your way anywhere particular?"

"No, not really." Brendan glanced at his wife. "We feel safer the further north we go. We are hoping to find somewhere to settle."

"So, you're an electrical engineer," Scott said. "Is there any chance ye are good at installing wind powered electricity generators and electricity storage batteries?"

"Well, I know how to install something similar," Brendan answered. "I haven't ever installed a domestic unit, but I know what they involve. Why?"

"How would you like to assist a 'Jack of All Trades' to install one?" Scott sounded casual, but Caitlin sensed his tension. "Free bed and board till it's done as payment."

Brendan and Bec looked at each other.

"I'll have to discuss it with my wife," Brendan said. "When would you need to know by?"

"Caitlin and I leave tomorrow morning, early. If your answer is yes, we need you to come with us then."

"Very well," Brendan gave a nod. "We will let you know in time."

Chapter Eighteen

"What?" Scott blinked.

Brendan and Bec had returned to the market to continue shopping. Caitlin and Scott were alone in the park.

"What?" Scott asked again as Caitlin maintained the expression of disbelief on her face.

"When were you going to let me in on your plan?" She tilted her chin up to him.

"Oh, that. Well, I was thinking on my feet and did nae have a chance tae ask you."

"You didn't think it was worth discussing with me first?" Caitlin moved her hands to her hips to join her chin in defiance. "Like, we will have strangers stay with us, for who knows how long, and you asked without consulting me? Me, your wife who has to live with them also?"

Scott hung his head, closed his eyes, and rubbed his brow with his thumb.

"I'm sorry, Caitlin." Scott looked up. "I forgot you don't ken them yet, like I do." He stepped closer. "They are good people, and we get on well with them. I don't regard them as strangers, aye? Sorry. You're right. I should have consulted you first. But it's a good plan, aye?" He raised his eyebrows and nodded vigorously.

Caitlin didn't answer his question. She had more. "Will they stay in the cottage with us?"

"Aye, in the room you are...were in. You should move your things into mine anyways now."

"And we have enough food for them?" she continued. "They will eat our stores that should last the two of us over the winter?"

"I had a wee peek at their vehicle. If I'm not wrong, they're loaded up with supplies of some sort. I'm sure they'll not mind contributing something while they stay."

"You said 'Free bed and board as payment'," Caitlin stated. "What if it takes a long time and they eat everything?"

"Caitlin, Brendan will make it possible for us to get electrical power! We'll make the food last! It shouldn't take more than a week at the most."

Caitlin pouted and didn't reply, trying to suppress a peeve at Scott not even considering asking her.

"I'm truly sorry, lass." Scott pulled her closer to himself. "I should have consulted you. Aye, you've raised some good questions."

"Valid concerns," she corrected.

"Aye, concerns. Valid ones an' all but I saw a solution to our problem and went for it. It's not like you have nae done it!"

"But I have never done it!" she protested.

"Oh, that's right, ye have nae yet. When you do it, you will understand why I did what I've done today. Sometimes leaders decide as they go and must wear the consequences."

***

Continuing to stock up on supplies at the market in front of the museum, they bought a bag of chicken feed to get them going, saddle soap, buckets and more seeds. Scott bought a few tarpaulins. He would need to wrap the windmill equipment in one for their journey home. Also, a few rolls of chicken wire. There was not much room for more.

"I would still like to know where this windmill will fit. When are you getting it?" Caitlin eyed their stock of supplies.

"At the end of the day," Scott answered. "I was thinking we may camp just out of town past the railway station. There's a nice quiet spot by the loch. We can carry it between us to there."

The windmill itself was ten feet in length. Scott planned to extend this when he installed it. The disassembled blades were each slightly over four feet. The batteries were large and heavy, and Scott had bought two. They made their way to the camping spot Scott had found and set up the tent and arranged the animals on the grass. It was drizzling, so he double-flied the tent to make a shelter for the goat, the chickens which stayed in their cages, and Scruffy. Scott wrapped the windmill, its fittings and batteries, and the saddles and stores in other tarpaulins and placed them closely alongside the tent. They secured the horses on a grassy patch by the loch's edge. Caitlin collected wood, made a campfire and put the camp kettle on to boil. She eyed the windmill parts and the storage batteries once more.

"Getting this home will be interesting. No—impossible!" Caitlin let her exasperation out.

"Dinnae fash, Caitlin. I'm hoping the Hamilton's will come to the rescue and offer to transport it in their vehicle."

"Oh... I see now. You're not as dumb as you look, are you Scott Campbell? Or am I meant to say 'Murray'? But what if they say *no*?"

"They'll accept," he said. "I ken them. He'll love the challenge, and she's tired from travelling. Bec needs a rest for a wee while. Besides, you and Bec have a lot in common. You work well together with medical things in the future." With a beaming smile on his face Scott added, "Bec delivered Angela."

"Who's Angela?"

"Our firstborn." Scott's grin expanded.

"Oh! Boy," Caitlin said. "I'm a terrible mother! I have never even asked you about our children."

Interrupted by the sound of a car engine and bright headlights directed at their camp, Caitlin slipped her hand down her right boot, and grabbed her throwing knives sitting in their sheath strapped to her ankle. Scott took his handgun from its holster around his waist. The group of loud youths at the market had eyed their purchases. Scott's nerves had seemed on high alert ever since, probably anticipating their appearance during the night. He also had that look in his eye, the one he always had when concerned for her safety. The headlights turned off, and the driver stepped out of the car.

"Only us, Scott." Brendan's silhouette emerged from the driver's side.

Scott's shoulders relaxed. Caitlin removed her hand from her knives.

"Well, good evening, Brendan and Bec." Scott said.

"We hope you don't mind us turning up, but we were wondering if you wouldn't mind if we camped with you two tonight. Safety in numbers, and all that."

"Aye right, so there is, Brendan. We would be glad of your company. Ye are most welcome to be with us tonight."

Bec and Brendan parked their vehicle next to Scott and Caitlin's camp and set up camp-chairs next to the fire. Caitlin pooled her resources with Bec and produced a fried dinner for four, cooked over the fire in Bec's cast iron frying-pan.

"Maybe we will have eggs for breakfast tomorrow!" Caitlin said.

"You think your hens will lay eggs in that cage? You're hopeful. Even a chicken needs to be comfortable and secure to produce an egg." Scott pointed at the cage.

"Guess I'd better read up on chicken keeping then." Caitlin made a face at Scott. It received the slight smile she was looking for.

"Have you heard much news of the goings-on then?" Brendan opened the conversation as they sat around the campfire.

"Only what we hear on the radio. I'm sure the government doesn't allow all that's happening to be broadcast." Scott fished for information. Caitlin sensed he was wondering where history was up to—the history *he* knew.

"Well," Brendan continued, "after the stock market crashed, everyone's wealth diminished. Some only by half, some lost all. Small businesses folded then even companies with large workforces went under. The 'less well off', shall we say, rose in protest to the Government. Some of them then took things into their own hands, like a revolution. Mobs ransacked a lot of private homes, and even stately homes run by the National Trust! The wealth stolen. Now and then, I've recognised something for sale on the black market, and even at these local markets, which looks like it's from such a place. Some wealthy people, who didn't have good security, were injured, and a few killed." Brendan's voice grew strained. "Lawlessness and violence are rampant. No shopping centre was exempt from looting, either. Goods are in short supply unless you know where to go. People live in fear and bar and defend their homes. We haven't felt safe anywhere."

Shivers ran their creeping fingers up Caitlin's spine as she listened to Brendan. She had followed the progression of events on the radio news and Scott's warnings of what would happen. But this from Brendan...

"It happened all over the Western world," Bec continued where Brendan had paused. "The governments of the developed countries are only just holding on, accused of weak leadership, a crisis of this nature only proved it. And well, countries, such as those found on the African continent, and," she added, "I hate to simplistically malign any country, but they have descended into absolute chaos. Probably never to return to normalcy."

"So, with people on the move there must be a lot of refugees then, aye?" Scott asked.

"Yes. Do you remember a few years ago, there were masses of refugees crossing the Mediterranean Sea and entering Europe via Italy?" Brendan paused while Scott nodded. "Also, there were millions coming from Syria due to the war there. Well, after the problems they had with terrorists who had snuck through posing as refugees, the British, European, and Scandinavian governments have closed their borders. The USA and Australia aren't letting anyone in. Having trouble enough with their own people. It's like a wall has gone up around these countries. All borders have a heavy military guard."

"Oh, the world is a bad place! This country is no better." Bec wrapped her coat tighter around her shoulders. "We just want to go somewhere safe and ride out the storm."

They sat staring at the campfire, each silent in their own thoughts. The fire crackled as the heat made its combustible way through the wood. It warmed Caitlin's face, and the smoke stung her eyes intermittently. Scott threw more logs on the fire and she watched the sparks fly heavenwards. Caitlin kept her head tilted back, looking at the night sky. An open fire and stars, two things which always aided contemplation.

"Those stars won't change," Caitlin broke the silence. "They'll still be there when this crisis is over. We need to hang in there and be ready; be what the world needs when it's time for order again. And we must preserve what we have before it is all lost and we have another Dark Age. Don't we?" She gazed at each of her companions, endeavouring to make eye contact with them.

Bec's mouth was open as she stared intently at her. Brendan also gazed at her; his head slightly tilted to the side. Scott looked directly at her, a smile at the corner of his mouth. Caitlin might have sounded profound—unintentional on her part. In her relaxed state, she had comfortably expressed herself. She now squirmed in her seat as no one answered her. Caitlin stared into the fire and the tightness of a frown pulled at her forehead. She was reluctant to speak further, as to do so would give Scott away. They watched the flames in silence as the fire crackled and sparked.

"Scott, I'd like very much to help you set up your wind generator. Is the offer still on?" Brendan broke the silence.

"Oh aye, certainly. I need your help and advice with it. Are ye able to come home with us in the morning? We have a five-hour journey, so we'll be leaving at dawn."

"Oh, we'll come with you," Brendan said. "But I have a question. How were you going to get the windmill and storage batteries home?"

"Aye, well." Scott's mouth stretched with a grin. "I'd try and rig something up between the horses but if you have a better idea, I'm most happy to hear it."

Chapter Nineteen

Scott tied the last of the windmill equipment to the roof-rack of Brendan and Bec's estate car then Brendan and Scott lifted the batteries into the back.

"We'll see you at the halfway mark." Scott nodded to Brendan.

A pale sun shone as they set off from their campsite near the ScotRail station of Fort William. Caitlin was used to walking, walking up and down the floor of the ED, but today would be long and tiring. Scott was silent for most of it. Something was bothering him, but she wasn't in the mood to ask. She hadn't slept well, and a slight headache lingered.

They arrived at Corran where they met up with Brendan and Bec and ate a quick lunch after which Scott beckoned Caitlin and Bec to the horses.

"Sorry ladies, but Brendan and I have to do the heavy work of unloading the windmill equipment when we get home." Scott shrugged as he handed Bec the reins of the horse she was to lead.

Scott turned to Caitlin, put his arms around her and held her close to him. She felt the pulse in his neck as her cheek rested there.

"Ye have your throwing knives, aye?" His deep, gravelly voice whispered into her ear. Caitlin nodded. "If you have any trouble, dinnae hesitate to use them. Just a limb, no' chest or head. Just to incapacitate, aye? Unless you feel your life's in danger, ken." Scott kissed her lips and got into the car. The car slowly drove away.

Bec and Caitlin walked in silence for a while, the two women led the horses laden with supplies which included cages holding chickens, and a pregnant nanny goat, while Scruffy darted between their legs.

We must look a sight.

"There's a wee bit of an age difference between you two, isn't there?" Bec asked after a mile or two.

"Yes, but we don't notice it." Caitlin stared straight ahead in the direction the car had gone.

"Scott is about our age, isn't he? His mid-thirties?"

"He's nearly forty, actually." Caitlin glanced sideways at Bec and caught the tail end of a stunned expression.

He doesn't look his age. A grin pulled at the corner of her mouth. Her horse nickered behind her.

"When were you married?" Bec asked.

"About four months ago."

"Oh, you're newlyweds then! Well, we won't stay long. Don't want to intrude." There was apology in Bec's tone.

"It's okay. We need the electricity. We'll appreciate Brendan's help."

"I didn't mean to overhear." Bec lowered her voice. "But Scott has such a deep voice I couldn't help it. Do you really have knives on you?"

"Yes. Why?"

"Do you know how to use them?" Bec frowned. "It's a wee bit dangerous, is it not?"

"Scott has taught me how to use them. He's training me in self-defence," Caitlin faced her companion.

"What if you injure someone?"

"That's the idea," Caitlin said simply.

"Have you ever had to use them?" A large crease sat between Bec's eyebrows.

"Yes."

"When? Did you hurt anyone?"

Caitlin rolled her eyes and lifted her head. Bec's disapproving manner grated.

"When I last used them," Caitlin said, "I killed two and injured one enough for Scott to shoot and kill him."

Bec stopped in her tracks. The horse she led bumped into her, almost knocking her over. It whinnied in annoyance.

"You killed two and Scott finished off the other?" Bec's eyes darted ahead and back to Caitlin.

"A pack of domestic dogs that had gone wild bothered us." Caitlin knew she'd better explain before she ruined this new relationship unnecessarily. "They killed our goat and were after the horses. When Scott tried to stop them, the alpha got him by the arm. So, I killed the dogs I could, and injured the one biting Scott enough for him to shoot it."

"Oh." Bec recommended breathing. "I thought you were saying you had killed humans!"

Caitlin *could* tell Bec of the intruders they'd killed, but she was still trying to forget about it. Bec was like herself, a professional with a vocation committed to preserving human life. Caitlin continued walking, keeping the silence that now surrounded them.

***

Scott and Brendan drew near to the pathway obscured by the small wood of Scots pines. They parked the car next to the 4WD and Scott scouted ahead of Brendan to ensure the cottage was safe, checking his perimeter markers, and others he had left at stages along the track to the cottage. Scott went to his vantage point, where he had set up the telescope he had retrieved from the attackers' car, giving an unobstructed view of anyone approaching and made a thorough viewing of their surrounds before he declared it 'all clear'. He returned to the car and helped Brendan unload the windmill equipment and carry it to the cottage.

"This is taking too long." Scott said as he and Brendan reached the cottage with a load of equipment. "I'll get the wheelbarrow to bring the batteries back in. That should quicken things up a wee bit. Then I'm going for the women while you finish up, aye?"

"I'll be fine with the barrow. You go on ahead and make sure they're okay." Brendan placed a bag of supplies on the kitchen table.

"Thanks." Scott walked out of the pantry, a box of shotgun cartridges in his hand, his lower lip pinched where he chewed it. "Och, I cannae leave it much longer. I'll take your car. I'll not be long. Dinnae want them on their own any longer. Have a bad feeling, ken?"

"On ye go." Brendan ushered Scott out the door.

***

Caitlin was only half listening to Bec's conversation. Behind them, the sound of many foot treads had followed them for some time. As they crossed the steel bridge at North Ballachulish, Caitlin glanced behind, feigning to admire the view. She recognised the group of youths who had bothered the Vermiculture stall, especially the one with the clashing paisley—his busy tattoo glaringly contrasting unfashionably with his shirt. They appeared to be troublemakers, but it was difficult to figure out how much trouble they could make. It was over an hour to home and the youths could follow them all the way and discover where they lived. The youths were getting closer and their comments louder. Amongst the mumbled comments to themselves, they spoke the name 'McSweeny' often. An unusual name, it reminded her of a musical.

Bec's one sided conversation petered out. "We're being stalked, aren't we?"

"Yes, but just keep walking and ignore them."

Ignoring them was getting difficult. Caitlin considered her options. Burned into her brain was Scott's first self-defence lesson. Live to fight another day, and run and avoid confrontation at all costs, were his key messages. So, her plan to ignore them, unless otherwise provoked, still held. It would be difficult to run with heavily laden horses, a pregnant goat and a companion who looked like she had not run in years. Bec limped slightly and her breathing got heavier as the afternoon wore on.

How close should she let them get before she'd throw a knife?

"There's our car." Bec's comment brought Caitlin out of her thoughts.

The car pulled up in front of them. Scott got out of the driver's side and pulled out his broken open shot gun and slung it over his arm as he walked toward them. Relief welled within her. Scott didn't make eye contact with her. He glared at the youths. The young men changed their tone. No longer brash and pestering, but now subdued, they ceased their advance. Scott handed Bec her keys and explained where to park the car and wait for him and Caitlin. Bec scurried to her car and drove away without looking back. Scott handed Caitlin the reins of the other horse.

"Start walking." Scott still didn't look at her.

"What if they have guns?" She whispered her question.

Scott's stare remained fixed on the young men.

"Start. Walking." He spoke through tight lips.

Behind Caitlin, the youths continued to talk amongst themselves. Their murmurings changed from defiant to resigned. She walked ahead, hearing the snap of the shotgun closing behind her. Caitlin's pulse sounded in her ears.

Behind her, all was quiet. Caitlin reminded herself she'd promised to do whatever Scott asked her to do, to stay safe on this journey. So, she kept on walking. It stayed quiet. She dared not glance back.

Quiet is good, isn't it?

Caitlin gulped. After a few moments—which seemed like a lifetime—footsteps approached from behind. She glanced around. Scott walked toward her. The youths were walking in the opposite direction, their backs turned. Scott walked backward for a while. His severe expression continued. He looked formidable, like someone you wouldn't want to cross. Caitlin recognised the scary side of her husband. She was thankful the young men weren't foolish and had heeded his silent warnings. He kept the shotgun cocked until the youths were out of sight.

Scott turned and walked beside her in silence for about a mile. Caitlin glanced sideways. He still seethed.

"I kenned it was a bad idea to leave you twa women on your own!" he said from between his teeth. "I saw the way those youths were staring at you when we were at the market. I cud nae think of any other workable options for getting everything home."

"Well, it worked out okay," Caitlin replied.

"Only because I listened to ma instincts and came back for ye!" Scott's voice rose.

"You aren't responsible for their behaviour. Thank-you for coming back. I was so relieved to see you." She kept her tone placating.

"Aye well, I'm not responsible for them, or Bec. But I am for you. And I take that charge very seriously."

"Scott." She put a hand on his arm. "It's okay. You looked after me. I'm safe now."

His shoulders rose with an inhalation and the tightness surrounding his mouth relaxed.

"That's what I get for having an extremely beautiful wife."

"You're biased."

"You don't realise how beautiful you are." He smiled at her, his head shaking ever so slightly.

Chapter Twenty

With Scott's further directions, Bec drove to the hiding place for the vehicle, while Scott and Caitlin continued to walk the horses. Once they met up with Bec, they hid the car behind the copse of Scots pines next to Scott's vehicle, and they walked home together. Bec looked appreciatively at the cottage and its out-houses and vegetable patch. Brendan greeted them at the backdoor where a pile of windmill parts and the equipment for its assembly lay against the back wall of the cottage.

"I want to get going on installing this windmill, ye ken," Scott said. "But we must secure these animals in permanent shelters first."

They unloaded the horses, rubbed them down and placed them in the yard until dusk, then led them into their cosy lean-to stable. They would house the goat and the chickens in their cages in the laundry until Scott made safe enclosures for them.

"That laundry will stink!" Caitlin commented as she walked past her husband at the backdoor. "No more spontaneous sex against a wall for a while then?" she whispered.

The edges of Scott's mouth curled as he continued out the backdoor without commenting.

***

Caitlin looked at her clothes in the 1960s style dresser in Scott's room, now *their room* officially, a half smile rising to her lips. The furniture was a musty, eclectic collection of mismatched styles. Scott had bought clothing her size and preferred style, enough to last for years. She held a red see-through negligee up to herself and turned to him.

"You prefer me in something like this, do you?" she kept her voice soft, conscious of their new friends in the next room.

"Well, in the future, we don't have any good clothing, ye ken. So, I thought it would be nice to, for once." Scott dragged his jumper off over his head, his hair now untidy. His T-shirt followed.

There were two very good dresses, like those in her previous wardrobe. Those clothes were sure to have been stolen with the ransacking of Uncle

Kieran's Country Estate. A knot of warmth lodged in the centre of her chest. When Scott bought these clothes, he had considered her taste for fashion.

"Scott, today you stared down those troublemakers. They could've injured or shot you, if they had firearms and were willing to use them. It scared me. They might have killed you." He moved to stand with her. "Well, I realised if you had died," Caitlin put her arms around him and tilted her head back to look him in the eye, "I'd have never told you I love you. And I do. Love you, that is."

"Aye, I ken ye do." Scott's expression softened. His warm arms encircled her. "It was inevitable really. Ye fell in love with me in the future, so why would ye no' fall in love with me in the past? We were made for each other, Caitlin Murray-Campbell, no matter what age we are, or what era we are in, we belong together." Scott placed his mouth on hers and pressed gently, then pulled back and rubbed her nose with his. "And I love you. Always and forever only yours." His eyes smiled. "Ye said that to me when we were married, the first time."

"Did I?" Caitlin liked the sound of it. Maybe it was something she would say. She held his gaze. "Everything you have done shows me how much you love me. And, you know you passed the test?" She fiddled with his chest hair.

"What test?" Scott frowned.

"Doing all you could to legally marry me was like the final test, to see if you were genuine or not."

"Oh, is that so?" he asked.

"Yes. Then I could be sure you didn't just want me for sex."

***

"Ye will have to be a little quieter now we have visitors in the next room, wife of mine," Scott whispered into her ear after they had made love. Caitlin lay in the crook of his arm, her head on his chest. "The walls are thin. They are only a partition to make this end of the crofter's cottage into two bedrooms."

"I'm not loud, am I?" Caitlin put a hand over her mouth.

"Hmm, ye are. You probably dinnae realise it when ye are in the throes of ecstasy." His eyebrows raised as he spoke, and his mouth developed into a grin.

Caitlin's cheeks heated, and the edges of her mouth turned up slightly. Then she remembered something.

"Oh, I've been meaning to say this to you. You know when we were sitting around the campfire last night and I spoke about preserving what was good for the future?"

"Aye," Scott nodded for her to go on.

"Well, I didn't mean to make it sound like they were all *my* ideas. We'd spoken about it together and they were as much your thoughts as mine. But I wasn't quick enough to think of a way to say this without giving you away, so I said nothing, as you know. But I don't want you to think I meant they're all my ideas." She leaned on him, to look directly at him.

"That's okay Caitlin, for they *are* all your ideas. You're the one who instigated the Community set up and influenced other survivors to do the same and ensured the preservation of knowledge and skills. Ye made sure people stayed educated and healthy. It was all you and your team. I heard it all from you."

"But I've heard it all from you!"

Scott shrugged. "Dinnae ken how it works, lass. Just telling you how it happened."

He pressed his lips to hers and eased her on to her back then he moved his lips to her breasts and worked his way along her torso, resting his lips above her pubic hair, where he spent some time kissing her belly.

Caitlin flinched. "Why are you focussing on there!"

Scott raised his head to look her in the eye. "That's where our bairns will come from."

"Oh, I am still a bad mother!" she cringed. "Tell me about our children!"

"Ye are *not* a bad mother, that's for sure. You have other things on your mind at present."

"Tell me about Angela. She's our eldest, right?" Caitlin asked.

"Aye, and a chip off the old block, she is too! She's you, with long red hair! A natural leader. Ye groomed her and she'll have a place in the Chief Council now that you've..."

"Now I'm dead?" Caitlin finished for him.

"Aye. In the future." His eyebrows drew together.

They were silent for some moments, Caitlin so conscious of Scott's pre-knowledge of her future.

"How old is she?" Caitlin finally asked.

"Nineteen." Scott moved back to be face-to-face with her.

"We've been married twenty years, and she's nineteen? We didn't wait long."

"We conceived Angela on our wedding night."

"What about the others? You said we have four boys," she asked swiftly.

Caitlin winced at the knot in her stomach. *Why am I feeling uncomfortable?* Was it because he was quite young when they married? Or was it the idea of parenthood? *But that is ages away.*

"Aye, the twins are eighteen," Scott continued. "Callum and Rory. Big strong boys. Take after me. They're in the Militia. They're both musical too. Rory lives up to his name. Ye ken we chose it because it means red king, aye? Well, he'll probably take over from ..." he trailed off again.

"Take over from whom?" She prodded him with her finger, and he flinched.

"From me eventually, I was going tae say. But now I'm no' there, and he's no' ready yet, I dinnae ken." Scott absent-mindedly rubbed where she had poked.

"You're a king?"

"No, I'm the leader of the Militia. Was." He took a thoughtful breath. "Rory's a redhead too. Ye have redheads in your family, aye?" Caitlin nodded. "Then we had Ceilidh," he tilted his head, "who lives up to her name and is the life of the party. Neither of us ken where *she* came from!" Scott chuckled. "She's also musical, and she plays with Callum and sings. She has a braw voice, aye. Ye made sure people had music. Got those who could play and had an instrument to teach the children and those who wanted to learn. Ye were most particular that music was nae lost."

Caitlin silently shook her head with each recollection.

Do I? How do I? I must remember all of this.

"Then we had the other two boys. More twins! First Brendan, named after his Uncle Brendan." Scott raised his eyebrows in response to her frown. "Aye, the very same Brendan in the next room to us as we speak. Mind, I told you we got on well with them?" He crossed his feet at the ankles, and he jiggled them as he spoke. "Then Murray, named for obvious reasons. Now, he's the scholar of the lot o' them. Our sixteen-year-old is a mathematician. Were ye good at maths? For I was nae," he continued without giving her time to reply. "He followed what Martin, your cousin and our physicist, was spouting aboot. Did nae understand a word o' it mysel'. Then our baby, Kelly." His smile broadened. "She's a braw lass. I felt the closest to her. Maybe because I spent more time with you and her when ye were sick, aye. We got close, ken?"

The rise and fall of her chest increased its rate as her subconscious spun with concern. It pierced through to her conscious thoughts.

What if they change things and that future never happens? And those children are never born?

No answer came, just the pounding pulse in her temples. She lay silent, not wanting to dispel the happiness his reverie gave him.

Scott paused, blinking, and his eyes were moist.

"You left them, to come to me!" Her throat tightened with a mixture of guilt and sadness for him. He missed them.

"Aye," he said. "But they are almost grown. They were okay with it. Or would be once they found out."

"What do you mean?"

"Kelly would've explained it to them. You remember I said I went straight from your deathbed to The Time Machine?" Scott paused as he seemed to be inwardly recalling the events of that particular day. "I had nae told a soul what I'd planned. Might've hinted at it to Rory. But Kelly *knew*. She followed me, stopped me in the corridor before I got to the barn where the machine was set up, handed me your ring and said, 'Give it to Mum when you see her.'" His voice held a note of wonder as he stared at the ceiling. "Aye, Kelly will explain it to them."

Scott looked at her so abruptly she flinched.

"Ye must have told Kelly." He spoke with wonder in his voice. "You knew I would go, but ye never said a word to me, lass."

Chapter Twenty-One

Invercharing Community. The Future

Relaying the story of how she'd met their dad had exhausted Kelly's mum. It was her idea of how to pass the time. Mum tired more easily and needed longer periods of rest in between the retelling as the weekend passed. Dad was away with the oldest twins. They were part of the Militia. Dad oversaw manoeuvres and there were reports of a bandit group nearby. He wanted the area safe and had taken a small troop of Militia to investigate. Kelly's chest constricted, and tears pinched at her eyeballs. Dad, being a Highlander, knew this area of the Highlands well, where they had set up the Invercharing Community. He was brave, and at times fierce, but always gentle and loving to her mum, brothers and sisters.

Kelly sat beside Mum's bed. The clatter of a dray going past, and the fresh scent of horses wafted through the open window, the breeze lifting the simple net curtains which brushed past the pictures of Van Gogh's paintings Mum had stuck to the wall beside the window. Mum loved Van Gogh. Kelly's chin dug into her hands. She hadn't brushed her long straight brown hair today. It fell untidily around her face, and she blew it away from her mouth.

Kelly's elbows left a dent on her knees. That sensation in her chest and throat welled up again. Should she believe everything Mum had told her about how she met Dad and their early life together? Some of it was quite fantastical. *Are the morphine tablets making her delusional?* Kelly thought. Aunty Bec, being a doctor, had personally taken on Mum's pain management.

It was upsetting the community to see their leader lose her fight with lymphoma. Everyone loved Mum. She was their own Caitlin Murray-Campbell, the Legend.

Kelly didn't understand how Dad went away when Mum was obviously going downhill, and fast.

Since the treatment stopped working, Mum had become very thin. Cachexia, Aunty Bec had called it. Mum now appeared small in her bed, her collarbones stood out, her cheekbones were more prominent, and she had dark circles under her eyes. Caitlin Murray-Campbell *never* had dark circles under her eyes. She'd always been a very beautiful woman who aged little, only the smile lines near her eyes showed her true age. Kelly wasn't the only one who believed she didn't look her almost sixty years. This had always been a good thing with a husband twenty years younger. But no one ever noticed. They were both exceptional people. Kelly being alone with Mum had happened a lot lately. It *had* been good to hear how they met.

Murray walked hesitantly into the room. Kelly was glad he'd been here too, often sitting by Mum's bedside as well. Kelly had to admit she'd needed him. It was funny how Murray was Dad's colouring but nothing like him, tall but skinny. Nerdy, not like the rest of her brothers. This time with him and Mum had brought them closer.

Murray strode across the plain carpeted floor to the chair on the other side of the bed and sat.

"Where's Dad, Kelly? Why's he not here?" Murray whispered over their sleeping mother.

Kelly shrugged.

"Can't he see she'll not be with us much longer?" Murray continued his whisper. "Dad should be here! He's in denial."

"What's denial?" Kelly asked.

"You know, the first stage of grief. Kubler-Ross and all that," Murray said. "What do you read, anyway?"

"Not what you read, that's for sure. Mum's been telling me how she met Dad."

"Oh, that's romantic," Murray said.

"No, it's been a bit weird. I think Mum's pain meds are making her a bit funny. Funny 'odd' that is. Mum said"—Kelly leaned over the bed to be closer to him and dropped her voice another notch— "that Dad travelled back in *time* for her right before The Stock Market Crash, to keep her safe till they got here."

"How did Dad go back?" Murray used measured tones.

"In a time machine they built here!" She almost laughed.

"Mum shouldn't have mentioned that!" Murray's whisper was harsh. "It's a secret project."

"What?" Kelly frowned.

"Nothing."

"What?" Kelly insisted.

Murray shook his head, his eyes slightly narrowed and his mouth a thin line—his expression one of *Don't ask!* But she had to.

"Murray, Mum's been speaking of a time machine, and Dad travelling back in time to when she was a young woman in her twenties. She claims he was almost forty. Like he is now!"

Murray gazed at their mother. He let out his breath, his shoulders slumping.

"Okay." He swallowed. "What I'm about to tell you, you mustn't tell anyone else. Especially not Angela, okay?"

Kelly nodded as Murray's Adam's apple bobbed a few times, then he spoke.

"So, there *is* such a thing as a time machine here in our Community compound. Uncle Brendan, some scientists, including Mum's cousin Martin, and myself, have been working on it for a while now. It's all set for human trials. It's a project only known by those on the team and the Chief Council. You know Uncle Brendan is an electrical engineer? Well, he devised a gadget for pinpointing places in time. We've tested it out on small animals going back and forward in time from a time zero, the present, for short-time distances. Then with larger animals, extrapolating results for humans. We haven't performed tests with humans, and we're still debating the ethics involved. We also haven't devised a way to make a return journey possible. Still more calculations and theory to think over. It's locked away, ready to go, set to the date of a month before TSMC."

Kelly's mind spun. Murray spoke as if it were fact. A time machine! Mum had said so. Murray said so. And Murray was smart, all the scientists in the community believed it. He'd never lie to her.

"What's the TSMC?" she asked.

"The Stock Market Crash! Don't you know anything? It's like, the reason the world is as it is now. Read your history girl."

Kelly knew her history, just not by the initials Murray used for that event. She wouldn't argue the point.

"Why you?" she asked. "Why are you part of the team?"

"Because I'm good at maths and I can use a slide rule for the complicated calculations. Computers can't do it all, like they say they used to."

"So, both Mum and Dad know about this?" she prodded.

"Yes. They check up on it regularly. Well, Dad does, anyway. He's fascinated by it all. Especially lately, as Mum has become sicker." Murray paused; his brow deeply furrowed. "You can't let him know you know, okay?"

Kelly nodded as Mum stirred in her sleep.

"Does Dad know that Mum is telling you all this? Does he know she knows he went back in time for her?" Murray's questions came rapidly.

"I've no idea. Should I ask Dad when he comes back?"

"No, no, no, don't ask Dad anything." Murray's voice strained. "We can't do anything to change history, past or present. If Dad goes, it must be because Dad goes. We can't do anything to affect it."

"What do you mean 'Can't do anything to affect history'? What's the time set to before TSMC all about? Isn't someone going back to prevent that?" Her voice rose at the contradictions in his statements. What was their idea setting *that* date?

Mum stirred and opened her eyes.

"Oh, sorry. Didn't mean to wake you." Murray looked down at her.

"Murray, that's okay. Haven't seen you for a while. How are you son?" Mum usually referred to Murray as her 'Little Einstein'.

"I'm fine. How are you?" he asked.

Mum's smile was weary. Murray bit his lower lip for a moment.

"Mum, have you been telling Kelly about the Time Machine?" Murray whispered.

Mum turned to Kelly. "I thought you realised that was confidential between us. You weren't to tell anyone, especially not your father. Do *not* tell Scott, please! He can't know. We can't affect what he does. What he will do." Mum shook her head as she corrected herself.

"Sorry." *Why hadn't I believed Mum in the first place?* "But I wasn't sure if you weren't just dreaming it or something. I needed Murray to confirm it's all real."

"It *is* all real," Mum said. "And it must happen. Don't tell your father I know, please."

"You mean, you *never* told him?" Murray's voice was loud in the small bedroom "You kept it a secret from him all these years?".

"He was so young and vulnerable when he arrived at this community." Mum sighed. "He was only eighteen. He'd been through an act of survival to get here. He'd lost everything and everyone and was emotionally fragile. He'd grown up quickly. He'd had to. The years passed, and I thought I might tell him, as it had been too soon when we were first married. He wouldn't have coped with it. Then I decided against it. When you know someone as I know your father—as well as I knew him as the mature man I had met previously—I knew he'd want to come back for me because *he* wanted to and had decided for himself. Not because I'd told him he did. And that still stands. Do *not* tell him." Mum sunk back into her bed, her speech exhausting her.

"We must make sure he goes, though. Without him realising that we are," Murray broke the silence. "Dad has to go, doesn't he?"

Mum's brow creased. So did Murray's.

"What's wrong, Mum?" Kelly placed her hand on Mum's bony shoulder. "Are you in pain? Do you need more morphine?"

"No." Mum shook her head. "It's just that if he doesn't go, then all this won't happen. Because it *has* happened, you see? I could only do all this because of what he taught me when I was a young woman, and he was the experienced man he is now."

"So, the space-time continuum will be safe?" Murray's knotted brow relaxed as Mum nodded.

"Time? Space?" Kelly asked. *What is he talking about?*

"Read more, sis," Murray said.

"When I die"—Mum's cool fingers reached out and rested on Kelly's hand— "take my wedding ring off my finger and make sure your father takes it with him. He also needs lots of cash." She turned her head to Murray. "Collect what you can and make sure he has it somewhere to grab quickly and that he takes it with him, please."

Kelly nodded and looked at her brother. His face held a grim expression.

Chapter Twenty-Two

The Present

C aitlin paused at the back window which looked out onto the back-yard. Scott enlisted the willing help of Brendan in not only installing the wind-powered electricity supply but building predator proof animal shelters. Brendan was a very capable and practical person, and—at this point in time—was of a similar age to Scott. The two strong and fit men worked well and efficiently together, being equal in many ways. Scott had previously prepared wood for timber to use on the stables and chicken coup, but they needed more.

The two men entered the yard after going further into the nearby forest and felling more trees. They used the Highland horses to drag the timber back. They'd completed the stables which comprised three stalls, one of which would house the nanny goat. The chicken coup was the next thing they would work on. The chickens were free range of a daytime and herded into the laundry at sunset. The daily laundry clean-out job would be over.

Caitlin turned back to the task which had occupied Bec and herself for the past few days. They'd looked through the medical supplies of both couples. Bec had theirs hidden amongst the boxes of stores they kept in their car. Swapping medical items provided a more complete medical kit for each couple. Scott had informed Caitlin that Bec, as a General Practitioner, was proficient in prenatal and postnatal care and delivering babies.

Her *own* babies in the future. Caitlin stifled the alarm rising in her chest, taking a deep breath to steady her heart rate. In a way it *had* already happened and turned out well, hadn't it? If they change nothing of this past, in the future she would have seven healthy children, who were late teens and young adults when their father left them. It was still *odd*.

Bec could also perform minor surgeries and administer anaesthesia. She showed Caitlin the small anaesthetic machine called a Boyles Machine. Bec held diathermy equipment, which Brendan had rigged to a large battery, and cylinders of oxygen and anaesthetic gasses. She gave Caitlin a brief rundown of how to use them.

"I can't do that." Caitlin stammered when Bec told her how to use a Boyle's Anaesthetic Machine. "It feels 'out of bounds'".

"You never know when you'll need to." Bec encouraged. "Go on. Try it."

Caitlin set the dials and fiddled with the ventilator section of the anaesthetic machine. She'd only spent a short time in ICU as a student, handling ventilators. This one seemed so much simpler. The monitor attached was similar to the cardiac monitors she was familiar with in the ED. To her surprise, she easily mastered it.

"A natural, you would say," Bec commented.

***

Scott appeared at the backdoor, eyes wide and speech rapid.

"When we were out in the forest cuttin' timber, we heard a horse!"

"What do you mean?" Caitlin turned from the table covered in medicines ranging from tablets to ampoules of morphine, which she and Bec had been sorting.

"I mean, lass, that there's a horse loose oot there!" Scott's eyes were alight at the prospect, his accent thick with excitement. "It's calling to our horses. I'm hoping it will be a domestic horse that's missin' the comforts of a home, so to speak. It's calling like one that's lonely, not like a stallion wantin' to steal our mare. I'm going to try to catch it. With everyone's help o' course. I'll need you ladies to help shepherd it into our corral, if we can."

They walked quietly toward the wooded area where Scott and Brendan came across the horse, and when almost there, the horse revealed himself. He was a young jet-black stallion with a full mane and tail and feathering to his lower legs and looked about sixteen hands in height.

"What if it's someone's horse?" Caitlin ushered the others into the shelter of the trees.

"Well, it *is* someone's horse, is it no'?" Scott said. "So, we'll secure him in oor yard and see if anyone comes looking for him. If no one claims him, he's *mine.*"

"Have to catch him first," Brendan reminded Scott.

The horse ran off at a gallop having sensed more humans.

"Aye right. Like that, is it?" Scott turned and addressed them, his accent lilting and burring. "Here's what we're going tae do. I'll go closer on my own. Just me, like. Ye all stay here behind trees on either side of this wee track here that I am going' to try and head him down. Aye? Then when I have passed you, come out from behind so we form a line of people and we, gently mind, nudge him into the yard. Aye? Keep quiet behind those trees when he comes past ye. He'll smell ye, but he may not be as spooked if he cannae hear nor see you."

They each nodded. Scott had left open the yard fence nearest this track and tied the horses next to some feed, as far in the yard as possible. He walked in the same direction as the spooked horse. Caitlin hid with the others behind the trees. After fifteen minutes, the young stallion came crashing through the trees near her. He trotted past them on the track. Caitlin and the others stayed silent in the cover of the trees.

Scott came from behind the horse, speaking the Gaelic softly, and walked slowly in the same direction as the animal, heading him toward the yard. The horse neighed, and the horses replied, spurring the horse on into the yard. He went straight for the oats Scott had placed by the horses, yet out of their reach. Caitlin and Bec spread their arms wide as the men replaced the crossbars of the fence. Scott continued to speak quietly in the Gaelic.

"Och, braw!" Scott hissed as he punched the air with both fists.

"He's beautiful!" Caitlin admired the animal.

"Aye, but he's lost condition." Scott never took his eyes off the horse. "I'd say he's not been in a human's care for a few weeks. His coat is a mess too. Needs a good brush. But aye, he's a beautiful animal. Hope no one comes looking for him. 'Finders keepers' 'n all o' that."

"Are you going to ride him?" Bec asked.

"Aye, well no' today. Give him time to settle into his new surroundings. I'll leave him till we get him into the stables tonight. I'll no' even approach him till then."

With the late autumn day, the light of the setting sun painted the stable and outbuildings golden. Caitlin followed Scott to the corral while Bec and Brendan trailed behind them. The air was crisp and the horses' breath misted around their faces. Caitlin hugged herself from the nippy air. Scott put one horse into the stable to encourage the stallion in. The remaining horse would stay with the stallion to act as a guide as it went into the stable. The horse didn't move. Scott approached the animal in his gentle way, quietly speaking the Gaelic. His deep, husky voice sounded melodic and breathy. The horse settled with his soft approach, but still didn't move into the stables. The last of the light was leaving their valley for the day.

"Oh, would ye just get into the stable, ye stupid beast!" Scott expressed his frustration quietly in English.

Caitlin snuck away inside determined to come back with a solution.

"Hey handsome." She whispered on her return and Scott turned to her. "Catch!" She threw something to him.

Scott caught an apple from the cold store in his left-hand. Twisting it in his strong hands, it snapped in two. The horse's ears pricked up. Breaking open the apple released its scent. The stallion's nostrils flared, and he tentatively stepped toward Scott, who walked slowly into the stable. The horse followed. Caitlin came behind to close the stable door. Scott led the horse into the empty stall and closed him in, still whispering in the Gaelic.

"Oh, you're a braw lass!" He gave Caitlin a hug, lifting her feet off the ground.

"It's my 'privileged upbringing' you know." Her voice muffled into his shoulder.

Chapter Twenty-Three

"We need to go shopping once more. Going to run out o' feed for the animals before the winter ends." Scott stood in the stable with piles of cut grass at his feet and more stuffed into the make-shift hay loft above him. He had enlisted everyone's help in hand cutting grass for bedding for the chicken coup and winter feed for the horses and goat.

"This wee amount of hay is nae going to last the winter. And it will be a harsh one. All signs in nature are pointing to it, especially the geese migrating south," Scott noted. "I have heard their honking high overhead in the sky much earlier this year. We must go to the market in Fort William. It should be on the weekend after next. We'll have the windmill installed by then, won't we?"

Brendan nodded in reply.

The ensuing week was a busy one for the men who earnestly tried to complete the wind-powered electricity supply to the cottage. It would generate enough power, albeit limited, for essentials such as refrigeration, water pumps, lighting and medical equipment when needed. They struggled, as some necessary items for installing had not been part of Scott's original purchase.

"He never told me I needed one!" Scott responded when Brendan pointed out the missing piece. "Now we must go to the market! Hope the energy stall is on this weekend."

***

"Need a lot more food for the horses now you've the extra mouth to feed." Caitlin leaned on the fence as Scott took the stallion through his paces. He spent most afternoons riding his new prize, the black horse, in the grassed, fenced area beside the stables; he'd made the yard into a menage. The stallion's coat glistened as his muscles rippled beneath it. Caitlin enjoyed the smell of horse, it brought back so many good memories. The stallion pranced and lifted his forelegs high. He led with his head to the left and Scott continually corrected him, the tack jingling with each slight tug.

"Aye but he's beautiful, is he no'?" he said.

"You're in love with him already. What are you going to do when his owner turns up?"

"He will nae," Scott trotted the horse around the yard.

"How can you be so confident?"

"Caitlin, if you owned a beautiful animal such as this, would you ever let him oot o' your sight?"

Caitlin shook her head and her thoughts briefly returned to her own horse. She hoped her mare had survived the stable fire at her Uncle Kieran's or was serving a kind master now horses were going to be in common use again, according to Scott.

"Aye, well," Scott interrupted her thoughts. "I believe this horse, which I am regarding as a Friesian, or part Friesian, was stolen then abandoned. Or escaped. Or somehow went missing after the ransacking of his owner's property. For only a person of reasonable wealth could afford such an animal, aye?"

Caitlin nodded while admiring her husband. Scott *did* sit a horse quite well. His back was straight and relaxed. He guided the horse's movements with subtle actions of his own—tightening a leg muscle, an imperceptible twitch of his hand. He appeared to be barely moving, but his body commanded volumes to his mount. Scott would have done well in dressage events.

"I think you're right. He steps out like a Friesian, he has a beautiful gait and he's good natured. He looks great now you've groomed him, and he's had a good feed. Which brings me back to my point. He'll cost us more in horse feed, if we can't grow enough of our own. Can we afford him? If no one claims him, we should sell him." Caitlin bit her tongue as she poked it into her cheek.

Scott, concentrating on riding and not looking at Caitlin, heard her serious tone. Scott stopped the horse so abruptly; he nearly lost his seat. The black Friesian snorted and reared slightly.

"What! Caitlin, mo chroi, ye cannae expect me to part with this horse! I mean, I will if the owner turns up. But how will they prove it?" he stopped and regarded her. The tension in his shoulder muscles subsided and the lines on his brow disappeared. "Ye'd think after twenty years of marriage you would nae catch me in your traps! Dinnae do that again about this animal, please," he laughed. "It's too close to my heart, aye."

During the week leading up to the market, under Scott's direction, they continued to prepare for the harsh winter he predicted. They turned their energy to stocking the woodpile. They tidied up and mulched the vegetable garden beds and secured the outhouses by making them sturdier. Scott had been hasty in some of his builds, being one man at the time, they had been difficult to construct to his satisfaction. The lean-to on the back of the outhouse being a case in point. No longer needed as a makeshift stable, it became a woodshed and goat house. The now heavily pregnant goat would have a place of her own—the three stalls in the stables now occupied by equine beings.

Brendan and Scott performed maintenance on the water pumps and other electrical equipment readying them for when they had power. Caitlin cleaned out the disused fridge and ensured it was ready for use. They checked the guttering and down pipes for leaks and the roof for water tightness. They checked the medical equipment of Bec's, as a courtesy, as regardless of who used it, it needed to be in perfect working order. Caitlin decided she would be on the lookout for a Boyle's Machine of their own.

The evenings had changed since their house guests arrived. Bec had brought a CD player and a supply of batteries. Caitlin missed music. Brendan and Bec had a collection of music from the 70s right through to the 2010s. They spent their evenings listening to music or playing chess, draughts, or charades. The fire crackled and Caitlin sunk into the dusty old couch after another hard day's work. The green couch had become surprisingly comfortable.

"I haven't had fun like this since I went to a party with my parents as a child," Brendan commented after a funny mime of 'The Dictionary' performed by Scott.

"Yes, and we didn't talk like we do now," Caitlin said. "I was always on my mobile phone. I must confess, I miss my phone. And my friend Jan, who I always texted; posted on Facebook. Tweeted... Wonder what's happened to her."

Caitlin surprised herself as she hadn't thought of Jan in a long time. Her friendship with Jan and her job at Edinburgh Royal Infirmary seemed a lifetime ago... and another world.

"You didn't stay in contact?" Bec asked. "Mobile phone relay towers have only ceased working recently."

Caitlin's eyes met Scott's. An imperceptible shake of his head accompanied his gaze. She wouldn't tell them Scott had confiscated it when he took her from her uncle's estate.

"Well, I left my uncle's home where I was staying in rather a rush," she said

"Oh, I see. Had to get away in a hurry? You were in a dangerous situation then?" Bec leaned forward in the green armchair.

"Yes. Well, I would have been, if it wasn't for Scott."

"Did I hear you say once that you had a privileged upbringing? That's how you know horses?"

"Well, I suppose you could say I did." Caitlin glanced at Scott.

He squinted one eye at her, and she read a warning in his expression.

"I was holidaying at my uncle's estate when the stock market crashed," she continued. "Scott took me away in a hurry. He saved me from harm..." she hesitated at the memory. "They ransacked my uncle's house."

"So, your husband came to the rescue?" Brendan enquired.

"Yes, but that was before you were married, wasn't it?" Bec answered for her. "Caitlin said they'd been married for four months when I asked her on the way here."

Scott looked at Caitlin, blinking widely but then quickly blanked his expression before the other couple had noticed.

"So, you got married after the crash?" Brendan looked from Caitlin to Scott.

"Aye well, we planned to elope." Scott took over the responses in this interrogation, friendly as it was. "The Stock Market Crash hurried it up for us somewhat."

There was an uncomfortable pause in the conversation. Scott creased his brow and his vision turned inward. Anxiety began to knot in her chest. What if they had heard Scott say they were married for twenty years? This could get difficult.

"My turn, 'cos I got the one about 'The Dictionary'," Caitlin stood and started miming 'The Lord of the Rings'.

Chapter Twenty-Four

Scott drove to the Fort William market, and in the passenger seat Caitlin mentally ran over their shopping list. As well as animal feed, they were to stock up on as much non-perishable food and any medical supplies they could find. The vehicle had a full tank and they had jerry cans for petrol. Scott wouldn't return without the items essential for the completion of their wind powered electricity supply.

They parked the vehicle at the Fort William market. The air wisped smoke from braziers surrounded by grubby-clothed shoppers. Along with smoke, the familiar scent of unwashed bodies assailed Caitlin's nostrils. The once pristine Old Museum, now a dilapidated and graffiti-abused building, was still the backdrop for the sparsely stocked stalls. Scrawny dogs followed scrawny children as they ran past her, splashing fresh mud on her jeans. The atmosphere was more tense than their previous visit, but Caitlin couldn't place the source of its cause.

They made their way to the black market pharmacy van, as Scott had called it.

"Well, hello handsome! Come back for more, have we?" The black market pharmacist eyed Scott with appreciation. She dressed as a Goth—black clothing draped her form and just as black eyeliner surrounded her eyelids. "Oh, ye brought your daughter with ye this time." Her dark outlined gaze directed itself at Caitlin.

Caitlin glanced at Scott. It was difficult to disguise his broad shoulders and athletic physique even under his thick coat, nor his good looks. His handsome face was always on display. The black market pharmacist's comments caught the ears of the stall holders nearby. The other female sellers' attentions remained on Scott, their eyes never leaving him, and smiles on most faces accompanied nods of approval and winks. There was a cat-call or two. Caitlin doubled-blinked.

"This is Caitlin, my *wife*," Scott corrected the pharmacists mistake. "Caitlin, this is the pharmacist who was so helpful when I was in Perth a wee while ago."

Caitlin stared coldly at the pharmacist. *How much pharmacology does this woman know?* Learnt on the job, post-crash, Caitlin suspected. The pharmacist smiled broadly and continued leaning forward over her stall, her cleavage prominent, as both Scott and Caitlin looked through the medicines and equipment she had for sale. They bought more local anaesthetic, antibiotics, and analgesics. Caitlin noticed general anaesthetics and cylinders of oxygen were in the back of the pharmacist's van and bought them as well.

"And you will probably be wanting more o' these?" The pharmacist held out strips of the contraceptive pill. "Your wife looks like she needs to grow up a wee bit before you get her pregnant." Her tone was derisive. Caitlin blinked but kept quiet regarding *that* remark.

"Scott, check all the expiry dates." Caitlin handed back two vials of lignocaine which were six months past their expiry date. "We don't want any out-of-date stock." Eventually, all the medical supplies available would be out-of-date, but she would not use them until there were no other options.

"Just let me know when you want a real woman." The pharmacist took the cash from Scott.

"That will be all, thank you." Scott caught Caitlin's arm and walked her to the renewable energy stall. As he spun her away from the pharmacy stall, a familiar face came into her view. It was the man-with-the-stare from their last trip to this market. Once again, the shabby middle-aged man never took his eyes off her. Or his fingers away from his mouth. She turned her attention to their shopping, trying to ignore the prickling sensation on the back of her neck, and stepped closer to her husband.

Scott bought the item needed to complete the installation of the batteries to store their wind generated electricity. As they walked to a food stall, Caitlin glanced in the direction of the man-with-the-stare. He now spoke to a younger man who vaped; the cloud of mist from his e-cigarette surrounded him like a fog with every exhalation. At the food stall she bought tinned foods and a small amount of dried fruit and nuts, a large bag of potatoes and onions. They also purchased more chicken feed and oats, and as many bales of hay as would fit in the back of the vehicle. Caitlin glanced again, but she couldn't see the man-with-the-stare or his vaping companion anywhere.

"That was ridiculous." Scott shoved the one jerry can of fuel in the 4WD.

"So was the price of everything else! Just as well you brought what you did, back with you." Caitlin referred to the cash he carried back through time with him, avoiding mentioning the word 'cash', which might draw unwanted attention, particularly of the man-with-the-stare.

Scott packed an old citizen band radio he found on a stall.

"Brendan may help me do something with this," he said, holding the piece of dilapidated equipment out for Caitlin's inspection. "In the future, it's an important means of communication."

The wind funnelled between the buildings and cooled Caitlin's face and hands. They walked to the hot food stalls for lunch and a warm drink. On their way, they passed two elderly gentlemen. They looked shabby, but Caitlin recognised the quality of the tweed jackets they wore.

"Aye! Terrible, so it is!" The elderly man had a broad Glaswegian accent. "Makes 911 look like a wee picnic, so it does!"

"Oh, aye." His companion's tatty tweed jacket hung loosely over tartan trousers.

"Excuse me, gentlemen." Scott addressed the elderly men. "But I cudnae help but overhearing ye. To what would ye be referring to now?"

The two men looked at Scott and then at Caitlin, shaking their heads slowly, both their brows a deep crease in between their hoary-haired eyebrows.

"And where have you been hidin' with your bonny wee wifey there," the older of the two asked, "that ye have nae heard about the terrorist attacks which have gone on around the world in all the major cities in these past two weeks?"

"What?" Caitlin glanced at Scott. He didn't look shocked.

"What happened?" Scott asked politely.

"Large areas of London and Greater London, Manchester, Birmingham, Cardiff, Glasgow and Edinburgh were bombed by vehicles blown up or suicide bombers! Nearly every major City on The Continent as well." The other man supplied the details.

"Oh aye," his companion continued, "and major cities in the United States. They say the terrorists have planned it since afore the crash but are taking the opportunity noo' the world is in disarray."

"Aye, ken, it's worse the noo', as there are nae emergency services to help, aye."

"Well, no so good as they used to be, aye," his friend corrected.

"And ye ken what smarts the most? They were home-grown terrorists." His face thrust forward as his bushy eyebrows raised themselves even higher.

"How do ye come to that conclusion?" Scott enquired.

"Well, ye ken there has nae been any immigrants allowed in for a wee while with the boarders bein' shut, an' all? Must be our residents responsible then."

Scott and Caitlin left their acquaintances still discussing the state of the world and went to stand by their vehicle.

"You guard the vehicle while I go get us some lunch." Caitlin omitted any comment on the news, or the man-with-the-stare.

No point in getting Scott edgy because she was being paranoid. Scott leaned against the vehicle, his coat tight against the winter wind and nodded. Caitlin soon returned with piping hot stovies and a mug of tea.

"Glad I bought the forty-pound bag of potatoes and the tins of corned beef," Caitlin commented. "I'll be able to make stovies for us now." At last, another item for their fast-becoming-boring menu.

Scott flicked his chin in reply as he began eating his pile of stovies.

"You knew this was coming, didn't you?" Caitlin asked. "It was like you've been expecting it."

Scott finished taking a bite of the hot stovies and blew out around them before swallowing.

"Aye." He took another hot mouthful.

"Want to add anything to what the gentlemen from Glasgow were reporting?"

"Well," he looked ahead with resignation. "Ye thought it was bad up till now. This is where it gets *really* bad. The Superpowers will do their usual vying for supremacy. The leaders with the most equipment left over from prior to the crash will do their posturing, while the average person trying to survive quakes in their hovel. From now on, we stay where we are. No more shopping forays. If there is anythin' ye see here and think is essential, get it the noo. We'll no' be oot in company for a long while. Safer that way, aye?"

Caitlin nodded mutely and began scanning the stalls. She spied a toiletry stall and finished her stovies and tea. "I'll be back. Been desperate for a nail file for a while."

Caitlin walked a few paces then glanced back now and then. Scott watched her go, smiling to himself over her comment about the nail file, most likely. He would be observing her, and anyone near her, as she made her way around the stalls for the final shop. She was safe with Scott watching out for her—no matter who stared at her.

***

Driving home was a quiet ride. The silence was palpable. She found herself stewing as she mulled over the pharmacist's behaviour toward Scott.

He glanced at her periodically. They were at the place near the Scots pines where they would hide the 4WD.

"Okay," Scott said. "What's the matter, lass?"

"Your friend the pharmacist." She didn't hesitate.

Scott glanced at her again as he parked the 4WD. There was such a burning begin in the centre of her chest and a hurt inside, so much so, she did not know how to express it, nor understand it herself.

"What about her?" He leaned on the steering wheel with his face fully toward her.

She sensed his stress. It was the way he breathed.

"Know her well, do you? In the Biblical sense, maybe?" She glared at him, unable to stop her words. They were like horses champing at the bit, and now they had bolted.

"Caitlin! What are you asking me?"

"It's only, the last time you saw her, you were in Perth."

"Aye," Scott answered calmly.

"And that was just after I'd refused you." She got out of the vehicle, slammed the door, and stormed to the back of the car.

Breathe Caitlin, breathe. Calm down.

Scott followed her.

"Are you seriously asking me if I had sex with the pharmacist?" Scott's neck was red and his voice tight.

"Well apparently, I'm not 'woman enough' for a man like you."

"That's her opinion. Not mine," Scott's tone remained hard.

"And it's an informed opinion, is it?" Caitlin's face burned, and her vision blurred.

Turning her back on him, she strode along the track to the cottage. She was within the copse by the time he had locked the car and caught up with her. The wind blew and caught her loose hair, which lifted about her face, whipping across her eyes. Scott grabbed her by the shoulders and spun her around to face him. He put his arms around her and spoke with his face very close to hers. So close, he was almost touching her mouth with his.

"Caitlin Murray-Campbell, you are the only woman I have ever loved! The only woman I have ever had sex with. The only one I will ever, *ever* be with. For all time. Aye? You get that?"

She nodded, tears ran down her face, wetting the strands of hair now stuck to it, but she said nothing.

"I *ken* I'm the only one you have ever loved," he continued. "Maybe I'm old-fashioned, for I must admit, I was a wee bit upset on our wedding night when I discovered you were nae a virgin. But well, you were in your thirties and a man cudnae expect a beautiful woman, such as yoursel' to wait forever. But now I know, you have only ever loved me. For I was your first and only. Aye?"

"Yes," she said softly. Was she lying? No, she knew she would never have sex with another man, not after having Scott for a lover.

Scott loosened his hold slightly and continued his intense stare.

"This is a part of you I have nae seen afore, lass," he said. "You're jealous, are ye no'?"

She didn't reply, only returned his gaze.

"Green-eyed Monster raising its ugly head? You have nothing to worry about, lass."

"You're mine!" she blurted out. Scott blinked a few times. "You are *mine*," she enunciated each word. "No one else's."

"Aye, that's so true. I've always been yours. When I arrived at the compound a tatty, dirty young wretch of a boy who had been living it rough for months, it was like you'd been waiting for me. Expecting me. And you took me in and cleaned me up. Instead of feeling like ye were mothering me, I fell in love with you. But ye already loved me that way, aye." He kissed her gently despite the strong grip with which he held her. "You have nothing to worry about. For I am yours and yours only." He raised his eyebrows slightly. "Always and forever. Remember that, lass."

Scott laid her on the soft, pine needle covered ground and made love to her in the privacy and shelter of their copse.

***

The day turned colder. The wind intensified as they returned to the car to unpack and take their stores to the cottage. Once they arrived at the cottage, Scott and Brendan went back to the vehicle to unload the rest of the supplies. They returned wet and cold and sat in front of the Aga. Caitlin and Bec helped the men take off their wet clothes, drink hot tea and warm up, having ensured the animals were safely in their proper shelters with feed—except the nanny goat, who was about to give birth. They placed straw on the laundry floor and held the goat in there. Outside, the snow continued to fall.

****

Fort William

McSweeny looked out of the one window of the office he had commandeered, the only window in the small office block which still had glazing. He looked down at the Fort William street below, the bright snow momentarily blinding him. The room was damp and musty, but it was a place to hold his business records and meetings with clients. He had to keep things normal.

McSweeny continued chewing his fingernails. His thumb hurt so he wiped his saliva sodden hand on the front of his blue jumper, his finger caught in the holes around the neck. The weather had made him postpone his trip south. He needed to clinch the deal, sign the contract or whatever you would call it these days. Tons of people had come up north, believing it to be a safer place. They were prime targets. Lonely and lost, most of them. Wasn't that what *he* had become? How could he be contemplating this?

He shook his head. Trade wasn't as good as he'd expected. To be on top he had to take risks. It was always the way he operated, wasn't it? But the goods he now contemplated trading...

"Mr McSweeny?" It was Brian. The kid was skinny and stank of vape, *Mother's Milk* probably, as McSweeny smelled strawberries. But the kid was sharp.

"What?" He took his index finger away from his teeth.

"The guys in the Borders sent a guy, and he's wanting to know what you're doing. And get a feed, ken." Brian sucked on his vape.

"Aye when this snow clears, I'll make the journey, not before," McSweeny said. "No' riskin' it in this weather. You still keepin' your eyes out?"

"Aye."

"Seen that blonde beauty again?" McSweeny asked.

"Nup." Brian blew out, the misty vapour almost filling the small office as it dispersed.

McSweeny grunted his acknowledgement. No one with any sense would be out in this. That chick was prime, just what they'd be looking for. A twinge caught the corner of his conscience; he batted it away. He was getting good at it. He tore the nail on his ring finger, again.

"An' stop vapin'. You look like a smokin' dragon."

"Ahh. It's hard to give up, you know. It's nicotine." Brian's hand was on the door.

"Well, it won't last forever. It'll run out one day. And you announce yourself from a mile away with your smoke signals!" McSweeny spoke to the shutting door and the kid's cloud chaser.

Chapter Twenty-Five

The Future

"Take me outside. I want to look at the mountains, please," Caitlin asked Scott.

He carried her to the outside seating area immediately past their bedroom door, wrapped in a purple rug. Caitlin's hands and feet were getting colder. She could tell she was so much lighter by the ease with which Scott lifted her. Ceilidh, Murray and Kelly sat on the bench-seat next to them. Their other children were on their way.

They knew.

Caitlin sat in Scott's lap as she gazed at the view of the grey-brown mountains opposite, their sides becoming purple with the heather in bloom.

One last time.

Caitlin loved *her* Bonnie Scotland. She called it hers, even though it belonged to no human. After a while, she turned her head to face Scott. She had waited for his return.

"*Gra mo chroi*, I should have come sooner. Forgive me." Scott's gravelly voice held pain.

Or was it regret?

Caitlin focussed on Scott. He returned her gaze, his eyes soft, with slight smile lines at the edges of red-rimmed, gradually moistening, piercing blue orbs.

My love, you are brave and heroic, but you won't cope with this. Sorry.

"Always and forever..." Caitlin breathed it out, barely audible.

His eyes searched hers, a look of foreboding started its journey across his features.

Now her vision went through him, her soul free.

Murray watched Dad shake. Dad's breath came haltingly at first, then progressed to uncontrollable, body-racking sobs. His tall frame shrank beneath his grief, his face buried in his wife's golden hair. After a brief time, Dad gently laid Mum's lifeless body on the couch outside and left without a word.

***

The living room was full of people. So full, mourners stood outside on the balcony, and even more were out the front where there was nowhere to sit. Murray's heart pumped louder in his chest and the muscles in his back and arms tensed as he brushed shoulders with yet another mourner. Murray made his way to the backdoor. Mum's wake was becoming too much. Did he *have* to endure it?

Why couldn't he just go to his room and pretend to be with Dad? It had worked so far, hadn't it? His and Kelly's subterfuge had convinced Angela and Rory that their grief-stricken dad wasn't coming out of Murray's room. Not even for the funeral. And amazingly, his bossy big sister had been okay with it. *After some convincing.* Even Aunty Bec had been okay with passing tablets through the door, so his 'distraught father' would get some sleep last night.

Murray approached the backdoor, where the minister who'd conducted Mum's funeral spoke to Angela.

"I have knocked on your brother's door to rouse your father," the minister said. "But he's no' answering. I'm concerned he may be in difficulty. Scott was staying in Murray's room, was he not?"

"Thank you, Reverend." Angela's deep red hair fell down her back as her shoulders bristled. "I'll get my Murray to open up and we'll get to the bottom of this."

Turning hastily, she nearly knocked into Murray.

"There you are!" Her wide blue eyes were inches from his face. "Come with me."

"What?"

"Come with me." Angela grabbed his sleeve and dragged him to his room where she demanded he open the door. There was no dissuading her.

"Dad! Dad? Where are you?" Angela called after Murray unlocked his door.

The room was empty. Angela whirled around to him and glared.

"Where's Dad? You and Kelly have been seeing to him, *so*, where is he?" Her voice was high pitched and strained.

"He must've gone to the funeral after all. Slipped in the back unnoticed." Murray shrugged.

She wouldn't believe the truth if he told her. And when they make him tell her, she'll kill him.

"Dad, unnoticed? You're kidding me!" she snapped.

Angela grabbed Murray's hand and dragged him back to their parent's quarters, one of the original farmhouses on the property. She scanned the living room full of mourners and well-wishers, her eyes darting in every direction at once. A dissatisfied expression crossed her face. Angela turned to Murray with a scowl. He opened his mouth. Giving him no time to comment, Angela faced the crowded room again and, seeing her brothers who were in the Militia, gave them a sharp wave. Callum and Brendan responded at once.

Rory finished his conversation with Dr Farquhar and, with a nod, made his way toward his elder sister. He was tall and muscular, with tightly cropped dark-red hair above intelligent eyes sitting in a freckled face. Murray gulped as he watched his oldest brother walk toward him, all confidence, fitness and strength—totally opposite to himself.

"Dad is not in Murray's room." Angela stared accusingly at Murray and then turned to his brothers. "So, would you please quietly search for him?"

"Where?" Callum finished the drink in his hand.

"Anywhere," Angela snapped.

The three burly young men quietly walked away. Murray followed on their heels like a puppy, glad to be away from Angela. Twenty minutes later, they returned to Angela.

"Nothing," Rory shook his head.

"Nothing?" Angela's eyes were wide. "Search further. The stables. The storerooms. Anywhere!" She flicked her hand dismissively.

Her gaze rested accusingly on Murray once more. It was one of *those* looks. Murray walked to the kitchen to ensure he was out of her sight. He wouldn't waste time pretending to look for Dad.

The room quietened, and most people in the room now stared at Angela. Murray peered around the corner. She couldn't see him, but he needed to keep an eye on her. She straightened her shoulders and moved to a group of mourners. They gave their condolences she moved on to the next group.

"Miss Campbell... Angela." A woman's voice from behind interrupted her conversation. Angela turned.

"I see your father is still not here. Is he well? Mr Campbell must be taking it very badly. I can't begin to imagine," the woman said.

"Aye." Her husband joined her. "I see you've sent your brothers off to fetch him. Do you need any help?"

Angela shook her head.

"No, really," the man insisted. "I overheard you telling your brothers to go find him. We'll be glad to help."

Others nodded and voiced agreement. Soon the wake dispersed and became a search party.

After two hours of searching for Dad, with no sightings of him, Angela called a family meeting. Uncle Brendan and Aunty Bec were there for support. Murray moved next to Kelly. He glanced at her, and she returned it.

"It seems our father is missing." Angela opened the discussion.

"Well, who saw him last?" Rory asked. They all turned to Ceilidh, Murray and Kelly.

"You said he was there when Mum died. Was he?" Rory asked Ceilidh.

"Aye, he was. He took her outside. She wanted to see the mountains..." Ceilidh melted into tears and couldn't speak further. Aunty Bec put her arm around her and gave her a gentle hug. Angela glared at Murray next.

"Well, he left when she died, and I had to carry Mum inside." He finished the story.

"So, has anyone seen him after that?" Uncle Brendan asked.

"Murray and Kelly have been taking him meals and seeing to him in Murray's room." Angela answered, glowering at him and Kelly in turn.

Everyone was looking at him and Kelly. They returned everyone's stares. Murray held his breath. *Time to face the music,* as Mum would say.

"Well?" Angela's lips pressed together, and her face was becoming the colour of her long straight hair.

"May I speak to Murray and Kelly alone? Would that be okay with you Angela?" Uncle Brendan's tone was placating.

He knew what Angela was like when over stressed. This situation fitted the description of *over stressed*.

Angela gave a reluctant nod, and Aunty Bec and Uncle Brendan ushered Murray and Kelly into their now vacant parent's bedroom.

Uncle Brendan sat them on the end of the double bed.

"Care to tell us what has happened?" Uncle Brendan and Aunty Bec stood in front of them.

"Well, Dad's gone missing," Murray answered.

I'll play dumb for a bit.

"We're aware of that. Tell us what we don't know, son." Uncle Brendan waited patiently in the quiet room. "Your Aunty Bec and I know more than you think we do."

Murray sat on the edge of Mum and Dad's bed. Kelly sat beside him, looking at the dull beige carpet, just like he was. Their conspiracy uniting them in silence.

Say as little as possible, sis.

"I have always admired your parents," Aunty Bec said. "They've brought you up to be loyal. I respect that. But if something significant has happened, you need to tell us, no matter what promises you have made."

Kelly rubbed her hands in her lap. Murray tapped his right foot rapidly, causing his whole leg to shake. And the bed. They both stayed speechless.

"Please remember we have known your mother since she was in her early twenties," Uncle Brendan tried again. "Long before she came here, and we all helped to set things up for this community."

Uncle Brendan was fishing, but Murray lacked the information to be sure of what his uncle referred to—though he could guess.

"You are asking me to break a promise which I've made to keep important secrets. Are you serious?"

It was a kind of code. If his Uncle Brendan was on the ball, it would signal to him that what had occurred had something to do with The Time Machine. His uncle would then understand whether or not to speak any further in front of the others.

Silence engulfed them, but not for long.

"You *know*?" Kelly gasped.

Shut up, Kelly!

"Know what, Kelly?" Uncle Brendan responded.

Murray glared at his sister. Kelly stopped herself from finishing whatever she was going to say.

"Don't let your brother prevent you from concluding what may be correct." Uncle Brendan held the palm of his hand up to Murray's face to stop him censoring Kelly. "Look, you two, we're on your side. We're on your parent's side."

Kelly glanced sideways at Murray. "You go first."

How much should he say? Confessing that he'd revealed The Time Machine exists was probably the lesser of three evils.

"I told her about The Time Machine." Murray waited for a reprimand.

The yelling didn't come. He opened his eyes and looked at his uncle.

"You would only have done that if you needed to. Did you need to?" His uncle's kind expression filled his view.

Murray screwed up his whole face. Agony. How would he say what he wanted to? Should he say it at all?

"Someone has discharged The Time Machine. A pod is missing, and they've used the journey to the past." Uncle Brendan came to the rescue. "Care to tell me what you know about that? You're not in trouble. I just need you to confirm my suspicions, son."

Murray opened his eyes wide. A mixture of disbelief and relief moved through him in waves.

"You say it Uncle Brendan, please."

"Okay." Uncle Brendan nodded. "Your dad went back in time."

Murray's shoulders eased. "Well, that's what Mum thought he would do."

There, he'd said it.

"Your mother knew?" Aunty Bec raised her eyebrows.

"Aye." Kelly now re-joined the conversation. "She spent most of her last days telling me how Dad had gone back in time to keep her safe."

"So, *you* guys knew?" Murray asked.

"We suspected," Brendan said. "You see, we spent a long, severe winter with your parents. We got to know them well and admire them. Your mother was quite young. A lot younger than your father, who looked about the same age as he does now. But we didn't know it was him then, the same man as now. We left them in the spring and did not see them again." He scratched his ear and screwed his mouth to the side. "Well, we didn't reconnect with your mother until about five years later. Caitlin was on her own and would not speak of what happened to your father. We thought of him as your mother's first husband. She stayed single for years and then your father, but as a young man, not far out of boyhood, arrived at the compound. He looked familiar to us."

Uncle Brendan glanced over to Aunty Bec for confirmation. She nodded.

"Your mother was enamoured with him right from the start," he continued. "As he grew older, we saw a resemblance to her first husband and assumed that was why Caitlin was attracted—he was so like him. But as the years passed, we saw the old Scott emerge, the one we'd known. Then, with the development of The Time Machine, we started wondering 'if'. I was on the verge of mentioning it to your father, but how would I say it? Then your mother became very unwell...and here we are. So, after today's events, the 'if' became a 'maybe'. You have now informed us it is actually a 'certainty'."

Chapter Twenty-Six

The Present

During the night, the wind died down and the snow it brought finally ceased to fall. Quiet settled after the snow had fallen—like a serene glow. Outside was white magnified by reflection. As the sun began to rise, the world glared through the front window, illuminating the inside of the house. The silence surrounded them. Caitlin peered out the window, her mouth slightly open at the view of glistening white extending to the horizon on every side.

Blinding.

As the back of the house had faced the weather, the snow had piled as high as the roof, jamming the backdoor shut with the heavy snow behind it. Scott and Brendan hastily dressed warmly and, after digging a small way out of the front door, made their way around to the back and started to dig out the snow from the backdoor to allow exit and entry.

The horses whinnied in the stables. Scott intensified his shovelling of the snow from the backdoor. When it was clear, he made his way through a seven-foot high snow drift to the stables, where he dug a way to the stable door. This took another half hour of concerted effort. Caitlin walked to the stables wrapped in a thick coat, sinking deep with every laboured step. Inside the stables it was warm as she helped Scott muck out the stalls and feed the horses. Scott soothed his prized black stallion with an extra-long grooming and brushed out his mane and tail affectionately.

"We only just got the animal feed from the market in time. Glad we did nae wait any later to get it!" Scott said.

They returned to the cottage where Bec had cooked a hearty breakfast of spam and powdered egg, as it was too cold for the chickens to lay. To make life easier for access to the horses, Brendan and Scott dug a wide path to the stables. Caitlin helped Bec stoke the fires, as both the Aga and the open fire in the other end of the cottage were burning, and brought in more wood, while the men cleaned up. Unable to attend to outside chores, they settled in to a day of baking and discussions inside and watching the progress of the new kid, which had been born overnight. On checking the animals in the laundry and commenting on how warm it was for them in there, Scott looked longingly at the stables.

"Oh, no you don't Scott C—Murray! Don't even think of it," Caitlin warned.

"What?" Scott asked as though he didn't know what she was talking about.

"You are not bringing the black horse into the laundry!"

***

It continued to snow on and off for the next week. Scott and Brendan finished installing the batteries that would store the wind-generated electricity in the well-ventilated shelter they had built to house them. They connected the power leads to the batteries and insulated and secured them to the electricity connection of the cottage. After digging the fallen snow from around it, Scott turned on the windmill with great ceremony. The blades slowly turned, and Caitlin joined in with the cheering. The lights inside flickered as they checked the other appliances to ensure all were working. Then they turned everything off to give the batteries a chance to charge. In the evening, under electric light, they enjoyed a celebratory dinner of tinned Haggis, onions, and potatoes.

They attended to the usual chores of feeding the animals and keeping the inside store of firewood stocked daily. After one such trek from the woodshed to the house, Brendan doubled over in pain. Caitlin and Bec stood beside him, Bec's concerned expression mirroring her own.

"I think it was because of how I was holdin' the firewood I brought in." Brendan dismissed them with a wave of his hand.

Later, he lay down on the floor near the open fireplace with his legs up on a chair. Bec walked over to him and blinked a few times on seeing Brendan's posture.

"What are you doing down there, love?" she asked.

"I am comfortable like this," he answered.

"On the floor?"

"Yes," he said with a slight grimace.

The afternoon drew on and Brendan sat in a more curled position on the couch. As Caitlin and Bec served dinner, Brendan walked to the table in a bent over posture. Caitlin stood with Bec, one on either side of Brendan, and put her arm under one of his; Bec did as well. They started to raise him up, but Brendan cried in pain. Caitlin faced Bec over Brendan's bent form, knowing they would think the same.

"Brendan, love," Bec said. "I need to lie you down and examine you."

"I'm all right." Brendan shook his head. His stomach muscles contracted, and he made a gagging sound as the contents of his stomach emptied onto the floor.

"You're fine? Really?"

They ushered him into their bedroom where Bec took a close look at him. Scott cleaned up the vomit.

"Wear disposable gloves, Scott. In case it's infectious," Caitlin called from the bedroom.

After cleaning up, Scott stood at the end of Brendan's bed. Caitlin flicked anxious eyes to him. Bec had the fingers of her hand digging deep into the lower righthand side of Brendan's abdomen. With his face relaxed, she released her hand from his abdomen. A howl of pain erupted from Brendan. Bec and Caitlin chorused a guilty 'sorry'. They left him to rest and went to the far end of the cottage.

"He's febrile." Caitlin held the thermometer in her hand.

"Yes." Bec drew her brows together and pursed her lips. Turning to Scott, she started giving orders. "I'll need you to help too, Scott."

"I've missed something here. Please enlighten me." Concern tinged Scott's husky voice.

"Scott, Brendan has acute appendicitis, and it needs to be removed," Bec answered.

"Will it no' go away?"

"No." Caitlin chorused with Bec, again.

"He could develop peritonitis and become septic and die if we don't remove it." Bec said. "We have no choice. You can help Caitlin and myself wherever you can. Caitlin will be tied up with the anaesthetics, so you must scrub in."

"Pardon? I've never done it for real before!" Caitlin tried to stave the panic rising with her pulse rate, but her lack of success revealed itself in the corresponding rise in pitch of her voice. "I'll be breathing for him! What if I do it wrong? I'm not intubating him!"

"Caitlin," Bec's voice was low and quiet, "you are a natural. You must do it. We are taking a risk in these primitive conditions, but we have *no other* choice. If he walked into my practice in his present state, I would have sent him to the nearest Accident and Emergency department ASAP, where he would have gone straight to Theatre." Bec tilted her head and put her hand on Caitlin's shoulder. "I'll do the induction and intubate Brendan, you only need to monitor him, Caitlin."

"One of ye will have to speak English for this mere mortal here!" Scott interjected.

"Scott, you need to scrub in and hand me whatever I ask for," Bec explained. She still had her hand on Caitlin. "Caitlin need not look so worried, as she will monitor Brendan after I have put him under."

"Oh, now I ken what you're on about! Although, can I no' have anything to do with the cuttin' and looking in bit? Not that I'm squeamish." He glanced aside to Caitlin. "For you ken well I've no problem with the sight of blood. It's just that, it seems like it's the, well, most important bit and I'm not medically trained."

"Because she's a nurse, Caitlin will be better at monitoring Brendan's vitals," Bec replied. "She will have more of an idea if things go awry. She'll notice trends and alert me before things go downhill, if that's what they'll do. We must be prepared for the 'worst-case scenario'."

The scrubbing brush in Scott's hand made a zigzag grating sound as he moved it back and forth across the kitchen table, now cleared of dinner. The kitchen smelled strongly of disinfectant. Catlin's arms were full of sterile packs and sterile surgical instruments. She placed them on the scrubbed kitchen bench and walked back into the pantry. Moments later, she returned wheeling the Boyle's machine to which she had connected the oxygen and anaesthetic gas cylinders. Biting her lip, she silently returned Scott's stare and exited the room. She came back with the diathermy equipment and sterile drapes.

"Caitlin, when you set up the IV, get the emergency drugs ready. 'If you're prepared, you never need them' I always say." Bec's manner was official but cheery, a contrast to the increasing tension building up inside Caitlin and dispersing into the room where she stood in front of the draped kitchen table. She started tipping the sterile instruments out of their packaging and onto the kitchen bench now covered in sterile drapes.

Bec talked Scott and Caitlin through the whole procedure, including the anaesthetic induction—several times.

"Any questions?" Bec asked.

Caitlin turned to Scott. He focussed Bec with intense concentration, swallowed and glanced at Caitlin. She returned a thin smile.

"Let's just do this," Caitlin said to Bec. "I'll leave informing the patient to you, though Bec."

Bec stood over Brendan; Caitlin peered over her shoulder. He lay curled up on their bed, his face pale and his skin clammy.

"I know what you want to do." Brendan glanced up at his wife. "What you have to do. I've heard you describe appendicitis in the past." "Just get on with it, please."

Scott supported Brendan to the table and laid him over the drapes. Caitlin put an IV into his arm. Brendan watched her push the needle through his skin and into the vein. He never blinked. Scott cleaned Brendan's abdomen with an iodine solution. Brendan flinched at the cool fluid on his belly. As Bec scrubbed her hands with the same solution, the earthy smell of iodine filled the kitchen, now a surgical theatre. Caitlin attached the blood pressure cuff, oxygen saturation finger-tip probe and ECG electrodes belonging to the monitor on the Boyle's machine to Brendan and started recording his vital signs. She then directed Scott on how to cover Brendan with the sterile drapes.

Bec administered the anaesthetics. Caitlin watched wide eyed throughout the whole induction. Bec also gave Brendan an anti-nausea and pain killer through the IV.

"Now those settings should be okay to stay the same"—Bec pointed to the dials on the Boyle's Machine— "Just monitor his vitals and tell me them regularly. You'll be fine, Caitlin."

Caitlin examined the dials, memorising the position of the indicators along them. She mentally counted to ten to settle her whirring thoughts and increase her focus.

Bec performed the incisions, through skin, muscle, fascia and mesentery, while Scott used retractors to hold the layers out of the way. The ventilator attached to the Boyle's Machine hissed and clicked in the background as it breathed for Brendan, a constant reminder to Caitlin of her responsibility to her unconscious patient. Bec adeptly located the inflamed appendix and double clamped at its base on the end of the caecum. She gently lifted it and packed gauze around and under it. Bec used the diathermy to cut and cauterised the green suppurative organ away from the caecum. She then placed it in the kidney dish, which she had instructed Scott to rest beside the incision. The appendix burst, and its yellow-green contents filled the kidney dish.

"Ooh, that's nasty." Caitlin's nose crinkled.

"Yes, that was close," Bec said. "If it had burst inside Brendan's abdomen, peritonitis leading to sepsis would have been almost inevitable."

How could Bec speak so calmly about her husband? *She's in doctor-mode*, Caitlin thought.

The acrid scent of burnt flesh permeated the room and made Caitlin's nose crinkle even more. Bec rinsed Brendan's peritoneal cavity with sterile normal saline solution. Under her direction, Scott suctioned out the debris and fluids. Scott and Bec counted all the forceps and used pieces of gauze to ensure they left none in Brendan's abdomen. Bec sutured and closed the layers she had opened.

"Now we wake him up," Bec announced after administering IV antibiotics to stave off infection.

When Brendan was fully awake, Scott assisted him into the bedroom and helped him into bed for his recovery.

Scott and Caitlin removed from the kitchen the last of the disposable waste they were to burn. Caitlin planned to wash the drapes and other cloth and steel instruments she could reuse. She would have to devise an autoclave of some sort for sterilising the equipment.

Scott and Caitlin leaned with their backs against the kitchen bench, now clear of surgical paraphernalia. She turned to Scott, who had begun a soft chuckle. Her mouth tightened in a smile, slowly at first, but more so as Scott's chuckle became a laugh.

"I cannae believe I just assisted in surgery. That was surreal. I feel like I can let 'oot a lung full o' air I've been holding in for a very long time." Scott shook his head.

"Huh! I've been an anaesthetic nurse!" Caitlin said. "Never thought I'd do that! Needs must I suppose."

"Needs very much must, Caitlin." A smile lingered on Scott's lips.

Chapter Twenty-Seven

The Future

After their private conversation with Murray and Kelly, Aunt Bec and Uncle Brendan brought them back into the main room of their parent's living quarters. All Murray's brothers and sisters were present; their faces reflected their day of grieving and farewells to Mum. The remains of the wake cluttered the living area. The smell of hot food gone cold and rubbish bins needing emptying, rose amongst the bare platters and plates scattered throughout the room.

"So?" Angela resumed her interrogation.

"Now listen, Angela, let Murray and Kelly say what they have to. Please?" Uncle Brendan made his request before Angela could go any further.

"You want *us* to tell them?" Murray asked.

"Yes," Aunt Bec replied. "It needs to come from you."

All eyes were on him and Kelly. Kelly looked to him to begin. With a resigned slump of his shoulders, he started.

"Dad's not here anymore."

"Where did he go?" The forced patience was clear in Angela's tone.

"Did he go back to Achnasheen to keep looking for those bandits?" Rory asked.

"I'll have to break a promise I've made to the Chief Council to explain everything to them." Murray directed his statement to Uncle Brendan.

"So be it. But everyone in this room mustn't say a word of the secret you're about to hear." Uncle Brendan stressed to all.

"Well," Murray hesitated, not sure where to begin. "Dad's gone back in time to be with Mum."

Dead silence.

"Oh, for heaven's sake." Angela's hand was on her hip as she swung her deep red hair over her shoulder.

"No, hear him 'oot," Rory encouraged. The two red heads locked eyes.

"We have a time machine here." Murray took a deep breath and ignored Angela's comments about the ridiculousness of his account and continued. "Dad's been part of developing it over the years. Mum and Dad knew about it and I was part of the team that developed it."

"So," Angela took great pains to emphasise every word, "there is a time machine and *you*, our sixteen-year-old *wee* brother, have been part of making it?"

"Let him speak, Angela!" Ceilidh shushed her older sister.

"Dad wanted to be with Mum. He went there straight from Mum..." Murray trailed off.

"So!" Angela recommenced her tirade, and nothing was stopping her, not even Uncle Brendan. "This is the stuff of fiction! We have a time machine *here?* This wee, under resourced and isolated Community in the middle of the bloody-nowhere-Highlands, have made a *machine* that transported our father back *in time* to be with our mother. Is that it?" Angela faced Uncle Brendan. "You expect me to believe *this*? Seriously Uncle Brendan!"

"Angela, The Time Machine is real. We can show it to you if you don't believe us. The only people who know about it are the Chief Council members and those, like Murray, who are part of the project team." Uncle Brendan now faced-off Angela.

"Why do I know nothing of it then?" she asked.

"Because you are not on the Chief Council."

Angela stiffened. It was true they would most likely ask her to be on the Chief Council now Mum had passed away. Mum and Dad had groomed her for it, in fact everyone had. Angela closed her mouth tightly and stayed silent for a time.

"Och no!" Rory's eyes were wide. "No! That's what he was on about! Shite, I'm as thick as two bricks!"

"What on earth's the matter, Rory?" Callum's brow crinkled in the middle.

Rory stood straighter and rubbed the back of his neck. Everyone stared at him.

Oops, somethings wrong. Rory never shows any distress.

"When we were spyin' oot those bandits, Dad asked me would I do anything to be with someone I loved again. Oh, no. *That's* what he meant." Rory shook his head. "If there truly is a time machine, he's used it. I'm sure o' it, if I know my father."

"He did," Murray began.

"One question." Angela raised her index finger. "Why you, Murray?"

"Because he's a genius," Kelly piped up.

"Where did Dad go then? Or should I be askin' 'when did he go to'?" Rory returned them to the real issue.

"The team set The Time Machine for one month before TSMC, but we were waiting to do human trials before we did anything as serious as send someone back to that time," Murray answered.

"That's The Stock Market Crash," Kelly deciphered for them.

"We know," Angela retorted. Murray suspected she was still smarting from not being privy to the knowledge of The Time Machine.

Ceilidh gasped and put her hand to her mouth. "They hadn't trialled it yet! What if he died trying to be with Mum again?"

"He didn't," Kelly revealed. "Mum spent most of her last days telling me how Dad came for her and took her away to somewhere safe, while all the dreadful things happened."

"Mum was delirious and on morphine. It's all hallucinations!" Angela shook her head again.

"It's true, Angela," Aunty Bec told them. "Your uncle and I met your parents years ago in Fort William. We think it was soon after they'd met. Your mother told me they'd been married for four months, so I expect it was how long they had been in hiding. Your father looked like he looks now. He was the experienced man he is now. On the other hand, we were pampered Westerners with every gadget and piece of technology to make life easy. We had grown soft and fat. We wouldn't have lasted a very harsh winter if not for your father's wisdom and experience in survival."

"Well, I am finding this *so* unbelievable!" Angela voiced. "Where is this time machine? Can I see it?"

"We must ask the Chief Council for permission," Uncle Brendan said. "I'll bring it up with them tomorrow. It's been a long and eventful day and we all need some rest."

"Do we have to let the Council know?" Murray asked.

"Of course, we do, Murray," Angela snapped, abruptly stopping the conversation.

"Maybe a good night sleep might help frayed nerves, and also help our sub-consciences to mull over the information we've just heard," Rory suggested, then they all dispersed.

***

They stood outside the tall wooden door of the old barn. Two of the Chief Council accompanied them. Dr Farquhar, an elderly, tough man who had survived all the hardships of the previous years and emerged as a leader of their Community, put the key in the lock of the paint-worn door and turned it. He had a grave expression on his face as he turned and ushered Murray and his siblings into the room which housed The Time Machine. Bec and Brendan followed.

The room which held The Time Machine was cold and barn-like and smelled of damp earth. It was familiar to Murray. The others looked around with interest. An army-green control panel comprising various knobs and dials set in a metal-desk was to one side. Wires extended from this desk to The Time Machine's transporter chamber and threatened to trip anyone who walked over them. One scientist involved in the machine's development was present when the group arrived. Angus, a dark-haired man in his thirties, was the one who had discovered the discharging of The Time Machine, the missing pod and the used journey.

"It will take us weeks or months to reset the machine and generate enough electricity to use it again." Angus pushed his glasses up the bridge of his nose. "This is tantamount to theft!"

The two Council members were silent, not revealing the identity of the time traveller.

Murray stood with his siblings. All except himself and Kelly stood open-mouthed at the evidence before them.

"Believe me now?" Murray asked as he wandered past his eldest sister.

Angela returned his stare but did not answer. It was another one of *those* looks. Murray wasn't the only smart one amongst them. Angela's mind would be miles ahead of the current evidence collecting exercise.

***

"I have been thinking over the information so far—all night, actually." Angela had called a meeting of her siblings in their parent's living room. "This morning's evidence confirmed to me what my next course of action must be." She had their attention. Anxious expressions met her stare. "I have to tell the Chief Council the whole story. They must know. And then I must, as a member of the Council, decide what to do about it."

"But you are no' a member of the Chief Council yet, sister," Rory commented.

"Oh, but *I am*. Mr George told me this morning that I will officially take my place at the next meeting." She stood straighter, shuffling her shoulders.

"Congratulations?" Murray said.

"Aye, congratulations sişter," Rory was more convincing.

"What does that mean, Angela?" Kelly sat straighter. "You telling them about Dad going back in time, I mean? Won't they be pleased? Their time machine works, after all?"

"Aye, Kelly," Rory turned to her. Rory was always kind to Kelly. She was his favourite wee sister. "Our faither has stolen something."

"But he's not here, so it doesn't matter, right?" she asked.

"If only it were so simple," Rory pursed his lips.

"Aye," Angela began, "and simple it is *not*. Our father has committed a crime and as the perpetrator, the Chief Council will call him to account."

"You're joking, right?" Murray couldn't believe it. But it *was* Angela, maybe he could.

"He took something that was not his. He used the Community's resources without permission. He has caused the Community to lose a great resource in removing himself from us for selfish gain—"

"Hold on, Angela!" Rory's hands were palm out toward his elder sister. "It's our *father* you're speaking of, no' some common criminal. He's a grieving man. He was no' in his right mind when he did it. You cannot be seriously considering charging him? How can you anyway, he's no' here?"

"I would not be an impartial leader if I let him get away with committing a crime." Angela flicked her head. "He won't avoid justice because he is our father. What kind of law and order would we have if we allowed that sort of thing? We may as well join those bandits you were after."

Yep. She isn't joking.

Chapter Twenty-Eight

The Present

"Hope I never have to operate on my man," Caitlin said to Bec a few days later.

"Brendan is recovering well, but *I'm* still recovering." Bec laughed.

With a break in the weather, Scott exercised his horse and let the horses out of the stables. He led them around as he rode the black horse, as the corral fence was still under snow. They kept the exercise area to the wide path they had shovelled in the snow between the house and the stables. Scruffy ran wildly in this space, enjoying the fresh air after the confines of the cottage. The dog did his 'business' in the snowdrifts at the sides of the cleared area and disappeared. Scott had to retrieve him on more than one occasion.

"You realise you'll have to name this horse?" Caitlin watched Scott riding. "How are you so good with horses?"

Scott looked up to make sure their friends were inside and out of earshot.

"In the future, we only have horses, ye ken? Due to the fuel shortage, there are very few vehicles. There're a few horses in our herd sired by a dark horse. They have magnificent natures and are very reminiscent of the particular animal which I'm currently riding." He raised his eyebrows and gave a knowing look.

Caitlin's mouth tugged in a broad smile. So, this horse had left its mark. And her husband had found an equine friend.

"I think you should call him Adam," she suggested, "as he was the first father. Just an idea."

"Hmm, aye." He nodded. "I like it. Adam, it is."

The evenings had become a time for reflection and discussion. The many terrorist attacks that had taken place around the world were still a shock to her and the others. Scott would quietly listen to her and their friends' responses. In the privacy of their own room he had told Caitlin he knew of these attacks as history, for he was an infant when they occurred. Scott recalled history reported that the world's population, at a point not too far away from the present time, was to diminish by approximately one half. This was due to the violence, an increase in warfare and terrorist attacks, poverty and disease, and starvation caused by the food shortages. It was his hope, he had told her, that tucked away in their haven, frugally managing their supplies and planning for their own food production, they and any companions, would escape the worst of it.

***

They sat on the green sofa and chairs. The fire glowed comfortably radiating the distinct scent of burning peat into the room.

"Law Enforcement and protection. Security. An army? Not too official and aggressive sounding. A militia?" Caitlin had sent her comment Scott's way. He raised an eyebrow, the lambent light from the fire caused his face to shine. "That's like the minimum a community requires, next to strong leadership."

"So, you think the model of one ruler is the best form of government?" Brendan asked.

"No." Caitlin shook her head decisively. "One ruler? Never. Too much power. History has proven it over and over."

"Democracy then?" Bec probed.

"Seems to have worked the best so far." Caitlin lifted one shoulder. "Couldn't imagine anyone around here going for socialism. And when I say Democracy, I don't mean to combine it with Capitalism, necessarily. I think a bit of community sharing and support, instead of competition, wouldn't go astray."

"So, group leadership, responsible for and to the people they govern," Brendan suggested. "An oligarchy then?"

"I suppose so, if I knew what it meant. Didn't study politics at school," Caitlin admitted. "These are only ideas. Nothing written in tablets of stone, yet."

"Form of leadership covered?" Scott moved the conversation forward. "Facilities?"

"Healthcare." Caitlin and Bec said it in unison.

"Power and fuels," Brendan suggested. "Can't do much without power. Windmills are the way to go, aren't they Scott?" The two men did a 'high-five'. "We must try to tap into Scotland's wind farms somehow."

"Aye. Very good idea." Scott had a knowing expression on his face. "Have to say though, it does nae seem like they will mass produce nor distribute fossil fuels for much longer. The Arab States hold their resources close, I think. Horses. That will be the mode of transportation." Scott waited for a response and received thoughtful nods. "I will breed from the stallion." He smiled. "That's assuming the owners dinnae turn up. They'd need to have papers to prove the animal is theirs, aye. Then pay me for keeping him for months."

"You'll breed him with your Highland Mountain mare?" There was amusement in Brendan's voice.

"Aye," Scott said. "Will make a strong and handsome horse."

"What's happened with the nuclear power plants. They can't just close, can they? Those nuclear rods release energy for a lifetime. Who's monitoring them?" A cold sensation centred in Caitlin's gut. What had happened to those potentially dangerous power sources?

"The government *probably* commandeered them and maybe use them for their power now they have gone underground." Scott looked directly at Caitlin.

"Probably?" Caitlin asked.

"Aye, probably," Scott continued his look.

Definitely then.

"The government went underground? What, like in bunkers?" Caitlin asked.

"Yes," Brendan said. "The government has been quiet for a while." They were silent for a few moments.

"Moving on—education." Caitlin remembered what Scott had told her of her own insistence on education for everyone in the future, especially those who had missed out due to the disruptions to normality. "Judaeo-Christian morals. They've held society in the West together for centuries, may as well stick to that. And we must secure any art, literature, music, historical artefacts." She counted these off on her fingers as she spoke, "and any precious thing saved from pillaging. We must ensure its preservation. Sorry. I'm on my 'high horse' again. I'd hate to lose any of it. I think of the Library in Alexandria, which in 48 BC, the Romans set alight and burned all the scrolls that were ancient manuscripts *then*. And all the art the Nazis stole from the Jews in Europe, they never recovered much of it. I don't want that kind of thing happening again!"

"That will require locked, safe storage. Where do you propose to have it?" Bec asked.

"Not in only one place, so it's easy to wipe out if anyone wished," Caitlin suggested. "It should be dotted around the world."

"There is probably something like this anyway," Scott said. "Surely someone's thought o' this? They've got an underground seed bank. There's one in Norway, is there no'?"

"What happened to that?" Brendan asked. "We'll need access to it for getting food production going."

"We need to write all of this down. We may forget some of our bright ideas when we get a chance to use them." Bec dug into a box of supplies in the corner of the living area and brought out a notepad and pen. "So, it seems this snow is here for a while. Our stay until we installed the wind-powered electricity supply may continue a wee bit longer. Is that okay with you two?" Being the practical person, Bec broached the 'elephant in the room'.

"Well, we could turn you out in the snow," Caitlin teased, "but we won't."

"Ye are welcome to stay for as long as you need to. It may be the whole winter, mind. I think I was correct in my predictions of a bad winter, aye?" Scott agreed.

***

It was warm and cosy in their bed together as Caitlin looked through the now curtained window. The world outside remained white and frigid, but no further snow had fallen so far that week. They were safe in their isolated haven, especially after their discussions of the evening on the contrasting state of the world. Snuggling into Scott, she smelled horses and pine. His muscles generated heat, and she moved closer to him; the bed clothes enveloped them both.

"*Tha gradh agam ort,*" she ventured.

Scott turned his head sharply and her head slipped off his shoulder.

"What? Would you care to repeat that?" He raised his eyebrows.

"*Ha gragh agum orshh,*" she said less confidently.

Scott's face lit up with recognition. "*Ha gragh ackum orsht, leannain.* I love you too," he responded in fluent Gaelic.

Scott chuckled.

"You don't know how long it's taken me to remember it!" Caitlin hit him in the ribs. "You're so unappreciative!"

"Oh, Caitlin, it was so bad." He flinched from her slap and shook his head. "But I'm touched that ye tried."

Caitlin opened her mouth to further complain about his lack of appreciation, but he cut her off with tender kisses. They had not made love for a while because of the proximity of their neighbours. It intensified her want for him. He would feel the same.

Scott ran his hands along the length of her back and down her legs. The exercise and self-defence training had honed her muscles and removed excess fat. Caitlin was lean and hard.

"I've missed you," she said between kisses.

"I want you. My body needs you," he whispered. "My heart and my soul need you."

Scott's kisses became more intense as he lay on top of her. He put his hand in the small of her back, in the gap now formed as her body rose to meet his in response to his touch. He parted her legs with his own and started making love to her slowly. Scott held his weight off her with his other hand as he gazed into her eyes.

"I love you," he breathed into her ear.

Shivers coursed through her as she ran both hands along the length of his back; it was all smooth skin over strong firm muscle. The fingers of her right hand ran through his soft curly hair and held it. Caitlin tugged his head back to face her. Scott kissed her again and pressed onto her lower lip with his teeth, gently. She let out a quiet gasp. He released her lip and grinned at the sound she had made. He covered her mouth with his. Scott's lips and breath were warm on her face. Their bodies joined as closely as their breath. Their oneness complete once more.

Scott rested his upper torso on his elbows and kissed her mouth, his lips soft and heated, and all-encompassing. His lips then traced a journey across her cheek until they reached her neck, then he lay to the side still holding her close.

"What part of that do you like best?" he whispered.

Caitlin turned to face him. "The part where The Universe explodes, and I see into your soul. And all I see, and feel, is you."

Chapter Twenty-Nine

The Future

A few weeks had passed since Murray's Mum's death and Dad's fake disappearance. Angela, on behalf of the family, announced that Dad had gone to visit another Community nearby to the south, believing a break from normal routine would help dispel his grief.

Angela and Rory held a quiet discussion in the hallway outside their parent's quarters. Murray watched from his bedroom doorway. It was intense. The two redheads bent close in conversation. Angela left abruptly after making a point, as only Angela could. Rory stood back, rolled his eyes, then turned to Murray.

"That looked serious," Murray called as Rory made his way toward him. Rory's eyes slitted. What had Angela done now?

"We *have* to have a family meeting." Rory's mouth became a thin line.

"When?" Murray asked.

"Now! Get your brothers and sisters together."

Within half an hour, Murray had assembled his siblings in the living room of their parent's quarters. They sat on the couch with the dining chairs turned around to form a circle. Ceilidh was red-nosed and sombre. His brothers were quiet. Rory sat with his arms crossed over his chest. Angela stood in front of them, wearing a navy-blue skirt suit she had found from somewhere, her neat attire matching her neat hair style. Rory let out a breath.

"The Chief Council, after much debate, have decided they will apprehend our father and bring him to justice." Angela opened the meeting. "All Council members agree that justice must be upheld. The Chief Council will make every effort to maintain standards and a sense of 'rightness' in our Community's society. Any breach of this would be the slippery slope into the chaos which now reigns in the world outside. Offenders will be punished, despite any position they hold."

Gasps and sharp intakes of breath made their way around the encircled chairs in a domino effect. Only Rory stayed silent.

"You knew about this, Rory?" Kelly asked.

Rory nodded, nostrils flaring.

"How do they propose to achieve this?" Callum enquired.

"Why do they *want* to achieve this?" Ceilidh asked.

Angela stood straighter; she had easily slipped into the role of Chief Council member.

"Justice must be done equally. No favourites. As to how," she looked at Callum. "We now know The Time Machine works. So, the Chief Council are proposing someone goes back to find and return our father."

Callum's face screwed up in disbelief. Rory, his twin, with almost identical features, raised his eyebrows in question.

"Well, that won't happen in a hurry!" Murray seemed to be the only one who could respond. "They've got to reset and recharge The Time Machine. It may take months. And then how will they bring Dad back—and whoever is to retrieve him—to serve Dad with justice? We haven't figured out how to do return journeys yet!"

"I agree with Murray," Rory said. "They can spout as much as they like about Dad being brought to justice, but they're impotent to achieve it at present, if ever."

The domino effect repeated around the circle of chairs, this time tense postures relaxed. But Murray didn't relax. It was impossible. They would cross these hurdles eventually. Being part of the team, he had access to this knowledge. And once they were over them, they could retrieve their dad from *any* point in time and return him for trial and punishment. Even if it wasn't in their lifetimes. Until they achieved his retrieval, a warrant for his arrest would stay on the files.

"When are they going to let the Community know what Dad has done?" Brendan asked. "They have nae said anything, just spun a lie."

"Aye," Rory's face reddened. "Not that I want Dad's reputation besmirched, but is that no' double standards? They want him punished for his crime but they'll no' tell anyone what he's done. They're lying."

"How can they tell anyone? Then they're required to admit to The Time Machine," Murray voiced the reason for their subterfuge.

Angela had stood quietly over Murray and the others.

"The Chief Council has been struggling with what to announce to the Community," Angela said. "If we define our father's crime, we would have to explain all. We will need more security around the machine, so no one misuses it again. People wouldn't understand what it involves or the machine's limitations. The Chief Council are yet to vote on it." Angela turned to Rory. "We need you to help us improve the security I just mentioned. Would you and George put your heads together with your best in the Militia please?"

Rory nodded. George Stobbart was the second in command of the Militia. In Dad's absence, he was Acting In-Charge. Mr Stobbart had been an ex-Royal Marine before The Stock Market Crash and had found his way to the Community. He was an older man with experience in leadership. His expertise had been invaluable. Mr Stobbart had trained Dad and the other young men and formed the security force for the Community. Rory admired him and had trained under him as well. Having talents that lay in other areas, Murray was thankful Mr Stobbart had never bothered him to join the Militia.

"Why'd he not say good-bye to us?" Ceilidh uttered. "We lost him as well as Mum."

Murray's two younger sisters, Ceilidh and Kelly, had silent tears running down their cheeks.

"They'll bring him back eventually," Ceilidh's expression brightened.

"That'll be years away." Murray tried to console his sisters.

"Aye, to put him in prison," Rory expounded.

Rory! Can you not be a bit gentler? It certainly isn't your strong point.

Ceilidh's shoulders slumped, and she began to sob.

"Any ways, the poor man did it in grief. No' in his right mind, like," Rory added a qualifier. "Surely he can plead insanity?"

"Dad's not insane!" Ceilidh cried.

"I don't mean he's mad, sis. It's a legal term. It'll give him a lighter sentence. May even get him off. Maybe." Rory looked at Angela and added, "Depends on if they want to make an example of him or believe they can't be seen to have favourites by being lenient." He continued looking at Angela. When she didn't reply, Rory shrugged.

Murray locked eyes with Kelly who cried silently, but with a thoughtful expression on her face. *What's she thinking?*

***

Murray sat at his desk. His paperwork was neatly piled to the left, textbooks to the right. The space in the middle, usually covered with an open notebook or papers filled with calculations and a slide-rule, was now bare and supporting his elbow. On the wall was a tatty poster of Einstein's head repeated in the style of Andy Warhol. The clock ticked rhythmically, mimicking his brain at work. Kelly sat on the end of his bed, elbows resting on her knees and an expression of anticipation on her face.

"So, you stall for as long as you can." Kelly sounded hopeful.

"I can only stall so much," Murray said. "They'll get suspicious if suddenly my calculations take twice as long. I'm a genius, remember!"

"Well, when they sound like they're getting somewhere with bringing someone back to the future from the past, try and misdirect them."

"But I don't know enough to do that!" he said.

"But you're a genius." There was snark in Kelly's tone.

"Ha, ha." Funny, *not*. "Only at calcs., not in theory."

The clock continued its ticking.

"Rory and George are good, aren't they?" Kelly asked.

"At their jobs, you mean?"

"Once they tighten security," Kelly said, "it'll be hard to get to the machine, won't it?"

"Why? What are you thinking?"

Kelly paused and shuffled on the edge of his bed, causing the springs to squeak, then she looked determinedly at him. Something was coming, and it would be momentous.

"One of us needs to go back and warn Dad," she put up a hand to stop his protests. "If we wait too long, we won't be able to!"

"One of *us* go back," he repeated. "Are you serious?"

"Yes!" she nodded. "Dead serious."

And she was. A sick sensation began in Murray's guts.

"You know how to work the machine. Don't you?" Kelly had been planning.

The question surprised and relieved Murray at the same time. "Yes. Although they've never let me near it."

"But when it's rebooted and charged and ready to go, you'll know what buttons to press or switches to flick. Or however it goes, yes?"

"Yes," Murray nodded.

"So, *I'll* go.," Kelly said. "You do the machine."

Murray shook his head. He wasn't sure if it was in disbelief at his sister's proposal, or in an authoritative way. "No," is what came out before he thought it through.

"Why not? I can do it." She thumped her hands on her thighs.

"Kelly! As it is, you won't get back!"

"Don't want to get back. I want to be with Mum and Dad!" Emotion strained Kelly's voice.

"So, that's what this is all about?"

"No! I want to warn Dad, so he can avoid whoever they send."

"It's too dangerous, Kelly. You won't be in a safe compound. The pod goes back in time to the very same place which they think is an abandoned farm, but it may not be yet, and the world is not safe out there!"

"You, big brother, will be in more danger than me." Kelly walked over to him where he sat and placed her hands on his shoulders. "If they catch you. I figured you could make it like the machine has accidently discharged or something."

Kelly stood over him. She meant it. She could do it, too—trained in self-defence, as they all were. Dad and Mr Stobbart had insisted all members of the Community could fight and defend themselves. Kelly looked girlish and weak but was a vicious fighter when her blood was up. It had made their dad proud. Murray had to admit, out of the two of them, she not only had more courage, but more ability. Kelly would survive in the past's chaos. He could 'do' the machine as she had suggested. Even make it look like an accidental discharge, as she had also suggested.

Kelly *did* have a good plan.

Murray was even willing to wear the consequences if they caught him. He was sure his other siblings felt as he and Kelly did about their dad being punished for stealing a time-journey. Except for Angela. Well, he was now contemplating the same. The idea of his dad getting into trouble was unbearable. Then another, more important issue came to mind.

"They *can't* send anyone back to get Dad," Murray said. "It would change the past. He *has* to meet Mum back then, protect her and make sure she makes it here. They can't stop him, or it will change all our futures. I mean presents."

"You must try and talk them out of it. Surely they have discussed all this?" Kelly took her hands off his shoulders and waved them around the room, pointing at nothing.

"I don't know. I'll speak with Angela. She'll have to *listen*," he added in response to the doubtful expression on his little sister's face. Secretly he held the same doubts. It *was* Angela after all.

***

Murray knocked on Angela's door. He and Kelly had decided to speak with her at once. The door opened. Paperwork covered the table in Angela's room—Chief Council business. Angela wore a smug expression, relishing her new role.

"Yes?" Angela's hand remained on the doorknob.

"We'd like to talk with you, Angela." Murray said.

"Well, Murray, as you can see, I have a lot on my plate at the moment. Still reading up on recent discussion topics. Things I missed out on before I was on the Council."

"It's important, Angela," Kelly said.

"Oh, come in then. Don't take long." Angela's voice dripped with impatience.

"Um... In all your discussions with the Chief Council about Dad..." Murray started, but Angela's narrowed eyes and downward tilted head made him pause. He braved her scorn and continued. "Well, have they considered the implications of bringing Dad back?"

"Meaning?" Angela straightened up, a wisp of deep-red fell across her face.

"Meaning, you can't because you'll change things."

"Change what?" The impatience stayed in Angela's voice. She pushed the strand of hair back behind her ear.

"Change everything!" Murray said. "If Dad doesn't protect Mum, then she'll not survive and get here. None of this will happen! *We* won't happen!"

"You can't prove that," Angela snapped.

"You can't risk it," he pleaded. "Did the Council even discuss this?"

"We did. But you see, you are forgetting something. If Dad did all that, why was he not here, in the Community, right from the start?" A smug smile erupted on Angela's face. "Why did he get here as a young adult a few years later?"

Murray had no answers. They were good questions. He'd asked them himself. Not consciously, but they'd been there in the back of his mind. Angela continued expounding the Council's hypothesis.

"We believe he was not here from the start because we had retrieved him from the past. You see, he *will be* called to account. We *will* bring him back just as soon as we are able."

Murray's mouth gaped, and he didn't reply. His legs wouldn't move straight away but when they did, he turned and walked his just as stunned younger sister out of Angela's room. The door closed behind them with a bang.

"Well, that makes me more determined than ever," Kelly said through gritted teeth. Their astonishment dissipated as they stomped their way back to his room.

"I'll figure out a way and let you know when. You'd end up here, at the Community Compound, thirty-eight years ago. We don't know where Mum and Dad are. How would you find them?"

"We don't know. But Aunty Bec and Uncle Brendan do."

Chapter Thirty

The Present

"Ye ken, apart from being dirty and some parts rusty, it is nae in bad condition, to say I got it from a junk stall, aye?"

The dismantled Citizen Band radio lay on the kitchen table. Scott and Brendan wished to see what condition it was in and if any parts were salvageable. Wires, cathodes and transistors lay in artistic disarray—metallic surfaces against raw wood, like a modern-art sculpture, industrial style.

"Well, it's definitely fixable," Brendan concluded.

A few hours, and some exasperated moments later, Scott and Brendan tuned into the wavelengths hoping to hear more than static. But there was nothing.

"There must be someone else with a gadget such as this," Scott declared.

Scott had told Caitlin there would be, and he wanted to be ready when people started communicating in this manner. Every day from then on, at Scott's insistence, they scanned the radio waves in search of communication from others.

The snow had continued to fall lightly over the previous weeks, keeping up the ground covering of snow and continually dusting the sparse tree cover surrounding their crofter's cottage. Inside the cottage was cosy and warm with the fires constantly burning. Things had been quiet for a few days.

"Let's go for a walk. I need to inspect the perimeters. See if we've had any trespassers," Scott asked anyone in general.

They all stopped what they were doing and turned to look at him.

"So, you want to make sure that *all* the people out there, who are off hiking in the *bitter* cold and constant snow, have not happened to cross our borders, which are in the depths of Glencoe?" Caitlin was the only one to speak.

Scott tilted his head to the side. "Caitlin, it's not snowing at the moment. Och! I'm going for a wee ride on Adam!"

He left the house in his warmest coat, hat, scarf and gloves with Scruffy trotting behind him.

"He's not serious?" Brendan followed Scott's progress to the stables from the kitchen window.

"Oh, yes, he is," Caitlin replied.

"Go with him Brendan," Bec urged.

"Please do. You can take a Highland horse."

Soon both men came riding past the backdoor with Scruffy in tow. The crisp, icy air misted around the faces of both men and beasts. The horses now taken from their warm stable, nickered, their tack jingling with every flick of their heads.

"We will nae be long lass. Dinnae fash." Scott leaned from the saddle and kissed her.

"Turn back if the weather changes," she insisted.

Caitlin and Bec were planning a Christmas dinner menu from their stores when the men came back on the horses, hurrying as much as the snow cover would allow. Caitlin stopped writing her list at the sound of Scott's hasty return.

"We must have intruders!" Caitlin grabbed her throwing knives and started opening the gun lockers. Scott jumped off Adam and ran into the cottage.

"How many are there?" Caitlin's anxiety made her tone sharp.

"Just one stag and he's braw. We're away after him! Fresh Venison for Christmas, he's a youngen, so will be tender, aye?" Scott grabbed the rifle and ammunition she had gathered for defence from intruders.

"Stag? No intruders then?" Bec sounded relieved.

"Yeah. Scott says the stag is weak from lack of feed, so it should be easy!" Brendan had caught Scott's enthusiasm.

"We will nae take the horses though. Nor the wee mutt. They might scare him off. We'll stalk him quietly. Will nae be long." Scott gave her a firm but distracted kiss on the mouth.

The men crunched off through the snow, reassuring the women they would be back well before nightfall. Scott had asked her to put the horses away. The Highland gelding followed meekly. The stallion was acting up. Lately, he had displayed the aggressiveness usual to stallions.

"Yes, I know your master abandoned you. You'll just have to be content with me." Caitlin tried to sooth him.

After putting the gelding in his stall, Caitlin removed his tack. Next, she tried to lead the stallion into his stall. He flattened his ears and pulled back. Caitlin undid his girth and removed his saddle but had to avoid a warning kick from the irascible animal. She tried once more to get him into his stall. The stallion's mouth clamped around her upper arm; hard teeth tightly pinched then pain shot into her shoulder.

"Ow! You beast!" she yelled and slapped him on the neck. "You can stay out of your stall for that. And your bit can stay in your mouth. See how you like it." Caitlin's eyes watered as she rubbed her upper arm. "I'll let Scott remove it." She tied the reins securely to the stall door and left, shutting the stable door firmly behind her. She put a cold compress on her arm once inside the cottage.

As the afternoon drew on, the snowfall became heavier, the sky became darker, with no sign of Scott nor Brendan. Caitlin returned to the stable with an apple and successfully got Adam into his stall still wearing his bridle. She wasn't risking another nip. Caitlin fed the horses then trudged through the snow to the cottage.

"They should be back by now. I'm worried." Caitlin shut the backdoor on the falling snow.

"Should we go looking for them?" Bec suggested.

"No! We have no idea where they are. As much as I want to look for them, we need to stay here. The weather is too bad for us to go out in, anyway." Caitlin halted as her stomach churned.

She put her hand over her mouth and ran for the toilet. She reached the bowl and vomited into it.

"Are you okay, Caitlin?" Bec followed her and stroked her back. "Don't get yourself so upset by this Caitlin. Your husband's a good woodsman and huntsman, the men will be okay."

Caitlin took deep breaths. She had to admit, she felt better now her stomach was empty.

"Even if they bring the stag home, the meat has to hang. We'll still need dinner and the men will be famished." Caitlin began making soup from a frozen squirrel carcass which had plenty of meat still on it, the remains of an earlier meal of squirrel pie.

The stock boiled in the pot for a while, and Caitlin lifted the lid to check its progress. She took a sniff of the brew. Oh, that sensation again, when her stomach wanted to come into her throat. She ran to the toilet and dry retched over it. There was nothing left in her stomach.

"You're not coming down with something, are you Caitlin? You'd better stop handling the food. And please wash your hands well."

"I feel okay now." Caitlin recovered quickly after each vomit.

Bec finished the soup while she rested on the couch. Caitlin stood and wandered to the backdoor often and looked out.

"You are letting the cold in Cait," Bec remarked every time she did.

It was now past dinner time. The men had not returned, and the snow continued to fall. Bec sat on a kitchen chair by the window and stared out. Caitlin paced, wandering back and forth. Her head ached, and it wasn't helping her stomach. Light-headedness came over her in waves, which she controlled by taking deep breaths to avoid passing out.

Where is he?

Food was out of the question and Bec ate the soup by herself. The rich gamey aroma of squirrel soup filled the main section of the cottage. Caitlin retired to her bedroom, after another dash to the toilet to dry retch. The smell of squirrel was weaker in her room.

"You must at least drink Caitlin," Bec cautioned. "Let's see if you can keep it down."

"No. Not yet. I'll be fine. I just want my husband back!" Caitlin burst into tears, unstoppable and continuing.

"Is your arm sore?" Bec sat next to her on the bed and gave her a hug.

Caitlin shook her head despite the pain on her upper arm.

"Like I said, your husband's a good huntsman and knows what to do in the woods." Bec rubbed her back. "My husband is not a silly man. They will hunker down somewhere and see out the night. You'll see, they'll be home tomorrow morning when it gets light again."

"Once, Scott went off to a market and he didn't return for a week. I thought he'd died! They have no provisions with them. Not even water to drink!" Caitlin's tears resumed, and her breath came out ragged. *Why am I so emotional?* "I need my man. He'd better come *back*. He's in trouble. Why's he so impetuous? They will *die* of exposure!" She sounded dramatic, even to her own ears.

"Caitlin!" Bec put on her most maternal voice. "The men will be okay. Okay?"

It didn't stop her crying. It took Caitlin a while to settle.

"Are you well, Caitlin?" Bec continued to hug her.

"Yes. What do you mean?" She looked at Bec's reflection in the mirror of the 60s dresser. "That's a funny question. You live with me. You know I'm well."

"That's not really what I meant to ask. Please don't think I am being too personal." In the mirror, Bec paused and looked down at Caitlin. "Caitlin are you pregnant?"

Caitlin sat straighter; her eyebrows furrowed. "I can't be. I'm on the Pill." She blinked twice.

"The contraceptive pill isn't infallible, you know," Bec stated. "When was your last period?"

Caitlin's eyes flickered as she did her mental calculations. "It was due three weeks ago. I'm never late, but I just put it down to the stressful situation we're in." She revealed her excuses for her menstrual tardiness.

"What about your breasts?"

"They feel like they do right before I get my period." Caitlin checked if they were still firm. They were.

"You know your body is preparing to be pregnant before your period, that's why your breasts feel like they do?"

"How can I find out if I am? Can't go to a Chemist and buy a pee stick!"

"No, we don't have any way of testing for Human Chorionic Gonadotrophin in your urine or your blood. But I could examine you. The good old-fashioned way," Bec suggested. Caitlin raised her eyebrows. "What they used to do before Ultrasounds," Bec clarified. Caitlin pulled a face, aware of the examination to which Bec referred. "Do you want to know for sure, or not?"

Caitlin nodded mutely.

"Well, I would say you are at least six to seven weeks pregnant," Bec concluded after examining Caitlin.

"But, oh, no! That will change everything!"

"Yes, they say having children changes everything. Life will never be the same!" Bec was cheery. Caitlin sensed her frown tight on her forehead. She should smile back at Bec, or something. But she didn't.

"Congratulations Caitlin," Bec added. "Scott will be so pleased. He strikes me as a natural when it comes to being a father."

"Yes, he *will* be an excellent father. Can't wait to tell him. Are you sure though? I don't want him to get all excited and then let down."

"Caitlin, I am as sure as I can be under the current conditions. Time will tell though."

Chapter Thirty-One

S now fell overnight. Outside Caitlin's bedroom window, fresh white powdered snow had topped up the winter beauty. Her room was cool. Caitlin huffed, her breath visible in the cold, then she got out of bed and dry retched.

"It's more from worry than morning sickness," she muttered to herself.

After attending the morning chores, Caitlin looked for a book that might have the method for making feta cheese. Caitlin tried to distract herself, but anxiety for Scott interrupted every thought.

Oh, Scott come back.

Caitlin made herself breathe deeply.

The weather had cleared for the moment. The sky was still dark with clouds and the wind howled in the trees nearby, but so far, no further snow. Caitlin crunched through knee high drifts and made a constant trek to the end of the garden from where she expected Scott and Brendan would appear. She nibbled on a dry biscuit, the only food that hadn't come up again that morning. As she peered across the snow-covered ground, three figures approached. It was Scott, and then Brendan. As the men got closer, the third figure revealed itself. It was the body of the stag tied to a sapling hanging between the men.

"Bec they're back!" she yelled as Bec came running out of the house with Scruffy close on her heels.

The dog made it to the men first and sniffed the dead animal, which was large and not too old. Red deer stags urinate on themselves. The ammonia rich dead animal smell wafted to her from twenty paces. The men were tired, hungry, and smelly from day old body odour and dead stag. Caitlin's legs dragged through the thigh-deep snow on her way to Scott; she wrapped her arms around him and held tight.

"Hello to you too, *mo chroí*." Scott said. "We got him! He would have been a twelve pointer in rutting season."

Caitlin buried her damp face in Scott's thick coat, and he returned her hug. She still hadn't spoken.

"We struck a wee bit o' trouble with the weather." Scott paused, waiting for a reprimand from her. Her head stayed buried in the lapels of his winter coat.

"We have been quite anxious for you," Bec now hugging Brendan, answered for both women.

"A snowstorm caught us soon after killing the stag," Scott admitted.

"What snowstorm?" Caitlin lifted her head. "There wasn't any storm this way. Where did you go?"

"Well." Scott glanced cagily at Brendan. "We followed the stag a wee bit farther than anticipated and ended up on the westerly edge of the mountain ridge there, and ye ken the weather's fiercer there."

Caitlin shook her head.

"But we've made it back, lass. And we've brought fresh meat!" Scott's eyes were wide, and arms open pointing to the dead stag now deposited on the snow.

"Caitlin," Brendan began, "your husband has mega-survival skills. I didn't doubt for one moment that we wouldn't get home. The weather started turning bad once we'd shot and gutted the stag. We dragged him to the woods nearby and found a spot to build a shelter. Scott showed me how to make an igloo. We were fine Caitlin! No need to be so upset."

"An igloo?" Bec questioned.

"Well, sort of. We made a shelter of branches and let the snow cover it. The sides were bricks of snow. Let's get inside and we'll tell yoo the rest." Scott was eager to get the meat under cover and be out of the cold himself.

He left the stag to hang in the woodshed, where it was secure ensuring no wild dogs would tamper with it before he butchered and stored it properly. In the house, the men removed their thick coats and warmed themselves by the fire. Caitlin helped Bec make hot tea, porridge and toast. Bec and Brendan went to their room for rest, their mumbled voices floating behind them.

Scott stood warming his back by the Aga. Caitlin put her arms around his waist and rested her head on him, absorbing his warmth. She sensed him move as he looked down at her. She had been quiet since their return to the house and held on to him, wanting to never let go.

"Caitlin?"

"Yes."

"Ye angry at me, lass?"

She didn't reply.

"I dinnae blame you if ye are. I did nae mean to be out overnight. But I'm home now. We made a shelter, and we were okay."

Still holding him tight, silent tears made tracks down her cheeks.

"Speak to me, Cait. What have you got to tell me then?"

Caitlin flicked her head up to face him. "How do you know I've got something to tell you?"

"I heard Bec whisper it to Brendan."

"Oh." When she didn't elaborate, he raised an eyebrow in question. "You won't believe this." She screwed her mouth to the side.

"Mm?" he said.

"I'm pregnant." Her voice was quiet.

Scott jerked his head back. "But..." His chest stopped moving as he held his breath.

"I know," Caitlin said. "According to Dr Bec, the Pill isn't infallible."

"How can you be sure?" Scott breathed in once more.

"Bec examined me," Caitlin said.

Scott frowned. She lowered her voice even further. "This will change the future, won't it, Scott? We didn't have a child your age in the future. Did we?"

Scott slowly shook his head. "Dinnae ken what to think, *mo chroí*." He continued shaking his head. "But we're going to have a baby." There was wonder in his voice.

"Apparently." She tightened her hug.

Scott returned it, then lifted her head with both hands and pressed his warm lips gently onto hers for a while. "We'll work it out, Caitlin." He then rested his chin on the top of her head. All the possibilities were probably going through his mind.

"I'm angry at you, though!" She wasn't speaking quietly anymore. "Why d'you go off like that with no contingency for the very strong possibility of the weather changing while you were hunting? You didn't even take water! You're so impulsive, Scott!"

His head jerked back again, and his brows crossed at her tone.

"Caitlin, that's me, aye?" His whisper was hoarse in her face. "And if I was nae 'impulsive', as you put it, I would nae be here! Would I? I'd be still grieving at your graveside, pouring my heart out to a gravestone. So, what would ye prefer?" He finished with a lift of his chin.

Caitlin continued to glare at him.

"Oh. By the way, your savage beast bit me. So, he's been in the stable with his bridle on since yesterday."

"What!"

Chapter Thirty-Two

The Future

"Thanks for taking some time to talk with me, Aunty Bec."

Kelly sat in Aunty Bec's kitchen. Uncle Brendan was away, involved with the Chief Council decision making and the general day to day running of the Community. Although Uncle Brendan and Aunty Bec were in their early seventies, they involved themselves as much as possible. As co-founding members with Mum, they determined to participate all their active days. Since mum's death and Dad leaving, the Community was down on manpower and leadership. The Militia felt it the most. Dad's shoes were hard to fill. Tightened security would test Rory and George Stobbart.

Kelly sat next to Aunty Bec at the kitchen table and ate one of her homemade biscuits. Aunty Bec had just got them out of the oven and the warm kitchen smelled of freshly baked ginger biscuits. Kelly's mouth watered before the biscuit reached her lips.

"It's all a part of working through your grief, love." Aunty Bec said. "I don't mind at all. It's good to remember things about your mother. What did you want to know?"

"Mum told me about her early life with Dad." Kelly said between mouthfuls of soft sweet but sharp ginger. "Could you tell me what it was like when you were with them? Uncle Brendan said you were with them for a whole winter." Older people like to reminisce, and she needed to find out stuff.

"Well. We met them in Fort William at a market that used to run ad hoc. Your father asked your Uncle Brendan to help him set up wind-powered electricity at their crofter's cottage. We'd just met them, but the two men hit it off at once. Well, we now know why that was!" Her aunt smiled at the remembrance.

Kelly smiled back. She was trying to be patient. She wanted to get as much information as possible, but her real need was the location of this cottage, and she was running out of time for a security-free attempt at The Time Machine.

"Where was the cottage?" she asked. "Was it far from Fort William?"

"Well, it's hard to tell as I walked most of the way there with your mother and it's difficult to gauge that way."

"Was it north or south?" Kelly prodded.

"Oh. It was down from Fort William. We crossed over the North Ballachulish steel bridge and kept walking east. Then your father hid our car." Aunty Bec paused. "I'm not sure how much to tell you of that journey to your parent's home. You see, this was the first time I had ever been truly scared."

Kelly sat back. Her aunt had never opened up before. Amazing what the death of someone close to you will do.

"It was when I found out your mother could defend herself with those knives she was so good with." Aunty Bec grinned. Then, just as quickly, her expression turned serious again. "And the first time I had witnessed the protective side of your father. I knew then that he was the type of man who would defend those he loved with his life."

Kelly absorbed Aunty Bec's observations but struggled to keep herself patient.

I have to get on with this.

"So, was it near there?" Kelly prompted.

"No. Your father then hid our car, and we walked quite a way more. Well, maybe not that much further." Her aunt put her index finger to her lips. "It seemed further as I was not very fit then. But after living with your mother and father for a while that changed. Your father taught us some martial art!" She laughed.

"Where did Dad hide the car?"

"Further east along the road, by a fence there was a small clump of Scots pine. We walked through it, I think. But that was nearly forty years ago. I don't quite remember." Aunty Bec stared at her.

"I want to know what their life was like. Dad is with her there now. I'd like to think he's happy with her then. Now," Kelly shook her head. "Whatever! It's so confusing." She tried to deflect. Was Aunty Bec suspicious?

"Well, they had horses and chickens and a goat. Oh, and a wee dog. Scruffy they called him. Aptly named. They were working on a vegetable patch, but it was winter and not much grew. We were cosy in that cottage.

Your parents had done well with it. And yes, they seemed very happy. Ideally so, despite what was happening in the world outside. They gave us hope for the future—that there were some decent people left in the world." Aunty Bec finished on that positive note and smiled.

Kelly leaned over and gave her aunt a hug.

"Thanks, Aunty Bec. I know Dad's happy there with Mum. I miss them both so much." Kelly's vision blurred. When was she going to stop crying?

"We are here if you need us, love. If any of you need us, just come." Aunty Bec's arms pulled her closer.

***

Murray wandered over to the building that housed The Time Machine. He checked either side of him. At the front of the next building, another barn, the smithy's hammer rang percussively as he made shoes for the horses. Two boys on paper making duty sloshed a long pole in a large barrel as they shredded and threw used paper into it. No one looked up from their duties.

Murray slipped through the door, as a member of the team he had a key of his own. The security step-up had not yet occurred. Once in the room that housed the machine, Murray walked over to the console, avoiding the cables on the floor, and examined the dials and knobs. The room was always cool. It seeped into his core, and he shivered. Murray ran through the process of setting the machine. The hairs on the back of his neck rose; footsteps came from behind him. Murray turned. It was Angus.

"Oh, hi," Murray said.

"What are you doing here?" Angus pushed his glasses up his nose. A piece of fine wire held the left arm of his glasses onto the frames.

"Just looking." Murray twisted his mouth. "Still intrigued by the whole thing. Didn't think we could ever be so clever. Man, that is. Being able to travel through time. Cool, hey?"

"Cool, until someone steals it." Angus' lip curled in a snarl. "Did they find out who it was?"

"Um oh. No, I don't know." Murray shrugged.

How much should he let this man know? He would need assistance; someone on the 'inside' willing to help.

"Whoever it is, is in big trouble." Angus had always been friendly to Murray; they were both nerdish and got along well. Angus looked around to make sure they were on their own. "They've asked me to check the machine wasn't damaged and to get it ready for a journey to see if all still works. Then we'll shut it down." Angus pressed his index finger to the bridge of his glasses and pushed. "We'll only start it again when we've worked out return journeys and can send the guy back."

"Which guy?" Murray asked.

"The guy who'll get the guy who stole the time journey!" Angus' eyes widened as he nodded.

"Oh, wow!" Murray joined in the nodding. "Who's it going to be, do ya know?"

"No, they're still deciding," Angus said. "We're now beginning our studies on how to do the return journey. Martin, the physicist, has some promising ideas, but, like I said, we'll shut the machine down until that technology is developed."

It must have made this guy's day, knowing this stuff.

"Wow," Murray repeated, still nodding. "When did that happen? Like, I've not heard about it."

"Oh, they'll let you know when they want you for the calcs. It's now a need to know basis only. Oh, and if you've got a key you have to hand it back, okay?"

"Well, I'd better leave you to it. See ya." Murray avoided the answer about the key.

Murray exited the barn and rushed to find Kelly. After searching her quarters without success, he made his way to one of the communal areas. Kelly was leaving Uncle Brendan and Aunty Bec's quarters. From across the walkway, he made a gesture to her to come over, trying to not look frantic.

"You need to go *now*," he whispered once Kelly was next to him.

"What! But I'm not ready."

"You have to be," Murray said. "Angus is setting The Time Machine up right now to check it still works. He says they'll soon shut it down until they can do return journeys. So, we need to go now!"

Kelly's hazel eyes peered at him closely. "I've always trusted you. It's no different now. If the time is *now*, I'll just have to go with the information I have. But I need to dress for it and get weapons."

That's why I'm proud of you, wee sister.

"Great. Meet me at the stables in five minutes," he said. "We're going in the back way."

***

Kelly was late. Murray paced. The scent of stable-needing-mucking-out surrounded him as she arrived dressed in khaki trousers with pockets full of equipment, a similar shirt and a flak-jacket. Kelly had a handgun and ammunition, which she must have got from Dad's room, and her knife in its sheath hung from her belt. She had slung a bow and a quiver full of arrows over her shoulder. Kelly would've grabbed them as she walked through the training shed on her way to him.

"Come on!" Murray shout-whispered. "Angus went for his lunch. He's away, but not for long!"

Opening the door and checking Angus was still at lunch, Murray led Kelly into the room that housed The Time Machine. Their footsteps echoed off the old barn's high ceiling.

"I'll set it ready to go for the March after Dad arrived," Murray said as he nudged Kelly forward. "You need to get into the pod now. Quick!"

Kelly entered the chamber and climbed into the pod. The chamber itself was an old shower cubicle from the farmhouse. Something so simple, no alarms and bells and sparking Tessler balls, as Murray had imagined from the Sci Fi novels he'd read. Their scientists had found the whole ability to time travel was much simpler than they originally thought. When TSMC removed modern technology, *science,* well this Community's scientists, were able 'to see the wood for the trees', so to speak, time travel had become obvious—to them, anyway.

The pod, which was already in the cubicle, was a brown resin capsule, large enough for an adult human to sit in a squat. Murray placed a backpack full of cash inside with Kelly, then she enclosed herself in the resin pod.

"Hey! What are you doing?" Angus' voice rang off the ceiling as he strode toward them.

Murray jumped, then stepped to Angus.

"Our father was the one who stole the time journey." Murray had both hands up in a placating gesture. "He went back in time to protect Mum. He took her to safety after TSMC. He *has* to be there. To stay there. We've got to warn him." His tone came out severe.

"The Council aren't listening to us," Kelly added. "We can't let them change the past or none of *this* will happen!"

"You mean they are going after *Scott*!" Angus looked from one to the other. "That's ridiculous! They can't do that. Not to him. We owe him almost everything." Angus gave an imperceptible shake of his head.

"Please let me go," Kelly pleaded.

Murray sensed Angus was on their side. After thirty seconds of decision making, Angus nodded.

"I'll say it accidently discharged when I was resetting it. It'll help us stall for time too." Angus directed his next comment to Kelly. "You've got to warn your father. You can't let them get him, okay?"

"Okay." Kelly closed the final clasp on the resin capsule.

"You'll be here thirty-eight years ago—" Angus bent down to speak to Kelly.

"She knows all that!" Murray interrupted. "Just start the Machine! We need to get her gone!"

Once enclosed in the pod, Kelly had a limited supply of oxygen, so it was imperative the time journey start. Angus pressed some buttons. Murray watched his sister disappear. How did Dad manage it alone? And why did Angus just help them? Murray turned to Angus, the question most likely obvious in his expression.

"Your parents did a lot for me. I owe them everything. In fact, I owe your father my life." Angus didn't elaborate further. "What's going on with the Chief Council?"

"Ambition." *Or rather, Angela*. "You know 'absolute power' and all that."

Murray stared at the empty time machine chamber, slightly empty himself. He'd never see Kelly again. Damn. In their rush, he hadn't yet considered it.

"Well, I'll have to account for the journey. Guess I'll blind 'em with science and explain an accidental discharge. You'll follow it all, won't you?" Angus asked.

"Aye, I sure will. Can give them the maths for it too, if they want," Murray said. "Seriously man, thanks."

Chapter Thirty-Three

The Present

C aitlin's day had taken on a new routine. Wake up, sit up, dry retch.

"How can I be sick when I haven't even eaten yet?" She sat in bed.

"Aye well, lass, get used tae it, for all your pregnancies began like this. The twin pregnancies were the worst, mind." Scott handed her a piece of dry toast. "This worked. Eat this before ye get oot o' bed. It always used to settle your tummy."

"Thank-you," she responded meekly. "And I do this five times? I *am* mad." She faced him. "This is all your fault, you know."

Scott stood at the side of their bed, grinning. "I sincerely hope so."

He had made the toast first thing and now stood in front of her wearing only his jocks. Their hard life had kept him lean and muscled. Scott's dark-blond hair was now long, and he wore it tied back in a ponytail and his bushy beard was full of red tinges. His summer tan had faded, and his scars were more noticeable.

"Haven't hurt yourself in a while," she commented as her gaze ran over his naked torso. "Keep it that way."

"Aye well, we've had enough excitement here for a wee while, have we not? You'll be all right then, lass?"

"Yes, you have done your husbandly duty. You are dismissed, wild-man that you are." Caitlin bit into the toast.

No butter?

"Wild-man?" he asked.

"Yes. The beard."

"Keeps my face warm, lass," he said. "It's a cold winter out there, in case ye haven't noticed." He dressed, gave her a quick kiss then left to do his chores.

Caitlin took her time rising, which helped ease the nausea. This morning there was a niggle in the left of her tummy. She dismissed it—again. It was surprising how easily she had come to terms with being pregnant. Scott was most attentive and supportive, happy at the unexpected extra family member. He'd been a father since he was nineteen. Perhaps he missed being a father here in the past, with their children in the future.

The days were shortening with the winter solstice approaching. Caitlin helped Bec prepare for the celebrations in earnest.

"Some semblance of normality, that's all I want," Bec declared.

"Yes, we need Christmas!" Caitlin said. "And Hogmanay! Would you put that holly over on the mantelpiece, please? I'll see if I can get through the snow to a fir tree and bring in some branches."

Once outside, Caitlin stepped her way through the still deep snow to the trees at the very far end of the grounds surrounding the cottage. To muck out the stables, Scott put the horses in the yard where the action of the horses and the slight snow melt had made an area for them to exercise, albeit a muddy one. Scott was on his stallion, putting him through his paces.

"How's your vicious beast?" she shouted at him as she walked past, her tender arm still hurt from his nip.

"He's fine thank-you. Only being a male," Scott said. "All that testosterone will do it to ye. We'll see some action come spring and I'll get him to cover the mare."

Caitlin smiled to herself at his anticipation of a herd sired by this one stallion.

Caitlin found lower, more easily accessible branches of the fir trees and, avoiding the resulting shower of snow, broke pieces off for decoration inside the crofter's cottage. She recalled her house as she was growing up. Its festive decorations involved the scent of pine branches and the soft glow of many candles. What would her mother make of her being pregnant? As she walked back, a stabbing sensation deep in the lower left of her pelvis made her bend over right as she passed Scott.

"Ye all right lass? Being sick?"

Caitlin held her shoulder. There was also a sharp stab of pain there. Then it eased a bit.

"No. I've got a pain in my tummy. Think I'm constipated. Better take something for it."

"Hello tinned prunes," Scott chuckled.

"Oh wheesht!" She was irritable and sounded it too, when she reflected on her tone to Scott.

What's happening? Her pulse raced, and her breath came faster.

Once inside the cottage, the pain subsided, and her breathing eased.

Caitlin continued decorating the crofter's cottage and Bec started baking. They had no mince fruit, so they had decided apples from the cold store would make pies for Christmas.

"Do we use all the frozen butter on shortbread?" Bec asked.

"Can't really. Don't know when we'll get anymore. Haven't got a cow. But there's an idea for a Christmas present from my man." Caitlin shook her head. "Never thought I'd get excited over a cow!"

Shaking her head caused the pain again. She bent over. It was the only thing that eased the tight stab in her pelvis.

"What's wrong Caitlin?" Bec asked. "You okay?"

Caitlin held her shoulder. The pain intensity was increasing with each episode. "I've had this niggle for the past few days. But today it's terrible."

"Where is your pain?"

"In my shoulder, just as much as my tummy. It's on the left. Wrong side for appendicitis." Her mouth tugged with a slight smile. "And this pain in my shoulder isn't where Adam nipped me. I think I'm constipated. May have to use a suppository. Sorry, too much information, but I'd better get on with it."

"Let me know if it doesn't settle Caitlin," Bec said.

***

Scott came in the backdoor as Bec took a tray of cooked pies from the oven.

"Hmm." Scott sniffed. "The smell of good things."

"They are for Christmas," Bec warned him.

A thud came from the inside toilet.

"You okay, Caitlin?" Bec called.

Silence.

"Is she in the loo?" Scott asked.

They both ran to the inside toilet where Caitlin lay on the floor of the confined space, pale, with beads of sweat on her brow. Scott's heart rocked in his chest as a cool numbness crept a journey down his spine.

"Caitlin!" Bec shook Caitlin's shoulder. She didn't respond.

Bec checked Caitlin was breathing, felt for a pulse in her neck then turned her onto her side with her head tilted to make sure her airway was clear.

"All good?" Scott asked.

Bec didn't reply at first, her mouth tight.

"Help me get her on your bed." Bec's voice held strain.

Scott scooped Caitlin up in his arms and carried her to their bedroom where he gently placed her on their bed. Bec got her stethoscope and blood pressure machine and wrapped the cuff around Caitlin's arm.

"What's going on?" The cool numbness he fought with was like the snow he'd walked through on his way from the stables.

"Her pulse is thready, and her BP is low. She's in shock," Bec stated.

"She was in pain outside just now. Said she was constipated. Not constipated, is it?" Scott watched as Bec examined Caitlin with skilled hands.

Bec pursed her lips as she made her assessment. "Lower left quadrant, so not appendix," she reported. "Associated shoulder tip pain. Early pregnancy. In shock. Shit!"

Scott narrowed his eyes. Bec had never sworn in his hearing.

"Get the kitchen ready for theatre," Bec ordered. "I must operate. She has a ruptured ectopic pregnancy. We need to hurry, or we'll lose her!"

"What!" Bec finished her diagnosis as Brendan reached the end of the bed.

"I'm sorry." Bec looked up at Scott. "I'm not an expert in pelvic examinations for pregnancy. It's all done by ultrasound now. I was correct she was pregnant, but didn't pick up it was in the wrong place. Sorry."

Scott didn't move, he clenched his jaw muscles and swallowed a few times, fighting off the frozen immobility which threatened him. His silence was brief.

"Tell me what to do!" he ordered Bec.

"Help Brendan get the kitchen ready to be an operating theatre just as we did for his surgery. Drape the kitchen table, get the diathermy equipment, suction and the Boyle's machine ready. I'll need a sterile procedure pack, forceps, scalpel, sutures. Scott, you assist me in the same way you did for Brendan."

Bec turned to Brendan. "Love, you can use the Boyle's machine. Remember how I showed you? Once I get her under, you monitor her for me. And help wherever you can. Both of you, please be quick."

Scott ran off to do as Bec asked.

In the room behind him, Bec had lowered her voice, but he still caught it. "Brendan, get me a cannulation pack and a bag of normal saline and a line, please. Be quick. Get the IV fluids and resuscitation meds in case I need them. Caitlin looks bad, but don't tell Scott."

Brendan came into the kitchen. Scott scrubbed the bench in quick swift motions, his knuckles white around the scrubbing brush.

"You okay, Scott?" Brendan asked.

Scott raised his head; his breath came out as snorts as his nostrils flared to suck in air.

"Got to get this set up quick."

Brendan turned to the storeroom and came out with the cannulation pack and IV fluids and ran back to Bec. On his return, he got the emergency IV fluids and medications Bec had requested and put them to one side. Brendan then retrieved the equipment from the storeroom, plugging it in as he went.

Scott watched Brendan out of the corner of his eye while he frantically recalled what he'd done when assisting in Brendan's surgery. That now felt like a lifetime ago. Scott threw the large plastic sheeting over the still damp table. He unwrapped the large sterile drape and flung it out flat. He ran to the bedroom, halting in the doorway. Caitlin lay curled on her side on their bed. Bec had put an IV in her arm and squeezed in the bag of fluid which she held up above Caitlin. Scott stood in the doorway, he puffed from his exertions, his eyes fixed on Caitlin. Her chest rose and fell rapidly, not from exertion, but in an attempt to survive.

"The kitchen's ready now." His voice was harsh. "I'll take her in."

"Get Brendan to assist you—" Bec began.

"No! I'll carry my wife in." Scott spoke curtly, his stress causing him to sound impolite.

Scott carefully lifted Caitlin off the bed and carried her to the kitchen table. She moaned as he placed her on the solid surface.

"What now?" He faced Bec.

"Drape her as you did Brendan while I put her under." Determination etched Bec's face.

"Brendan, come here and help. Put the BP cuff and other monitoring equipment on her." Bec's tone was equal to her position of authority.

Scott covered Caitlin with sterile drapes while Bec and Brendan performed the induction. He turned away when they started putting the tube down her throat. Caitlin was so vulnerable and weak. Not like *his* Caitlin. Scott grabbed the sterile equipment Bec had asked for and began opening it onto a draped sterile tray, in the same manner he had seen Caitlin do for Brendan's surgery. He leaned on the table by her side and forcibly calmed himself. His hands shook.

Get a grip, man! Hands need to be steady to hold instruments.

"Scott, because this pregnancy is probably not in the uterus but in a fallopian tube, I must remove it." Bec looked over the drape once she had anaesthetised Caitlin. "Sorry, but the baby is already lost. I have to do it to save Caitlin."

Scott swallowed and returned her stare. "Save her."

He glanced at Brendan, now sitting behind the green drape that screened his wife's face.

"Ye ken I can only do this now because of what we went through with you, Brendan."

Bec and Scott both scrubbed well with the iodine solution. Scott sniffed, the earthy scent brought back memories of Brendan's surgery. Once gloved and gowned, he looked across his wife's anaesthetised form to Bec.

"Just like we did with Brendan, only a lower incision, Scott." Bec raised her eyebrows, most of her face covered by a mask. "Retract what I show you. Okay?"

Scott held layers aside with retractors and suctioned any bleeding as Bec tied and diathermied the vessels. Once in Caitlin's pelvic area, Bec found a ruptured fallopian tube, which was bleeding. Bec tied and cut it away from the pink muscled-looking thing—Caitlin's uterus. Bec tied off the vessels which bled and used the diathermy rod on the smaller bleeding vessels. The kitchen began to smell of burnt flesh. Scott swallowed.

"Kidney dish, Scott," Bec ordered.

Scott flinched as he stared into Caitlin's pelvic cavity. He grabbed the kidney dish and placed it beside the incision. Bec put the swollen ruptured fallopian tube into it. Scott sucked in a breath.

Our child.

The forceps pinching the end of the tube clattered into the kidney dish. His hands shook again, momentarily.

Focus!

Brendan called out Caitlin's blood pressure and pulse at regular intervals.

"Her pulse is creeping up Bec, and her BP is only sitting at eighty."

"Put up another bag of fluid and squeeze it in," Bec ordered. "You've got the line with the hand pump attachment, haven't you?"

"Yes."

"Squeeze it in! I've ligated and diathermied the bleeders. She should settle after this. Scott, more suction here please let's clean her up and make sure we've got them all."

Once certain she had cauterised all the bleeding blood vessels, Bec irrigated Caitlin's pelvic area and then started closing it. Scott, recalling the suturing from Brendan's surgery, helped to close Caitlin's incision. Bec injected the cut with local anaesthetic for pain control. Scott glanced often at the kidney dish, which Bec had placed on one of the sterile trays. He blinked away tears. His greatest fear would be to lose Caitlin. She was not yet out of danger.

Bec started waking Caitlin. With the tube out of her throat and Caitlin breathing normally, Scott allowed Brendan to help him carry her back to their bed. Bec devised an IV pole from the bedpost as she wished to continue IV fluids and give her more pain relief.

"For a bit more fluid," Bec said. "I want to be sure she won't drop her BP again."

Bec and Brendan cleared the kitchen. Their voices travelled into the room where Caitlin lay on their bed. Scott stood beside it, looking down at her. His pulse raced like he'd been fighting with all his strength, but he'd never been so powerless.

"What do I do with this, Bec?" Brendan asked in the kitchen. There was a clank of the kidney dish.

"Leave it. Put it in a plastic bag in the fridge. They'll want to bury it and say good-bye." Bec's voice came through the door.

Scott laid himself behind Caitlin on their bed. Their own familiar scent, embedded in their duvet, surrounded him and Caitlin. She lay on her side, still waking up. Scott's breath stirred the small hairs at the nape of her neck. She moved her shoulders and he lightly put his arm around her.

"Are ye okay, *mo chroí*?" he whispered into her ear.

"Hmm," she sounded groggy.

Scott sniffed and brushed away the tears which spilled out of his eyes.

Caitlin woke more fully. "Whas wrong?"

Scott didn't answer her.

"Scott, whas wrong?" she slurred again.

"You're all right. That's all that matters." Scott held her gently, not wanting to cause her more pain.

"What happened? I feel odd."

"Bec had to operate on you, *mo chroí*. We lost the baby. Sorry lass," he said softly.

Caitlin looked surprised and blinked a few times. "Is that what the pain was?"

"An ectopic pregnancy," he said. "Bec called it that."

Caitlin woke further, a look of recognition on her face as Bec entered the room to assess her patient's recovery.

"Bec. Where's my baby?" Caitlin spoke with clarity.

"Has Scott told you?" Bec stood by their bed holding a BP machine.

Caitlin nodded. He did too.

"Caitlin, I had to remove your left fallopian tube," Bec said. "The pregnancy had ruptured it. You were in shock. You can't save an ectopic pregnancy."

"I know." Caitlin seemed to sink further into the bed. "Where's my baby?"

"We've kept it," Bec fiddled with the BP cuff. "We thought you and Scott would want to say good-bye when you were feeling better."

"So, I've lost a fallopian tube. Can I still get pregnant?" Caitlin gripped his arm around her waist and tried to get up.

Scott held her more tightly and shushed into her ear.

"Yes, of course you can!" Bec quickly answered.

Bec glanced at him as well. He must have looked alarmed, so he tried to hide it.

"The human body is an incredible thing. Your one remaining fallopian tube, your right one, will swing over to your left ovary and pick up an egg when it releases one. They take turns, you see." Bec smiled.

"It will be harder to conceive though?" Caitlin asked.

"They say it doesn't make much difference. You rest now, Caitlin. You've been through an ordeal. You need to recover. We could've lost you." Bec's expression turned even more serious. "You're a brave and strong woman, Caitlin. I'm so proud of you."

"Bec," Caitlin grabbed her hand. "Thank-you. I know I wouldn't have survived without you."

"You're welcome, Cait. Your husband and Brendan helped too. I couldn't have done it without them. You both rest now. It's been an ordeal. I'll come and check on you regularly."

***

Three days had passed. Scott bent over Caitlin as she lay on the couch. Caitlin's whole body felt heavy with tiredness.

"Are ye feeling up to a wee walk, *mo chroí*?" he said softly.

"Yes. Why?"

"There's something you and I need to do." Scott wrapped her in the blanket she lay on, lifted her off the green sofa and carried her out of the backdoor.

The sun shone but not brightly, its dimmer switch on halfway. Scott crunched through the snow, now only ankle deep, a solemn look on his face. The lines beside his eyes were a little deeper today, and a furrow was making its way to permanency on his brow. All this has stressed him.

"I *can* walk, you know," Caitlin said.

"Aye, I ken ye can. But if you slipped, those stitches of yours might rip. Dinnae want to ruin all Bec's hard work, do ye now?" Scott glanced at her in his arms and smiled.

I must look better today. The strength was returning to her limbs, despite the heaviness of fatigue.

Caitlin turned away from Scott. He carried her to the far end of the garden where the tree line started. Directly in front of them was a large fir. Underneath it was a small wooden box beside an equally small grave, a dark gash in the white snow-covered ground.

Scott stopped and gently lowered her to a standing position. The chill came through her slippers. Caitlin stared at the tiny box. She then gazed up at the tree. There had been a slight snow melt. The usual blanket of frozen water covering the trees was now tiny, translucent droplets dangling like chandelier crystals from the ends of the pine needles.

Like our tenuous hold on life.

The random *pat pat* of the droplets falling to the ground punctuated her thoughts. Blinking, she looked down again.

"I suppose we should say a few words," Scott interrupted her sombre reflections.

He placed the small box in the ground.

"Good-bye little one. Mummy and Daddy love you." He lifted the shovel full of dirt and carefully covered the small box in the ground.

Silent tears ran down her face.

"You sound so brave." Caitlin's voice muffled as she turned and hugged into him. Scott returned her hug and held her close.

"I'm no' brave. Just being practical, *mo chroi*."

"Will we see him or her again, do you think?" she asked.

"I know we will." His husky voice was gentle. "When we get there, we will find a wee girl, or boy, who will run up to us and shout 'Mummy' or 'Daddy'. Whichever of us gets there first."

They both wept. The moments passed in silence.

"That will be me. I get there first," she said.

Scott nodded as he stifled a sob. "We lost a child. Something we never did in the future. But I nearly lost everything, Caitlin. I nearly lost you." He buried his face in her hair and his tears fell freely.

Chapter Thirty-Four

The Future

"We will send a member of our Militia back in time to retrieve Scott Campbell, who will then return to our present time and be brought to trial for his misdeed." The most senior member of the Chief Council, Harold Farquhar, read the outcome of the Chief Council's earlier deliberations.

The Chief Council sat at their long desk, in what had once been the living room of one of the dwellings on the original farm. They discussed the progress of their action plan. The Chief Council consisted mainly of the older members of the Community who had leadership experience; their varied attire attested to their diverse backgrounds. Encouraging mentoring, the Chief Council had included Angela at a young age, her potential recognised and nurtured.

Harold addressed George Stobbart, the Acting In-Charge of the Militia. George, dressed in buckskin leggings and a shirt made from home-spun cloth, the Militia's usual garb, stood tall to attention, his middle-aged frame still bore the strong and disciplined physique of a military-trained man.

"How are your preparations for this journey going? Have you decided on the man to send? And how are the extra security arrangements for The Time Machine coming along?"

"Well, sir, Council members," George nodded in their direction. "We are reinforcing the security around The Time Machine. We will complete this shortly. Please remember sending a man back to the past for the retrieval of Mr Campbell will depend on the ability to bring both the retriever and the offender back to the present. Currently, this is not possible."

"Yes, we understand this, but we must be ready the minute it is," Dr Farquhar countered.

"It is a priority, is it not, Mr Stobbart?" Angela added her voice to the discussion. "We must attend to justice."

"Aye, well, regarding the progress of The Time Machine's capabilities, you will need to make your enquires to the scientists involved. As to the priority we place on this matter, I can assure you there are more pressing security concerns on our doorstep."

The meeting then closed. George exited and made his way to Rory who was due to return from a training exercise.

***

Rory stood on the Militia training green, after completing a twenty-mile hike with the younger members of the Militia, its purpose to improve their fitness. The dishevelled young men and women arranged themselves untidily on the grass in front of him. They wore khaki—military clothing and equipment obtainable on the black market, or home-made clothing. Some stood; most had collapsed on the ground. The scent of sweat wafted into Rory's face.

"You've got to be kidding, man!" A scrawny member of the group puffed their protest.

Rory's facial muscles tensed in an enthusiastic smile, having regained his resting respiratory rate. He thrived on exercise and fresh air. His close-fitting shirt was damp at the armpits, neck and down his back. His brow cooled as beads of sweat collected there.

"Tomorrow, we will run it again." Rory paused, interrupted by groans from the participants. "And we will carry our twenty-pound backpacks!" More groans and expressions of disbelief sounded, particularly from the participants lying on the grass. "You are dismissed!"

Turning, his cheeks still tight from a large grin, Rory spied his mentor.

"George! How goes it?" Rory's facial muscles relaxed at the expression on George's face.

"Need to speak with you, son. In private," George said.

Rory led his mentor to the nearest cabin and shut the door behind them.

"What's gone on? You've been at a Chief Council meeting, aye?"

"Aye," George replied. "And you won't like it."

"Tell me."

"Your sister!" George sat and rested his elbow on the table covered in Rory's exercise spread sheets.

"You don't need to tell me," Rory said. "I know what you'll say."

"Angela's a concern! She's pushing it." George shook his head. "It's as if she's got something to prove."

"She's got tae prove she's 'the best man for the job' and is nae on the Council just because of who her parents are." Rory exhaled loudly, frustration boiling in his chest. "She's verra mad at Dad for embarrassing her.

Anyone would think she wants to punish him for that more than the theft of a time journey!"

"Aye," George agreed. "She complains about your father having wasted resources, and she wants the security team to concentrate its efforts on The Time Machine! We have other pressing matters, such as defending our perimeter."

"Not to mention the power the thing uses when it goes off," Rory said. "There are more vital things to run, like the medical centre." Rory's lip pinched between his teeth as he stared out the window at his junior Militia members returning to their quarters.

"Rory, lad, when it comes time to send someone back, you must be the one who goes, aye?"

Rory mulled over the implication of himself being the retriever. A pang of tightness caught his throat. Rory missed Dad, who wasn't only his father, but a mentor, an ideal and a best friend. He missed their conversations long into the night on watch whenever on manoeuvres.

"I have wondered if I should be the one." Rory's voice caught in his throat. He coughed to clear it. "Angela would be against it. She'd say I'm biased and wouldn't do the job."

George shook his head. "When the time comes, do all you can to be the one," George ordered. "I would definitely give you the command, but apparently, the Chief Council seem to think they have a say in who goes, it being a special case and all."

"I'll try," Rory said. "It may be more than a wee while yet. They've still to develop the return journey. Might ask my wee brother where they're up to with it."

After showering and changing, Rory took a detour and returned to his quarters via the room which housed The Time Machine. Standing in front of it, he shook his head at the trouble it was causing his family, and at how unlikely looking an object it was. A scientist he was familiar with, Angus, had allowed him entry. Angus got along well with Murray. Well, they were both nerds. Martin the physicist was present as well and examined the board of switches for setting and discharging The Time Machine. Martin and Angus conversed intensely.

"How do you mean 'accidentally'?" Martin's tone was sharp.

"Well, I don't know. I must have knocked it. It just went off! Sorry." Angus pushed the stray strands of his black mop of hair behind his ears.

"It can't just 'go off'!"

"Must be a loose wire. I'll check under the console." Angus began unscrewing the console cover.

It didn't sound good. *Is this a security issue?*

"What's going on, guys?" Rory asked.

"Seems like there has been an accidental discharge of the machine," Martin replied as Angus removed the console cover.

"Ah! There it is!" Angus lifted the loose wire in question.

"So, The Time Machine has gone off accidentally? Is that what you're telling me?" Rory rested his hands on his belt as he stood directly in front of the scientists. The two scientists nodded in unison.

"That's a shocking waste of power!" he yelled. "You must inform the Council."

Two heads bobbed unison again.

"Anyways, are you any nearer making the return journey possible?" Rory asked.

The scientists glanced sideways at each other.

"We're making our report to the Chief Council regarding this," Martin said.

"Okay then." *So, I am too much of a minion for access to this level of knowledge.* "Write this incident in that report, would ye? And how you're rectifying any such shameful wastes of power re-occurring in the future, aye?" Rory turned and left.

Rory usually passed Murray's room on his way back to his own. This time he would stop and speak to his younger brother. He knocked on the door. Murray opened.

"Murray! You're in. Got time for a chat?" Rory brushed past his much slighter built younger brother and left him standing at the open door.

"Um... Yes." Murray closed the door, came into the room, and sat on his bed.

It squeaked. Rory sat tall in the chair by Murray's desk. His elbow knocked the neat pile of textbooks on the right, causing the stack to tumble to disarray in the bare space in the middle.

"So, brother," Rory said, ignoring the books and glancing at Warhol's Einstein, "you seem to know what goes on with the time machine more than anyone else. What's the situation with the return journey? Do they ken how to do that yet?"

"How would I know?" Murray asked. "It's a need to know basis only now. They'll only ask me to do the calculations when they need them."

"There's a theme beginning to emerge here." Rory scratched the new growth on his cheek.

"You mean they're purposely keeping us out of the loop?" Murray sat straighter. "Us Campbells, I mean."

"Except for our big sister," Rory said. "Being on the Chief Council she'll be privy to everything."

"You gotta speak to her," Murray pleaded. "Tell her to lighten up about Dad and bringing him to justice. *Please* say something to her."

"Can't." Rory shook his head.

"Why not?"

"I would love to grab that sister of ours by the scruff of the neck and shake some sense into her and some self-importance out." In front of him, Rory held an imaginary Angela by the throat. "But, if I did, I would blow any chances I have of doing an important job that I must do when the time comes."

"What important job?"

"I will be the one who goes back for Dad," Rory said.

"Oh." Murray gulped.

"So, we'll see what happens when it happens." Rory stood to leave, stopped and casually added, "Oh by the way, there's been an accidental discharge of The Time Machine. They only let me know because I was there when they were trying to figure it out."

Murray's mouth tensed slightly.

"Looks like they put it down to a loose wire," Rory continued. "Shameful waste of power. They need to get it fixed pronto."

Murray's mouth relaxed.

Rory left his brother's room, casting one last suspicious glance as he closed the door behind himself. What does *he* know?

***

"You made it, Rory," Angela sounded pleased. "Where's Kelly?"

The rest of his siblings had met together for dinner and seated themselves around the dining room table. They all looked at Murray. Rory let his stare linger.

Aye, where is she, brother?

"Why ask me? Am I my sister's keeper?" Murray flicked both hands palm outwards.

"You spend the most time with her out of all of us," Ceilidh stated the fact.

"Okay then." Murray stood and strode out of the dining room.

Five minutes later Murray returned. "She's not feeling well."

"What sort of not well?" Angela demanded.

Murray's face pinked. "You know...girl stuff."

"Oh." Angela didn't enquire further.

Little conversation occurred between the six siblings as they consumed dinner. Rory kept his attention on Murray, glancing between mouthfuls of meat and potato pie, having placed himself opposite him. Murray's eyes flicked to Rory's intermittently. After the meal, he followed Murray back to his room, which was next to Kelly's. As Murray entered his room, Rory knocked on Kelly's door.

"Kelly. Can I come in?"

"She's probably asleep." Murray ventured.

Rory raised an eyebrow. "Asleep?" He placed his shoulder against the door. It only took one shove.

"Hey, you can't do that!" Murray followed him into Kelly's darkened room.

Rory shut the door behind them both and turned on the light which showed an empty bed, and a room deficient of Kelly. Most of her possessions were there, the scent of the outdoors and horses coming from a pile of dirty clothes abandoned by her bed.

"Where's our sister?" Rory challenged his younger brother. He would get it out of him.

"I don't know—"

"Aye, you do," Rory interrupted. "Where is she?"

Murray didn't reply but stood biting his lower lip.

"Let me guess. It has something to do with the 'accidental discharge'"—Rory made quotation marks in the air with his fingers— "of The Time Machine today. Am I right?" His stare burned into the top of his younger brother's head.

"Murray!" Rory shouted, as his brother continued to observe his feet.

"You're not Dad. Stop speaking to me like a father," Murray spat out.

Rory took a breath to restrain his temper.

Does this kid not realise how serious this is?

"Murray, I need to know. I could do this officially, but I want to know what happened before I make it official."

"Please don't," Murray blurted.

"Don't what?"

"Make it official," Murray said.

"I may have to."

"When I tell you, you may not want to." Murray screwed his mouth to the side.

"Tell me, then."

"It's Kelly," Murray said. "She's not here."

"I may not be the brightest of us, but I had got that already, aye?" Rory crossed his arms and tapped his left bicep with the fingers of his right hand.

"She's... gone back to warn Dad." Murray screwed his eyes closed. Silence.

The stupid fools!

Murray ventured to open his eyes and looked up at him. Rory remained standing in front of Murray, nodding soundlessly, a heat forming at the back of his neck.

What did they think they were doing?

"Thought so!" Rory exploded. "Fool has gone back in the pod which has only been proven to work once! You don't even know if she survived it!" He stepped closer to Murray and spoke directly into his face. "Do you realise you may have killed *our* wee sister?"

"It worked for Dad, it will work for her!" Murray justified.

"How do you ken it worked for Dad?"

"Mum told Kelly," Murray said.

"Aye, and did Mum mention that Kelly was there?" Rory asked.

Murray was silent. Rory raised his eyebrows at his brother. *Smart but not so smart. Hasn't thought of everything, has he?*

"Well?" Rory asked again.

"No, but she didn't tell Dad either, in case it changed their minds and they didn't go, or they went at the wrong time."

Rory closed his mouth tight, silent.

Calm yourself Rory, mind what your father always said to ye. He fixed his eyes on Murray's and flicked from one to the other, over and over, as he mentally counted to ten.

"*When* in time was Kelly sent to, then?" Rory finally asked.

"Six months after Dad went, so she missed the bad winter."

Rory continued shaking his head. "I hope she's okay. As to her mission, warning Dad, it is nae going to change the fact that we'll go back for him. Only make my job harder!"

"Are you going to tell them?" Murray asked.

"I don't know. But people will wonder where she is. We must try and stall it for as long as we can." Rory rubbed his forehead with both hands. He needed to remove the pressure building up there. "I don't enjoy being deceitful. But the Campbells have stolen something, again!"

Chapter Thirty-Five

The Present. Spring

Outside, the morning was white, calm, and serene. The quiet was palpable, the glare eye-aching as the early spring sun shone on the last snowfall of the season.

"March! 'In like a lion, out like a lamb.' Isn't that what they say?" Brendan stood at the window with Scott. It had snowed heavily the previous evening, another white-out. Brendan and Bec had said they would like to leave within the next few days; the overnight blizzard delayed them.

"We must have a farewell dinner." Caitlin pushed her shoulder against the backdoor, now jammed shut with the pile up of snow. "We can have roast venison. I'll get a cut from the shed and bring it in to defrost."

In the evening, they ate their last dinner with Bec and Brendan. A bright cloth covered the large kitchen table, and they served the meal on a miss-match of tableware. The roasted venison, well-seasoned with dried rosemary, Caitlin cooked in the Aga oven, the aromas having permeated the cottage for the past few hours. Roast potatoes and pumpkin went with the meat and tinned peas.

"Can't wait to get the spring planting started. Need some fresh greens. Getting tired of tinned vegetables. I'll make some cloches to get a head start." Caitlin's face was warm from her time of cooking on the hot range.

"Aye well, we have nae any glass cloches." Scott's eyes flicked with thought, his mind in creative overdrive. "But you can devise something from the transparent plastic we've been salvaging from everywhere we can think of, aye?"

"To our hosts." Brendan held up his glass filled with a dram of twenty-one-year-old Scotch.

"The beautiful Caitlin who always has a smile and looks like a million dollars no matter what she's wearing! Who works hard and has made this old crofter's cottage a home." Brendan lifted his glass higher as Caitlin smiled appreciatively. He continued, "And to her man Scott, without whom, I honestly believe, we would not have survived this winter. The huntsman and horseman extraordinaire and handyman, who can devise anything from junk and make it useful! Thank-you both for your hospitality and friendship. May we meet again and always be friends."

Glasses clinked as they touched.

"*Slainte Mhor,*" Scott said.

"*Slainte Mhor,*" echoed around the table.

Dogs barking and the frantic clucking of startled chickens halted their toast. Scruffy growled. Caitlin leaned down and held him by the collar. They rose from the table as one to the clamour erupting in the backyard. Scott retrieved his shotgun and ran to the backdoor. Caitlin looked out the kitchen window. In the yard, a pack of dogs attacked their chickens, their dark forms visible against the snow-covered ground. The dogs dug under the deeply buried chicken wire. They removed the chickens, one by one, from their sheltered hut. Feathers and blood sprayed in all directions. Growls from dogs and shrieks of chickens resounded in the night air.

"Oh, no you dinnae, ye bastards!" Scott said under his breath as he took aim.

Two shots rang out in quick succession with two dogs down. Brendan grabbed a handgun and dispatched three more. They both stayed near the backdoor of the cottage.

"Don't move too near those wild dogs. Aye? They'll go at ye, Bren," Scott told his companion at arms as he reloaded the shotgun.

The domestic dogs-gone-wild scattered and attempted retreat. Scott and Brendan moved from the doorway and pursued each one until they killed them all.

"Better be the last o' that lot!" Scott shouted after he shot and killed the final fleeing animal.

"They looked like pet dogs!" Bec stood next to Caitlin in the backdoor way as they peered after the men.

"They were," Scott replied. "But it's a thin veneer of domesticity that our wee pet doggies wear, that's for certain!"

"Remember that's how we lost our first goat," Caitlin said to Bec as she began to make her way to the chicken coup.

"No, lass." Scott stopped her. "Let me make sure there is nae any still lurking about. Dinnae want a repeat o' last time, aye?'

"What happened last time?" Bec asked.

"The pack leader attacked Scott," Caitlin explained. "Its teeth didn't sink into him. Only got the sleeve of his coat. But they're vicious animals now."

Scott declared the coast clear, then he and Brendan assessed the damage. The men threw the dog's bodies in a heap near the yard fence. They would burn them later. The rooster and two hens survived.

"I'll have to restart my poultry venture. Could've been worse," Caitlin said. "Scott, was that the same pack?"

"Dinnae ken. Need to make the lock to the hen-hut more secure. There's sure to be more than one pack. Wonder why they're moving back here," he said more to himself than anyone. "I'll check the boundaries tomorrow."

Scott and Brendan lit a fire to burn the dog and chicken bodies. Caitlin watched from the kitchen window as the flames lit up the backyard, melting the snow surrounding the pyre. Transfixed by the yellow and orange display, she absent-mindedly washed the dishes in the sink.

"Brendan and I have decided we'll leave tomorrow if the weather stays fine," Bec said as Caitlin handed her another plate to dry.

Caitlin had a twang of guilt at her relief that their friends were going. At times the cottage had been a small place for two couples over winter.

"I'll really miss you, Bec," she said.

Caitlin couldn't hold back the sob that escaped her throat. But it was time for their friends to move on. They were part of their future, according to Scott, and *not* their present.

"Me too." Bec returned the hug. "But we'll see you guys again, I'm sure. We'll make certain of it."

***

The next morning Scott stared at Caitlin as she stood outside the back-door next to Bec. Bags of their belongings hung from each arm. Caitlin looked at her friend, her eyebrows creasing in the middle. She did it when she tried to decipher her thoughts or feelings about something. Caitlin looked conflicted, but she was right. It was time for Bec and Brendan to leave.

"Bye. We'll miss you both." Caitlin wrapped her arms around Bec's shoulders.

Scott took Bec and Brendan to the edge of the property. They walked behind him, carrying what he couldn't place over Adam's back. Near the copse of Scots pine, Brendan helped him remove the camouflage from their vehicle. He'd offered them some petrol, but they declined, saying they had enough fuel and wouldn't take any of his. Scott helped them load their car, placing the citizen band radio in the back. He had given it to them to ensure they had contact with others. They planned to continue their journey north in search of a place suitable for them to settle and had promised to send word if they had found and set up such a place.

Caitlin stayed back at the cottage. Scott made Scruffy stay, as 'an early warning system', he liked to phrase it. Scott spent the next few hours checking the boundaries and inspecting his markers which he set to determine if anyone, man or beast, had passed. Scott found most of the markers buried by snow and needing resetting. He spent some time over them and peered at the surrounding countryside through the small telescope with 50-times and 100-times lenses, which he now carried with him for regular use.

On one such sweep, a group of men on foot headed toward the copse. He watched them for an hour. They were stationary, with no clear intent to move forward, so he returned to the cottage.

***

"Just want to go back and determine if they are staying or movin' on. I'll only be a wee while," Scott reassured Caitlin after explaining about the men.

"Okay. But could you please get the plastic you were talking about down from the roof space before you leave?" She gave a pleading smile. *It always seems to work.* "I'm eager to make my cloches."

Scott grimaced and hurriedly climbed up into the roof space. His legs dangled from the manhole in the ceiling as he passed the rolls of plastic to her. Scruffy began to bark frantically. Scott leaped from the roof space and looked out of the window into the back garden.

"No!" he snarled. "It's the same group of men I saw in our copse."

Scott retrieved his rifle from the kitchen bench where he'd left it on entering the cottage and took the safety off his handgun, while grabbing a magazine of ammunition from the pantry.

"Stay inside," he ordered her. "Do *not* come out. Stay down out of sight. If something happens to me, lock yourself in. *Don't* come out. Get the handgun and be ready to shoot to kill. Okay?"

Caitlin nodded mutely. Her heart pounded, the pulsation loud in her ears. Scott shut the door behind him. She breathed rapidly and had to focus to slow it down. She needed to find out what was going on.

"Good afternoon, gentlemen." Scott's voice came through the window. "What brings you to this part of Glencoe?"

Caitlin peered through the large old-fashioned keyhole of the backdoor. Scruffy stood beside his master, growling. The men were a shabby, thin, dirty, and savage looking group. Some of them carried guns, all were armed with knives or a sharp object of some sort. This dozen men appeared relaxed, except for one at the back of the group who was fidgety and restless, with eyes darting everywhere at once. He was not wearing a paisley shirt today, but his neck covered in tattoos was very familiar. Standing next to him, looking casually at everything from the damaged chicken coup to Scott's prized stallion, was another familiar face. Once again, a cloud of vapour surrounded the man as he exhaled. He held a silver square object in the palm of his hand. From their position, they could view the cottage windows.

Scott stood in front of the kitchen window, legs wide apart and shoulders braced. His hands tight on his rifle and his pistol tucked in his belt at the back. His imposing frame guarding his home and woman.

"Well, *helloo*." The tallest and skinniest of them answered as spokesman. "Nice wee set up ye have here. How long ye been here for then?"

"Long enough." Scott was curt. "How can I help you be on ye way?"

"Oh. I am surprised!" The man's accent was mild, that of a Lowlander. "I'd heard Highlanders were famous for their hospitality. And with this severe weather we've been having! I thought we'd be more welcome than this."

Scott did nothing to improve the welcome previously extended.

"Had problems with your chickens, I see." The man from the Boarders commented.

"Aye. Wild dogs. Will nae be a problem anymore." Scott indicated with his chin to the funeral pyre near the fence.

The smell of burnt flesh and the distinctive stench of singed animal fur still hung in the air. Ashes swirled as a slight breeze blew, lifting them into the air and the faces of the unwelcome guests.

"So, that's what you do with your unwanted guests, is it then?" The spokesman coughed and waved a swirl of ashes away from his eyes.

"How can I help you be on your way?" Scott repeated.

The leader raised his head at the unyielding nature of the man before him. "My friends and I have been travelling for some time and, well, we are quite hungry. Could you possibly spare us something to eat and then we will be on our way, as you wish?"

"You are on my property uninvited," Scott said. "I will give you some provisions and you will leave the way you came and not cross my boundaries again. Understood?"

The spokesman nodded slightly, never lifting his eyes from Scott, who backed into the cottage. Ducking low, Caitlin made her way to the pantry and gathered non-perishable foodstuffs for the men. Once the sack was half full, Scott took it and indicated for her to lock the door once he left. Scott returned outside to the men who had not appeared to move. Scruffy continued growling. She peered again through the wide keyhole.

Adam had wandered, nibbling grass. Scott whistled quietly. The horse returned to him and Scott mounted, still holding the half full sack of provisions and his rifle, never taking his eyes off the men.

"Ye will all stay put for a wee moment, while I give this to your friend here." He lifted the sack in his hand. "Then ye will all turn around and walk back the way ye came. I'll be watching ye all from a distance, aye."

Scott rode to the spokesman and handed him the sack.

"Thank-you, kind sir." The man took the sack from Scott. "Highland hospitality *is* all they say it is."

They turned and wandered off in the direction from which they had come. This was not the direct path, but across a nearby field and through a boundary fence covered in snow. Scott continued to follow them from a distance. When they were out of her sight, Caitlin carefully stepped out of the cottage and gazed in the direction they left.

She walked to the garden shed. Its door was slightly ajar. She peered in; some hooks on the wall were now empty. A shiver went down her spine. *How did they...?*

Scott soon returned.

"They appeared to be halting at the copse of Scots pine, so I indicated they were to continue," he said. "They were soon well out of sight. I viewed them through the telescope moving farther and farther away."

"They took some things." She pointed to the shed.

"What! When? I barely took my eyes off them, except for when I was in the house and then I was checking them through the windy' all the time," he shook his head. "What's missin'?"

"Shears, pruners and some other sharp things," she replied. "I don't like those men!"

"Aye," Scott's mouth hardened. "I dinnae think we are finished with those felons yet."

"I recognised two of them. They've been at the market in Fort William."

"Which two?" He asked.

"The one with the neck covered in tattoos and the guy who vaped," Caitlin said.

"Vaped? Oh, the lad surrounded by smoke?"

Caitlin nodded.

"Well, now." He held her by the shoulders. "I'll ride the boundaries regularly from now on. The weather is improving, and people are on the move. I'll be more vigilant with my surveillance of our property. When I'm away, you carry a weapon always and never be too far from the house where you will lock yourself in if you see a stranger approaching, or if you see me with someone you dinnae ken and if I look concerned or anything's amiss. Okay?"

She wrapped her arms around her husband's waist and held him tight, his solid frame pushing away the icy dread inside her.

"We'll be all right, Cait," he said. "Just need to be more careful."

***

Fort William

The door slammed shut behind him and the room filled with the sweet smell of strawberries.

"You're back at last." McSweeny turned in his chair. Brian's hood partially covered his face, and the last wisps of vapour surrounded him. "You saw the Lowlander at his headquarters then?"

"Aye." Brian put his square silver vape battery in his pocket and pulled his hood away from his face.

"Legit then?"

"Aye," Brian replied. "We stopped by a property on the way down."

"And?" McSweeny turned fully in his chair now. The kid sounded like he had something interesting to say.

"I've seen the guy who lives there before, at the sometimes-market here at Fort William." Brian smirked.

"And?" McSweeny raised his eyebrows. *Honestly, sometimes it's like extracting teeth.*

"I did nae see her, but she was there, must have been. It was the guy who she was with when she's been to the market." Brian's smirk broadened.

"And 'she' is?" McSweeny asked.

"The blonde chick."

The blonde chick—that beauty. At last she was in sight. McSweeny took his finger out of his mouth. He had no nails left to bite, anyway.

"Next time you are passing, you get her. Okay?"

"Aye, but the guy she's with won't let her go without a fight," Brian said.

"Be ready to fight then," McSweeny ordered.

Brian tilted his head and left. McSweeny looked at his fingers. He had bitten them to the quick and his thumbs bled again. What *was* he doing? He bit his lower lip. *It's the market.* He was doing what he had to do to survive. He had to round up more units before settlement of the deal. Plenty of people were gradually coming into debt, and now with no banks to bail them out with tide-you-over loans, loan sharks were everywhere. It was amazing what people would sell to settle a debt when their lives were threatened.

Chapter Thirty-Six

K elly landed with a squelch in the still inhabited farm. The cow pat in which the pod landed was at the feet of the cow who had produced it. The large full barn sheltered the animals from the last of the chilly weather. She broke open the pod and carefully removed herself and the duffle bag of cash from it, avoiding the warm waste products of the creatures living there. The scent was unavoidable though. The cattle lowed and scattered at the sudden arrival of the pod. Trying not to cause more of a stir amongst the cows, she searched for the nearest way out. The farmer, alerted by his animals' frantic bellowing, walked over to the stall Kelly had exited moments before. She scuttled out of sight behind a stack of hay bales as the flannel-check shirted farmer greeted his cows.

"What's going on the noo' ladies? There, there. Och!" The farmer's muffled voice continued as he bent low. "What's this again? Another one! Where do these thingmys keep comin' frae?"

Kelly grinned and silently slipped out of the enormous barn and started her journey to Fort William. A fresh fall of snow covered the ground. It wasn't deep and didn't hinder her progress any. If her estimates were correct, in clear weather, it would take her five days to walk to Glencoe where she would search for the crofter's cottage that Aunty Bec had described. Kelly hoped the weather would improve as she hadn't come prepared for the harsh winter that had supposedly just finished.

You'd better be right, brother.

Kelly trudged through the ankle-deep snow that still lay. The sun's warmth melted it to slush. Her wet shoes made heavy going. The first day's travel south was slower than she had predicted. Snow still dusted the moss-covered dry stone walls that edged the winding road. Dirty mounds of mushy half melted snow skirted the narrow road in places. The wind blew cold across her face as it passed over the hills covered in the white remains of winter. That evening she made herself a shelter out of bracken ferns in the forest near Beauly. Kelly had kept close to the river and settled down to a cool night's sleep after a dinner of cold rations.

The next two days she travelled toward, and then alongside Loch Ness. She'd never seen it in real-life, only in pictures from old calendars and magazines. Kelly's parents never took them on family trips. They said people used to go on outings to tourist attractions. But the world wasn't safe enough for anything like that anymore. Life was too dangerous outside of the Community. She stayed acutely aware of her surroundings and the other people nearby.

The sun shone off the water of the dark, deep loch. Her parents had told her of the Loch Ness Monster, that it was probably more than one animal—possibly a plesiosaur pair who had managed to reproduce and continue the line. Undisturbed for the millennia, successive plesiosaur pairs would have kept the line of 'Loch Ness Monsters' going. The cold, deep waters of the loch were ideal.

"I wonder," she said aloud as she admired the view from the ruins of Urquhart Castle.

"Ow!" Distracted by so much to look at, she had walked into an old piece of iron pole which had been part of the information stands dotted around the base of the castle ruins. Kelly pressed her hand onto her leg. The slash from the sharp pole began to sting. It was a deep cut to her shin. Her mother would *make* her wash it. Kelly spent time getting to the loch's edge where she washed her cut shin and then dressed it from the supplies in her small first aid kit. First aid reminded her of mother. Her eyes stung, and her vision went blurry as she wound the bandage around her leg.

Kelly walked faster and tried to not let her scenic surroundings distract her from her mission. It was taking too long to get to Fort William. That night, she went deep into the woods beside the road away from other people. She snared a squirrel and cooked it over an open fire and settled next to the coals for warmth under a clear night sky. The stars were her view as she lay trying to sleep; her reflections of her journey so far kept her awake. The people she'd encountered appeared to be eager to be about their own business and not bothered by a youth travelling on his own. Her boyish figure and plain features had made her unremarkable.

Kelly started her journey early the next morning, determined to get to Fort William by the end of that very day. She set herself a hard pace and reached the outskirts of Fort William by late evening. There were a lot of houses along the road now. She'd never seen so many. The light from candles and lanterns burned in most but coming to a small house off the road she found it was empty. Cold and slightly damp, but empty, and a sheltered place to stay the night.

Kelly lay on the carpeted floor. For the first time on her journey, the coolness of uncertainty edged her thoughts. She'd learned in school that people lived in large towns at this time, but she'd never actually seen one, only photographs. Members of their Community were convinced towns were places to avoid, and now she was about to walk into one.

Kelly must have fallen soundly asleep as she woke to daylight what seemed only moments later. The cut to her shin was hot with the edges red and angry, and there was pus on the dressing when she changed it. And it throbbed. She packed her belongings and snuck out the backdoor.

Kelly made her way toward the road. There was a great number of people walking the road to Fort William's centre. Their conversations revealed that there was to be an impromptu market that day. She passed a large single storey building where lots of people had slept the night. They still lay on cardboard boxes broken and laid out flat, their bags of belongings beside them. The building had a sign—Fort William ScotRail. Rail...a railway station. Trains! She'd seen photos of trains on calendars, but there wasn't one anywhere.

Kelly followed the crowd past tall stone buildings, dark stone with black stains on most of the fronts. She walked on the concrete footpaths beside dark bitumen roads and travelled a long way past groups of these tall, many storeyed buildings. She craned her neck to look up at the windows; most of them broken or boarded. The streets were damp and scattered along the footway at the side was something that looked and smelled like poo.

The crowd at the market was in poor shape. The majority were thin and hungry, dressed shabbily and needing a wash. Compared to these, the people she lived with in the Invercharing Community were in excellent health.

Some looked friendly, most looked desperate, and many had weapons. There was a group of a dozen men who stayed close together. They all had weapons of some sort. The guy who looked like their leader was a skinny young man who blew out smoke, lots of it hung around him. He looked in her direction, but not for long, as Kelly moved herself out of his sight and lost herself in the crowd. She remembered her father had often mentioned people smugglers.

Making her way around the stalls, Kelly bought hot chips and gravy, which she wolfed down hungrily. *So good.* It warmed her insides. There was a van which sold medicines. Kelly made a beeline for it as she might find antibiotics. Her mum said they used to sell them as tablets, not make it from bread like Aunty Bec did. The youngish woman sitting in the back of the van, dressed in black, had heavy dark makeup around her eyes. The woman appeared ghoulish, but it didn't put Kelly off.

"Antibiotics you say?" the woman asked as she looked at Kelly's shin wound.

"Aye. Do you have any? I want to get on top of this," Kelly asked.

It would be black market, like everything else at this market.

"Aye, here you are. Erythromycin would be best for a skin wound." The woman handed her a week's course. "That will be fifty pounds please, lass." The deep purple lip-sticked mouth emphasised the 'lass.'

Kelly reluctantly handed over the money.

"Be careful, lass," the woman said. "There are bad men around here. I've seen 'em looking at youngsters such as yourself. Be wary, aye? They kidnap girls and sell them for slaves. Not joking. It's rife the noo'." The kohl outlined eyes held a stern expression, then the expression changed to a curious one. "You seem familiar. Do you have family around here?"

"My parents live nearby," Kelly answered. "They've been to this market. You may have met them."

"Och. No!" the woman said with recognition in her voice. "You're no' related to Scott are ye?"

"Do you know Scott's surname?" Kelly asked. Caution made her wary; even if this weird-looking woman seemed friendly, she must be suspicious of everyone.

"Aye. Campbell. He's got a funny wee wifey. She's way too young for a man like that. She's not your mither, for she's no' much older than yoursel'. You must be his from another woman, aye? But you're his all right,' she said with a tilt to her head. "I ken it by your attitude as well as your colouring."

Kelly smiled. This woman may be her best chance of further pinpointing her parent's location.

"Would you have seen them lately?" Kelly asked.

"To be honest now, I have nae seen them since afore the winter. They live a fair way from here by foot, so they may not have been wantin' to venture oot. It bein' a harsh winter an' all. But Glencoe's easy enough to find now down the A82. I ken they've vandalised the signs but it's the only road south. Just as well for you, aye? You no' seen your faither for a while then?"

Kelly thanked the woman and moved on, grateful for the information. She couldn't spend all day talking. Kelly continued out of the market and through Fort William on to the A82. The late afternoon sun was casting tall shadows on the road. Her whole body lagged. Her journey had been a long one and today's walk was no exception. This was a strange place—a city, so big and full of people she didn't know. A pang of longing started in the centre of her being. Her parents had made a safe place for her and many people. From what she'd seen so far, the world outside was *not* a great place. The longing was growing with the thought of her mum and dad. She had to find them, and soon.

Sparse but constant traffic passed. Those market attendees fortunate enough to have a vehicle, and fuel to run it, passed infrequently. Most vehicles were of the horse-drawn kind, all making their way south. The unfamiliar scent of petrol-exhaust fumes wafted in Kelly's face when the motor vehicles over-took her. They had one or two vehicles at the Community, but they used them rarely.

People travelled in the same direction and Kelly heard footsteps behind her, as there had been for most of the day. The gentle clanging of metal now accompanied them. The shadows of those following her nudged at her feet and she briefly turned to look. She picked up her pace as behind were two men from the group of well-armed men at the market. Kelly's mind cleared as she removed her knife from her belt.

"Oh well, pretty one," the voice came from behind her. Kelly flicked a glance back. There was a lad with tattoos up his throat. He was trying a friendly approach. She lengthened her stride.

"Come now. We just want to talk to ya," his companion joined him.

Kelly picked up her pace. Rapid footsteps came behind her. A quick glance back confirmed it was her pursuers. She also ran, but not as fast as the young men who were gaining on her.

Kelly spun, and in the same motion, threw her knife. It hit the tattooed pursuer in the left shoulder. He screamed in pain and astonishment. His accomplice stood still. Kelly ran and gained some ground. Her surprise offensive move had only angered the uninjured youth. He sprinted toward her. So intent on her would-be abductors, Kelly hadn't noticed a van travelling behind her and her pursuers. It now accelerated and, knocking her closest threat over, pulled up next to her. The passenger door flew open.

"Get in lass! Quick!" It was the woman from the black market pharmacy.

Kelly sprinted to the van and jumped in the front seat. The van skidded away. The side mirror's view showed the injured lad sprawled in the middle of the road—his friend making his painful way toward him, still with her knife in his shoulder.

"You okay?" The dark rimmed made-up eyes of the pharmacist were wide and round. "Do you realise how close you came to them capturing ye!"

"Thank-you." Kelly's voice was quiet. She *was* aware and very grateful. Her journey back in time to her parents almost wasted but for the actions of this weird-looking woman. "I mean it. Thank-you."

The pharmacist nodded and checked in the rear vision mirror for her would-be slavers.

"That's got rid of them," she said. "I think I know where to drop you off close to the place where your father lives. Well, where I thought he lived last time I saw him before the winter we've had."

"Could you take me there, please?" Kelly asked.

Chapter Thirty-Seven

Pale beams of early spring sunlight shone through their small bedroom window, hitting the dust motes which danced around the room otherwise unacknowledged. Caitlin lay on top of Scott, the length of her naked body stretched out on his, her head on his chest—her favourite place.

"I love hearing your heartbeat. The rise and fall of your rib cage is relaxing too." Her voice was soft and husky as she spoke into his sternum while chest-hair tickled her face.

"Ye were rather relaxed last night, lass," Scott said, "You let yourself go all right. Lack of neighbours, aye?"

"You, Mr Campbell, weren't silent on the matter, either!" Caitlin raised her head and looked him in the eyes. "I love you. What is it you say? *Always and forever only yours.*" She brushed her lips softly against his mouth. "I love your blue eyes. You're quite handsome for an old man." She flinched. The gentle slap on her buttocks stung. She ignored it. "Except for the beard! Winter's over now. When is *it* going?" She gave his beard a tug with her fingers. Disregarding Scott's pained expression, Caitlin continued, "And I love your Highland accent, which apparently, I've said *before* in the future. Ow! Leave my bottom alone! You've already had your fill of it. We should get up and feed our animals." She lifted herself off him but struggled to extricate his hands from her bottom.

"Love you too, always and forever. And *you* said it first, my beautiful wife," Scott whispered in her ear as he released his hold on her.

After they had breakfasted, dressed and fed the animals, Scott rode off on Adam to check the boundaries, his daily, sometimes twice daily, task. He'd go at various times of the day in case he was watched, and any routine noted. He made sure there was no set routine, and he varied his route. Today he started at the back of their property and worked his way to the east boundary, where the unwelcome group of armed men had gained access. The snow had melted, and the ground was wet and semi-flooded in parts and very muddy as Adam's hooves sloshed through it.

Scott came to the small wood of Scots pine. It was the nearest point of entry from the closest road. A figure moved behind a tree. This person had got close without him noticing, until now. He kicked Adam to a gallop as he raised his rifle to his shoulder.

"Show yourself!" Scott called. "Drop any weapons you have! *Now*!"

The person threw a bow, a quiver full of arrows and a handgun, then stepped out slowly from behind the tree, with hands in the air. Scott looked down the double-barrel of his rifle at his youngest daughter. He lowered it at once.

"Kelly?" He blinked a few times. "Kelly? Is that you, Kelly?" he shouted as he swung his right leg over and jumped off Adam. The black horse snorted.

"Dad!" Kelly ran toward him.

They met, and he held her close in a warm hug.

"Cannae believe it! How'd ye...? Why d'you...? What on earth are ye doing here, child!" Scott held her by the shoulders and tried not to shake her. "Ye are here, so ye have come through a time machine which may not have worked for yoo!" Bending lower to look her directly in the eye, he continued his tirade. "What if it had nae, lass? Ye'd be dead, child! Ye should nae ha' done it!" He yelled, shaking his head, trying to stop the alarm welling up inside him.

"But Dad, I came to warn you! You're in danger. They're sending some-one back to get you."

"What! Surely no'. Why?" Scott shook his head.

"Because you stole a time journey," Kelly replied.

"They will actually send someone?" His skin above his nose bunched, tightening his brow. "What? To arrest me? They cannae take me back, so they'll be trapped here. Wha's the point o' that?"

"Eventually they will do return journeys," Kelly said. "So, when they can, they'll come for you."

"Really? It will take years of developing the technology—findin' the technology—and the resources." Scott put his arm across Kelly's shoulder as they walked side by side toward Adam. "They would've forgotten about me by then."

"Well, Angela is adamant about it."

"Angela?" he asked. "Why? What's she doing?"

"She's on the Chief Council now. Thinks she has something to prove. Like justice has to be done no matter who it is."

"Well. She's right there," Scott conceded. "But my own daughter is 'on my case'?" He found *that* hard to digest.

"Yeah, Dad. You've embarrassed her. Murray says the power's gone to her head."

Scott hugged his youngest daughter again, then grabbed Adam's reins. Leadership, power, all those things Caitlin spent hours discussing with Angela. *Was she no' listening?*

"Well, I cannae say I'm no' disappointed in my eldest havin' a vendetta against me, but I suppose she's just doing her job. You must have had help," Scott said after a pause. "Ye ha' stolen a time journey too, daughter o' mine!"

"Yeah, well, Murray helped me."

"Oh, no," Scott's shoulders tensed. "We will be in big trouble. He'll get it in the neck for you back there."

"No, Angus helped us," Kelly said. "And they know how to cover up. Hopefully, they have."

Still hugging Kelly, Scott shook his head, his eyes staring. How will they not miss her not being there in the future? What will happen now she was with them, here and now? For she could not return.

"What's in there? Is it money?" Scott pointed to the duffle bag she carried.

"Aye. Cash," Kelly said.

"There were two bags o' cash waiting for me in the pod afore I left," he recollected. "Did you put them in there?"

"No, Murray did."

"You gave me Mum's ring, just before I left." Scott spoke over her head. "So, you and Murray knew what I was about to do? She told yoo, aye?"

Kelly looked up at him. "Yep. She asked us to do those two things for you."

"Your mother knew I was coming back, and she never said a word to me, all those years." Scott hugged his daughter and swayed gently, enjoying their embrace. Then he tensed. "How will I explain this to your mother?"

Scott rode Adam to the crofter's cottage via the back route so as not to pass by the kitchen window as usual. Kelly rode behind him on the stallion. Once in the stable, they dismounted Adam.

"Now you stay here. Brush him down for me, will ye? I'll break this news to your mother." Scott turned to go, then turned back, the discomfort in his stomach surely showing on his face. "Don't know how this meeting will go. Mind, your mother is nearly forty years younger than when you last saw her."

"Okay."

"Dinnae ken how long I'll be afore I return for ye." His grin was tight.

"It's okay, Dad. I'm not going anywhere." Kelly smiled.

***

Caitlin stoked the fire under the Copper to heat water for the weekly wash. She looked up when Scott entered the laundry.

"You're back early. Any trouble?"

Scott stood close and pressed his lips to hers for a while.

"I have a surprise for yoo," he whispered in her ear when he released her mouth from his.

"Oh well, I'll need to do the washing first," Caitlin said. "Anyways, did I not tire you out enough last night? Honestly Scott Campbell, you are insatiable!"

"No, I dinnae mean *that*. I have a surprise for ye. Just dinnae ken how to tell ye." His shoulders drooped.

"Whatever's the matter, Scott?"

Scott shook his head. "Ye'll no' believe me but," he took a breath, "here goes. Kelly our youngest is here," he finished quickly, his accent thick with his stress.

Caitlin stared back at him. Long moments passed.

Scott raised his eyebrow. "Did ye hear me, lass?"

"Yes," she swallowed. "Our youngest daughter, the one you are closest to, is here."

Scott nodded.

"Are you sure you're not just missing her too much?" she asked, frowning a touch.

"No, Cait, I'm nae imagining things! Kelly has come back through time, for to be with us."

"But why?" Caitlin asked.

"Well, apparently, they're after me for the time journey I stole," he finished very quietly.

She did a double blink.

"They are coming back in time to arrest you for stealing a time journey and she's come to, what, protect you?" her voice rose. "Misdirect them? What?"

"Probably all o' that, aye. Kelly says she came back to warn me. But she'll most likely stick around. She's a handy lass to have. Good with knives, like her mother."

Scott sprinted to the stable after directing her to the living area to wait.

Caitlin sat on the green sofa near the fireplace. The room was warm, as it had been all winter long. The smell of smoke, ash, and raw wood pervaded the room and its contents. She looked at her hands in her lap. Kelly was their youngest. Another time traveller in the family. Must be brave like her father. Footsteps coming through the backdoor disturbed her. Scott walked in with a tall slim teenage girl dressed in army camouflage, her hazel eyes and long light-brown hair matched her attire.

Kelly was nothing like herself in her teens. Not a trace of makeup in sight. Caitlin rose to meet them, staring intently at her youngest daughter, blinking often, trying to hold back tears developing from the confusion of emotions within her.

Kelly barely reached the doorway when she spied Caitlin. Running toward her, Kelly burst into tears and enveloped her in a bear-like hug and appeared to be not for letting go. Caitlin returned the hug and raised her eyebrows at Scott. She had no words; the swirling emotions within her became warmth and an inexplicable love for the girl who now held her tight. Kelly cried loudly for a few moments.

"Are ye all right lass? Your mother's pleased to see you," Scott's tone revealed his concern. Kelly's crying continued. Scott removed Kelly from Caitlin, sat the girl on the sofa, and put his arm around her shoulder. "Whatever's wrong, Kelly? I thought ye'd be happy when ye saw her."

Kelly looked up at her father through tear-soaked eyes. "You said to remember Mum's almost forty years younger than when I saw her last. Well, it's not just that. When I saw her last, she was dead! I'm so glad to have my mum back, whatever age she is!"

Kelly returned to Caitlin and resumed the hug. Over her daughter's shoulder, Caitlin shook her head imperceptibly at Scott.

Kelly finally settled, and Scott made a pot of tea. Caitlin examined her daughter.

"You're so like your father!" she said. "Am I in there somewhere?"

"Oh, Mum, I love you. I've missed you so much," Kelly answered through more tears.

"You were there when I died?" She ventured. Kelly nodded. "No teenager should have to do that. I'm so sorry, Kelly." Caitlin put her arm around Kelly as she sat beside her.

"Mum, I spent a lot of time with you when you were sick. We got close. I wouldn't have missed it for the world."

Caitlin started crying silent tears. They weren't tears of sadness. They were tears of pride at the young woman she had just met—the impressive young woman who called her 'Mum'.

Chapter Thirty-Eight

The Future

"So where is she, then?" Angela asked in officious tones. "Where is our wee sister?" she asked Murray once more. "I haven't seen her for days. No. Correction. *None* of us, except *you*, have seen her for days!"

Murray recalled the plan he and Rory had devised. "Well, you know we have cousins near Glencoe?"

"Aye. Not that we've ever seen them. Come to think of it, I've never even spoken to them, but do go on," Angela said in her most encouraging but impatient voice.

"Kelly's taken Mum's death badly. She was pretty close to her before she passed," Murray said.

He and Rory had tried to put as much truth into their lie. 'Makes it more believable' Rory had said.

"Well, she was so distraught one day," Murray continued, "that Rory suggested she stay with them for a wee while. He had some things to get at the sometimes market at Fort William. They met them there, and they took Kelly home. That was on Saturday."

Rory had, in fact, had an errand to run at the Fort William market, and so they incorporated this into their plan, as cover.

"When is she returning then?" Angela asked.

Murray shrugged. "How do I know? I'm really not my sister's keeper, despite what you all think!"

***

After two weeks, Angela, concerned her youngest sister may overstay her welcome, hailed the Community at Fort William on the citizen band radio. She asked to speak to her cousins.

"Oh aye. I'll get him for you. Ahh. 'Over'. I ken I should say that," an elderly man on the other end of the Citizen Band radio said.

Moments later, another man's voice came through on the hand piece.

"Hi Angela, I'm Alistair. I'm married to your cousin, Kim. She's busy at present, but can I help you? Over." A man with traces of a Canadian accent and who sounded middle-aged was at the other end.

"Hello. I'm Angela Campbell. It's nice to meet you, even if it is by radio. Is it still okay for my sister to be there? Over."

"Kelly's fine," he said. "What a wonderful girl! She can stay as long as she wants. She's been an immense help here. Quite a wide skill set. She's fitted in fine. We're quite falling in love with her here! Over," Alistair's voice oozed enthusiasm.

"Oh, well, if she isn't any bother. Over."

"None what-so-ever. Over." Alistair's reply was quick and emphatic.

"May I speak with my wee sister? Is she around? Over," Angela asked.

"Okay, one moment while I get her. Over."

The radio went quiet for a brief time and then Kelly came to the radio.

"Hi, Angela. How are you? Over." Kelly sounded tired.

"I'm fine," Angela spoke into the handset. "How are you? Over."

"Good thanks. Over."

"You enjoying yourself there? Not causing trouble? Over."

"No. Over."

"You want to stay there for a wee while longer? Over." Angela's grip on the handset tightened.

"Aye. Over."

"You helping out with the work and no' free loading? Over." Angela's voice rose.

"Aye. Over."

Angela, impatient with Kelly's monosyllabic answers and all the 'Overs', finished the conversation.

"Okay then. You thank your cousins for me, and I'll speak to you again sometime. Over."

"Aye, I will. Bye. Over," and Kelly was gone.

***

At their evening meal that night, Angela mentioned she'd hailed their cousins on the citizen band radio. Murray paused and briefly exchanged glances with Rory. He and Rory had made a gamble and were about to find out if it had paid off.

"You mean our cousins in Glencoe who we've never met?" Ceilidh asked.

"Aye. He's a Canadian, I think," Angela reported. "So, Kelly's welcome there for as long she likes, from all accounts."

"How's it we have a Canadian cousin?" Brendan asked.

"Married to our cousin, a relative of Mum's Aunt May and Uncle Kieran." Rory gave the link. "Mum often spoke to them by radio. They'll be missing her too. Maybe Kelly's a comfort to them, and vice versa."

No one asked further questions about Kelly's sojourn with her cousins. Murray and Rory walked casually to their rooms together wearing expressions of relief that their gambit had paid off, shared only between themselves.

"When you go back," Murray whispered to Rory. "Don't know who you should prime for that, but you'd better warn them."

Chapter Thirty-Nine

The Present

The day after Kelly arrived, so did Spring. Caitlin stood outside the backdoor, her back turned to the sun, heat easing her shoulder blades. Scott walked out into the sunshine, his rifle over his shoulder with Kelly not far behind him.

"Did you have any trouble on your way here?" Scott turned to Kelly. "How did ye find us, anyways?"

Kelly recounted her journey to Fort William and her meeting the black market pharmacist.

"Oh yes, that Goth would know anything of your father's from fifty paces!" Caitlin couldn't prevent the annoyance present in her tone.

Kelly looked at her.

"Dinnae mind your mither." Scott brushed her comment aside. "I'm glad the black market pharmacist recognised you as mine. Helped you the rest of the way did she, then?"

Kelly hesitated.

"Tell me everything, lass," Scott demanded.

Kelly described the encounter with the two men who would have abducted her if it weren't for the pharmacist's intervention.

"We have a lot to thank the pharmacist for," Scott said. "But we also must be more alert. Ye say the lads who were attempting to grab ye, were part o' that group ye saw at Fort William?" Kelly nodded. "They sound verra much like the group o' men that came here casing the joint. Kenned we had nae finished with them." Scott's eyebrows drew together. "They'll be back. Both dangers are real. Slavers abducting my two beautiful women, and the retriever from the future getting me. We can never afford to drop our guard."

"We'll do the boundaries with you today then?" Caitlin looked up at Scott, anticipating a day out riding in the spring sunshine.

They saddled up the three horses, mounted and made their way back to the burn, their favourite fishing spot. The snow was melting high upon the mountain peaks and their gentle burn was now a raging torrent of swirling brackish, brown, ice-cold water. With their speech lost in the water's roar, they retreated a way back where Caitlin and Kelly found rocks protruding from the heather and sat. Scott squatted in front of them while the horses grazed lazily near-by and Scruffy frantically sniffed everything.

"So, what are we going to do, Dad? Someone will come back for you when they finally have the know-how." Kelly plucked a sprig of heather and lifted it to her nose.

"Aye, I ken. I also ken it could be anytime." Scott faced Caitlin. "So, we have to be ready."

"Which means?" Caitlin prompted.

"We must always be alert to strangers."

"But we *are*." She pressed her lips tight, holding in the frustrated words which threatened to spill out but would do no one any good.

"More so," Scott said. "We must pack and be ready to flee on horseback at a moment's notice. Need to go east, not north. They'll come from there and will expect us to return that way, as I ken it well. Most likely, whoever comes will be someone we know."

Their eldest daughter, Angela, believed she was doing the right thing. Angela was a perfect stranger to Caitlin, but she and Scott would bring her up to be the responsible leader one day, right? Was this a consequence of that, and Scott's actions?

"Always looking over our shoulder. Is that how life is to be?" Caitlin's brow tightened in a frown.

"Afraid so. It's Kelly's birthday soon." Scott tilted his head in Kelly's direction. "Sixteen!"

"Wow, I'm only six years older than you!" Caitlin turned to Kelly. The bizarre sensation returned.

"Yeah. It's weird!" Kelly gazed back at her. "You are so beautiful, Mum."

"Thank-you."

"You've always been beautiful," Kelly said. "Even when you were sick, you were still beautiful. Everyone said so."

Caitlin lowered her eyes and scrunched her mouth, a slight blush warming her cheeks. Scott was silent, his attention still on both women.

"No wonder Dad had to fight those three men for you." Kelly spoke as if it was common knowledge.

"What?" Caitlin raised her eyebrows and her cheeks cooled.

Kelly looked at Scott. "Didn't you tell Mum?"

Scott shook his head, avoiding eye contact with her.

"Tell me," Caitlin stared at him directly.

Scott's mouth was a thin line.

"Go on, Dad. Tell Mum," Kelly ordered.

Scott looked from one woman to the other and shuffled his weight from one foot to the other as he remained in a squat. An expression of resignation appeared. He wouldn't win this one.

"Well, you ken I was a scrawny youth when I arrived at the Community?" Scott paused.

Caitlin nodded. So did Kelly on the rock beside her. Kelly wouldn't be hearing the story for the first time, but she seemed eager for the retelling.

"There were a few men in the Invercharing Community who believed they had more right to the beautiful Caitlin's affections than I." Scott fixed his gaze on Caitlin.

She raised her eyebrows once more, encouraging him to continue.

"Well," he said, "they challenged me. All three of them."

"Aye and they still talk about it today! How he fought off three men with knives all at once! Oops sorry, Dad. Spoilers." Kelly pressed her tongue between her lips.

"There was fighting amongst our community members? With weapons?" Caitlin double blinked. "I can scarcely believe it. I thought we were a peaceful group. Or will be."

"Well, they were deadly earnest, *mo chroi*," Scott confirmed. "They approached me all at once in the forecourt outside the main building, seriously going at me with knives and switch blades. You did nae ken what all the hullaballoo was aboot till you came oot o' the building and saw everyone crowding around me. The three strongest men in the place surrounded me. All wanting *you*. My arrival had only brought it to a head, ye ken. I won, being younger and more agile, and having had more recent experience of fending for mysel' in the big bad world out there. They cut me. Aye, they cut me. It was the first time ye sewed me up, lass." He smiled. "But I disarmed them and kicked the crap out o' them, if you'll pardon my French, ladies. They never challenged me again. About anything!"

"That is *so* medieval!" Caitlin said. *Unbelievable*.

"But *so* romantic Mum! They talk about it still." Kelly looked adoringly at her father.

"You're proud of your father, aren't you?"

"And you, Mum," Kelly corrected her. "You're both, like, super-hero material. You're both great leaders."

"Your father there," Caitlin directed her gaze at Scott, "always says *I'm the great leader in the future.*"

"He's being modest, as usual. You're a team. You're one and the same. You're nothing without each other." Kelly then chewed her lower lip.

Caitlin locked gazes with her husband. Kelly's comment reminded her of her death in the future, the springboard for Scott's journey to the past, to be with her once again.

Boy, I love this man.

Scott's gaze softened his features and his lips gently curved at the corners.

Returning to the cottage, after Scott did his check to ensure there were no intruders, Caitlin and Kelly started the spring plantings in the vegetable garden. Scott turned over the ground and Kelly broke up the sods, while Caitlin sorted the seeds they'd acquired.

Adam had been attentive to the Highland horse mare while they had been out on their ride. Scott went to the horses to check if the mare was coming into season. He walked back to them with a grin filling his face. She glanced at him.

He's chuffed.

"Carrots, onions, spring onions, beetroot, swede, tomatoes..." Kelly went through the list of seeds to plant.

"Oh, no! Too soon for tomatoes," she advised.

"Ladies," Scott interrupted. "I'll get Adam to cover the mare soon!"

"That horse of yours looks like most of ours, Dad."

"Well, that's because he's the sire of most of them." There was great pride in his voice.

"Don't 'count your chickens'," Caitlin reminded him.

"Aye. Well, plenty of time."

***

Caitlin sat on the outside bench underneath the kitchen window with the warmth of the afternoon sun on her face. She liked to catch the last of the sunshine before it descended behind the mountains to the west. Her muscles ached from another day of weeding and staking tomatoes and runner beans. Kelly often surprised her; for a teenager she was hardworking and never refused a job. She appeared to have spent a lot of time with animals and was a *natural*. Kelly was a natural at other things as well. Caitlin's cheeks tightened and her mouth tugged, and she tried to relax as Scott walked with Kelly from the chicken coup. Kelly held more eggs in her hands.

"These chickens are happy, Mum. Look at this." The smooth shells shone in the sunlight.

Scott came to a stop behind Kelly. "And what is the grin on yoor face all about, woman?"

"Nothing." Caitlin's face grew tight again, all attempts to hide her grin failing.

"What, Mum?" Kelly's voice held a laugh, Caitlin's smile was infectious. Scott glared at her.

"If you really want to know"—Caitlin sheltered her eyes with her hand from the lowering sun— "I'm glad there is someone who can finally slaughter your father at chess."

Scott shook his head slowly, a knowing smile on his face.

"You help us all the time with the animals in the future, Kelly? And you're not texting your friends all the time you're doing it." Caitlin asked.

She recalled a summer trying to teach her younger cousins to ride. It was difficult with their focus on the glowing rectangular object in their hands and often interrupted by selfie-shots. Her comment slipped out before she had thought it through.

"Texting?" Kelly raised her eyebrows in question.

Beside her, Scott's smile continued as he tilted his head.

"So, you've never text and you truly don't know what Facebook is?" Caitlin watched as Kelly maintained a bewildered expression. "Twitter? YouTube? Snapchat?" Kelly shook her head in the negative for each one.

"Apart from the fact that there is nae wee phones to *text* with, Kelly was too busy learning how to ride and use weapons to have time for any 'o that." Scott stood tall beside Kelly. "She's been out with the Militia a couple 'o times. Plenty o' bandits around to deal with."

"*You* let her ride with you when you were after bandits!" Caitlin's jaw dropped. "But she's just a girl!"

"Aye. But I've trained her in weaponry. She's a soldier in the making," Scott replied.

"But she's just a girl!" Caitlin repeated.

"Mum, I'm okay," Kelly said. "The other militia members always made sure I was safe."

"But she's a mean fighter Cait, you'd be proud o' her." Scott put his arm around Kelly's shoulders.

***

Caitlin rode the gelding toward the target. Scott insisted she became proficient in throwing while riding. The last two passes had found her knives in the ground and none in the bale of hay covered in the hand-drawn bullseye.

Focus.

Flick. *Got it!*

"Och! Well done! At last." Scott's laugh didn't hide his comment.

"I heard that," Caitlin said.

"Aye well, you're getting there Cait. Oot the way, Kelly's comin'."

Caitlin wheeled the gelding out of Kelly's path as a *thwack, thwack* came behind her and Kelly rode past on the mare. Caitlin turned. In the red centre of the hand-drawn bullseye were two arrows, close together.

"Wow!" Caitlin looked at her girl.

Kelly cantered the horse around for another go, her quiver of arrows sat by her leg from a belt around her waist. Kelly held two more ready in her right hand as she held the bow in her left. She guided her horse with her legs.

"The arrows are so close together," Caitlin said.

"Kelly uses the old Mongols technique." Scott smiled and nodded. "Found it in a book." He raised his eyebrows. "Works well, aye?"

"Yes. Pretty awesome." Caitlin replied.

Kelly *was* the good fighter her father had said she was.

Scott strapped an old scythe to a shortened rake handle. In the middle of the medium-sized grassed-area near the vegetable patch, he forced the post of a straw dummy into the ground. Particles of straw of various sizes floated through the air. Caitlin's nose tickled, threatening a sneeze.

"What do you propose to do with your scarecrow?" Caitlin asked Scott.

"It's a mark, isn't it, Dad?" Kelly answered for Scott.

"Aye, he's my enemy and I'm going tae kill him." Scott's head was at a tilt and his mouth pursed.

Scott mounted Adam and wheeled him around for a charge. He held his reins loosely in his left hand and his makeshift sword firmly in his right. Once he had gained a distance, he turned Adam sharply. His focus was entirely on the straw man he had constructed for this purpose. He kicked Adam to a canter, then once more to a gallop. By the time Scott reached his target, his sword pointed low, and he held it tight. It connected with his intended target, jolting Scott's shoulder only slightly and decapitating the straw dummy.

"You look like a medieval knight, Dad!" Kelly exclaimed.

"I'm concerned regarding all this violence, Scott," Caitlin said.

"What have I told ye, Caitlin? There are bad people out there! If those men come back, they'll attempt to take you. I've told ye I'm serious about your protection, Kelly's as well now." Scott jumped off Adam and approached her. "Dinnae be feeling guilty on me again. It is imperative that we defend ourselves, even if it means killing them. It will be us or them. What do ye want Cait?"

"I understand where you are coming from," she said. "But it feels like cold-blooded murder, that's all." There was a niggle of guilt and an ache of sorrow in her heart, that now her life was like this.

"Aye," he responded, turning on her. "And it will be *your* cold-blooded murder, if you are nae able to defend yoursel' and be willing, and able, to kill if ye have tae. Cait, it's a war now."

Chapter Forty

One Year After The Stock Market Crash

Caitlin wiped the sweat off her brow. Her top stuck to her chest so she pulled it away and flapped it so the air cooled her a little. Her face was warm from the Aga. Caitlin had finished preserving the apples which had grown in abundance and placed the jars to cool on the spare shelf in the pantry. Tomatoes sat in the plastic box by the backdoor. She would make them into sauce before they started to rot. The Scottish summer had been warm and long, and Kelly had helped her with the vegetable patch, as she always did. It surprised Kelly that the tomatoes had ripened in the sun. Kelly spoke of greenhouses for food production at their Community in the future. The day's work had tired Caitlin again. Harvest time was exhausting. Scott spent hours cutting and storing the hay after he had carefully pulled the wheat heads off the stalks. They would mill the wheat heads into flour later, by hand. Not a job she was looking forward to. Kelly divided her time between helping her and Scott.

Caitlin glanced out the backdoor at the newly constructed smoke-shed. Smoke creeped out of the minute cracks in between the wooden slats. Inside hung strips of salmon and venison. Her mouth began to water. Smoked salmon was her absolute favourite. The last time she'd tasted any was Uncle Kieran's birthday. Wow, that was a lifetime ago!

Scott ambled back to the kitchen from the stable with Kelly beside him. They had checked the Highland mare, now in foal.

"Should have got a billy goat for your wee nanny," Scott said with real regret.

"You love all this 'self-sufficiency', don't you Scott?" Caitlin asked.

"'Self-sufficiency'? It's how we live in the future, is it no', Kelly?"

Kelly nodded.

"Well, I think I like it better than going to the super-market for food, that's for sure," Caitlin said.

It always brought a sense of satisfaction when she placed a meal on their table comprising meat caught hunting and vegetables grown in the garden. It hadn't happened often, but if life stayed as it was now, it would become a regular occurrence. It would have to, as the supplies Scott had brought originally wouldn't last forever. There would come a time when all they had would be what they grew or caught.

Caitlin looked out at the garden, from where their plentiful harvest came. The windmill spun lazily above it, generating their electricity. Yes, they had what they needed. Life was simple, but it was good; harder but better. She looked again at Scott and Kelly. They were the reason for it all—always.

***

"I think the mare needs to rest a bit," Caitlin said.

Kelly had ridden her hard during defence practice. The mare was flagging toward the end of the session. Scott walked her to cool her down while examining her, concern crossed his face as he led her into the stable for a closer inspection.

Scruffy ran off barking and wouldn't return when called. Kelly went after him.

"We'd better give her a rest for a wee bit," Scott said. "If we push her any harder, she may miscarry."

Scott turned from the mare as Caitlin joined him in the stable. She regarded the tired horse closely and ran her hands along the smooth coat of the mare's belly, which showed signs of her gestation. The mare snorted as she placed her weight from one hoof to the other.

"Those men are here!" Kelly yelled as she burst into the stable.

They erupted into action and mounted their horses bareback, as they had removed the saddles. Scott plied Kelly with questions.

"How many?" he asked.

"About five."

"How close?" he asked.

"They were halfway between the copse and the front gate when I saw them. That's what Scruffy went after. I can't see him now. I heard one shout something and then Scruffy yelp. I think they killed him."

Scott looked at Caitlin and then Kelly, a decision clear on his face. "Swap horses with your Mum."

Kelly got off the mare and ran the few strides to Caitlin as she jumped off the gelding.

"Caitlin, you go into the house and hide," he ordered her. "Get the guns ready. Bar the windows and man the door. Kelly, you ride the gelding. Your mare's in no state for fightin'." Then Scott addressed them both. "These men are no' here for afternoon tea. They're probably here for yoo both. So," he bore his stare into Caitlin, "we are defending ourselves, and that means to their death, if we have to."

"Do nothing heroic." Caitlin glared back at him.

Scott was in protection mode and would take risks.

"Either of you!" She put command in her tone.

Caitlin snuck her way through the vegetable patch and into the house, ducking low behind runner bean poles and staked tomato plants almost empty of their fruits. The men were now close. From behind the kitchen window, she counted five, as Kelly had. One of the unkempt number led a lad with restraints on his wrists. He was young, in his early twenties she guessed, and dark-haired. He looked thin and pale, sporting bruises in various stages of healing, as if they'd mistreated him for a prolonged period. They all dressed shabbily, were dirty and carried a weapon. Except for the bound man. Caitlin recognised one or two faces from their earlier encounter, the tattooed one was amongst them. She was certain now they were slavers.

"Hi friends! We're back for more Highland hospitality," the leader shouted.

He stood at the edge of the raised garden beds with his men tucked behind him in the path between the beds. An empty yard and silence answered him. "We know you're here. Come out, come out wherever you are! Oh, and sorry about your wee doggy."

Keeping herself hidden, Caitlin peered through the kitchen window, handgun at the ready. The stable door was half open. Scott would evaluate them and discuss his plan of attack with Kelly.

"I have it on good authority that you have two pretty women here," the spokesman yelled. "You lucky man, you." After a brief period of silence, "And I *want* them."

Scott and Kelly exploded from the stables like racehorses from the starting gate. Brandishing weapons, they sat confident, bareback on their charging horses. The leader of the slavers shouted his men into defensive action. The men with firearms raised them to aim and shoot. Those brandishing knives braced themselves for combat.

Scott fired the handgun. He always carried it loaded. Kelly shot arrows from her bow, her quiver full of arrows hung at her waist and she held two in her hand. The air reverberated with the sound of Scott's gunfire. The intruders were slower to get their firearms into action. The young lad, bound by plastic ties, ducked and laid low next to the raised bed at the rear of the group.

Scott aimed for the men with firearms first, attempting to negate the greater threat. He hit one in the neck. The man put a dirty mitt to his throat, trying to staunch the flow of blood. He sunk to his knees, gurgling cries for help from his companions. None turned to him. Scott hit a man close-by in the shoulder. The man yelped, clasping his shoulder. His arm now flaccid with severed nerves dropped his gun to the ground. Kelly shot two arrows in the centre of his chest. Mouth open in shock, he fell forward in slow motion.

The mild acrid scent of propellant wafted into the kitchen. Only two men remained a threat, as their prisoner stayed on the ground, silently observing all that took place.

The gunfire ceased, and the young captive lifted his head. He peered ahead to the ground before him and began to crawl. A hunting-knife lay beside the man Scott had shot. The young man grabbed the knife and cut his bonds.

The remaining men started yelling. It was like a war cry coming from their throats. Scott, undeterred, wheeled Adam around and prepared for a charge. Scott had put his handgun aside and now brandished his scythe-come-sword. He'd honed its edge razor-sharp. Kicking Adam to a canter, he moved toward the vegetable patch where the remaining assailants were shielding themselves.

Scott was like a sheepdog with sheep, manoeuvring his opponents out of the protection of the vegetable patch. This enabled him to have a good run and charge at them. Kelly came at them from the rear.

These combined tactics were successful in moving one intruder. The other man didn't budge. The young lad, with his hands now free and holding the hunting-knife, moved forward. The man who refused to move, stared ahead, never taking his eyes off Scott. Without hesitation, the hostage took his opportunity for retribution. He approached the man who had led him along like a dog, stabbed him in the back with all his might. His victim gave a short yelp of surprise. Blood spurted from his mouth as he collapsed forward to the ground.

Scott got a man into a position where he could advance on him. Guiding Adam with his knees and subtle shifts in body weight, Scott held the scythe-come-sword with both hands. Scott galloped Adam toward his target, who had no time to devise a counter move.

Scott descended on the man like a Celtic warrior from ancient times. His long hair flew behind him. He held his weapon out in a firm grip. Scott cleaved the man in two. His 'sword' sliced straight through the intruder's body at mid-torso. Scott brought Adam to a swift halt. The stallion reared as it came to the vegetable beds.

Scott yelled, loud, deep, and husky, as he threw his leg over and dismounted. He gazed around for the remaining assailants. Scott spied the last man standing—the young, dark-haired lad, still in the vegetable patch. He hadn't witnessed the youth kill his captor and was unaware he was effectively on his side. Scott began his charge on foot.

No Scott, he's innocent. Don't kill him!

Caitlin ran out of the backdoor toward Scott, heart pounding, mind whirling with the possible outcomes of this encounter. Undaunted, she rushed forward.

"No! Don't Scott!" Caitlin continued shouting and waving her arms to attract his attention.

Scott's blood lust was up. Ropey arms held his bloodied sword; his blood-spray covered shirt stretched over his chest; his massive shoulders rose and fell with each breath; his nostrils flared, and his eyes were slits. She *had* to stop him. Scott was *that* scary man once more.

Caitlin stood directly in front of him putting herself between Scott with his bloodied, makeshift sword and the lad. Kelly shouted at her father to cease his charge and brought her horse as close to the young man as possible in the confines of the vegetable patch. The young man had flattened himself to the ground. Kelly joined Caitlin in barring the way to this last intruder.

Scott pulled himself up sharp. He turned to Kelly, then back to Caitlin. Scott's expression regained some sanity. She and Kelly were side by side in front of the boy, hollering their unified warning.

"Scott, he was their captive." Caitlin now lowered her voice. "I saw him bound. He freed himself and then killed *him*." She pointed to the corpse in front of the young man.

Scott glanced at the body, and then at the young man. He pointed at the youth with his sword, still dripping with blood and the intestinal contents of the man he had cleaved in two. Scott's ribcage heaved.

"You will remain still while you answer my questions." His voice was gruff, his tone threatening.

His captive remained prostrate and put his hands in the air slowly, nodding his compliance.

"Who are you?" Scott asked.

"My name is Alistair McKinnon," the young man stammered out in a North American accent, his voice muffled into the grass. "These men captured me three months ago."

"Where are you from?"

"Vancouver. I was here on summer vacation when the stock market crashed, and I found it impossible to get a flight back."

Scott stood stock still, his expression severe, unmoved by the lad's explanation.

"Please, I don't mean you any trouble," the lad continued. "I'm not anything to do with these guys. They were going to sell me. They knew about you and your women, and they planned to sell us on the black market. I've nothing to do with them. Please, you've got to believe me!" Alistair's whole body trembled, and he briefly glanced up at Scott.

Scott took a step. Caitlin moved closer to her husband.

"Scott," she whispered to him, "I think Alistair is genuine. I saw his desperate attempts to escape and his bravery in killing this guy." Caitlin again pointed to the man's body.

Scott never dropped his sword. He looked from her to Kelly, who remained on her horse in guard-like fashion near the young man. Scott's gaze went to the youth. His jaw muscles tightened and then relaxed. The veins in his neck became less visible. His breath rate slowed. Her husband was calming and thinking. The scary Scott was gradually replaced with *her* Scott.

"Remain on the ground, face down. Spread yourself," he ordered Alistair.

After Alistair had done so, Scott handed Caitlin his makeshift sword to hold. She took it. *Eww!* Guts hung off its edge. Scott searched Alistair for weapons. He found none. He examined Alistair's chafed wrists. The emaciated lad smelled like he had not washed recently. Scott seemed somewhat satisfied.

"Stay there," Scott commanded once again. "Watch him."

He took his makeshift sword from her and then walked toward the shed. He soon returned with a shovel and his reloaded handgun.

"Kelly, come with me," he called to her.

"You, stand up," Scott ordered Alistair and Alistair did so. "Ye will dig some graves for your friends while I decide what to do with you. Ye still have to convince me, aye."

Scott turned to Caitlin. "Ye can come if ye want."

My calm, self-controlled man is back.

"But ye may wish to get all the useful things ye can from the bodies, okay?" he asked. "Kelly and mysel' will find a spot aways from here to bury these misfits." Scott looked around him at the four bodies and snarled, "I want tae get rid o' the stench o' 'em. I'd let the wild animals eat them if I did nae think it would then attract them to us and our animals!"

He walked off in disgust, dragging Alistair by the arm. Kelly followed on the horse.

The vegetable patch and the grass beside it were strewn with blood and body contents. Caitlin searched the bodies, periodically looking to see where Scott and the others were. The adrenalin-rush manifested itself. Her mouth was bone dry, and she started to shake. She sat on a clean patch of grass. The scent of crushed tomato leaves and bowel surrounded her. But the all-pervading stench was of stomach—vomit. She turned her head to her right. She had sat next to the upper torso of the tattooed man Scott had cleaved in two. Turning her head back to her left, she took deep, slow breaths, trying not to lose the contents of her own stomach. She replayed the events of the previous twenty minutes through her mind. So close. *So close.* She burst into tears, warm saltiness ran down her face, washing the emotion away.

When she'd drained herself of tears, emptiness settled in her chest. So, this was her life now? Kill or be killed? People were bad. They *will* hurt you. She had to defend herself and those she loved. Scott was right. He knew.

Oh, how he knew.

After an hour or so, they returned. Scott was much calmer, and Kelly watched Alistair closely. A fine layer of dust covered his emaciated frame, his hair was matted, and dark circles circumnavigated his eye sockets. He staggered as he followed behind Scott. Dirt covered everyone.

Caitlin walked inside, cleaned her hands well and got drinks for everyone.

"You all need a wash," she announced when they had finished their drinks.

"After we bury these," Scott waved his hand to encompass the bodies strewn around the yard. "You picked them clean I hope."

"Not the most pleasant of jobs." Caitlin clipped her reply.

"We'll be back afore long," Scott assured her, his gaze intense.

Scott re-saddled the gelding and then got a tarp and tied it with a length of rope to the saddle. He dragged the bodies and dumped them on the spread-out tarp. The two halves of the one man he flung onto the sheet, spraying more stomach contents as he did. The gelding pranced as Kelly held his bridle, his eyes wide and his nostrils flaring at the scents.

Caitlin shook her head. Scott needed to be more careful.

The tarp dragged behind the gelding as Scott led him to the large grave. Kelly and Alistair followed. Caitlin stood where she was and watched. On their return, Scott led the horses to the stable to brush them down. Kelly took Alistair to the cottage.

At the backdoor, Catlin gave Alistair a stern look up and down.

"Bath," she ordered.

Kelly still holding the handgun to Alistair, ushered him into the bathroom while Caitlin ran the bath, using the entire contents of the hot water Copper.

"Strip," Kelly said.

"What?" The young man tensed, his dark eyes wide in his dirty face.

"Yes, take your clothes off!" Caitlin confirmed the request. "I can see the fleas jumping on you from here. Your clothes are putrid. Think I'll burn them!"

"I'm not gonna strip in front of you women!" Alistair looked from her to Kelly and back again, a deep red developing under the layers of grime.

"Kelly, stand out for a moment. But be ready if I need you, okay?" She directed Kelly out of the bathroom and half averted her eyes as the young man stripped and entered the bath.

Alistair sank deeply into the hot water. From the sigh he let out she imagined it was something that had been lacking in his life for some time. She handed him soap and Alistair started washing himself. She picked up his clothes and took them away, while Kelly stood guard. After throwing them on the floor in the laundry Caitlin returned, viewing Alistair in the bath from the living area to give him a little more privacy.

"Oops!" The soap slipped out of Alistair's hands and Kelly strode forward and retrieved it from the end of the bath.

Alistair sat up, his hands covered his groin.

"Oh, don't be shy," Kelly said. "Nothing I haven't seen before. I have four brothers." Then she gasped. "Mum! He's got lice! I can see them crawling oot his hair!"

"Okay," Caitlin called back. "I'll bring the de-licing shampoo."

In the small cottage, no conversation was private.

Caitlin went to the pantry.

"Did you call her Mom?" Alistair asked.

Kelly ignored him. Caitlin returned to the bathroom and handed Kelly the de-licer, and Kelly started washing his shoulder-length dark hair with the treatment. Scott returned to the cottage and walked into the bathroom as Kelly scrubbed Alistair's back.

"What on earth's going on here? He did nae come here for a Day Spa!" Scott shouted.

"He's full o' wee beasties, Dad!"

"Would you rather we got infested with fleas and lice?" Caitlin added.

"Oh, aye then," Scott conceded. "But dinnae come to expect the ministrations of my women every time ye wash, okay?"

"Yes sir," Alistair replied meekly.

Every occupant of the cottage was now stood in the bathroom.

"Come on, we'll leave you to your ablutions." Caitlin ushered everyone out.

Scott beckoned Caitlin to go outside the cottage. "So, you think he's genuine?"

"I'm sure he is," Caitlin answered. "The poor lad's been through an ordeal and a half. You should give him a break."

"Aye well, we must leave here for a wee bit. The leader of the slavers will wonder where his goods and men have got to. We'll have to go camping until the coast is clear. Start packing a few things. We are all going. With the horses, of course. Leave the chickens and goats enough feed for a few days. Lock them away." Scott sighed. "I found Scruffy's body."

"Poor wee mite. Going to miss him," she said.

If it was the worst that came out of today's excitement, she could cope with it.

"Me too," Scott said. "The mutt had his uses."

"What about the animals while we are away?" she asked.

"Just have to risk it," he said.

"You're next, by the way." Caitlin tapped his arm, avoiding the stains on his sleeve.

"What?" he asked.

"Bath! Time to clean up, my Celtic warrior, you're covered in gore and blood splatter."

Chapter Forty-One

The Future

"We are still uncertain of the conditions the time traveller will encounter on his return. Or whether the farmer is yet to abandon his property." Martin the physicist stood in front of the Chief Council as they sat at the collection of tables which passed for their bench, in the dull-green living room of the old farmhouse. With a concerted effort by the scientists and mathematicians, a return journey from the past was now possible. "The Retriever has a month to find Mr Campbell and bring him back to the same place where The Time Machine landed him, put Mr Campbell in a pod where it can detect him and bring him forward. We will then return the Retriever."

Rory stood at the back of the room, he wore full camouflage gear and had trimmed his hair and beard for the occasion. He had matured in the last five years; he recognised it in himself. Rory was stronger and fitter; the disciplined life of a soldier agreed with him and filled him with confidence. The other Militia members looked up to him and the older men respected him. Still, Angela was part of the selection panel. He needed to have her vote, and he wasn't sure how he felt about it. A burn followed by an icy touch collected in his guts, like he'd swilled down scotch on the rocks, cubes and all.

"Well, we are all very pleased with this progress, and that it has only taken five years to get where we are today." Harold Farquhar thanked the team for their report.

Now to the crucial stuff. Rory's back stiffened as his sister spoke.

"Who do you suggest as a candidate for the position of Retriever?" Angela, now fully initiated as a Chief Council member, asked George Stobbart, who then walked to stand before the Council.

"I truly believe the man for the job is Rory Campbell." George glanced briefly at Angela.

Angela shook her head and opened her mouth as if to protest.

Why am I not surprised?

Rory gritted his teeth and leaned against the back wall.

"Would the Council please hear me out?" George asked.

Dr Farquhar and the other Council members gave a nod. Angela closed her mouth.

George continued, "Rory Campbell is an outstanding member and emerging leader of our Militia. Over the past five years, I have witnessed him grow into strong manhood. Rory exhibits all the qualities and skills required of the Retriever. I believe he will be faithful to his mission and unbiasedly search and find Scott Campbell and then ensure his return."

Angela's eyes narrowed. The other members of the council smiled and nodded as they asked Rory to come forward. Rory looked directly at the Council as he stood to attention, but avoided eye contact with Angela.

Dinnae let her put you off.

Dr Farquhar asked Rory to give an account of himself.

"I believe I am able for this task," he began. "I can stand the rigours of fending for myself without support. I am resourceful. I ken the Highlands and the conditions often encountered in them. I understand how The Time Machine operates. I know the offender and how he thinks. I am sure I can trace his steps and recover him with minimal difficulty and, importantly, with no disruption or change to the past."

"Where do your loyalties lie?" Angela asked.

"I am loyal to the Invercharing Community," he answered the expected question. "I believe we must uphold justice despite the status of the offender. I promise I will bring my father back to face his misdeed. I know I can convince him. I will return or die trying."

"A little dramatic, brother?"

"Surely you are not unaware of the time and the place to which I'll return?" Rory smothered the annoyance he felt towards Angela. "It's one of the most dangerous times in recent modern history."

While you sit safely and comfortably in the Community our parents forged, flexing your authority muscles, sister.

"I can't make promises for unforeseen circumstances," Rory continued. "I can only vouch for my own actions."

Despite Angela's misgivings, George's choice for Rory as Retriever impressed the Council, and they appointed him.

Rory made his way to Murray's room, the tension easing from his shoulders. He and Murray had had the previous five years to develop their plan. It was imperative that Rory made the journey back in time. Murray had stalled the scientists developing the return journey technology. In fact,

Angus and the physicist had not been far off the theory five years earlier when his father had stolen the time journey. With Angus' sympathies lying with the Campbells, and having a profound respect for his father, Angus had dallied in producing his contribution to the theory which would advance the process. Murray delayed equations and key calculations along the way. They had procrastinated as much as was conceivable. Rory knocked on Murray's door. His brother let him in and shut the door quietly behind him.

"You've teed it up with Angus then?" Rory leaned against Murray's desk.

"You'll return eighteen months after Dad arrived and seven months after Kelly." Murray sat on the end of his bed, jiggling his right leg so rapidly the whole bed shook.

Rory regarded his younger brother. Murray had also grown in the past five years. He had filled out and his voice was deeper. And, if Rory wasn't mistaken, their subterfuge and planning had livened the boy up a wee bit.

"Aunty Bec said they were in Glencoe?" Rory went over the available information. "Well, I hope they are still there. It'll be fair annoying if they're no'."

***

Rory spent the night so far lying on his bed staring at the ceiling without sleep coming. Thoughts of his parents kept him awake. He would see his mother again, but young. About the same age as him. *Huh.* His laugh echoed in his quiet room.

His best friend would be there. No one understood him as his father did. It would be braw to be with them again. He realised how lonely he'd felt without them. What will they think of Angela? They'd understand; his father did something wrong. Rory wished he'd recognised what his father was up to when they'd had the conversation before his mother died. Rory would've stopped him. But that was history now. He gave a short laugh at his pun.

Rory got out of bed, walked to the kitchen and reached right to the back the cupboard, behind the jars of preserves. Aye, it was still there. His father's bottle of 21-year-old Scotch. He poured a glass, more than a dram.

"Here's to reunions."

No one answered as Rory lifted his glass to the air and sculled the amber liquid, smooth in his throat and warm in his chest. He lay back on his bed. Sleep came eventually.

***

Dressed in full combat gear, sub machinegun over his shoulder, and a full pack on his back, Rory stood in front of his sister and the whole Chief Council. Behind him was the control panel for The Time Machine and the scientists who would operate it. Murray stood amongst the on-lookers.

"Really, Angela? You don't trust me?" The barn's high ceilings echoed with Rory's questions.

"Just do it." Angela raised her eyebrows. That expression of hers. Best not to argue.

"I, Rory Campbell," he placed his fist over his SAPI vest. "Do solemnly swear that I will fulfil my duty as Retriever and bring back from the past the perpetrator of the crime, 'theft of a time journey', Mr Scott Campbell, to face the appropriate justice."

Angus, now the head handler of the machine, set the time journey. Heavily armed, carrying a large amount of cash and two spare pods folded in the backpack, Rory settled into his pod.

"Remember, one month after you arrive, you must be back in the very same place to send Scott back and then yourself," Angus recapped.

"Aye," Rory said. "I've got it."

Rory and Murray had discussed the possibility he may not return. Rory knew from his parents how dangerous those years had been, but he would take the risk. It was all a risk. The Council's insistence on justice had made it so. With the machine charged, Angus pressed the buttons and Rory disappeared.

"Goodbye brother," Murray whispered.
A lot rides on this time journey, and you.

Chapter Forty-Two

The Year After The Stock Market Crash

Caitlin gazed around at the secluded place Scott had found to camp for a few days, or as long it took him to be convinced the slave traders wouldn't trouble them. They had one two-man tent and Scott had erected an extended fly, which he and Alistair would sleep beneath. Scott kept an eye on Alistair and kept Caitlin and Kelly from him. Scott viewed the cottage and surrounds daily with the telescope from a high ridge nearby. Every alternate day he went to the cottage and fed the animals, all the horses being with them at the camp.

"So, we can cook bannocks on this griddle." Caitlin stood over the hot coals.

The heat bathed her face as she held the cast iron implement. A camp table set up under a separate fly thrown over a rope tied between two of the pines they camped beneath became the outdoor kitchen.

"And then we'll have fried eggs. That's a decent breakfast, is it not?" Contentment came from her core, despite being away from their cottage. The change of setting was fun.

"Mum, did you never go camping as a girl?" Kelly asked.

"No." Caitlin looked up from the glowing coals.

Why had she never gone camping? she asked herself.

"We have enough tinfoil to bake the rabbit your dad caught," she said to Kelly. "Oh, Scott, when you get back to feed the hens would you pull some carrots and tatties, so I can bake them also?" Caitlin licked the dough off her floured hands.

"Okay. But ye ken, when you are camping, you eat what ye have, not keep going home 'n getting what ye no' have?" Scott grinned at her.

His gentle reprimanding warmed her heart. Kelly smiled at them both. Kelly would have a man who loved her that much one day, maybe. Who knows what this life would bring?

The week had passed with no sign of the slavers, but Scott remained cautious and insisted on camping for at least another week. During this time, he spoke to Alistair often and discovered Alistair was an Agricultural Science student who grew up on a farm and came from a large family.

Caitlin was cooking at the campfire as usual, while the men sat near her.

"Why don't you trust me?" Alistair asked Scott. "What can I do to you? Man, you're awesome. I mean, *really* scary. I promise you, I wouldn't even consider doing anything."

Kelly stood behind the men, pretending to help Caitlin but listening to the men just as intently as she was. Their conversations had become, well not friendlier, but at least civil in the last two days. Scott was still down on him.

"Ye could find out all ye can about us," Scott narrowed his eyes. "Then escape and eventually lead them to me and my family."

"*Really?* You think I could do that?" Alistair's voice rose. "Or even try? Man, meanin' no disrespect sir, but you've got trust issues!"

"Have ye no' been payin' attention to the world you now live in, son?" Scott's voice was firm.

Alistair stiffened.

"My dad is just cautious." Kelly interrupted and sat in between them.

"I think I need to go relieve myself." Alistair stood and walked away.

"Dinnae ye go out o' my sight," Scott warned.

"Dad, can I say that I think Alistair is trustworthy and everything he says he is?" Kelly said.

"You think I'm too hard on him? Ye can never be too careful. And he's with *my* family. He needs to ken I'll no' tolerate any bad behaviour toward my women. Will nae hurt him to learn some respect either." Scott looked closely at her then. "Why? Ye like him?"

Kelly blinked. "He's okay. I just think he's genuine and we're safe with him, that's all."

Alistair returned.

"Go help your Mother for a wee bit," Scott said to Kelly.

Alistair sat next to Scott as Kelly left. Kelly came back and stood by Caitlin. Kelly looked at her, not speaking. Caitlin then continued observing the men. Something was going on, a turning point in the relationship between them. Caitlin wanted to hear what they said. Kelly would be the same. The men were quiet for a while. Scott faced dead ahead and from the set of his shoulders, she knew he wore one of his severe expressions. Alistair plucked at the grass beneath him.

"I think you're legitimate." Scott broke the silence. "I will trust you with mysel' and ma family." His gravelly voice was exceptionally stern. "If ye betray my trust in any way, I *will* kill you. Do you understand me?"

Alistair nodded in silence. His shoulders relaxed, but his back was still stiff. Caitlin chewed her lower lip.

Alister had better believe every word of Scott's threat.

"Do you have questions?" Scott asked Alister.

"Yep, a few," the young man answered.

Scott turned his head to Alistair after a silence, his eyebrows raised in question. "Well, ask away."

"What are you going to do with me?" Alistair looked straight at Scott.

"Ye will stay with us for the moment until I see any other options. You'll be handy on our wee farm. Winter is on its way and ye'll nae be able to do much travelling until the spring. So, I imagine ye'll be with us for a wee while." Scott's fist was on his hip, his gaze intently on the young man.

Alistair's head turned back to the view in front of them. The mountains in front and behind dwarfed them. They were tiny specs at the base of a behemoth.

"Can I ask a more personal question?" Alistair enquired.

"Aye, ye can ask it. I may not answer."

Alistair took some moments to formulate his query. "Kelly calls Caitlin 'Mom'. You just told her to go to her mother. But Caitlin is probably not much older than me. What's the go with that?"

Scott looked at Alistair for a moment, his left eye twitched.

"Like I said, ye can ask. I may not answer." Scott stood and walked to the fire.

He paused slightly as he passed Kelly but said nothing. Kelly watched Alistair's back and bit her lip.

During the weeks of camping Caitlin learned camp-cooking and Scott had a break from the cottage surrounds, except for his regular checks on the animals. Not attending to the odd jobs around the cottage, as was his habit, and spending most of his time with her around the campsite was a good break for him. By the end of the second week he even looked rested. It was a sort-of holiday.

***

Kelly and Alistair rode the horses and took in the views of the surrounding Highlands—after Dad had given his permission. Alistair had not seen this area of Scotland before 'hell broke loose', as he called it. They rode the horses part way up the mountainside above their secluded camp and sat in their saddles, speechless. The mountains here were so much larger than near the Invercharing Community. Nearby were The Three Sisters, a group of mountain peaks behind which, and high up, was a green valley. It looked like another world. The horses snorted from their exertions and their tack jingled as they chewed at their bits.

"Your bruises are healing; you are filling out and you look more relaxed," Kelly commented, turning from the vista. After two weeks of freedom, the difference in Alistair was noticeable. "You look like you are recovering. I can't imagine what it was like for you."

Alistair turned his intense dark brown eyes to her. "I never want to go through that again. They were evil." His Adam's apple bobbed a few times.

It was hard to imagine what he'd been through. Any recollection of it still shook him. She admired him and how he had recovered. And how he managed her dad. He wasn't easy on him.

"I killed one, Kelly. I killed a man," he whispered.

She reached across from her horse and grabbed his hand. It was warm, but the skin was rough. Alistair trembled. He would take a while to get over this... if he ever did.

"It was him or you. Self-defence." Kelly held his hand tighter. "No self-respecting person lets their life be taken from them without a fight, unless they have good reason."

"You and your dad are awesome fighters!" He glanced at his hand in hers. "Your dad is terrifying." Then Alistair's gaze went to her face. "You're a scary warrior woman on horseback!" He laughed.

"That's the first time I've seen you smile, Alistair."

From their perch halfway up the mountain, they watched the weather gradually change throughout the day. A bank of dark cloud, heavy with rain, approached the valley where they camped. They turned the horses and picked their way down the steep hillside.

Kelly and Alister cantered the horses into the campsite as Caitlin roasted grouse in the coals of the cooking fire, totally absorbed by her task.

"Where's Dad?" Kelly asked, now leading her horse with Alistair beside her.

"On his way back from checking the cottage," Caitlin answered.

"Hope he's back soon. Look at the weather, Mum."

Caitlin turned to the approaching clouds. The wind had picked up, coming ahead of the imminent rainstorm. Caitlin covered the fire with a large up-turned pot to protect the coals from the weather, so there would be some to stoke once the rain had passed. Then she secured the equipment while Kelly and Alistair led the horses deep into the trees and tied them.

She faced the direction Scott would come, scanning the forest at the base of the mountains.

"Ooh Scott, come back soon! I hate it when your father's not here and something like this happens."

They put on their thicker coats. Alistair fitted into Scott's clothing. It was a little loose but the right length. He now wore a waterproof coat of Scott's.

"Batten down the hatches!" Caitlin called through the wind.

They weighted down any loose items around the campsite and, after checking one last time for Scott's approach, settled into the tent.

Outside, the wind howled, and the rain battered their tent, like rocks hurled at the canvas roof. Alistair had tightened the guy ropes and thrown and pegged storm guys over the tent to prevent it taking flight.

"You've camped before, then?" Caitlin asked once Alistair settled in the doorway of the crowded tent.

"Yeah. My dad and me used to camp in The Rockies," Alistair smiled.

"It's nice to see you smiling, Alistair." A slow warming began in Caitlin's chest. Alistair had been through an ordeal. "Please don't fear my husband, he means no harm. He's only being protective."

The chatter helped. It distracted her from her concern about the storm outside and that Scott was possibly out in it.

"You aren't mom and daughter, right?" Alistair dared his question. "She's your step-mom or something, yeah?" he asked Kelly.

"Yes, that's it." Caitlin answered for Kelly. "Scott's first wife is Kelly's mother."

"Must be weird having a mom almost as young as you?" Again, Alistair directed his question to Kelly.

"We don't notice it." Kelly said in a harsh tone.

The tent door started flapping more vigorously. Alistair grabbed the canvas door and held it shut as it flapped more and more wildly in the wind.

"Are ye goin' tae let me in or no'?" Scott shouted from the other side of the tent door.

"Scott!" Caitlin flung herself past Alistair and wrenched the tent flaps from his hands, opening them for Scott. He only half entered, as there was little space left in the tent and he still held Adam's reigns.

"We tied the horses to the trees out back," Alistair told him. "Want some help?"

"Aye, you stow the saddle while I take Adam to the other horses," Scott said.

Outside, the men yelled over the roar of the wind. The trees, picking up the wind in their leaves, sounded like an ocean roaring above and behind their camp site making the horses skittish, their alarmed and nervous whinnies came through the tent wall. Once back in the tent, the men took off their soaked coats. The heavy rain continued for hours. Caitlin would resurrect the roasted grouse another time. Dried biscuits were dinner instead. All four, now cold, huddled next to each other in the confined space.

"Well, that's it. We go home tomorrow!" Scott said.

The horses were saturated and cold when Scott and Alistair fetched them from the trees very early the next morning. They had slept little, as none could lie fully with four in the two-man tent, especially with the large men inside it. Kelly helped Caitlin pack up the equipment and they loaded the horses and made their way home. The warming sun made steam rise off the horses' coats as they walked back to the cottage.

"Your job will be to keep the wood-pile for the fires stocked up." Scott walked Adam beside Alistair. "And ye can muck out the stables. Ye need to ken horses a wee bit better than ye do."

Alistair walked silently next to Scott.

"Are ye hearing me, lad?" Scott asked.

"Yes, sir." Alistair nodded as he made eye contact with Scott.

Caitlin's mouth tweaked in a grin. Her husband the Militia leader was coming to the fore.

"Have ye ever done any fighting?" Scott enquired.

"Like martial art? Yes, I have a Brown Belt in Karate." Alistair walked taller.

"Karate? Hmm." Scott let a flash of appreciation form on his face, but not for long. "It's a start. What about weapons? Guns?"

"Ahh... I've hunted with my dad."

"Aye, that'll be handy." Scott walked on in silence and Alistair glanced sideways at him now and then.

Caitlin looked over the neck of the gelding she led. Kelly smiled back at her. Yes, it was a start.

Chapter Forty-Three

M cSweeny scanned the street, finger in mouth, chewing. Where were they? His frustration boiled. He expected them three days ago. Four guys, and they'd got the kid from the States with them. Or was he Canadian? Young and fit, he'd sell. The buyer asked for women, but young guys were in demand too. Oh yeah, he'd sell.

A mist blew around a corner followed by Brian who lifted his head as he walked past the street women.

"Hurry up!" Impatience burned in McSweeny and he sounded terse. What did he care? He'd stopped being *mister nice guy* ages ago. "Where are they? What's gone on?"

More vapour surrounded Brian as he shook his head. "Can we go inside, boss?"

So, he wouldn't be happy with what Brian would say. "Tell me here."

"I warned you the guy who has that blonde was a tough one. There was no one there when I checked the cottage out. Like, *no one*. I looked around a bit. There were fresh graves way down the back. But no one there. I think he killed them all."

"On his own?" McSweeny screwed up his face. "He killed five men on his own? What *is* he?"

Brian took a suck of his vape and shook his head. The *crackling-click* was getting annoying. He surrounded them both in vapour.

"Get back to those market traders and find out more," McSweeny ordered. Like where he is now and who's with him. He's got to have help or something. Maybe he's gatherin' an army like some are startin' to do. And stop that bloody vapin'!"

Brian turned away toward the stalls with a smirk on his bony face. Mc-Sweeny would have to try again when he had more information, and now he'd have to wait till the next shipment was due. He needed to move the ones in the holding house on to the buyer. And he'd all but promised that beauty too. Makes him look bad. He didn't enjoy looking bad. Definitely *not* good for business. He decided then and there he would be with his men on the next attempt. 'If you want something done, do it yourself,' his mother used to say. Well Mum, you were bloody right!

***

Tinnitus enhancing static was all the citizen band radio had emitted for weeks. Everyday Scott tried to contact other citizen band radio receivers. This morning Caitlin manned the airwaves while Scott explained to Alistair what it involved exactly to keep the woodpile stocked. She turned the dial to 27.8125 MHz

"Breaker. Breaker. This is 109 Bravo Bravo Hotel calling. Anyone out there?"

The voice was Brendan's.

"Scott!" Caitlin shouted out the backdoor.

Scott ran inside and stood next her as she sat by the small table set up in the pantry for the citizen band radio. Kelly came and stood behind them both in the doorway.

"Breaker. Breaker. This is 109 Bravo Bravo Hotel calling. Anyone out there?" Brendan repeated several times.

Caitlin met Scott's gaze. They could connect with their friends. She turned to see the look of recognition on Kelly's face. Yes, Kelly was close to them in the future and probably missed them. But how would they explain her?

Caitlin moved her hand to the switch, but Scott placed his own large hand over hers and held it firm.

"No. Dinnae," he ordered.

"It could be okay. We just never mention Kelly."

He shook his head slowly and grimaced. "Dinnae ken, lass. I feel we should nae. Not yet, anyways. Ye dinnae ken what it will mean for the future."

Caitlin frowned. "Okay. If you're sure."

"Aye," his look was grim. "Sure enough, for the moment." He turned around and stared straight at Kelly.

Chapter Forty-Four

The days were cooling with autumn on its way. Pale, warming sunshine streamed through the open back door. Scott put the sandwiches and wrapped strips of dried smoked venison into his backpack. Their bedrolls, two rifles, and ammunition stood next to the door.

"Bonding exercise?" Caitlin stood close and worked her way past his coat to put her hands on his solid, warm chest. His body heat seeped through his jumper. He always felt warm—and alive.

"Hunting. That's all." Scott tilted his head to look her in the eye. Dark ginger stubble covered his chin. "He says he's been hunting afore. Let's see what the lad kens. And how he rides."

Alistair walked from his make-shift bedroom in the shed, carrying the backpack she'd given him, and wearing a heavily water-proofed coat. Kelly was by his side, as she had often been lately.

"Be nice," Caitlin ordered in a whisper as the two young people headed toward her and Scott. "Give him a chance."

Scott nodded slowly, his eyes wide. "Aye, missus. He's hanging around ma daughter. I need to ken what he's made of."

Caitlin screwed up her face. "He's okay."

She reached up and kissed Scott on the lips. He'd shown her a side of him she never seen before—his paternal protective instincts. They'd dominated since Alistair's arrival.

"Ye ready?" Scott turned to Alistair, who nodded.

They made their way to the stable. The plan was to ride the horses and make camp, then stalk deer.

"See you tomorrow." Scott mounted Adam.

He'd loaded the saddle with gear, his rifle hooked over the pommel. He leaned from the saddle and kissed Caitlin, then kicked Adam to a canter.

Alistair waved and hurried after Scott.

"He's hunted before. He'll be okay. Hope Dad isn't mean to him." Kelly stood with her, watching the men ride through the back of the property and head toward the moorland where Scott had spotted a stag and his harem. "Just us girls for a night, Mum."

***

Scott had promised Caitlin an overnight stay, and that's what it was. Caitlin was hanging the washing on the line when animated voices of the men travelled from the back trees. She and Kelly had kept an eye out for them since breakfast. Caitlin recalled the last time she waited for Scott after stalking deer. *So* different this time.

"Mum, they've got something." Pleasure tinged Kelly's voice.

Caitlin abandoned the washing and strolled toward the returning hunters. Alistair sat straight in his saddle, his shoulders broad and head held high. Behind him, Scott rode closely. The animal they had caught lay slung on a sapling and hung between them.

"*That* must have taken some co-operation." Caitlin leaned against Kelly and pointed with her chin, indicating the manner in which the deer was being transported.

Kelly kept her gaze on the approaching hunters. They halted the horses near the shed and Scott dismounted.

"Doe this time." Scott looked at Caitlin, an eyebrow raised, as he untied his end of the sapling.

Alistair dismounted the gelding and, untying his end, began to take the weight of the sapling and doe. He kept bunching his mouth as if to repress a smile, his dimpled cheeks giving away his efforts.

"Glad it's a doe. The stag was so tough and took ages to finish." Caitlin said as she opened the wood-shed door. "Which one of you caught it then?"

The men walked in with the deer carcass. Scott tilted his head in Alistair's direction.

"You shot it, Alistair?" Kelly followed them into the wood-shed and stood closer to the carcass, and Alistair.

"Yep. I *have* hunted before." Alistair sounded a little defensive, but his face filled with a smile.

Caitlin caught her husband's attention, raised her eyebrows then inclined her head to the young man. 'Congratulate him' she mouthed. Scott's eyes narrowed slightly, and he screwed up his mouth. 'Go on!' she mouthed again.

"It was well done, Alistair. Ye can hunt, I'll grant you that. Dinnae leave it too long to see to your horse and unpack your gear, aye?'

"Yes, sir."

"And mind to clean your gun."

"Yes, sir."

Caitlin helped Scott lead the horses to the stables.

"Learned anything new on your camping trip?" Caitlin removed the saddle from the gelding.

"Alistair can hunt, and he can ride." Scott pointed at the saddle. "Ye should leave that for him!"

"Oh, give him five minutes with Kelly. I hoped you'd have learned to give the guy a break! Did you have good man-time, *hunter-gatherer*?"

Scott rocked his head from side to side and pursed his lips while he removed Adam's saddle and bridle. Then he grabbed her from behind and placed his warm lips on her neck.

"Aye, I learned a lot aboot the young man." One hand went to her breast the other held her waist. "But I also remembered why I like my home, cosied up next to my warm, sexy wife."

***

"Man, your dad's a hard one!" Alistair turned to Kelly as they stood by the doe's carcass hanging in the cool woodshed. "I finally found something that impresses him."

"You probably impress him more than you realise. You've done well picking up the training and skills we use in our Militia. Oh!" She put her hand to her mouth.

Too late. It was out.

"What Militia, Kelly?" Alistair asked.

"Oh, you know. Dad and I joke about our own little army." She cast her gaze downward, her boots apparently the most interesting.

Alistair tentatively put his hands on her arms and gently turned her to get her eye contact.

"Okay, I've been with you guys a few weeks now," he said. "Every now and then, one of you lets something out that just doesn't add up. If I'm going to be here, long term, I need to know what's really going on."

Kelly returned his intense stare. Then she hung her head, eyes closed and took a deep breath.

"Okay. Come with me. It's about time you knew. Where's Dad?"

They found Dad grooming his prized animal in the stable. Mum had returned to the cottage.

"You've told him *what*?" Dad yelled.

"I've told him nothing yet. But I think it's time we did."

Dad rubbed the back of his neck, then dropped his hand to his side. "Get your Mother."

***

They sat on the green couch beside the open fire. Alistair stood opposite them.

"So, you're from the future." Alistair pointed at Kelly, his hands clasped, and his index fingers directed at her like a pistol. "And you're from the future." He did the same to Scott. "But you"—he pointed at Caitlin—"are from this time, like me? And about the same age, yeah?"

Each person at the end of Alistair's pointing finger nodded at the appropriate statement. Alistair began to run his hands through his dark hair from front to back, which Caitlin realised was his habit when he was a little distressed. He was still trying to make sense of it and his thick black hair sticking up made him look slightly comical.

"Knew we should nae have—" Scott began but Alistair interrupted him.

"No, I get it. And your secret is safe with me," he assured them. "I'm just trying to take it all in."

He looked at Kelly next and smiled. Kelly looked back at him, grinning. Something passed between them. Like, understanding. Like, *now I get you*.

"You came back through time for Caitlin." Alistair smiled directly at Scott. "That's romantic even," he finished, a slight tinge of disbelief in his voice.

Scott grimaced.

"Of course my dad can be romantic! He loves my mum." Kelly was on the defence.

"Oh, I never meant he couldn't be." Alistair held his hands up, palm forward.

"Anyway," Scott began, "I dinnae remember you in the future, so I dinnae quite ken where you fit into all o' this, but for now, ye are with us. Okay?"

"Okay."

"And as you know the truth about us, your loyalties must lie *with* us, aye?"

"Aye. I mean, yes."

"Verra well. Kelly, you can enlighten our friend on what you wish about the future, but ye dinnae have to tell him everything aboot the family, okay?"

Chapter Forty-Five

Scott and Alistair walked through the trees, which marked their back border. Kelly stood beside Caitlin in the drizzle, the air misty grey with rain. Previous days of a clear sky had allowed Scott to do more training with Alistair, this time honing his gun skills. Scott was eager to stock the larder with more meat before the cold weather brought snow. He was reluctant to leave her and Kelly but now with an extra mouth to feed, a large male one at that, more stores of protein were essential. The backs of the men were dark-wet already. Their hunting of small game should be successful, causing their soon return. Scott had spent time that morning looking through the telescope on his vantage point and had given it the all-clear.

"But still be vigilant, mind." Scott had ordered Caitlin before he and Alistair left. "Ye both have your knives on ye? Keep a gun handy." He had looked at Caitlin sternly. "Kelly's a braw fighter. If any trouble comes, fight." That nod of command again.

Caitlin followed Kelly into the stable, conscious of her throwing knives tucked in her right boot. Kelly had hers on her belt and carried a handgun. They would clean the tack and give the horses a good grooming.

"You can do Adam. He seems to like you." She told Kelly as she made her way to the mare.

The mare was leaning her weight from one foot to the other and panting hard. Caitlin ran her hand over the mare's coat and bent to feel her belly. Warm horse scent filled her nostrils. The mare's gestation was obvious, and under her hand Caitlin felt the mare's belly tightened on and off.

"Oh, no. Way too soon for this mare to be in labour. She may lose it." Caitlin's shoulders sank.

Scott would be so disappointed. With no veterinarians around, she'd have to let nature take its course.

Rain pelted on the roof; the stable reverberated with its noise, reminding them of the damp day outside. The mare continued to show discomfort and blood stained mucous came from her rear as the stable filled with the metallic scent of blood.

"Will she be okay?" Kelly stood by the mare's head, stroking her neck.

"Yes, if she gets rid of it all." Caitlin then shook her head. "But the foal will be too young."

"Poor Dad." Kelly's brow creased in the middle.

"Poor Dad? Poor horse!" Caitlin said. "I'll have to be midwife! Never done that before."

The mare's steady wander around the stall continued, pausing to shuffle from one foot to the other now and then. After a while, liquid gushed out and membranes covering tiny hooves protruded from her rear. The horse snorted, and Caitlin felt a tension in the horse's belly under her hand. Then a full sack of membranes fell onto the straw-covered floor of the stable with a wet splat. The horse stepped away to reveal a small, still form wrapped in membranes trailing a placenta. The mare bled slightly. The scent of the warm amniotic fluid brought back memories.

"Ah, I remember when I did my Midwifery secondment, if the woman bleeds you had to tickle her tummy. Suppose I should do the same." Caitlin reached down to the horse's belly and started to rub where she gauged the top of her uterus would be.

"See if the foal's alive or not," she instructed Kelly.

Kelly stepped over to the membrane-covered form. It was motionless.

"Break the membranes. You never know." Caitlin continued leaning under the mare's belly and rubbing.

Kelly grabbed a piece of the slippery clear membrane in each hand and ripped. A tiny horse's head peek through, lifeless and making no attempt to breathe.

"It's too small," she said. "What a shame."

"Yes, it is a shame. But that's life, isn't it? Shit happens." The voice came from the stable door.

Caitlin jumped with a start and her heart began a wild ride in her chest as rain-soaked strangers piled into the stable. A tall skinny lad whose dark hoodie partially covered a bony face held a shiny rectangular object in his hand. He stepped forward and stood in front of her.

It was the guy who vaped.

Slavers for sure.

Cold joined the wild ride in her chest.

The intruders glared at them, looking both women up and down. Most of the men had guns, and knives glistened at their belts. They filled the stable, their large forms invading her and Kelly's space and blocking any exit points; their unwashed bodies and clothing emitting an overpowering odour, squashing the scent of horse and amniotic fluid. Caitlin glanced aside at Kelly who slowly stood taller and viewed each man in turn, her mouth a thin line, her expression giving nothing away.

The man who spoke was middle-aged with a gut which hung over his belt; his jumper had holes around the neck. Caitlin checked his hands for a weapon. His fingernails were bitten to the quick, but no weapon. She then glanced at the handgun Kelly had placed on the top of the stall post. Kelly reached for her knives in their sheath hanging on her belt. Caitlin lifted her hand off the mare at the same time.

"Now stop right there unless you want to lose your lives," their leader commanded.

In unison the men surrounding him held their guns ready.

Caitlin and Kelly raised their hands in the air. Kelly held her knives out to surrender them. Two other men approached, one went straight to Caitlin and bound her arms behind her back. The other stepped toward Kelly and reached out to grab her knives. In an instant, Kelly lunged forward close into the man, stabbing him high in the ribcage with the three thin blades of her throwing knives.

"What the—?" The man gazed at his upper chest as Kelly flew past him and aimed for the next man.

"Grab the bitch, you idiots!" McSweeny yelled at his men. "Don't shoot! You'll hit the blonde!"

The butt of a rifle landed between Kelly's shoulder-blades, and she crumpled to the floor on her knees. Another grabbed her flaccid arms and wrenched them behind her back, securing them tightly with a cord. Kelly's victim pressed his hand near his collarbone, blood seeped through his shirt—a flesh wound. Kelly groaned.

"Don't you hurt her!" Caitlin cried as the scrawny youth who had tied Caitlin's arms, made sure they were secure, pulling the plastic ties tighter.

The ties clamped around her wrists and aggravated her skin, her heightened nerves sent pain messages double-time. Caitlin willed herself to ignore the pain. She turned her attention to the leader. He looked so familiar.

The vape-guy took the handgun from the stall post and then dragged Caitlin from behind the mare who whinnied and ran to the far side of the stable. Adam and the gelding snorted and shuffled in their stalls. Vape-guy thrust her in front of the leader, whose yellow teeth exuded an unpleasant halitosis. Caitlin dry retched.

"That's amusing. I heard Scott Campbell's women were tough." The leader with the pendulous abdomen sneered at her. "Yes, that's right. We know whose place this is. We've been waiting quite a while for you to be unguarded. Off to market, is he maybe? And the dark-haired Yank."

"Canadian, actually." Kelly lifted her head and now, with her breath returned, spoke with unmasked disdain.

"Whatever he is, he's mine too." His eyes narrowed. "Aye. They said you were the spit o' your father. Not as beautiful as her"—he lifted his chin in Caitlin's direction— "but you'll do."

"Who told you about us?" Caitlin held her head high.

She would *not* be cowed by this scum.

"The stall holders at the Fort William market," the leader said. "People will do anything for money and such these days. But that means little to you now."

Fort William Market. That's where she recognised some of these reprobates from.

And the leader was the man-with-the-stare.

"You disgust me. What are you going to do with us?" Caitlin looked from one face to another, memorising them.

"Well, we don't usually give captives the itinerary, and I'm making no exception *now*." The man-with-the-stare grabbed Caitlin by the hair with one fist, and Kelly with the other. He dragged them both outside into the rain and toward the cottage.

The rain pelted on Caitlin's back. She'd removed her coat when seeing to the mare. Her drenched jumper seeped cold wet onto her back. His men followed and stood behind them as the man-with-the-stare dragged Caitlin and Kelly into the kitchen. Vape-guy clicked his vape and exhaled. The kitchen filled with strawberry smelling mist.

"Show us where your medical supplies are. We require some," the man-with-the-stare said.

He pushed Kelly into the hands of the man who vaped. Caitlin indicated in the pantry's direction. He snapped orders to one of his men who found the items. They took food supplies as well. The man-with-the-stare tightened his fist further into her hair. Caitlin's scalp grew taught and the skin beside her eyes pulled. The cold chilled her back muscles, but it was nothing compared to the burn she felt at the sides of her face.

"I hear Scott Campbell always has plenty of cash when he goes shopping," he said. "Where is it?"

Without giving Caitlin a chance to answer, he shook her by the hair. The tears sprang to her eyes. The tightness was now full-on reverberating pain.

"It's also in the pantry." Her vision became watery.

"Get it!" he yelled to his minions.

The scrawny youth obeyed. "There's not much here, McSweeny," he said.

"Where is it?" The leader shook Caitlin by her hair.

Her scalp burned. She cried out. "Ow! Scott must have taken it with him."

"Leave her alone!" Kelly yelled at him, trying to take a step forward but now held back by her hair in the tight fist of the man who vaped.

McSweeny! Not a name you would forget. So, this guy had been after her for a while. Bet he was chuffed with himself. *Let's see how chuffed he'll be when Scott gets him..*

Ignoring Kelly, McSweeny directed his question to Caitlin only.

"Where else do you keep it?"

"What do you want money for? It's useless," she ground out through her discomfort.

"Maybe now," McSweeny said. "But once the world gets its act together, thems that have it will have the power, will they not?"

"You can have it all if you let us go." She chanced a bargain and was rewarded with a fist in her belly. The sudden crush to her abdomen made her double over and vomit. It landed right on McSweeny's shoes. The acid burned her throat.

"Ahh! That wasn't nice! Where's your money, *bitch*?" McSweeny yelled to her bent-over form.

His bad breath wafted past her ear and made its way to her nostrils, threatening another emesis.

"In the... mattress." Caitlin answered in between gasps.

With a smirk, McSweeny ordered his men to cut open the mattresses in both bedrooms in search of the cash. They tore apart every cushion in the cottage. After finding the cash, the men dragged Caitlin with Kelly behind them and made their way to the road. Caitlin, now saturated with rain, turned her head to Kelly. Kelly's hair was wet and stuck to her face, dripping.

Past the copse, covered horse-drawn wagons were parked and waiting. Female voices came from inside the one to which they led her. Caitlin glanced at Kelly again. Kelly's eyes were wide, and she gave Caitlin a slow nod. Scott would come for them as soon as he found out. Caitlin pretended to make a run for it and brushed herself against the lower branches of a pine tree. Her soaked jumper caught and tore.

"Come back here." Vape-guy dragged her away from the trees and forced her and Kelly into the wagon.

Caitlin glanced out, threads of her green jumper hung on the stub of an old branch.

In the dark interior, the rock of the dray and the *clip clop* of the horses' hooves indicated the start of their journey to *who* knows where.

Chapter Forty-Six

The rain eased while Scott and Alistair were returning, its *plip-plop* on their coats a slower rhythm now. They had caught three ducks, but with the rain heavy and unrelenting, their pickings were lean and getting further cold and wet would not be worth it. Always the way, now they were almost home, the rain was easing.

Alistair walked beside Scott. He wasn't a bad lad. Aye, he was hard on him, Scott admitted to himself. Never hurt, as the lad could do with learning some manners. He'd had to stop himself from slapping the lad for his insolence at first. Scott would never have stood for it with the youngsters in the Militia. But that was another place and time. Things would change.

The grounds were quiet as they approached. Scott loved the way Caitlin always came out to meet him when he returned from a hunt. No Caitlin today. A whinny from the stables caught his ear.

"Let's see what the women have been up to," Scott said. "Surprise them, bein' back early an' all."

They both entered the stable, Alistair held the brace of wild ducks to show them. The women were not in the stable and the horses were skittish and snorted. The mare was wandering around out of her stall, mucous and blood coming from her rear.

"What's happened, Scott?" Alistair's tone was wary.

Scott placed his rifle by the door, stepped over to the mare and felt her belly. His heart sank. He walked to her stall and inspected the straw on the floor. At the back of the stall lay a tiny horse, perfectly formed, covered in membranes, but not alive.

"No." Scott hung his head, groaning in disappointment.

"I'll go to the house and let them know we're here?" Alistair lowered their catch.

"No, we'll both go," Scott said. "The mare looks okay. She'll clean herself up. Wonder if Caitlin kens."

"They were cleaning tack and stuff today," Alistair said. "That's what Kelly said they would do, 'cos it's raining."

They made their way to the cottage through the rain. It had started again. They stepped through the backdoor, the contents of the pantry were strewn around the kitchen. Opened boxes, which usually contained their medical supplies, were lid-less and empty. Cushion and mattress stuffing lay everywhere, and the living-room furniture turned upside-down.

No women. Not good. Scott suppressed the body-draining-dread which formed in his core.

"What's that smell?" Alistair's eyes were wide. His voice held a note of alarm. "I know that stink."

Scott sniffed. "Body odour."

"No. Not only that. Strawberry." Alistair threw the ducks on the kitchen table and began searching the floor.

Scott raised his eyebrows. "What ye looking for, lad?"

"Can't you smell the strawberry?" Alistair sounded frantic. He shuffled through the junk lying on the floor.

"I can, faintly. But I fail to see the significance of strawberry and nae women." Scott took a breath to forestall frustration, as it wouldn't help.

Scott ran out the backdoor. "Caitlin!"

Only the patter of rain on the yard and its low thunder on the rooves of their sheds answered him.

Alistair came out behind him. They both stood in the rain, their wet-weather gear getting wetter.

"Found it." Alistair held up a small transparent plastic container with a short spout at its neck. "A bottle for vape liquid." The dread in the lad's voice sent Scott into high alert mode.

"What are ye tryin' tae tell me, lad. Come oot with it! Now!"

"I'm pretty sure slavers have Kelly and Caitlin," Alistair gulped.

"How?" Scott asked.

"The slaver's assistant vaped." Alistair held Scott's gaze.

I've got complacent. Too comfortable. *Damn the Bastards!* A plan was forming. Scott raced to the gun locker, opened it and took out a shotgun and two Glocks. After stuffing the handguns in his belt, he filled his coat-pockets with boxes of ammunition.

"I'll take the vehicle!" Scott turned and ran out the backdoor before Alistair had a chance to comment.

"You won't be able to do it on your own! Wait!" Alistair shouted behind him.

Scott wouldn't wait for the lad.

Not turning back, Scott ran for the 4WD hidden in the copse nearby.
Footprints had disturbed the pine needles which carpeted the copse floor,
plenty of them. Cartwheel tracks, as well. Horses' hoofprints trailed away
from the edge of the copse toward the road. Scott stopped himself for a
second.

Think Scott.

He scanned the ground, wanting to get as much information as he could.
One wagon, lots of feet...a dozen men? No motorized vehicle? No, wait.
He walked to the side a little—there were tyre tracks.

Scott leaned against the tree, his heart pounding and reaching his temples. His worst nightmare. His beautiful Caitlin and his Kelly. Scott rested
his head against the tree as he regained mastery of his pulse and breathing.
He needed his adrenalin and wouldn't let it control him. He looked down.
Snagged on one of the branch stubs which surrounded the lower parts
of the Scots pine, was a piece of green thread. Caitlin wore her green
jumper today. *Good lass.* He smiled to himself. His brave, smart woman
was keeping her head.

The tyre tracks and cartwheel marks led north. Scott ran to the camou-
flaged vehicle and removed the tarp and foliage. Luckily, he had over half a
tank of fuel in it. Jumping in, he turned the key. It took three goes to get it
started. He skidded into reverse, then made his way north.

***

Alistair ran back into the cottage. The gun locker was open. Just as well,
as only Scott and Caitlin had a key, and they never let it out of their sight.
He grabbed more bullets and shotgun cartridges. He then removed every
weapon from the armoury. Well, nearly. He wasn't going to stand by and
let those bastards get Kelly and Caitlin. Alistair shoved the ammo into a
saddle bag as an idea formed.

Alistair ran to the stable. The horses were still skittish. He'd never ridden
the black stallion. He approached him gingerly. The horse snorted as he
patted his nose but then settled. Alistair had rubbed shoulders with Scott
all day, maybe his scent was on him. He hoped it was. He needed his plan
to work.

***

At the bridge at Ballachulish, Scott had an intense conversation with a
group of people by the side of the road. They'd been helpful, but it was
still not enough information. The clatter of hooves caught his attention.
He turned away from a couple amongst the group. Alistair rode Adam
through the persistent rain, the gelding trailed behind the stallion. He'd
loaded both horses with weapons and bulky saddlebags. There would be

ammunition in those if the lad was on-the-ball. Finishing his conversation, Scott thanked them for the information and walked toward Alistair. His chest was tight, and his breathing came hard.

"By all reports, there has been a group of slave traders through here tha' day," Scott reported to Alistair. "They take 'em off in covered horse-drawn wagons. These people dinnae ken where to, mind. Think I'll make my way to Fort William. Somebody's sure to ken there."

"You need me." Alistair pointed to the armoury he'd brought on the horses.

Scott's mind spun. He needed the horses and arms but also to get to Fort William quickly. Alistair had done a braw job thinking of more weapons and ammo. Scott had some in the vehicle. But what would they be up against? Time was of the essence. Speed won.

"We need to get to them afore they sell the women on, or something happens to them." Scott sucked in a breath.

He wouldn't go *there* in his mind. He recalled the state Alistair was in when they freed him. What must *he* be feeling? But there was no time for that.

"The vehicle's quicker than horses, aye? I'll ask around at Fort William and meet ye there. I have enough fuel. If you're no' there when I find out, I'll drive back for ye and we'll go from there. Aye?"

Scott sped off in the vehicle, leaving Alistair to ride the horses at a canter to Fort William.

Chapter Forty-Seven

At Fort William, a handwritten sign on a torn piece of cardboard tied to a post with string stated the market would be held the next day. Scott searched through the groups of traders who had arrived early. He went from one to another asking about the slavers. Most were tight-lipped, many would not engage in conversation and some even turned their backs to him.

Odd. Something's up. There was a familiar face. The black market pharmacist was always keen to let him know what she knew.

"Aye, handsome, I do ken," she said. "Well, I've heard there's a house a wee way back the way ye came from, off the road like, where in the past they have kept them afore they move south with 'em. Hope that's a help to ye. Your wee wifey and your lassie ye say?"

Scott gave a grave nod, then reached out and hugged her.

"I never thanked ye for saving my daughter that time. Well, I thank ye now." He finished with a brief nod and turned to be on his way.

Scott soon halted at the sight of the young man standing before him, a reflection of himself in his twenties. The tall man stood to attention, dressed in full combat gear, holding a helmet in his hand and with a machine gun strapped over his shoulder. He was wet with the rain, which dripped through his deep-red hair, down his face and through his neat beard. He blinked as the side of his mouth curled.

"Dad!" The young man's face broke with a smile as he stepped forward and embraced him.

"Rory?" Scott recognised the firm, ropey arms around him, now even stronger. "Rory, is that you? Ye have grown up son!"

"Dad, it's been five years since Mum died and you left." Rory's blue eyes searched his.

"Well, son you are just in time." Hope welled in Scott's chest. "Slavers have stolen your mother and sister. We've got to get them, now, before it's too late."

Rory had arrived at the best moment.

Rory blinked a few times and shook his head. The rain pattered on the shoulders of his SAPI vest.

"Okay, Dad, but we need to talk. Where can we go to have a quick private conversation?" Rory looked around at the gathering audience of admiring stall holders.

Rory's exceptionally masculine appearance was now the centre of female attention. Not to mention the stares his military-kit received from the male onlookers. Scott took Rory by the arm and briskly walked to the 4WD.

"Son, oh, it's braw to see you. But I dinnae want to waste time talking. I need to get to your mother!" His hope now wrestled with his impatience.

"Kelly met up with you, then? Did she tell you they want to prosecute you for stealing the time journey?"

"Oh aye, she said they'd send someone back. Will it be soon? Did ye come to warn me too?"

"No, Dad. They sent *me*."

Scott stopped mid-stride and stared into his son's vivid blue eyes, so like his own when he last looked in a mirror. *Him?*

"*You* will take me back? Why... No, I understand why. It's the why *you* I dinnae understand." Rory opened his mouth to speak but Scott cut him off. "Dinnae have time for this! Will you please help me get your mother and sister back? Then we'll discuss it!"

Scott and Rory got into the vehicle and drove south out of Fort William and continued along the A82 the way he had come. They travelled halfway along the road beside Loch Linnhe where Alistair now approached with the horses. Scott drove the vehicle off the road and hid it by some trees. Alastair followed with the horses.

Scott and Rory stepped out of the vehicle as Alistair dismounted Adam.

"Rory this is Alistair... our boarder." Scott wasn't sure how to describe the lad. Boarder would have to do.

"Alistair, this is my son Rory... from the future." Scott made the hurried introductions.

The young men shook hands.

"Pleased to meet you," Alistair said in his Canadian accent.

Rory stared at Alistair with wide eyes. "You're our Canadian cousin in Glencoe!"

"I am?" Alistair asked.

"It's a long story," Rory said. "I'll tell you later."

"Aye," Scott interjected, "because we have miles to cover and a job to do."

How could they be talking general chit-chat when they had their women to save? He clenched his fists at his side to control his annoyance. Anger wouldn't help now. Well, not just yet, anyway.

"So, I've found out there's a holding house," Scott spoke firmly. "It's supposedly down this road and off a wee bit. And I'll take no argument from ye both. I'm offering myself as a trade."

"But why, Dad?" Rory asked.

"I can go on the lines of experienced mercenary," he replied. "They may get more on the black market for one. Leaders, or those who think they're important, have their own private armies now, ye ken."

"No Scott," Alistair spoke up. "*We* can do it. Rory looks like he knows what he's doin', and you and I know how to fight." Alistair pleaded into his face. Then he turned to Rory. "What do you say, Rory? We'll storm the place, yeah?"

"But..." Scott tried to interrupt. *The lad believes he can fight? But Rory can.*

"No, Dad. If they don't accept your offer, you're captured." Rory pointed out.

"And Kelly and Caitlin still won't be free." Alistair said.

"We'll end up storming the place anyway and you won't be able to help us." Rory explained.

Scott bowed his head and nodded. He hadn't thought it all through. He was *so* glad Rory had arrived. What a level-headed soldier he had grown to be. If he had time and room enough in his emotional space just now, he'd be proud.

Scott and Alistair rode to the holding house on horseback, and Rory ran beside them.

"Wow, you're pretty fit, Rory," Alistair commented.

***

They reached the outskirts of the property and settled under a large oak tree which gave them a view of the run-down crofter's cottage, the supposed holding-house. They tied the horses behind the tree and began their reconnaissance. Rory looked through his high-powered binoculars.

"This holding house is the usual abandoned wreck," Rory said. "It's got a roof, only just. The glazing in the windows is non-existent." Rory moved his binoculars to view each section of the cottage. "There's a guard front and back. I reckon eight men inside. Mostly women captives. I think I see Mum and Kelly. Wow. Mum's young! I know that's obvious but knowing it and actually seeing her is something else!"

Scott grabbed the binoculars from Rory's hand. "Where?"

"Back window, near the kitchen sink. They must be on mess duty." Rory's voice was in Scott's ear, the binoculars still strung around Rory's neck.

Scott pointed the binoculars in that direction. Caitlin and Kelly collected water and then sorted crockery for the evening meal. Scott gave the binoculars back to Rory, who then counted fifteen hostages and ten slavers in total.

"What's that? A fire? No...smoke and lots of it." Rory shook his head slightly. "The guy doesn't seem to be bothered though."

"Lemme see?" Alistair held out his hand for the binoculars, his fingers wriggling with impatience.

Rory took the binoculars from around his neck and handed them to Alistair. Rory's brow was a ridge of furrows. Alistair grabbed the lenses and hurriedly put them to his eyes.

"Thought so. It's Brian, the guy who vapes. McSweeny's second in command. Arrogant bastard, excuse me. Now we're *sure* it's slavers. We've *got* to get them out of there!" Alistair spoke directly to Scott, his eyes wide, his gaze flicked from Scott to Rory and back again. "Now!"

"We will, but we need a plan, son. No rushing in and getting ourselves and our women killed." Scott stared the lad down, they needed cool heads for what they were about to do. "We draw as many slavers out as we can and dispose of 'em. Then we go in for the rest. When they hear the action, Caitlin and Kelly will grab a weapon and join in or lie low. Either way, their safety is our priority. Shoot to kill anyone who gets between us and our women. We wait till almost dark," he commanded.

He may have been foolish with his original plan, but he *was* in charge.

The men crept closer and hid behind a large boulder in the grounds, and observed for the next hour, waiting for the half light of dusk. They would begin their attack once the slavers started their meal.

***

Caitlin's damp clothes still stuck to her. Now in the shelter of this abandoned crofter's cottage she was drying out. The slavers had assigned Caitlin and Kelly cooking duty and moving around would help them warm up. The kitchen had running water, amazingly. Photographs of the family who'd lived here were still on the wall. The tattered calendar had a picture of the Kelpies near Falkirk and the month was November 2017.

"McSweeny's gettin' hungry. Hurry up, bitch," the vape-guy spoke.

His name was Brian, but she'd never call him that. Caitlin glanced over at him. He watched her every move.

"We've been waitin' a while for you. Make sure you're worth it," he said. "McSweeny lost good men last time. Won't happen again."

Boy, this guy was cocky. McSweeny was tough, and angry—a simmering anger. She'd seen it before in patients and their relatives. Something had happened to him.

Well, something had happened to everyone.

The simple meal was rice, the expiry date was last year sometime, and a meat with tomatoe sauce. Caitlin didn't even want to look at the expiry date on *that* can. She prepared this for McSweeny and his men. What were the women going to eat? They were tied-up in the living room, except for the one in *the room*.

Caitlin served the meal.

"Get a plate. The largest one, aye. He's got a good appetite." Brian led her to the room where McSweeny sat at a table.

There was only one chair.

"Let's see what sort of cook you are." McSweeny looked up from his paperwork. His gaze was dark. He addressed her guard. "The other bitch can serve you and the men out there. Keep your eye on the merchandise, Brian."

Brian shut the door. Caitlin walked over and placed the plate on the table in front of him and stepped back. She scanned the room—peeling wallpaper, a partially boarded window, the dirty table and chair McSweeny sat on, gun on a holster over his shoulder, body odour permeated the room. She flicked her eye back to the handgun, probably a semi-automatic. A Glock.

McSweeny picked up the fork that stuck in the rice and stared at her beneath his eyebrows while he shovelled the food into his mouth. His blue jumper had holes around the neck, and it looked like he'd worn it for months, years maybe. Tomatoe dribbled out of the side of his mouth and down his chin.

"You look disgusted." McSweeny startled her out of her assessment of him.

She didn't answer.

"You wonder how I got here," he said. "Well, so do I."

What? Was he going to give his Confession to her now? He must think she was condemning him by her silence. Well, let him.

"I didn't choose to be like this, just trying to survive in a mental world." McSweeny shovelled another fork-full into his mouth.

So, he wanted to talk. Well, she'd talk. "We all lost someone dear to us."

He flicked his stare back to her. She'd struck a chord.

"It's how we respond to it that determines who we are," she said. See what he makes of that. See if he had any conscience left.

"You think I'm unfair," he said. "Well, like you said, we all lost something when the stock market crashed. Stuff happened to me, why shouldn't it happen to anyone else? Don't begin to judge me." His face contorted in disgust. "You don't know what's been dished up to me by fate, the Universe, God... whatever you want to call it!"

Close proximity gunfire sounded through the walls. He stopped speaking.

Chapter Forty-Eight

S cott crept to the pile of rubble near the backdoor and tossed an old tin near the doorway. A man came out to investigate its clatter. Without making a sound Scott stepped behind him and grabbed his hair. The man gasped. Scott pulled the man's head backward, exposing his throat. He ran his razor-sharp hunting knife across it, severing his windpipe. No more cries from that one.

Alistair dispatched the man who followed his friend with a throwing knife to the left chest.

Well done, lad.

The three men then quietly made their way to the backdoor. Two more slavers came out. Rory fired shots from his submachine gun, point-blank, dropping those two slavers to the ground.

Rory's submachine gun alerted the slavers to their presence. Rory led the way through the kitchen. His S.A.P.I vest and helmet provided the best protection. Rory would aim at slavers only, minimising unwarranted deaths. Kelly was in the living room. Rory pulled her behind him. Alistair grabbed Kelly's arm and ran past Scott. Taking her to safety. Moments later, Alistair returned behind Scott once more, still holding a handgun.

Ahead of Scott, Rory fired some rounds. Men dropped, the one who vaped amongst them. Scott leaned forward and started slicing the plastic ties around the wrists of the women who sat cross-legged on the dirty carpet.

"There are more of us in the rooms down the passageway," said the girl he released from her plastic ties.

She pointed behind him. The lass was young. *Too young.*

"Aye, thank you, lass." With his chin Scott indicated the passageway to Rory. "Rory! Ye go ahead." Scott turned back to the girl. "You women slip out the back way, aye, and *run!*"

He looked sternly at them all. They obeyed.

Scott followed Rory as he led the way along the door-lined passageway, Alistair behind him.

***

The gunfire startled McSweeny. He fumbled with his gun holster.

He must've always stayed safely behind his desk.

Another round of gunfire was very close, right in the house. McSweeny's handgun fell to the floor. He gazed at the door, hands limp, mouth open, eyes blinking.

Caitlin ran forward and grabbed the handgun and pointed it at him. His eyes were wide as he remained immobile. Caitlin racked the slide. An unspent bullet flew out, but she had to be sure the Glock was loaded and ready. McSweeny looked at the gun in her hand then up at her face.

His head bobbed as his eyes registered understanding.

"Oh, that's how he did it," McSweeny said. "He's trained you. His little assassin, are you?" He'd regained his composure.

But *she* had his Glock.

"Yes. He's trained me. He's the very noise you can hear out there. You've underestimated him, McSweeny." She aimed for the centre of his chest.

"What you waiting for? Get it over and done with then," he sneered.

Caitlin's heart pounded. It rocked and tried to fight its way out of her rib cage. McSweeny was so close. All she had to do was squeeze the trigger, and he'd be gone. Wasn't that what he'd do to her in this circumstance? If the shoe was on the other foot? The gun in the other hand? She wouldn't let him take advantage of her hesitation. Her lips pressed tight, her eyes squinted—but still she didn't pull the trigger.

His shoulders relaxed, then he shook his head slightly.

"What are you going to do? *Not* shoot? Show me mercy?" His eyes narrowed as he took a step closer to her.

Is he right? Did she want to be merciful? She couldn't answer that one. She was certain he was another soul trying to make sense of it all but had got lost along the way.

"I would sell you to a man who will have men pay to hump you. You know that? And you'd show *me* mercy? *Fool!*" McSweeny took another step forward.

The door burst open, then a loud crack of gunfire filled the room. McSweeny buckled and fell to the floor. Caitlin turned to the door. Alistair stood there, holding a handgun, face blank.

"Come on Caitlin, get out of here." He grabbed her arm and tugged her out.

***

Scott walked along the narrow corridor behind Rory. Scott kicked open a door to an empty room. He moved to the next door. He kicked twice before it burst open. Inside was a naked woman on a dishevelled bed. The whole room smelled of... stale sex. Gagged and bound, her eyes implored as she looked to the space behind the door. Two loud thuds came through the door beside him. Scott grabbed for it, searching for the source of the noise. Two more thuds hit his belly. He shot through the door at chest height with his Glock. From behind it, a naked man slumped to the floor.

"Get out o' here young woman," Scott ordered gruffly.

He cut her bonds and helped her loosen her gag. He paused, his hand to his abdomen, the initial numbness in his gut was wearing off. A dull burn began at each hole. His hand came away from his shirt, covered in his own blood. Scott waited for the volley of gunfire from his son's machine gun to cease.

"Rory," he yelled.

The four dull burns joined and encompassed his entire abdomen.

"Aye, Dad." Rory's voice came from the next room.

"Have you got your mother?"

"Alistair took her." Rory was now in the doorway, staring at his bloodied clothing.

"Time to go!" Scott squeezed out the words.

***

At the large tree on the periphery of the property, Kelly and Caitlin waited with Alistair. The screams of the women hostages and the cries of the wounded and dying men were amongst the ever-present background sound of gunfire.

The crack of gunfire ceased. The only sounds in Caitlin's head were the ringing in her ears and the pounding of her heart as she waited for Scott's return. Some liberated women made their way past them and thanked Alistair. Through the dimming light, two figures make their cumbersome way toward the tree. Scott walked stiffly, supported by another man who wore army gear.

"Scott looks hurt," Alistair stated the obvious.

Caitlin took a shivering breath and ran to meet him. She supported him on the other side and helped move him to the cover of the tree. Scott smelled of a mixture of propellant and blood.

"Light! I need light," Caitlin demanded.

Torchlight shone on Scott as he lay under the tree. His face was pale. Sweat clung to the hair on his forehead. His shirt stuck to his abdomen. Caitlin lifted the blood-soaked shirt and swiftly put it back in place. She pressed her hands to his abdominal wounds.

"It's not good Scott." Caitlin looked Scott in the eye. "I haven't any medical equipment to do what I need to do in a hurry, but I'll try with what I have.".

Someone placed a small first aid kit before her and Caitlin began to open the blood coagulant powder to stop his bleeding. She used all they had, but it only stopped the surface wounds. Scott would continue to bleed internally from the bullet-wounds to his abdomen. This knowledge sent the arctic to her belly. Scott grabbed her hand as she applied the last combine dressing to one of his many wounds.

"It's not enough Caitlin, *mo chroi*," he said. "It will nae work. Dinnae bother anymore."

Caitlin searched around frantically for more dressings.

"We have no more, Mum." Kelly's voice came from behind her.

"They stole some of our medical equipment." Caitlin referred to the equipment in the slaver's belongings. "But I'd need blood or blood replacement product, and I need to operate..."

"Dinnae waste time, *mo chroi*, talk to me." Scott grabbed her other hand and held them both in his. They were both covered in his blood.

"Oh Scott!... I don't want to be without you. Please don't go. Don't die. I love you." Caitlin spoke through tears of desperation and frustration.

She'd rather still be captive than have him die because he'd freed her. She wasn't going to voice her thoughts. She wouldn't have him die with self-imposed guilt or regrets. Or mad at her. Scott would *never* have left her there.

Despite his pain, Scott held her to him. His strong arms, not so strong. His gravelly voice, quiet and gradually getting softer.

"Dinnae be sad for me," he whispered into her face. "I have had more time with you than I ever imagined. Remember Caitlin, that in my life's time-line, where I go now, you're already there." Focusing on her eyes, he added. "Always and forever..."

"Only yours," Caitlin whispered back as she held him close.

The remains of his breath and lifeblood slipped out. Scott was dead moments later. Caitlin held him tightly, cradling his head against her, fondling his curls with her fingers, pressing her lips to his forehead. Don't be gone.

Don't be gone!

Her breathing began to rock her whole body as she inhaled.

No! She wouldn't do this now. They weren't yet out of danger.

"Mum, we need to get going. Just in case they have anyone else nearby who's on their way." An unfamiliar male voice spoke urgently from behind her.

The man's voice penetrated her grief. The accent was Scottish.

"Who's calling me Mum?" she asked.

Alistair and Kelly didn't answer. They were holding each other, looking at Scott's lifeless body cradled in her arms. Caitlin turned her head, the voice belonged to a young man who was the spitting image of Scott. The dark-redheaded man wore army combat clothing.

"Mum, it's me, Rory," the young man said.

"Rory?"

"Mum, we must get moving." Rory looked to Alistair. "Get one of the horses. We'll put him over the saddle to take him back."

"No!" Caitlin commanded. "You're not hanging him over a horse. His face will go livid with the blood settling in it. I'll not have him looking like that when I bury him." She said, determined her man would look his handsome self when buried.

"It will only be to the 4WD," Rory said.

"No. Not over a horse," she cried.

"I can't believe we're arguing about this, man!" Alistair interjected. "I'll ride with Kelly to the vehicle and drive it here."

They mounted the horses and kicked off at a gallop, leaving her still embracing Scott's body. Rory stood guard with a watchful eye for any adversaries.

Caitlin's gaze wandered the full length of her son then returned to Scott. She took more calming breaths. Not now.

Not now. Stay clear. They were not out of trouble yet. She had to take charge. She was the matriarch now. And the young man standing there was their *son.*

"You're quite a man, Rory. Brave and smart. Like him." She kissed Scott's cooling forehead, calm and stoic. "How did *you* not get shot Rory?"

"My S.A.P.I. vest," Rory tapped one of the light armoured squares inserted into the sections of the vest which he wore over his camouflage shirt. "You know, the Israeli Army ones from the black market?" he added as she returned a blank stare. "You insisted we buy them. You insist we get anything on the black market that is Israeli Army."

"No, I don't know any of that. Something I do in the future, yes?" Caitlin said numbly.

Rory nodded without replying, not ceasing his scan of the surroundings, his machinegun always at the ready.

Alistair returned with the vehicle and a tarp. Caitlin still held Scott tightly. Alistair gently lifted her hands off him and placed him in the tarp with Rory's help. Caitlin stood still, empty and unable to move. Rory and Alistair lifted Scott's body into the back of the 4WD. Alistair held out his hand to Caitlin. She flinched into action and got into the vehicle.

**

Kelly arrived at the tree, riding the gelding and leading Adam. Alistair and Caitlin set off, leaving Kelly and Rory to ride the horses home. As they kicked the horses into a gallop, a woman ran from behind the tree and waved them down. She was gaunt, wearing only underwear and desperate, her cut bonds still hanging from her wrists.

"Please take me with you," her model-like features looked up into his face.

"You can go home now," Rory replied.

"I don't have a home." She burst into tears and sat heavily on the ground before his horse, exhausted.

Rory jumped off Adam, took off his S.A.P.I. vest and shirt. He handed his shirt to the young woman, who put it on and thanked him.

"Can you ride?" Rory asked her as he got back on the horse.

She shook her head. "Well, get up here behind me," he suggested.

She tried to jump up onto the horse's rump. Reaching short, she landed on the ground beside the horse with a thud. Rory leaned from the saddle and offered her his hand. With his help and direction, she mounted behind him. Ensuring she held on tightly, Rory kicked the horse to a gallop.

Chapter Forty-Nine

Alistair helped Caitlin lay Scott's body out on the kitchen table. Caitlin removed his wedding band. She used warm soapy water to wash away the blood, dirt, coagulation powder, which had become a blood-soaked gel, and other bodily fluids now leaving Scott's corpse. The others arrived home. Kelly and Rory walked in the backdoor. Caitlin hastily covered Scott's dead body with towels. A young woman followed behind them.

"Ahh, Mum this is Mandy. She asked us for help." Rory shrugged.

Mandy stood in the doorway; her eyes fixed on Scott's covered corpse.

"There is plenty of hot water," Caitlin turned and said to Kelly. "Why don't you run a bath for our guest? And find some clothes to fit her."

"Okay, Mum." Kelly ushered Mandy into the bathroom.

Caitlin leaned on the table then lifted her gaze to Rory.

"She's desperate, Mum," Rory said. "She had nowhere to go. We always give help when needed."

"I don't really know what the circumstances were, but she was in a room," Caitlin said.

"What do you mean 'in a room'?"

"The slavers went into the room, one at a time," she answered. "I can only imagine what degradations this poor woman has gone through."

Rory's eyes narrowed. Caitlin uncovered Scott's body and started to dress him for burial. Rory helped.

"We'll have to make a coffin." Alistair had stood to one side, watching.

"Mum!" Kelly interrupted their conversation.

Caitlin responded to the anxiety in her daughter's voice and ran into the bathroom. Rory followed. From the door Caitlin could see the bathwater was blood tinged. She stopped Rory at the door.

"Out! Women only." Caitlin shut the door in Rory's face.

The bath water was a deepening red. Mandy bent over in the water, holding her belly. Caitlin turned to Kelly. "Quick. Go get a medical pack from the pantry."

Kelly ran out of the bathroom, got what she needed and ran back in to help Caitlin.

"What's going on?" both men asked through the partially open door.

Kelly shook her head at them as she closed the door in their faces.

Caitlin's attention was on Mandy, but the scraping of furniture over the wooden floors of the cottage came through the bathroom walls. Once Mandy had passed her miscarriage, Caitlin left Kelly to support her. She'd had enough blood and trauma for one day.

Caitlin walked to the kitchen to find it empty of its long table bearing her husband's body. A shard of ice hit her gut.

No, the boys moved him.

The room seemed to lose its oxygen. Caitlin went outside to sit on her bench and draw in the fresh mountain air. She halted at the doorway.

Rory was outside alone. He sat on the bench seat at the backdoor which faced the mountains, now dark with night. The stars were showing themselves. Caitlin lifted her head, her rapid breathing settled.

Rory must recognise familiar constellations from another time. The night-sky hadn't changed. The air was cooling, and Rory shivered. Caitlin was sure the day hadn't gone as he'd expected. Out of the corner of her vision, Rory's head bowed, and his shoulders shook.

Caitlin sat next to him and put her arms around him—the first contact she'd ever had with her twenty-three-year-old son. They both shook together, as her breath caught in her throat and no words came. She had no thoughts either, only blank numbness.

After a few moments, Rory composed himself.

"We started making a coffin." He wiped his tears off his face. "We need to cut more timber." He wiped his cheek with the heel of his hand. "How is she?" Rory needed to change the subject.

Caitlin shrugged a reply and stayed silent.

"What happened, can I ask?" Rory's concern pushed her out of her fog and prompted her to answer.

"That young woman has been through hell." Caitlin would be breeching a confidence but continued regardless. "She just miscarried. Mandy said she had been with those slavers for about three months and abused for most of them. I would estimate the foetus was about seven weeks."

The muscles in Rory's jaw tightened, like Scott's had when he was angry.

"Will she be okay?" he asked.

"Yes, probably," Caitlin said. "I think she's made of strong stuff. She should recover. With time, the support of a Community and the love of a good man, she might make it." She regarded her son for a moment, then returned her focus to her own trials. "Where have you put him?" Her voice was quiet, barely above a whisper.

"Come with me, Mum." Rory rose and took her gently by the hand.

They entered the rearranged bedroom. Rory and Alistair had placed the kitchen table with Scott's body on it near the open window where the cold air would come in. Due to the Aga, the rest of the cottage was always warm. After covering it with a sheet of plastic, they had packed his body with ice from the freezer.

Caitlin went to Scott's body and bent over his head, quiet for a few moments. She tried to pray. Once again, no words came, only emotion. That was enough. An all-powerful being, who knew everything, did not need to hear her words when she had none.

Caitlin's lips brushed Scott's forehead "Thank-you for being your brave, loving self and coming for me, as I knew you would." She finally said. "Wish it hadn't ended this way." She allowed her tears release. "I love you. Goodbye my incredible man." She kissed his cold forehead; her breathing became difficult. Her arms embraced his cool shoulders and stayed there for a while.

***

Rory and Alistair brought the coffin into the house and placed Scott's body into it.

"We'll bury him near the burn," Caitlin announced. "He loved fishing there."

The next morning Alistair and Rory dug the grave. On their return they carried Scott's coffin to the grave and placed it beside his favourite place in the Highlands of Scotland. Mist covered the steep sided mountains of Glencoe. The wind blew high on the mountain peaks, shredding the clouds as they passed.

Like my soul, Caitlin thought as she wandered back to the cottage.

***

"Mum, you know why I am here, don't you?" Rory asked later that day as he sat on Caitlin's bench. She now shared her favourite place in the garden with her eldest boy.

"You were here to take your father back," she answered.

Rory nodded. "I had a month to get it sorted. I've got two pods, and I must be back at the abandoned farm at a certain date. The farm will be our Community in the future."

Caitlin turned her face to him. The afternoon sun peeped below the clouds and warmed her cheek as it made its decent in the sky. "Rory, I'm so proud of you. You're brave and disciplined—a good soldier."

"Dad taught me." His voice threatened to break. "I am what I am because of him."

"You are very much like him. You look like him. I think you're very handsome, but I'm biased." She laughed.

"Remember, I'm a twin, Mum. Callum and I are identical."

"Wow, two handsome men like you in the world. God *is* good!" Caitlin smiled again.

A flickering of guilt at being happy for a moment, when sadness was expected, threatened to spoil it. *No.* She would never see this beautiful young man like he is now, ever again. She would die before he grew to full manhood. How wonderful that she got to see him now.

"So, you are returning?" she asked.

"Aye. I have a place there, Mum. And a job to do. I'll miss you. I'll miss you both." Rory's eyes filled with tears and began to overflow.

"I'll miss you too," she whispered, holding him.

***

During the next three weeks, Caitlin and Rory were often in each other's company, quietly conversing. Rory assisted Alistair with the running repairs to the cottage and grounds, and the energy supply, and to bring in the last of the harvests as well.

Rory spoke with Alistair in the privacy of the stables.

"Sorry, Alistair but I can't stay. I have a job to do in the future."

He had become close to Alistair in the past weeks.

Bonded.

"I need to make sure they never try to come back for Dad," he said. "Just want to leave the past as it is."

"Yeah. It's... tragic... losing Scott." Alistair scuffed the straw covered stable floor with the toe of his boot. "Who knows what havoc it would cause if things of the past changed further? You're taking Mandy with you, aren't you?" Alistair lifted his eyebrows, wiggling them slightly.

Rory gave a lopsided smile but didn't answer.

"Man, you *are*. I can tell," Alistair said.

Rory's neck heated then his face followed.

"You look after my wee sister. I ken you love her, genuinely." Rory kept his eye contact with the dark-haired young man until he responded.

"Yeah, I do." Alistair's face screwed up a little. "I don't know if your dad would be pleased."

"Why not?" Rory asked.

"He was down on me. Gave me a bit of a hard time."

"He was testing you. Figuring oot what you're made of. He trusted you with the rescue. You saved Mum, killed McSweeny. He would've thanked ye for it."

After a pause, Alistair nodded.

"Help Mum when the time comes, please," Rory asked. "She knows what supplies she might require. She'll need assistance and protection getting to Invercharing. I've given her directions and described the state it's in. She's no' ready yet but, if I know my mother, she will go soon."

"Can't imagine being here without her," Alistair said. "Kelly won't be happy."

"Nae choice really, brother, aye?"

"Yep." Alistair picked up a curry comb and started grooming the stallion. "Doesn't make it any easier."

Chapter Fifty

The Future

Murray stood next to Angus beside the control panel for The Time Machine. They'd given him permission to attend the return of the Retriever. Angela, Mr Stobbart and the other members of the Chief Council were present in the cold earthy-scented barn. Angus activated the machine for retrieval.

"It's engaged," Angus said. "That means he's there with Scott at the right time."

All was going to plan. The Time Machine discharged, and a pod appeared. Limited available oxygen in the pod meant time was crucial and the traveller was at risk of suffocation. Murray ran over and broke open the pod. He stood back in surprise. An attractive young woman peeled the pod away from herself.

"Hi. I'm Mandy. Um, Rory is in the next one," Mandy explained as her long legs slipped out of the resin pod.

A stunned silence filled the barn. Angus let out a low whistle as he reset the machine. It discharged again, and Rory returned.

"Where's Dad?" Murray demanded, his face twisted in confusion and his chest empty with the absence of his father.

Those present looked accusingly at Rory.

"Things didn't go as planned," Rory stated.

"I knew it! You couldn't bring him back, could you?" Angela's tone exuded justification at her misgivings of Rory as the Retriever.

"Aye, I did nae bring our father back," Rory faced his eldest sister. "And do you want to know *why*, Angela?" Angela took a step back as Rory breathed his vehemence in her face. "I couldn't bring the offender back," Rory continued loudly, "as he died saving his wife, your mother, from slave-traders."

The barn was silent.

"You're just saying that because you wouldn't let Dad face his crimes," Angela accused.

Rory's shoulders rose with a breath as he struggled to maintain control. He must have expected Angela would be hard to convince, Murray guessed. She *was* so infuriating in her lack of compassion.

"Did you want me to bring his *head* on a spike as proof of his death?" The high-ceilinged barn rang with Rory's shout.

Angela stood silent, her mouth open. Murray spun and left, brushing past Angela. Silent tears were falling down her cheeks.

***

Rory placed Mandy in suitable accommodation, then made his way to the communication centre where he hailed the Community at Glencoe on a citizen band radio.

"It's Rory Campbell here, from the Invercharing Community. May I speak to Kelly and Alistair McKinnon please? Over."

Chapter Fifty-One

The Past

C aitlin sat by the open fire. The weather was cold out. She had completed her chores for the day and now the green couch was as good a place as any. She'd have to vacate it before long as, due to the season cooling, it was now Alistair's bed. Caitlin couldn't let him freeze in the shed another night. She lowered her gaze to the book in her hands, reading the same line, yet again. She didn't look forward to another night in the double bed... without Scott.

Laughter wafted from Kelly's room. They'd become close. They were in love. Kelly was so young, but she was a sensible girl. If they were in another time, she'd say wait. But why? If you're in love with the right person, don't waste time. Be with them. Yes, she'd suggest they formalise things. Uncle Robert at Bridge of Orchy was sometimes on the citizen band radio. Maybe they could make the journey. Or do it by proxy. *You can do that, can't you?*

***

Two Years After The Stock Market Crash.

"You know I must go." Caitlin sat at the table after the evening meal.

Kelly and Alistair's baby had settled. Kelly was a natural mother, and luckily breast feeding had worked out for her. The birth had been routine as well. Caitlin recalled from her maternity secondment that younger first-time mothers usually did well. Kelly stared at the remains of her dinner. Alistair paused briefly in his chewing.

"Now little Murray is three months old," Caitlin announced, "I'll gather what I'll need, but I must ask you a great favour, Kelly."

Kelly swallowed hard. The possibility of Caitlin starting her journey north had hung over their heads since Rory left a year ago. Kelly looked up from her plate.

"Please, would you both come with me for protection while I travel to Invercharing?" Her daughter glanced sideways at her husband. "Are you okay with that, Kelly? I must go north and start setting up the Community."

Kelly stayed silent, her eyes glistening, now staring back at her dirty plate.

"I've got to stay alive and make a place for when your father gets there." Caitlin placed her hand over her daughter's as she rested it on the kitchen table. "We hear Brendan on the CB often. I'll radio Brendan and Bec the minute I arrive."

Shaking her head to dispel the tears, Kelly stood and hugged her.

"I may never see you again, Mum." Kelly's voice muffled into her shoulder.

"We can keep close contact by radio. When you have your next baby, if you have any trouble, I can come." Caitlin smiled over at Alistair. "Your husband did a wonderful job helping me when Murray was born. You'll be fine." Her throat was tight. "We can't risk it ever being discovered that you are adult Kelly. It would ruin everything. Change the future and the past in one hit." She rubbed her daughter's back affectionately. "We must be careful."

***

Caitlin started gathering the items on her list she'd made with Rory.

"You won't see your grandchildren grow up." Kelly leaned against the bedroom door. "Even when they are older, you can't let Dad or even young me see them."

Caitlin's shoulders slumped as her gaze fell on her packing. "Yes, I know. We'll talk often on the citizen band radio." She fought the hollowness starting in her chest. "I'm still coming to terms with it all myself."

"When will you go?" Kelly asked.

"As soon as I can before the weather turns."

***

Alistair found enough petrol to fill the 4WD for one return journey to Invercharing. It was the last of their fuel supply. He loaded the vehicle with food, suitcases of clothing, medical supplies, books, small items of furniture, bedding, another citizen band radio and an antenna, which he found in the roof space of the cottage. Caitlin and Alistair armed themselves well.

Caitlin rode Adam, who now behaved himself for her, while Alistair drove slowly behind with Kelly and the baby. They left early and reached Fort William by lunch time.

They travelled through the town, with their heads down to avoid attracting attention. The town was almost deserted as it was on a non-market day. There was a sparse crowd of about twenty people standing by the railway station. Security-type men surrounded an older couple. She pulled Adam back to speak to Alistair through the car window.

"I think I know those people." Caitlin jumped off Adam. "Hold him for me." She threw Adam's reins through the vehicle window and ran over to the group.

"Wait! Caitlin," Alistair shouted.

She didn't reply.

Caitlin approached the couple, but a burly man with a gun halted her. The man of the couple pivoted to see why his guard had reacted, and looked into Caitlin's face.

"Uncle Kieran!" Caitlin cried.

The man blinked and stood open-mouthed for a moment. The woman turned, and not saying a word, ran to Caitlin and embraced her.

"Aunty May!" Caitlin said into their hug. "I thought you were dead!"

"So did we...for you! We gave up hope months ago, after all our investigations came to dead-ends." Aunt May held Caitlin at arms-length and peered closely. "Oh, my beautiful girl, are you not a sight for these sore old eyes?"

A tall, slim young man stepped from within the group. "Caitlin?"

"Martin!" She hugged her cousin, her heart bursting with relief at finding her family again.

Caitlin introduced Alistair and Kelly as helpful friends she'd met during the crisis. Anything else would give too much away. She had to bend the truth, so she lied to the best of her ability. How *could* she tell them of Scott and Kelly's time travel?

What might the implications be if I did?

"I couldn't find you, Aunt May, once the mob had entered the house," Caitlin said. "So, I ran. You weren't there when I came back, and the mob was still around and wrecking the place. I wasn't safe anywhere. I got a lift to the Highlands and found a cottage in Glencoe. Alistair and Kelly have been with me since. Oh, and for a while some other friends stayed too." She added in case Bec and Brendan ever encountered her aunt and uncle.

It was getting complicated. She'd have to remember all this. She *had* to keep Scott and his time travel secret safe.

Throughout Caitlin's recounting of her time since the attack on the mansion, Aunt May silently shook her head in wonder.

"When it all calmed down, we looked everywhere for you on the property," Aunt May said. "Your Bonny was gone, so we thought you'd ridden off on her. Somewhere safe, we hoped. But you were nowhere... Well, Caitlin, you're with us again now and you are safe." Aunt May was always so good at taking charge. "We are heading north. We've heard there are some safer places up there. You'll come with us. What about your friends? They are most welcome."

"Thank you, ma'am." Alistair's Canadian accent seemed thicker. "We're quite content to go back to our cottage in Glencoe. Actually, we better get going. We have animals to tend to, and I don't want to leave them for too long. Thank you, anyway. Really nice meeting you."

"People have been setting up secure communities all over the world," Caitlin said.

This had happened already, and maybe this idea would inspire her aunt and uncle. If they were the same people, unchanged by the difficult world they now lived in, they would be.

Caitlin continued, "Where people are safe and can ride out this storm, which seems to go on forever. I've heard there are a few abandoned farms up north. I know the location of a decent one."

Caitlin omitted the fact her son from the future had given her directions to the exact place where they had set up this Community already, in the future.

"We had planned for your other cousins to meet us when we found somewhere." Aunt May squinted her eyes in thought. "I like the idea of a safe community. It's logical and meant to be. We'll pool our resources and go to this abandoned farmhouse you know of."

Relief floated through Caitlin. They transferred Caitlin's supplies from the 4WD to her uncle's vehicles. Uncle Kieran and Aunt May had a company of twenty people and plenty of supplies with them.

"Well, I haven't kept you from your home for too long." Caitlin leaned against the vehicle as she cradled her grandson. The moment had come to leave all behind. To see her daughter, son-in-law and grandson for possibly the last time. Still holding the baby, she gave her daughter a wordless hug.

"We'll keep in touch. I love you..." Kelly choked off the last words.

Caitlin handed baby Murray to Kelly and turned to Alistair. "I know my daughter will be safe and secure with you. You remind me of Scott." She hugged him, conscious of an ending and a new beginning.

Alistair, his smile from the compliment fading, waved solemnly from the vehicle's window as he drove the old 4WD out of Fort William.

Chapter Fifty-Two

Five Years After The Stock Market Crash

C aitlin strode along the covered walkway between the large sheds. The men were working on more accommodation blocks. The noise of hammering and sawing flitted past her ears as she moved along. She entered the storeroom. The 5.0 silk was in here somewhere. The sharp end of snapped-cut wire had torn the young boy's face. His mother said it happened this morning, less than six hours ago, so Bec had decided to suture him straight away. Caitlin was glad Bec would do it. The human face has so many delicate structures and tendons—

"Caitlin. It's so hard to find you on your own," a man with a Highland accent spoke behind her.

She jumped, then turned to see a well-muscled man with slightly greying hair.

"George, you scared me. I didn't see you there."

"Sorry, but you're rarely alone and ... well I've been wanting to know," He said, "Would you like to spend time with me?"

"I do, George, we work together a lot," Caitlin answered.

She'd anticipated where this was going and expected it for a while. How could she not hurt him? George Stobbart was a fine man. Similar to Scott. But *not* Scott.

"No, Caitlin, I mean... have a relationship." George gave a cock-eyed smile.

"You know I don't have time for that." She spied the suture material in the box beside her, grabbed it and quick-paced out.

Part way along the corridor, she turned. George was ambling out of the storeroom, his head bowed and shoulders slack. Unusual for him with his military posture.

"George, you're ex-British Marine, aren't you?"

"Green Beret, actually." George's posture regained its straightness, his shoulders broadened once more.

"I'd like you to formally train our people in self-defence," she said. "We need more than the security we already have."

People had come. News of the Community had spread, and they had arrived. But not all were friendly. In the early days, the men and women who repaired the farmhouses and constructed more buildings had worked with a hammer in one hand and a gun in the other.

"Please train and lead a militia for us, George."

George's eyes lit up. "Aye, Ma'am." He stood straighter, if it was at all possible.

Caitlin returned to the crowded room designated for medical treatment, where the most recent arrivals waited. Dr Farquhar, a retired paediatrician, examined a teenager. He was invaluable. This new group comprised mostly of children who had lost parents in the terrorist bombings and linked up while they lived on the streets. They were malnourished and full of lice and fleas. Caitlin said another prayer of thanks that nearly every new arrival had brought possessions and resources and, most importantly, their skills. She would mobilise the teachers among them now.

Aunt May organised the sorting and storage of these resources. Uncle Kieran was the store-master and banker. He had an uncanny knack of knowing what was available on the black market and how to acquire it. Everyone put their differences—class, gender, education-levels, ethnicity and vocational-expectations—behind them and pulled together. It was a condition of entry to the Community—the willingness to work for the common good.

Brendan devised a way to tap into the many wind farms dotted nearby and electricity was available for medical and security purposes at first. Now they could store the perishable food they grew in their market garden effectively. These key people would one day become what Scott called the Chief Council. But for the present they were the administrative team.

As the afternoon rolled on, Caitlin went outside for fresh air and stood by the guard at the gate who held a sub machinegun and scanned the surrounding countryside continually. He smiled at her. He was a very handsome man, and she smiled a friendly smile back.

"Lovely evening, Miss Murray." The guard walked closer.

"Yes, it is. And so fresh out here." She hugged her arms and looked along the road. Their wide valley in between green sloping high hills was still. A rain cloud broke over the near-by forest, emptying its load of rain.

"So, maybe we could sit together for dinner, Miss Murray...or, may I call you Caitlin?"

She turned her head sharply. Two on the same day? She was getting the reputation for being cold. It wasn't easy. This life is a two-person life.

Sorry guys, but my man is on his way.

Seventeen Years After the Stock Market Crash

I t was a cold, bleak afternoon when he arrived.

Caitlin stood by the guard at the gate. A lone figure approached through the gathering mist that hugged their hidden valley. In her free time, Caitlin was in the habit of standing at the gate and watching.

Caitlin chuckled to herself as it had happened again today. People had commented behind her back after her polite refusal of one of the newer men. Her nickname was *Ice Woman*.

The tall, emaciated youth staggered as he ambled toward the gate. His clothes were dirty and his long dark-blond hair a mass of knots.

Caitlin took in a sharp breath.

The guard at the gate gave the lad a cursory glance. "I'll send him away, Miss Murray."

"No, you will *not*! Open the gate!"

Caitlin strode purposefully toward the youth. He had piercing blue eyes. He stopped his advance, either from fatigue or uncertainty at her approach.

"Hello. I'm Caitlin. What's your name?" she asked, despite knowing the answer.

After a moment's hesitation, the young man replied through a dry mouth and cracked lips.

"Scott."

"It's okay, Scott." She held out her hand. "Come with me. You're home now."

The End

Reviews are an important part of letting others know about books.
If you enjoyed *Stolen Time*, please leave a brief review at your online book seller. *Thanks*

Acknowledgements

Halfway through 2016, a story came to me. I wrote the first draft in two months. Its characters were so real and vivid, I often felt like an intruder in their lives. Writing was a hobby then, just for me. But that would change. I'm grateful for the support of indie authors who believed in and encouraged me. My editor, author Annie Seaton, a wealth of wisdom and experience and so easy to work with. Thank you for loving Scott and Caitlin's story and helping me get it out for others to read. Alli Sinclair, who has always encouraged me and was the first author to say my writing sounded like a writer wrote it. The Romance Writers of Australia, the Aspiring Author's loop, their Online Writing Labs, the competitions, and the annual conference were all a major part of my development. The craft books of Jeff Gerke, and Ted Dekker's course, *The Creative Way*.

I'd like to thank the members of my long-suffering family. Our daughter Gillian has read every draft of this story. Thank you for your enthusiasm which spurred me on to believe. Thank you to our daughter, Emma. You are so talented and such a resource. I don't know where to begin to list the help you've give me, from basic writing skills to what images suit best. Our son Frank, my martial-art, survivalist, and general does-that-sound-okay-from-a-guy-point-of-view? person. Thank you. Our son-in-law, Richard, who kept me right with the Scots tongue and Scottish history. Our niece, Vicky the vaper, thanks for the insider information. Many thanks Leanne Prosser, for checking the horsey stuff and Sally Sewell for double-checking the surgery. Thank you to the rest of my family, friends and workmates who always encouraged and never scoffed.

Special thanks to my critique partners, Mindy Graham and Laurelle Kinsman, for all the back and forth emails. Your opinions are always helpful and encouragement always spot-on.

Finally, I wish to thank my husband Frank, for his unwavering support and encouragement. He has missed out on many hours with me, so I could share this story with you.

Jenn

About the Author

DESTINY RELATIONSHIP COURAGE

Retired nurse Jenn has travelled extensively and lived on three continents. Although Australia is the land of her birth, Scotland always called her back and remains her source of inspiration. She lives with her husband, and family nearby. Jenn loves walking through a forest and climbing a mountain to experience the view. Or exploring a castle ruin and soaking in the history. Her only disappointment in life is that time travel is not possible... apparently.

Award-winning fantasy author, Jenn's latest release, *Of High Kings and Mages: Arlan's Pledge Book Three,* achieved Semi-Finalist stage in the OZMA Book Awards for Fantasy Fiction 2024 CIBAs. *Of Warriors and Sages: Arlan's Pledge Book Two* achieved Semi-Finalist in the OZMA Book Awards for Fantasy Fiction 2023. Longlisted in the Realm Awards 2025 Fantasy Section. Manuscript *The Quest* reached the Top 10 in Ink & Insights 2021. Lees' Best Selling novel, *Of Myths And Portals: Arlan's Pledge Book One* achieved First Place Award (Gold) in The BookFest Fall 2024 Fiction-Romance-Fantasy, Second Place Award (Silver) in The BookFest fall 2024 Fiction-Fantasy-Magic, Myths and Legends, and Fiction-Christian-Fantasy. *The Crossing: Arlan's Pledge Book 1* (re-released as *Of Myths and Portals*) achieved the finals in the OZMA Book Awards for Fantasy Fiction 2021. *Restoring Time: Community Chronicles* Book 4 reached the finals in the CYGNUS Awards for Science Fiction 2021.

Arlan's Pledge 'Perfect for anyone who ever wished Outlander had dragons' Book for Thought review

Find out more about Jenn Lees and her novels. Sign up for the newsletter and receive *Running with the Stags,* a free novella in the *Arlan's Pledge Series.*

www.jennleeswriter.com

Want more of Jenn Lees? Support Jenn Lees Fantasy Author on Patreon.

https://www.patreon.com/c/JennLeesFantasyAuthor

Also by

www.ingramcontent.com/pod-product-compliance
Lightning Source LLC
Chambersburg PA
CBHW030632110726
47901CB00002B/422